CRITICAL PRAISE FOR *THE MED!*

"Update *The Caine Mutiny* and *Away All Boats*, move the action to the Mediterranean, throw in some Arab terrorists with American hostages, and you've got *The Med*...a naval thriller at full speed!" —*St. Louis Post-Dispatch*

"A POWERFUL STORY, as honest as it is imaginative...Readers will be gripped...realistic, and indeed uncomfortably topical." —*Publishers Weekly*

"One of the best seagoing novels of the decade. YOU WON'T BE ABLE TO PUT IT DOWN!"
—William P. Mack, Vice Admiral, U.S. Navy (Ret.), Co-author of *South to Java*

THE MED is the only contemporary novel being taught in associate professor Herb Gilliland's *Literature of the Sea* course at the U.S. Naval Academy.

"*The Med* gives a feel of what it's like to be out on a deployed ship during an operation, and that's particularly valuable for budding naval officers to be able to experience." —Herb Gilliland

The colossal acclaim continues...

"This is the Commodore speaking. A few minutes ago this ship, this formation, was overflown by a Russian bomber. We had no warning. No one detected it. . . ."

Harisah took a last drag and flicked the cigarette to the desert floor. He raised his weapon above his head and looked down on his men. Their enemies did not have the ultimate weapon. He did. His enemies were not ready to die . . .

St. Martin's Paperbacks Titles
by David Poyer

THE MED

THE GULF

THE MED

DAVID POYER

ST. MARTIN'S PAPERBACKS

THE MED

Copyright © 1988 by David Poyer.

All rights reserved. No part of this book may be used or reproduced in any manner whatsoever without written permission except in the case of brief quotations embodied in critical articles or reviews. For information address St. Martin's Press, 175 Fifth Avenue, New York, N.Y. 10010.

ISBN: 0-312-92722-3

Printed in the United States of America

St. Martin's Press hardcover edition published 1988
St. Martin's Paperbacks edition/September 1989

10 9 8 7 6 5

ACKNOWLEDGMENTS

Ex nihilo nihil fit. For this book I owe much to James Allen, James Blandford, A. J. Campbell, Kelly Fisher, Marilyn Goldman, Judith Haynes, Richard R. Hobbs, R. P. Lucas, Robert Kerrigan, Llewellyn Williams, George Witte, George Zabounian, and many others who gave of their time to contribute or criticize. All errors and deficiencies are my own.

In Greece 1949
Suez 1956
Lebanon 1958
Jordan 1970
Israel 1973
Cyprus 1974
Beirut 1983
Libya 1986
You were there.
This novel is dedicated to all those who serve in peacetime,
But especially to those sailors, officers, and marines
—And their families—
Who served through the long cruises
The liberties
And sometimes, the actions
Of the Sixth Fleet.
We sent you to keep the peace for us.
Some of you never came back.

Every discussion of duty has two parts. One part deals with the question of the supreme good; the other, with the rules that should guide our ordinary lives.

—Cicero, "On Moral Duties"

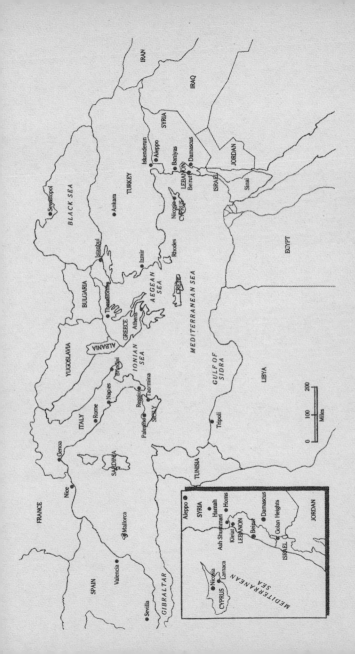

I

LINE OF DEPARTURE

1

The Central Mediterranean

FORTY MILES FROM LAND THE SEA heaves in predawn darkness. No buoy, no man-made mark interrupts the undulant glitter of stars on an easterly swell.

The destroyer is a sharp-edged shadow against Cassiopeia. Since midnight she has cruised slowly before the prevailing sea. But at 0400, suddenly, she heels as her rudders bite water. The hum of turbines rises to a whine, the sound rolling out into blackness, and a phosphorescent waterfall shoots from the screws. As she gathers speed she begins to pitch, dipping her bow to the swell, then lifting to shake hissing spray into the sea. Above her wake a stain of smoke unrolls against the sky.

The Line of Departure for an amphibious assault is drawn not through dark waves, over the mirror of stars, but across a Navy chart in number-two lead. On one side, in the minds of men, is peace. And on the other, the irrevocable commitment to battle.

The destroyer crosses the line still accelerating, sonar pinging into the deep, radar sweeping the sky. Its gray sides fade to black. A single dimmed stern light retreats into the night. The waves of its passing widen and then disappear, merging at last with the unchanging sea.

Half an hour later six gray ships slowly lift into view to the east. At first only their masts show above an empty horizon, against the faint glow that precedes morning. Then they grow closer. Not speedily, but with a steady and inexorable pace.

They are not so sleek, nor so fast, nor so heavily armed as the destroyer that escorted them, ten miles in advance. But they are larger, swelling with displacement curves rather than the fine lines of speed. Instead of guns and missile launchers, their decks are cluttered with helicopter pads and replenishment stations, stacks of containers and nested landing craft. In the faint light rises deck on deck of superstructure, topped by the vertical spikes of booms and funnels.

Flung wide across miles of sea, the task force moves across its face with ponderous eagerness; and from each ship, above the antennas and signal lines, streams the red-and-white-striped ensign of impending battle.

The landing has begun.

U.S.S. *GUAM* LPH-9

High in the island of the helicopter carrier, a stocky man in khakis thrusted his face angrily into binoculars. He raised them with the ship's roll, leaning into the coaming, examining a shadow that steamed parallel to her, four thousand yards away. The glasses remained level for several minutes; then Captain Isaac I. Sundstrom, Commander, Mediterranean Amphibious Ready Group, jerked them down. He muttered into the fresh wind of a twenty-knot passage, and turned for the interior of the flag bridge.

"Commodore's on the bridge!" At the shout officers and enlisted men looked up from dimly lit charts, flickering radars. They glanced at one another, but only one man—a lieutenant, junior grade—moved cautiously toward Sundstrom, his hand rising automatically to his helmet, saluting unseen in the darkness.

"Good morning, Commodore."

"Dan. Morning." The words were short with anger and fatigue. "What's going on? Are we ready to hit the beach?"

The lieutenant's name was Dan Lenson. Seen by the faint radiance of a vertical plot, he was taller than the commodore and almost unnaturally thin, hair somewhere between sandy and dark. He too looked tired. Rubbing a sun-bleached mustache with the back of his hand, he pitched his voice above the roar of wind, the hiss of radios.

"Commodore, we're on two-eight-zero true, speed nineteen. The amphibs are in circular formation for movement to assault. *Guam*'s the guide, in station zero. *Barnstable County* is dead ahead; *Newport,* on the starboard beam; *Spiegel Grove,* starboard quarter; *Charleston,* port quarter. *Coronado* lagged back during the night; I shifted *Charleston* to her station at 0200. Screen units: *Ault* is twenty thousand yards ahead of the main body, sanitizing our track in to the beach. The other destroyers are deployed along the air threat axis." His eyes shifted to a board behind the commodore. "Equipment status: Both of *Coronado*'s boilers are on line now and she's catching up, eight miles astern last time I looked. *Ault* has an anchor casualty that's being worked on right now. *Barnstable* reported radar trouble again—"

"She'll need that during beach approach. Damn it," said the commodore, looking out at the darkness.

"Yes sir." The lieutenant waited, then went on when his senior did not continue. "Other than that, all units of Task Force 61 and embarked marines report ready for the assault. We're at H minus one hundred now."

"Where are we on track? Are we up with intended movement?"

"I hold us dead on so far, sir."

"I think we're falling behind. Let's play it safe. Goddamnit, I don't want to be late again!"

"That will make it harder for *Coronado* to catch up, sir. If she isn't in position for that first wave—"

"You heard me, Dan. I don't like to give orders twice."

The lieutenant studied him. Dawn was coming. He could make out the sagging, lined face under graying hair. "Aye aye, sir," he said at last. "I'll signal another knot speed increase. Mr. Flasher—"

"Got it," said a voice from the darkness.

"Dan, you've got to keep me informed. I'm not getting the proper reports."

"Sir, the chief staff officer was up here most of the midwatch. I thought he was—"

"Don't count on that zero, Dan. He's disappointed me too often."

"Uh . . . yes, sir. We're ready to go, then, as far as I can see."

"Have you talked to the *Guam*'s bridge yet this morning?"

"Just a few words, Commodore. Would you like me to—"

"Forget it," said the older man. His face settled, his head lowering itself toward his chest; his eyebrows drew together. "I told you last night to keep close tabs on that brownshoe son of a bitch. Remember how Fourchetti screwed things up in Bizerte, when that helo went into the drink? That's not how I want things run. When my captains look bad I look bad. And I don't like to look bad. That's the name of the game, Dan."

"Yes, sir."

"*I'll* do it. Just like I have to do most of what gets done around here."

"Yes sir," Lenson said again, to the commodore's back.

As the door to the bridge wing opened a blast of sound hit them. Fifty feet below, on the flight deck, ten helicopters were beginning their flight checks. The roar of their engines warming up made Lenson cover his ears. Several of the near aircraft had engaged transmissions, and their blades began to whip around, slowly at first but then faster until in the dim deckedge lights they blurred into misty disks. The smells of exhaust and kerosene and hot metal mingled with the wind that blew back along the deck from the sea.

The commodore seemed not to notice it. Below him, around him, something massive was taking form out of the night. Leaning over the coaming, he swept his gaze along the length of his flagship.

From her blunt, rounded bow, where the flight deck stopped abruptly, aft along a flat sweep of deck to the forest of antennas and nets at the stern, the carrier teemed with men and machines. Men ran in the growing light among the vibrating fuselages. Flight-deck personnel in comm helmets and colored jerseys bent to check chocks and unplug starter cables. Armorers rolled bomb dollies toward four streamlined attack helos that now were adding their scream to the symphonic din that pounded along the deck, spilling out over the sea. Marines in drab utilities clambered in and out of cockpits. Another helicopter came into view, rising from the red-lit hangar below; the elevator locked and a tractor swung in, towing it toward its launch station. Hatches slammed open, and from deep in the ship more men streamed out onto the flight deck. In dull green helmets, packs jogging on their backs and rifles held nursing-close to their chests, the marines bent low beneath the revolving swords of the rotors.

Sundstrom raised his glasses, and after a moment, so did Lenson. Ahead of them, beyond four thousand yards of rushing sea, was the same frenzy of activity. *Barnstable County* was a tank-landing ship, an LST; she was smaller than the *Guam,* but at seven magnifications her decks, too, were busy with sailors in faded dungarees. Aft of her, on the horizon to their right, was another ship, too far and small to see movement, though it was there; and two more gray specks, far back; destroyers and frigates, escorting and protecting the larger ships that now moved and readied themselves here in the center, the heart, of a vast formation that had flung its moving nets of steel and data, radio waves and sound over three thousand square miles of the central Mediterranean.

Lenson, looking at the commodore, saw his lips move.
He leaned toward him, careful not to brush his arm; Sundstrom disliked being touched. "SIR?" he shouted, into the
mounting roar of engines.

"Sloppy . . ."

"Sir? Do you want me to—"

But he had already turned away, disappearing up a
ladder leading to the bridge deck; *Guam*'s captain held
sway there. Lenson straightened, and half-smiled. He
went back into the flag bridge, pausing to dog the weather
hatch against the steady beat of engines.

"Dan?" It was a chubby lieutenant with overlong hair.
His helmet strap was unbuckled and he had shoved it
back. "Where'd he go now?"

"Hi, Red. Up to see Fourchetti, I guess."

"What for?"

"Probably wants him to go to general quarters. He does
it earlier every landing. I think—"

The ship's announcing system blared out just then, jerk-
ing their heads around. "FLIGHT QUARTERS,
FLIGHT QUARTERS. ALL HANDS, MAN YOUR
BATTLE STATIONS! SET MATERIAL CONDITION
ZEBRA THROUGHOUT THE SHIP."

A gong began to sound, strident, insistent. From below
them came the thud of running feet. The red-haired lieutenant, buckling on a lifejacket, shouted, "Want me to
take it for you? You haven't had breakfast, have you?"

"No, been up here since 0100 . . . I ought to check on
SACC too. Thanks, Red."

"I hear ya. Now get outta here."

"I stand relieved."

Three decks down, deep in the steel labyrinth of the ship,
Lenson groped through a litter of maps and overlays,
messages and green-bound Marine Corps artillery pubs
for the cup he had left wedged there at midnight. The
coffee was cold, but thick with sugar. As he sipped at it
he slumped backward in his chair.

"Tired, Lieutenant?"

He bobbed upright; seeing a second-class petty officer old enough to be his father, with the seamed face and graying hair to match, he smiled. "A little. Between here and the flag bridge, I forget what my rack looks like. You getting the circuits up, Mac?"

"Sure, Mr. Lenson. What's the skinny?"

Turning, they both looked straight ahead, to where one end of the compartment was covered with a huge map. Fully nine feet by nine, it writhed in five colors over the bulkhead: sea blue, shading toward green near the shore; yellow of beach, of sandy plains; the crowded green terrain of foothills, black Vs of washed-out gullies, red lines of roads. Glossy plastic protected the dozens of symbols and numbers that had been drawn over its surface in the last forty-eight hours.

"We still got over an hour to H," said Lenson. His voice was a murmur over the ceaseless hissing from the speakers; the petty officer had to lean forward to hear him. "Anyway, when the rest of the team gets here, get your comm checks started. You should have the gun ships— *Ault, Bowen,* the two Turks, and the Italian can—coming up on the Gunnery Coordination Net. The Turks may take a couple of calls to answer. They weren't very cooperative at the presail conference. So—" He glanced at his watch and got up—"You've got her, Mac. Be back as soon as I can."

Lenson paused in the passageway to dog the door, then broke into a run. He turned at a stenciled arrow and slid down a metal ladder. A hundred feet on, the corridor narrowed and filled with breakfast smells. By a door marked OFFICERS COUNTRY a row of khaki and green caps stirred like impatient guests as the carrier rolled. In the wardroom he pulled out a chair between two other men, both of whom were eating as fast as they could. "Anything good, Stan?" he asked the one to his left.

"It's all good," muttered the supply officer.

"It all tastes the same, too."

"Lay off, Dan. It gets old after three months out here."

"Hey," said the man on his right, a marine major. "You just come down from the bridge?"

"Flag bridge. Not ship's bridge. Why?"

"What's going on? How far out are we?"

Lenson reached eagerly for the cup the steward rattled down at his elbow. "Uh—another hour to H—we're twenty miles from the coast yet."

"Shit," said the marine.

"Eager?"

"Drivin' those Cobras is better than sex. And they pay *you*. What do you do aboard?"

"I'm with the staff," said Lenson, not enthusiastically. "You know your supporting fire—ships' guns, aircraft, artillery?"

"Sure."

"I coordinate that. We keep the opposition's heads down as you go in, take out positions that threaten the ship-to-shore movement, then cover the marines as they head inland."

"Staff, huh? You work for Ike Sundstrom?"

"That's right."

"I hear he's kind of hard to get along with."

The lieutenant stared at his coffee. "He's the man in charge," he said at last, his voice hard. "He wouldn't have four stripes if he didn't know what he was doing."

The marine stared at him for a moment, and seemed about to speak. Then his look dropped to Lenson's heavy Academy ring. Then continued on up the left bicep, where it emerged from the short sleeve, showing the puckered flesh of an old third-degree burn. He nodded, looked away, and said nothing more.

A plate appeared in front of the thin j.g. He began to eat rapidly, greasing the food down with coffee.

Seven minutes later he was in his stateroom. Throwing himself on the lower of two bunks, he covered his eyes with an arm for a moment, and then removed it.

Under the upper bunk, wedged into the webbing, a

photograph lay fixed six inches above his open eyes. The woman was dark-haired, and she was in bed. Her arms were crossed under her head, and the wary alertness of her eyes contrasted strangely with her teasing smile, with the way her bare nipples poked erectly out toward the camera.

A few minutes went by, and he lay motionless; once he checked his watch. The ventilators breathed air into the tiny room. His shirt and trousers were soaked with old sweat. I need a shower, he thought. No, I need sleep.

But he knew there would be no sleep. Not that day. Any minute now, he thought, lying rigidly in his bunk. Any minute—

"LIEUTENANT LENSON, LAY TO THE FLAG BRIDGE," said the ship's announcing system suddenly. It hissed for a moment and then went on: "ATTENTION, ALL HANDS. H-HOUR HAS BEEN DELAYED ONE-HALF-HOUR BY THE COMMANDER, AMPHIBIOUS TASK FORCE. I SAY AGAIN, H-HOUR HAS BEEN DELAYED ONE-HALF-HOUR BY THE CATF. MAKE ALL PREPARATIONS FOR H-HOUR AT 0630."

The depression in the bunk that had taken Lenson's weight was already gone. He was halfway back to the radios, the charts, and the short angry man who paced impatiently high above the sea.

U.S.S. *AULT,* DD-698

Ten miles ahead of the flagship, a huge-bellied man in khaki trousers and grease-smeared T-shirt thrust himself through a hatchway and into a tiny compartment. Elbowing away a knot of equally dirty sailors, he aimed his face upward toward a mass of gears, shafts, and cables that came through the overhead and continued down through the deck.

"Where's the flashlight, Steurnagel? You think I'm a friggin' owl?"

One of the sailors hastened to thrust a light at him. The big man flicked it to one side to examine a handwheel and brake assembly, then forward, into the very bow, to the chain tube. The anchor chain itself filled the locker beneath their feet, fathoms of rusty tumbled links each five inches across and twenty pounds in weight. Then he aimed it upward, to the massive mechanism that fed it onto the forecastle, to the ground tackle. He stared for a long moment, then turned so quickly that the three other men in the closet-sized space flattened themselves against rusty steel. "Polock!" he bawled aft, through the hatch. "Mason! Lay back to the gear locker. Biggest prybar you can find, two lifting hooks—six-inchers—and a hundred feet of twenty-one thread. Smee!"

"Yeah, Chief."

"Operator's station, up on the fo'c'sle. Tell whoever's on it to cut power to the windlass—don't ease out, don't haul in, just stand easy. *Move!*" Men turned instantly, pelting aft and upward, boots echoing from steel amid machinery crowded so close they had to turn sideways even as they ran. "Stewie! Haul ass up to the bridge. Find that new ensign. Or Mr. Jay, or the XO if you see them first. Tell them Chief Wronowicz has a jammed shift mechanism on the—no, better keep it simple. Just say a casualty on the anchor windlass."

When the first class, too, was gone the large man sighed. He reached up to touch the gritty, half-greased surface of a cam, and his teeth showed under a half-growth of dark beard. Behind him, unseen by him, the two sailors who were left exchanged apprehensive looks.

"Blaney," he muttered.

"Chief?"

"I want BLANEY! Get that slack-wristed scumcock down here on the double!" His roar echoed around the compartment, and the men crouched as if a steam line was about to break. He had his mouth open again when a sudden humming came from the windlass motor, beside him, and he jerked his hand free and danced back with the lightness of a squirrel.

"Watch it, Chief."

"I'll have 'em shut down, Chief," said one of the men, and he, too, disappeared. Wronowicz, rubbing one of his massive, greasy hands with the other, glowered at the jammed mechanism, then glanced up and around him.

The *Ault*'s wartime designer had built her forepeak for thin midgets. Gear lockers and paint lockers and ground tackle had been crammed into the sharp stem of the old destroyer. The bulkheads and overhead were lined with cableruns and piping; the deck was slippery with oil. This far forward, the engines' whining roar was deadened to a rumble, but the vibration of the seas as the bow shattered them a few feet ahead made the confined air tremble around the waiting men. The stinks of grease, rust, paint thinner, and the powerful smell of Wronowicz himself mingled in a miasma of confusion and disaster.

The humming died. The sailors dispatched aft came running back, swearing as they tripped over knee-knockers, hanks of heaving line, cans of red lead. Immediately the chief set them to work. As one hastily connected a sound-powered telephone, two others braced themselves around the windlass mechanism and began to maneuver the pry, a tapered nine-foot iron bar, into place with its sharp end under the jammed assembly. Wronowicz, meanwhile, had been looking around. He found a wooden block and wedged it tightly under the bar, against the winch housing. As he stepped back he bumped into someone behind him, and barked, "Jesus, get your ass out of here! Wronowicz don't need a goddamn audience of thousands when he's working."

"Chief?"

The voice was hesitant. His head still turned away from it, the big man's face altered; then he turned, moving an inch or so to give the other room.

"Ensign Callin," he said, his voice flat.

"One of the men said you were having some trouble

down here," said the officer. He was husky too, though nowhere near the size of the chief; he was clean-shaven, with a truculent look, though his voice had none of the confidence of his build and expression. No more than twenty-one, he wore a set of gleaming, oversized gold bars, and his new khakis were creased and clean. "What's the, uh, problem?"

"Brace yourselves against the roll," said the chief, looking at the waiting men, two of them hanging on the lever end of the pry, the others standing ready with wrenches. One, looking scared, was holding a hammer he had taken out of his belt. "Got a jammed anchor winch, sir," he said to Callin. "This motor here turns the wildcat through these gears. This handwheel shifts between the wildcat and the capstan. The lower part of it here engages up into these notches. There's a lot of slop in 'em now and this pawl here, see, didn't engage right. Plus I think that handbrake assembly's hosed too. The way the wildcat—"

"The capstan, you mean?"

"No, sir. Line goes on the capstan, chain goes on the wildcat. Anyway, it's jammed tight as an Irishman in a Hong Kong whore. Stewie, is she dead now? Breaker open?"

"Main deck says yes, Chief. They didn't understand before. They were trying to rock it out."

" 'Rock it out.' I'll rock that asshole's . . . see if they have the stopper on."

"Says it's on."

"Fuckin' well better be. All right, let's put some Swedish steam on that bar."

"Chief," said the ensign quietly, "what are you doing up here? Isn't this first division's space?"

"Those fuckin' deck apes can't find their butts in the dark with both hands, sir. If somebody don't get this jam cleared we can kiss off standing in close this morning." He motioned to the bar. "Okay, girls. Hop to it."

Two men heaved at the pry. It moved slightly under

their weight, then stopped. The pawl moved a bit, then slid back between the notches.

"Ask them topside if they've got the brake on."

"Yes they do, Chief," said the man with the phones.

"We need some slack. Who's on the control?"

"That new guy—what's his name, the black kid—"

"Take him off. Get the petty officer on the switch. Tell him I want her backed off about three inches. Just that much. You two, get away from that pry."

"Chief," said the ensign again, "how long—"

"Look, Ensign, I can't tell how long it's going to take to fix until I fix it. This always happens when the goddamn BMs gundeck their maintenance. Sometimes it takes coupla minutes, once it took a day. I had to unbolt the axle frame and take it all apart. You better get out of the way, sir, there's likely to be a lot of grease and shit flyin' around in here."

Callin's face closed even more. He set his lips, then moved back. "Go on, then, Chief. If it doesn't work in a couple of minutes—"

"Yeah, good, sir." The motor hummed again, and the chain rattled and scraped in the hawsepipe. The humming stopped. "The other way," said Wronowicz, watching it. "A cunt-hair will do it." The motor reversed itself. The gears made a grinding noise, making them all start, and then reversed too.

"Hands to it, now," said the chief, drawing a massive forearm across his mouth. Black grease smeared his beard. "Heave!"

Again the men set themselves against the rolling ship. Again the bar gave for the first inch or two and then set solid, wedged tight, giving not at all. The sailors strained, their necks rigid, muscles bunched, sweat starting on their faces. Nothing moved.

"Chief," said the man at the sound-powered phones, "they got a problem with the steering engine aft. Can't tell if it's controls, or what."

"Call an electrician, tell them."

"Say they did. He don't know what's wrong with it, he says."

"Jesus H. Christ," bawled Wronowicz to the universe. He stared at the sailors; they had slacked off, unable to put their full strengths to the bar for long, but afraid to take their hands from it so long as he was watching. His massive shoulders slumped, but it was a slump of exasperation, not of defeat. Not yet.

"Get off that bar," he said to them.

"Chief—don't you think a block and tackle, get some multiplication of force on it—?"

"Yes sir, Mister Callin. Multiplication of force. Lots of room down here for that. Just let me make love to her once first."

The sailors moved apart silently, and Wronowicz put his shoulder to the bar. He tested it, waggling the end to be sure the pointed shaft was deep inside the mechanism, just where it refused its greasy union, and braced his grease-spackled boots.

The bar suddenly sank into the fleshy part of his arm, just above an old tattoo. Wronowicz grunted deep in his chest and shifted his legs to one side, so that he leaned forward, into the ship, the bar coming out of his shoulder and into the guts of the winch. Slowly, he began to straighten. The bar bent, arched, the iron set as stubbornly as the massive back that bent into it, that humped in swelling muscle under the filthy T-shirt, dark with sudden sweat between the wide shoulder blades.

"Chief—"

He grunted again, mindlessly. His eyes, turned from the others, were squeezed closed. His lips drew back, showing dental gold and decaying teeth, and his breath hissed out between them.

Callin bent through the hatchway, his face dark. "Chief! Leave it," he muttered. "Let the boatswain's mates do it. Go back to the engineroom. We need you there."

". . . Can do it."

"Get aft!"

The sailors exchanged looks. That had been an order. But not a muscle of the chief's body changed, only to lean harder, harder, into the rigid metal, as if will alone could force matter to yield.

". . . Coming!" he grunted.

With a grating sound, the bar stirred. The chief relaxed slightly, took a new hold, then levered his whole weight upward and then down on the quivering hilt. The bar bent slowly, and the mechanism rasped and moved slightly and then suddenly gave a bang like a pistol going off. The ensign jumped.

Wronowicz stepped back, sweating mightily, and the iron fell with a clang. "Hand me that light," he panted. "Yeah . . . there. It's in. Steurnagel, finish her up. Grease this fucker good; that's prob'ly what caused the jam. And get all this crap out of the locker before you secure, or it'll lop some poor fucker's head off next time we drop." He turned, and his eyes met Callin's for a long moment.

"You say there's more trouble back aft, sir?"

When they had left, the big man a pace behind the one in khaki, one of the sailors went down on a knee to pick up the iron. An inch and a half thick, it had bent near the end of the shaft through an angle of thirty degrees. The men looked after the two figures. "God *damn,*" whispered one of them.

"Pretty good," said one of the others; then added, in a low voice that nevertheless carried clearly to every man who stood there, his hands dangling by his side:

"—for a old man."

U.S.S. *SPIEGEL GROVE,* LPD-12

Ten thousand yards astern of the *Guam,* deep in the belly of a squat old ship, a private first class named Givens sat nodding in the midst of a score of other marines, hunched like fetuses in the dim red light, jammed together like subway passengers at rush hour.

Wherefore, as by one man sin entered into the world, and death by sin; and so death passed upon all men, for that all have sinned. . . .

The operating handle of a machine gun dug into his left side, the curve of a mortar baseplate into his right. The shelf he sat on was steel; the low overhead, also of metal, crisscrossed with insulation and swaying with lifejackets, pressed down to the crown of his lowered helmet. Strapped to him, wired to him, part of him, he wore the issue pack, haversack, blanket roll, two canteens that sloshed with the roll of the ship, a pistol belt and Colt, first-aid kit, gas mask, and poncho. Two canisters protruded above his pack, and he carried a third under his arm. They held mortar shells. His polished black boots were planted solid and motionless on the gritty floor of the amtrac. His face was expressionless except for tension at the corners of thin, tightly closed lips. His bony scarred hands rested on the oiled barrel of the 81mm mortar that he carried clamped between his legs.

Will Givens, age eighteen, swayed motionless, his eyes closed. On one side of him a corporal named Cutford snuffled in his sleep. On the other Sergeant Silkworth, the mortar team squad leader, whispered mad obscenities to himself, polishing his battalion-famous profanities. The closed interior of the amphibious tank stank of diesel oil and old vomit. The twenty marines had been sealed there without movement for two hours now.

Nodding there, half-asleep himself, Givens dreamed his way back into the morning.

Fourth platoon had had reveille passed on them at four that morning by the gunny. Will had rolled out faster than usual, knowing this was the day. He'd been pulling on his second pair of socks when Corporal Cutford leaned out of the blinking light of the overhead, his face blank and lightless as the inside of a mortar tube, and said:

"Fuckhead. You."

"What you want, Corporal?"

"You, Oreo. Shit detail."

"I had it yesterday, Cutford. And the day before."

"And you got it again, Oreo. Dee-dee into that head. You hear me? *Haul ass, fuckhead!* We hittin' a beach today. No time waitin' breakfast for shit-eatin' prives."

He finished dressing, enough for the detail at least, his worn soft trousers bloused into unlaced boots, skivvy shirt from the day before. In the head he bent to draw water into a scrub bucket amid the Niagara roar of urinating marines, then pulled swab and disinfectant from the cleaning locker. The solution rushed over the terrazzo, chasing into rusty dark corners under the thrones, islanding the men as they squatted. He swabbed away grimly, ignoring curses and threats. Today no one lingered; the head emptied as quickly as it had filled. Givens lifted the swab, swirled it to separate the gray strands, slapped it down to the deck, drew it along in swift parallel lines, taking up the gray water. Under it the terrazzo came clean, white base and green and red and blue flecks of color showing sharp and clear in the sour ammonia tang.

"Will. I'll finish up."

Givens looked up. The marine lingered uncertainly in the hatchway, his face white as porcelain. Pimples showed where his uniform collar rubbed, and though he was no older than Givens his skivvy shirt showed a line of blond-fuzzed gut above his belt.

"Cutford told me to do it."

"He did? Naw, I'm on the list for today. He's just on your case again, man."

"Yeah . . . all right, Washout. Thanks." He straightened, passed over the swab, and went out to the bunkroom to pick up his blouse.

The chow line was short; two cooks in ketchup-stained "Spiegel's Eagles" T-shirts were ladling out the last scraps of sausage and dry toast. Givens got the last egg and slid into a seat with some infantrymen. They glanced at him without welcome, but kept eating. The upcoming operation was making everyone silent, and they were all tired; the heavy seas of the past few days took a lot of energy from men cooped belowdecks, stewed in the same sweaty air, heat, damp, and boredom. . . .

He came back from memory to reality, to now, at a sudden snarl from the amtrac's engine. The marines stirred as the starter whined again and then the diesel, not ten feet from any of them, burst into clattering life. A dim blue light came on over Cutford's head, like an infernal halo, and the corporal leaned forward. Sweat glistened on his skin, and against the hair at his open blouse Will Givens caught a twisted gleam of gold. He leaned too, tensing, to look forward to where the A-driver crouched in his turret.

The gears meshed with a bang and the 'track began to roll. Its treads clawed at the steel deck, jolting over tie-downs, sending every slam and lurch straight up their backbones. Givens wedged himself into the seat, tightening his hands on the mortar. Low and heavy, the amphibious tanks floated with only a couple of feet of freeboard. Sometimes, he remembered, when they hit the water they didn't float at all. The men locked inside didn't have much of a chance then.

Any minute now . . .

Twenty-five tons of steel and men launched itself into the sea. He felt a moment of falling, then heard the clatter of the diesel change timbre, become a heavier mutter. The exhaust burbled like a drowning giant behind them. Received, then yielded up again reluctantly by the sea, they leaned with a slow waterlogged roll. Givens stared across the aisle at Washman—"Washout"—and the white boy stared back at him, his face sober. They looked at each other for several seconds and then Washman managed a scared wink. Givens smiled slowly and then winked back.

The amtrac began to turn. The big 'tracks, efficient and fast for something of their weight on land, were under-powered and logy in the water. He felt his body grow light, and then crash down. They were in open sea, on their way to the beach. A single ray of sun came shooting back from the A-driver's viewport. With the twenty other captives he stared at it as it danced along, briefly gilding the pronged barrel of the machine gun, swaying to Silky's bulging crotch, Harner's vacant grin, the tops of Cutford's white socks, Givens' long fingers splayed over the spiral threads of the tube, and then fled out of their dark compartment as the track turned once again. He steadied the mortar with his knees and reached up to wipe his forehead. His hand came away dripping and he used his sleeve next. His mouth began to water. He slipped off his helmet and pulled from the liner the candy sack he had saved against this ride.

At the sound of his retching the other marines groaned. The lifejackets danced in close gloom as the track corkscrewed. The seas grew steeper as they closed the beach, bottlenecked by the rising bottom, and the 'track soared and plunged and rolled. The air stank of diesel fumes. Givens had started it, but most of the troops were sick now, using utility caps, paper bags, shirt pockets, anything to keep it off the deck of the amtrac. They had swabbed it up too many times before. Only Silkworth and Cutford leaned back against the vibrating steel, the squad leader watching with a smile of disdain, the lance corporal with an expression that could be either contempt or hatred.

U.S.S. *GUAM*

Eight miles to seaward of them, high on the bridge of the flagship, Isaac Sundstrom dropped his binoculars to dangle against the rows of ribbons on his tropical khaki.

"Lenson! Get me Haynes."

"Sir?"

"Colonel Haynes. Where is he?"

"I think he's in Helo Direction, sir, or he might be—"

"Find him. Ask him if it's convenient for him to come up to flag bridge."

Colonel Stephen Haynes, USMC, was in charge of the two thousand-plus marines in MAU 32. His troops were embarked in all six amphibs, and directed from Haynes' command center on the *Guam*. When he came up Sundstrom was staring landward again, his binoculars on the leading wave. The coast was a line of brown, the surf a strand of white caught between blue sea and a climbing slope of foothills. Between the flagship, sixteen thousand yards out, and that seemingly motionless line, nine ships stood closer in. Two of them were the LSTs, *Newport* and *Barnstable County.* The third and fourth were *Spiegel Grove* and *Coronado;* the LSD and LPD carried both amtracs and assault boats. They were underway, steaming parallel to the beach while black specks tumbled from their sterns in plumes of spray: the second assault wave. Beyond them, low and black against the land, the destroyers rode close inshore. *Ault, Bowen,* the Italians and Turks. Their guns pointed toward the empty hills. And beyond them, closest in of all, a line of dark dots yawed and threw foam, streaming blue smoke as they wallowed almost imperceptibly toward the surf.

The two men watched tensely, silently. A rumble grew above them and suddenly two jets flashed overhead, canted lazily away from the beach, and slanted down above a headland to the east. Metal glittered beneath them, tumbling, then dirty smoke leaped up. Moments later came the *brrump* of a stick of bombs.

"How do they look, Steve?" said the commodore at last, not turning.

"Not too bad. Scattered, but that could be the seas. Surf height's four at last report. That's pretty rough for the mike-sixes."

"You think so? I think they're dropping the goddamn ball on us. The boat group commander's four hundred yards left of where he should be. That's why none of them are on track!"

"They look pretty close on the screen," said the colonel. "You're a perfectionist, Ike. That's what they told me about you before we met."

"Somebody has to be," said the commodore, but

Haynes' words might have pleased him; at least he smiled. "Other than that, how are we?"

"Some problems. Nothing we can't iron out. We've been at this for a while."

"You'd think after three months in the Med . . . but some people just can't get it straight. Like this chief staff officer of mine, Hogan. Like my intel team. Nothing personal, Steve, but a few of your men, too. And the ships' commanding officers don't have the big picture either. Their noses are down in their own little rice bowls. They don't understand somebody has to quarterback the whole pie, make sure the operation doesn't fall through the cracks. And frankly, anyone who doesn't realize that— well, he isn't worthy to be wearing khaki." The commodore leaned back against the coaming. "Fine day, though, isn't it?"

"Except for the surf," said the colonel. He stared to landward. "Some of those bulldozers, when they come off the causeways . . . this beach is notorious for soft patches in the sand."

"You've warned them about it? Ordered them to wear lifejackets?"

"Of course, Ike," said Haynes quietly. "I've seen drowned men before."

"Is everything else on schedule? When they hit—how soon can you be ready to pull out again?"

"I'll be *ready* anytime. But I'd hoped to get a couple of days ashore. The men get antsy cooped up. Forty-eight hours—"

"I want them to prepare for a quick withdrawal. As soon as objective is reached."

"Understood," said the colonel, losing the agreeable look he had worn since he arrived on the bridge. For a moment he and the commodore stared at opposite ends of the beach.

Below them at that moment, two decks down, Lieutenant Lenson was repeating himself for the fourth time, shouting over the whine and static of unsynchronized transmitters at a Turkish destroyer.

And inshore of them, deep within one of the warlike silhouettes that rode gray against white of surf and brown of hills, Chief Wronowicz, squinting against fluorescent light, grunted a warning about voltage regulation to the nervous watchstander in front of Number One switchboard in the forward engineroom.

Four miles inland, the skids of the first helicopters slammed into the dirt at the landing zone.

And Private First Class Will Givens and nineteen other seasick marines felt the scrape of beach under the treads. They seized their weapons as the nose lifted. The engine roared anew, shifting gears to maneuver inland, and then two dozen tons of amtrac skidded sideways as the driver braked. The hatch banged down into a blinding wall of daylight, and they pounded down the ramp, yelling as they dropped to their bellies onto sand and scrub, jacking cartridges into their rifles.

A long blast of fire ripped out ahead of them. Givens saw the muzzle flashes between the dunes. Burdened with the mortar, he drew his pistol clumsily. "Machine gun," screamed Cutford, beside him. The dark face was distorted. "Ready—advance!"

"Oorah!"

They charged forward. He fled over scrub brush, air hot in his throat, the sand turning his run into a nightmare stumble. Ahead of him the hidden gun chattered steadily. He fired wildly, not aiming, just making noise, and at that moment something caught his foot and he fell. Fell hard, knocking the wind out of him with agonizing force. He lay there for a long moment, watching the sand and trying to breathe. So many grains, alike from a distance, but up close each unique and only itself . . .

A man walked toward him across the dunes. His eyes found Givens, steadied on him. Givens stiffened. He started to get up. The man walked up to him.

"You're dead," he said.

Givens sagged back into the sand. The umpire strolled on. A marine ran by him, shouting. The umpire caught his arm. The man crumpled. He grabbed at his leg and began shouting for a corpsman.

Cutford returned, cursing him. Pulling the mortar from his unresisting arms, the corporal ran on under a double load, not looking back.

And the whole immense mechanism of Task Force 61, over two thousand marines, three thousand sailors, eleven ships, forty aircraft, continued the strike inland toward a dot on a map, toward an imaginary enemy somewhere in the silent sweep of sere and empty hills.

For it was all an exercise. It was all a game. Every man knew that; just another in an unending series of practices in a Navy that—it sometimes seemed to them—had been built and manned and maintained for forty years of peace, five thousand miles from home, just for drill. It had been the same through three months of the six-month deployment. This was just another exercise. It would go well or badly; some men would make mistakes and be reprimanded, others would do well and be complimented. But then it would be finished, and then there would be liberty. And then it would be over, and could be forgotten; because it was a drill, and none of it was for real.

This time.

THE BAQA'A VALLEY, LEBANON

The air over the camp blazed with light; it boiled with windless heat above flat asphalt, off the tin roofs of the wooden barracks—built by the British, one of the men from the Committee had told him. The tall man thought it a sign, the dark humor of a God beyond history but determining it all, who fought for those who fought for Him. The desert air boiled above the obstacle course, the barbed-wire gate, the dusty road that stretched off toward the firing range.

Hanna Abu Harisah crouched in full sunlight, blinking sweat from his eyes. In his pocket his thumb found the stopwatch.

"Begin!"

The assault pistol leapt of itself into his hands. Short-barreled, with a collapsible stock, it had a moment before been invisible beneath his civilian jacket. In the same motion he was at full sprint across the tarmac.

Running. Ahead, the glint and shimmer of aluminum. Behind, the thud of many pairs of boots. When the flat pop of automatic weapons began he flinched but kept on. His back felt naked. He ran as if to outdistance bullets. His own weapon jerked in his hands and spent cartridges leapt up to brand his forehead, glittering like broken-off bits of desert sun. They were past practicing with blanks. A man-shape sprang up to his right and he sprayed it without stopping, hearing three rounds clang off plate steel.

Ahead, the boarding ladder. He went up it three steps at a time, screaming through scorched lungs, pistol extended and hammer back. Inside, darkness. Shredded upholstery, overhead luggage bins racked by bullets. A second manshape. He swung and triggered without thought. After two rounds the striker clicked on an empty chamber but he had anticipated that and his free arm swept up. The lever popped free as it left his hand and the grenade hit the cutout in the chest. Behind him he heard firing, thuds, muffled screams from the crew compartment.

A whistle trilled faintly outside and he paused, panting. It was over. He retrieved the dummy grenade and watched his men as they filed down the boarding ladder. Dark-haired, sweating, they clutched their gleaming new weapons, pantomimed deadly jabs with their hands at each other. Some grinned; some looked bored; one, a new recruit not used to exertion in the heat, was vomiting over the handrail as he descended. Another had cut his forehead, and dabbed at blood with the corner of his *kaffiyeh,* which had come partly unwound.

As Harisah lit a cigarette he searched their eyes, their gestures, evaluating them against men he had known and fought beside in years past. Four had been tested already, on a border raid four months before. The rest were unblooded. But they had spirit. They had responded well to the physical and political training, accepting the trade: his harsh discipline, in place of the apathy and squalor of the camps of the Transjordan.

They'll do, he thought. Not all of them; as with any group a few would be flawed, cowards or too foolhardy. But only a mission would find them out. All in all, he was content.

He took a deep drag and silhouetted himself in the open door.

"Skhot'!"

They stared back at him, turning to hear, gripping their weapons.

"Thirty seconds, from a hundred meters distance," he shouted, looking down into light-filled desert, into their upturned faces. The language he used was neither classical nor dialect; it was the new medial speech of the radio station, the newspaper. They were from many lands; it was their common tongue now.

"So. Do you know why you are doing this?"

They stared at him, heads lifted, eyes alight.

"I will tell you. Should you be assigned to seize a plane in flight, be aware: They have trained teams to take them back on the ground. They are as skilled and as well armed as you. Yet if you know how they will attack, you can defend—or better yet, prevent them from attacking by using your hostages.

"Very well, return to your places. We'll do it again, up the rear ramp this time."

As they filed away, the tall man glanced across the terrain, past the barracks huts, the wire. From here, from the top of the ramp, he could see far across the desert, see to the mountains that danced above the hot plain.

Beyond them, and beyond a plain and another range of mountains, lay his land.

His people's land, taken now by others. These others owned many things. Jet fighters. Missiles. Tanks. Some said, the atom bomb. There were not many of them. Yet they were rich. They had power.

But there were ways yet to fight them.

Harisah took a last drag and flicked the cigarette to the desert floor. He raised his weapon above his head and looked down on his men. Staring at the mountains, he opened his throat to the sky.

"Sharaf! Majd! Khulud!"

Sweaty, exhausted, their teeth gleamed whitely as his men looked back and up to where he stood. Their hoarse shouts, their upthrust fists echoed his. *"Sharaf! Majd! Khulud!"*

Honor. Glory. Immortality.

Their enemies did not have the ultimate weapon. He did.

His enemies were not ready to die.

II

THE LIBERTY

2

Taormina, Sicily

LENSON WOKE EARLY THAT FIRST MORN-
ing ashore, roused by a golden triangle of sunlight.

He watched it for a long time, not moving, after he
opened his eyes. The ray crept across the crumpled sheet
toward him, so slowly it seemed not to move at all. It was
quiet in the room. There was only the sound of two people
breathing, and the cry of gulls.

When the sun reached his eyes he blinked and raised his
head. Turning in the bed, he looked at the woman beside
him.

His expression of wonder grew. She slept peacefully,
lips parted, a strand of dark hair across her cheek. His eyes
traced her face in the ruthless morning light. The lacing
of veins at her nose; the curve of her neck; a slight tired
crinkle of skin at the corners of her closed eyes; the fine
features, the delicate complexion of Asian blood. Raising
himself gently from the rumpled bed, he stood naked by
it for a long time, looking down at her. She had wrapped
the upper sheet around herself, and in the quiet light her
face was like a sleeping child's.

At last he turned, catching his breath as his bare feet left
carpeting for tile, and crossed to the windows that opened
on the balcony. He leaned out, feeling the stone morning-
cool against his bare arms.

Rubbing at the scarred flesh of his shoulder, he stared out, over the crystal blue of the Mediterranean.

The Hotel Vecchio frowned down from the heights of Taormina like a captain from the bridge of his ship. It was a traditional hotel, a dignified hotel. Its walls were solid stone, and the curule chairs at each landing looked as if they had carried Caesars on holiday here by the blue Ionian. She had chosen it, days before, when the wives had arrived to await the ships. He thought it was too expensive, even in declining lire, but he had to admit she had chosen well. Its outdated calm would mirror the perfection of the coming days, the halfway point of the deployment. Here with her he could forget for a time the fatigue, the monotony, the loneliness of three months at sea. Could push away, ignore, the thought of three more months without her.

For four days, he would be happy.

He glanced back into the room. She was still, one arm outflung in the rising tide of golden light. He did not want to wake her. Their night had been passionate. Instead he leaned out again, absorbing himself in the play of light on rock and sea, the gradual repossession of the world by the sun.

Sicily was awakening. Gulls cried in sleepy hunger from the paling sky, and waves lapped against the cliff below the hotel. A squad of small boys, naked as puppies, clambered from rock to rock. One dived into the blue, coming up to swirl water from his hair. Beyond them, miles out, the sun was turning a flat and perfect sea to liquid bronze.

He lifted his face to the light. It took so much work to deserve, this sense of peace; and it came so seldom. Life was filled with a thousand negatives. Boredom, anger, sometimes terror. But happiness was part of it too, if you did what you had to do. If you did that—only what was right, and did it with all your strength—then the good could come.

Surely nothing truly evil, nothing irredeemably ugly, could exist in a world with this capacity for beauty.

A fishing boat, chugging slowly out to its day's work, drew its silhouetted bow through molten copper, shattering it into a million glittering diamonds.

Shattering it . . .

Before his gaze, silently and tremendously, the bow, the cutting edge, grew to fill the sea, blot out the sky. A steel cliff. At its foot a line of white gleamed cruelly, like bared teeth.

The bow of an aircraft carrier, towering sudden and tremendous in the night.

No, he thought. Not here! Sweat pricked his bare arms. He swallowed, fighting memory, hallucination, nightmare. It was morning! Italy—Susan—

He could not avert it. His fingers cramped suddenly on ancient stone, transformed, in his seething mind, into the steel splinter shield of a destroyer.

The *Reynolds Ryan* had been in company with a carrier task group. Late at night, several hundred miles west of Ireland, Dan Lenson had been on her bridge, junior officer of the deck.

Someone had made a mistake.

He stood frozen on the balcony for long minutes, looking out with unseeing eyes. The first wind of morning stirred the hair on his bare chest.

The recording, like a tape in his head, ended at last. The North Atlantic, the cries of burning men receded, thinned, vanishing like a dream. The trawler was turning away. Men moved tranquilly about its distant deck, laying out their nets.

Against his will, he looked toward the harbor. The curve of the town blocked his view, and that, too, was fine, as fine as the morning. He swallowed again.

He did not really want to see the *Guam*.

Behind him, later, he heard the bed creak. When he turned from the sea she was sitting up, watching him, her eyes intent and unsmiling.

Just seeing her stirred him after the months of longing. It was not her hair, dark as oiled walnut, swept back with

one hand to lie across the pillow, that stirred him, nor the
revelation of nudity as she pulled back the coverlet to
invite him in. It was not her bare legs, tanned dusky to the
thighs, nor the small breasts, pale with a hint of saffron.
It was true that compared to her other women seemed to
him oversized, hairy, and common. (He had never said
that aloud to anyone. But he had remarked to Flasher one
night on watch that he had never looked at another
woman with interest since he had met her; a remark that
Red, for once, let pass in the darkness without a guffaw.)

"Morning, babe," he said, and smiled.

"How long have you been out there, Dan?"

"Not long."

"Isn't it peaceful here? I love to get up early and just
stand there, like you, and look out. Are the boys swimming?"

"Yes," he said. He ached to go to her, but he stayed by
the window. The wind was cool on his back. It was good
just to look at her, and let the hunger for her wait, whet
itself into pain. It would be all the better to join her, feeling
like that. . . .

"I know one of them. Erculiano. He waits tables at
dinner. I'll introduce you."

"No. Don't get up yet," he said, giving in. As he slid in
beside her they came together thigh to thigh, breast to
breast. She was sleeping-warm and smelled of the night's
love, and her shoulders were small and smooth in his
hands.

"Are you happy?" she said into his shoulder.

"To be with you? Yes."

"And to be in Italy?"

"Yes. It's lovely."

"I think so, too. I'm glad you made us come."

"I didn't *make* you come, babe."

"That's true. I wanted to," she whispered quickly. She
glanced around the room, then smiled. "I was looking for
Nancy . . . forgot where she was for a minute."

"It was good of Mrs. Hogan to take her. That was above and beyond the call of duty."

"Alicia's all right. And Nan likes her."

"How is she, traveling? Hard to handle?"

"No, she's good most of the time. For her age." Susan laughed a little, raising her eyebrows.

"It's good for both of you. I think you were right to come out. You can make up your class work. You can't always come to the Med."

"I have to keep studying while I'm here."

"I know," he said, feeling her go away from him somehow, although she did not move at all; he felt he had phrased his remark wrong, about her work, and tried to retrieve it. "You can study here, and between ports. You have your books. I don't want you to fall behind."

"Yes . . ."

She snuggled close again and he rubbed her shoulders and back, wondering, as he always did in the all-too-short times they were together, about how delicate and fine and at the same time strong and proud her body was; how close to him and silently wonderful. It seemed so seldom, he was away so much; and yet when she was there, it was all-encompassing; it made him happy. And from it, somehow, they had produced a child.

He did not understand at all what he had done to be so lucky.

She muttered something then. Her head was on his chest and he could not hear it. "What?" he said.

"I said, I don't like being away from you, Dan."

"I know."

"I get afraid."

"I know."

"I said . . . when you hold me like this, it feels . . . it feels like nothing bad can happen to us, not ever."

He moved to hold her more tightly, feeling salt sting his closed eyelids. A wave of tenderness made him tremble as he caressed her back, from shoulder down the soft curve of thigh. He felt like telling her how much he loved her.

But he did not say the words. Instead his hand hesitated, then moved again, downward.

She stirred. "What are you doing?"

"Nothing."

"You don't want to make love, do you?"

"Who, me?"

"You feel like it . . . down here . . ."

"Well, we already did."

"But that was last night."

"Oh yeah. This is another day, isn't it."

"Wait a sec," she said, a few minutes later. "Let me up. I'll be right back."

But when she came back she had to smile. She was ready for him, but he was asleep. Sitting beside him, she touched his face lightly, feeling the rough stubble of beard, tracing his mustache. Seeing how tired he looked in the growing light.

And then the annoyance came, unasked-for, unwelcome. This was good, being together. But it came too seldom. For the last hundred days—she had counted them one by one—she had been alone. Yes, she loved him. But this wasn't what she'd expected from marriage.

She frowned, in the light-filled room, and tried to push the thought away. She did not want to spoil Taormina.

Susan Lenson turned angrily in her bed, and reached for a book.

They'd met at the Academy, at one of the mixers that introduced the midshipmen to "suitable" girls. She had seen the notice on the bulletin board at the student center, and thought the trip might be fun. Some of the other girls had been there, and although they thought the "mids" handsome, they said it was dull. Nowhere to go but the campus, nothing to drink, and they felt like toking would be a federal crime . . . certainly not in front of all the straight-arrow midshipmen. But they also said Annapolis was a pretty place, especially in spring, and so she had thought to see what there was to see and then go back to the bus and study.

But it turned out to be a military operation. Before the bus could start they had to check names against the sign-up list. Then there was a kind of inspection; one girl had to leave; she was wearing shorts. Susan almost got off right there, and would have except for Moira Lieberman, her roommate. "The Ox" was eager to go, and when Moira wanted something, no one could turn her off. So she stayed, too. When they arrived, a man in uniform—she had no idea what he was—escorted them straight from the bus to the dance. There had been no chance to duck out, so she and Moira had stood in the big hall and waited, smoking.

When the mids came in she saw immediately that they were all alike. The same hair, the same uniform, the same face. "They're robots," she whispered to Moira, who laughed. "Men of steel," her roommate said out loud. "I hope."

She stood in the middle of the room and smoked as they circled in. She hated mixers; you stood and hoped and waited and then drew some goob with bad breath . . . her friends fell one by one to the robots, and she kept smoking, nervous now at the thought of not being asked to dance at all. She would have left, but the place was so big, she had no idea how to get back to the bus. . . .

"Excuse me," said someone behind her. "You're here from Trinity?"

"No. Georgetown."

"That's in D.C., right? Hi. My name's Dan."

"Mine's Susan—Susan Chan. Some of the girls call me Betts."

"Hello, Susan. Want to dance?"

"I guess so."

He was a robot. Tall, as good-looking as most of them, but he scared her a little. They were so different from the boys who came around in jeans and beards to drink beer with them on the steps in front of the library. This man

wore a black uniform with gold on the sleeves. His hair
was incredibly short. He danced as if unused to it, but after
the second he seemed less threatening—or threatened.
Later she was willing to go down to "the steerage"—that
was the name of the snack bar—and sit waiting for him
while he bought (honest) two milk shakes.

"So what do you do here?" she asked him when he came
back, holding the milk shakes carefully away from his suit.

"Student. Same as you."

"Come on. Aren't you in the Army?"

He winced. "*Navy.* Yes. Or sort of. I will be, in a year."

She poked his sleeve. "What do these stripes mean?"

"I'm a segundo. A junior." He grinned as he said it, at
her, and she didn't like his tone. She decided that he was
a prick. They all were; this was a Fascist citadel, and it was
stupid for her to have come here when she could have been
studying.

"And what do you do?"

"I'm in archaeology."

"A junior?"

"Sophomore."

"Oh. So, have you dug up any fossils yet?"

"Archaeologists don't 'dig up fossils.' That's a paleon-
tologist," she stated, and started to get up. "I think I'd
better—"

"No, wait. Don't go. I'm sorry," he said, and she saw
suddenly that he was uneasy too, shy of her in a different
way than she of him, but still shy. "I don't know the
difference. What is it?"

She hesitated, half to her feet, and then sat down again.
She explained, and he asked questions. He didn't know
much about the social sciences, but he was smart. She was
warming to him, until she took out her pack and offered
him one. "No!" he said, raising his eyebrows. "You don't
actually inhale those things, do you?"

"Jesus. You make it sound like a moral judgment."

"It's not good for you."

"It's none of your damn business, frankly."

"I know, Susan. You asked me."

"I didn't ask you anything!"

"Okay," he said, looking puzzled and little-boyish; and again the change was so strange, so sudden, that she found it funny. He looked so serious and regretful. He was a character.

She decided that he was cute.

It was all, she thought lying there beside him, very strange how rapidly, how easily, everything had happened after that. A year later she had accepted his miniature, a little Academy ring she never had had the courage to wear at school. When she graduated they lived together for six months. Except for one nasty scene with Mr. Lenson—his father hated anyone, Dan said, who didn't look just like him, which meant white—it was all right, and one day they were married. Almost offhand, as if she had accepted it without thinking. Then Nan . . . she had not been planned; nothing was 100 percent effective, but they had never discussed not having her.

And so Susan Chan, who was once going to be the Margaret Mead of archaeology, was in Italy at last. But not for field work. Instead she was a Navy wife, a mother, following the gray ships from port to port. . . .

"Come on," she said, shaking him. "It's eight o'clock, sleepy. I want some breakfast."

He came awake like a tiger, and she gasped once and then reached to guide him as his long body moved over her. And the miles were no more; the long parting was forgotten, almost, and they were together.

After breakfast they walked together through the hilly town. He wore civilian slacks, a jacket, a short-sleeved shirt. Susan left her traveling jeans and pack for a navy skirt and tweed coat. The tables were already set out in front of street cafés. Trellised roses arched above the tables; the heating sky arched above all. She matched her stride to his long legs, glancing up at him. It was always like this, she thought, when they met again. Joy, but with a sense of strain. As if they had grown out of step during the months apart, and needed to rematch their pace. It takes awhile, she thought, to feel close to someone again.

And then, as usual, it would be time for him to leave. . . .

"So how was the trip?" he asked her. "Did you mind traveling with Mrs. Hogan?"

Susan made a face. "Alicia's okay, but I can't take that bunch long. All through France, don't do this, don't drink that, I got sick in this hotel once, why don't you wear something more ladylike . . . oh, I'm sure they're real people, Dan. But I had to get away. I left them at Nice."

"You came here from the Riviera alone?"

"It wasn't hard. Nan was good. We met a lot of people on the train." She told him an amusing story of going through customs at the Franco-Italian border between Menton and Ventimiglia, of Italian paratroopers in the second-class car smuggling wine under the skirts of fat peasant women. "And then I stopped in Genoa, and saw the city, and spent most of the next week in Rome. That was tremendous, the Museo Vaticano, the digs in the subway. I went down to see Dr. Biccari's team at work. Then Alicia and the others came through and I came down here with them."

"Where are they staying? Here?"

"No, no. They're down in Giardini, closer to the fleet landing." She laughed. "But I came up here on the bus, I couldn't resist it. The view! And it gets you away from the ship, doesn't it?"

"It sure does." He grinned down at her. "You know what I need, all right. So you've had a week to see the town?"

"I haven't seen squat. We stayed in our room and I read François Bordes and Nan watched 'The Three Stooges' in Italian and we waited for you."

He reached out to her in the middle of the street, and looked down into her dark eyes; laughing, slightly hard for everyone but him. She was so vibrant, so alive, that she made him feel stiff and dull. But in spite of that he loved her more intensely than he had ever thought he could love a human being.

"Give me a kiss."

"I thought you Navy types didn't like affection in public."

"Pretend I'm a civilian, just for today, all right?" He joked. She put her face up then. But her remark had spoiled something, and he lagged behind as she roamed through the high town.

In the afternoon they became suddenly purposeful, and went sightseeing. Susan dragged him around San Pancrazio, telling him the walls dated from the third century B.C.; the Greek theater; the Naumachia, which reminded him of a model-towing tank. He trailed along with his jacket slung over his shoulder, sweat soaking his shirt, and took pictures. He wanted to put together, at the end of this cruise, an album of all the ports Comphibron Six had visited, along with a few paragraphs of description in his own and Susan's hands. He imagined that someday, when they were old, they would look through it together. At four the sun grew too much for them, and they went back to the hotel and took a shower together and made love again and then napped.

When they woke they had a short but surprisingly bitter argument over where to go for dinner. He wanted to try the hotel dining room. She was sick of it and wanted to go out. In the end they compromised. Dinner at the hotel, and the night out in Giardini, at the base of the hill.

They found a noisy knot of the bachelor officers at the Hotel Naxos bar. He ordered gin and tonics. That was the only drink Susan really liked. The bachelors welcomed them, but Dan felt the conversation become awkward. Once you were married, in the Service, you moved out of their circle and into that of the married officers. After one drink he nudged her and they went out into the night again. They found a bench at the seawall, overlooking the water. It was cool, welcome after the heat of the day, and the wind came in sweet and heavy off the sea, smelling of salt and faraway storm.

"You didn't like them?"

"They were all right. Just . . . I'd rather be with you."

"You're sweet," she said, looking away toward the sea, and his eyes followed hers, out into the dark.

Dark, but blazing and twinkling with lights. The evening was clear. Across the Strait of Messina, only twenty miles wide here at the meeting of Italy and Sicily, Reggio and Pellaro and Porto Salvo glowed like heaps of fallen fireflies. He made out four ships, moving slowly against the fixed lamps of the far shore; a green sidelight, red; two bound south, two north. The traffic would get even thicker as they neared the neck of the strait, a few miles north. He remembered taking the squadron through there a few weeks before. It had been a hairy evolution.

Closer in, swinging a mile or so out beyond the breakwater, *Guam* had dressed ship. The electricians had been climbing about when he left the night before, and now the ship was a pyramid of lights. They stretched white from bow to truck, truck to stern, and multicolored lamps glittered along the edge of the helo deck. It was beautiful to see, a twinkling palace suspended in the darkness; beautiful to see. . . .

"What's the matter?" she whispered, leaning on his arm.

"Nothing."

"Yes there is. You're quiet. When you get quiet . . . come on, talk to me. Is it the *Ryan*? Is that still bothering you?"

"No. I mean, it still bothers me, yes. But that's not all of it."

"Is it this ship? Is it old Crazy Ike?"

"Yeah," he said, his voice so soft she could hardly hear it above the sigh of wind.

"He's giving you a rough time?"

"Not me, so much . . . I think he likes me. Red was his fair-haired boy on the way across, but now—"

"Red? Which one is he?"

"The chubby guy—he was the one juggling apples at Stan's party."

"Oh, him. Lieutenant Flasher, right? He's so silly! I liked him."

"Anyway, all of a sudden Sundstrom turned against him. I have no idea why, but since then I've moved up to favorite."

"That can't be so bad. Isn't that what you wanted? Isn't that why you volunteered for sea duty again, after the court-martial?"

"You don't know what it's like." His voice hardened, and she felt afraid, a little. He never spoke to her like that; it was another side of him, the Navy side.

"What do you mean?"

"Forget it. I shouldn't have mentioned it."

"Dan . . . don't clam up on me. Don't pull that Academy bullshit. It wasn't your fault! There's nothing to prove! The Board said—"

"I don't care what they said! I keep thinking—damn it, I knew the maneuver was risky. I was only an ensign, but if I'd spoken up, argued with the captain, it might, it might not have happened."

"Dan. Don't, please. They cleared you and the man above you."

"The Board hung it on Captain Packer because he was dead and it was neater that way. But none of us on the bridge came off clean, Susan. With that letter of reprimand in my jacket my career is shot unless I pull four-ohs from here on out."

"Then why are you worried, if *he* likes you?"

"It's nothing I can pin down. He just lets things get on his nerves; he worries, all alone there in his sea cabin . . . then he gives these crazy orders. He ridicules the officers on the bridge, in front of everybody. He treats the chief staff officer like a plebe. I've never served with a guy like this before. Commodore MacInroe would tear your ass off if you screwed up, but at least you knew where you stood. He wanted a tight squadron, good performance, and he knew what he was doing. I try to give Sundstrom the benefit of the doubt. He's only had the job three, four months. But he seems to be getting worse, not better." He fell silent, still looking out to sea, toward the ship that was swinging now into the wind. "Don't worry. I can take him all right. But sometimes I wonder . . . if something happens while we're here in the Med, I hate to think what it'll be like with him in charge."

"Don't say that! I don't want to hear about that. Nothing's going to happen, is it?"

"Not that I know of. But that's what we're here for, Susan."

"I don't know what you're here for. I don't know what business the Navy has this far from America anyway."

They both sensed the argument coming, and neither of them wanted it; they dropped the subject tacitly. She turned to look across the bay. "There's yours—the big one," she said. "And that other one—didn't you say there were six ships in the squadron? Where are the others?"

"You don't put the whole task force into the same place for liberty, not in the Med. The port authorities don't like it, too many sailors at once. And it's not a good idea if we're attacked."

"Where are the other ships?"

"Scattered around. *Guam* and *Barnstable County* here . . . *Newport* and *Ault* in Naples . . . *Spiegel Grove* and *Coronado* in Palermo . . . *Charleston* in Civitavecchia. We'll join up after the port visits for the next exercise."

"I'd like to go to Greece. And maybe one of the islands, look at some of the digs. Moira's on a project in Cyprus. She wrote me about it."

"Our next port is Iskenderun. Turkey. I guess you could go through the islands on the way."

"And Yugoslavia . . ."

"I don't think that would be a good idea."

"Why?"

"It's a Communist country, Susan."

"So what? They allow tourists."

"You say that like it doesn't matter."

"That they're Communists? Dan, don't be ridiculous. You act like we were at war with them, or something."

"I just don't think it would be a good idea."

"Well, is Turkey any better?"

"That's a good question," he said, thinking of the last exercise. "They don't seem to want to play on our team anymore, as Sundstrom would say. They can't even answer their radios right."

"I don't see why they have to," she said. "Here we are, in their ocean—"

"It's everybody's ocean, Susan."

She twisted, to look up at him. "Dan. Speaking of that—have you thought about what we talked about, before you left?"

"What's that?"

"About your getting out of the Navy."

He didn't answer for a while. He was looking out at the bay. At last he said, "Some."

"You promised me you'd think about it."

"I know. And I am. I'm just not ready to talk about it yet."

And again they both stopped, unwilling to go farther, and looked out to sea in silence. After a time he put his arm around her, felt the coolness of her bare shoulders. "You getting cold, babe?"

"A little."

"Want to head back?"

"I ought to stop by and pick Nan up. She'll get worried if she has to go to bed again without me."

He saw her, just for a moment, not as a wife or lover, but as a mother. He smiled. He had wondered, when Nan was coming, how she would adapt. But she had. "Okay," he said. "Let's go back to the bar. Jack Byrne has a rental car. Maybe he'll give us a lift up the hill after we pick her up, and we can show them Taormina."

"All right," she said, hearing the meekness in her voice

and wondering at it. Where did it come from, when she was with him? All her friends said she was so independent, so sure of herself. But when she was with this tall man— her husband on and off, he was gone so long it seemed like that—it all changed. *She* changed, became someone different. She did not like it; she reacted with resentment, and then in surprise heard herself arguing, complaining. . . .

She made herself stop thinking about it. This was his liberty, and they would enjoy it. They went out of the wind, out of the uncertain reaching and drawing back that was always there when they were together, into the hotel to look for the others.

3

Palermo, Sicily

YOU COULD SMELL SOUTHERN ITALY, Sergeant Silkworth had told the mortar squad, long before it came over the horizon. He had described the flies, the heat, the sewage that fouled the soft crystalline air.

And then, relishing the open-mouthed attention of the privates, he had described its pleasures.

Sweating that morning at formation, Private First Class Willard Staunton Givens, U.S. Marine Corps, slid his eyes beyond the flight deck of the *Spiegel Grove*. Past Corporal Cutford's broad back, beyond the life nets, to where a line of palest blue trembled in the early light. He sniffed.

Once again, the sergeant had been right.

"Ten-hut!" bawled the Top, and the two hundred marines of Bravo Company came to instant and complete attention. They stared out over the starboard side, ranks swaying with the roll of the old landing ship as the officers strolled out. Givens watched the back of Cutford's neck darken. It happened whenever the assistant squad leader saw brass. He glanced sideways at Harner, but the Kentuckian was looking straight ahead, his narrow face as still and empty as a worked-out mine.

"Have them stand easy," he heard one of them say.

"Bravo Company. At . . . *ease!*"

With two hundred other men, Givens went back to parade rest with the joint-cracking snap that every marine carried from boot camp and never let decay. Above them, looking down from a crane, two sailors snickered, then went instantly silent as a score of eyes swung up to memorize their faces. The company executive officer—Will could never remember his name—stepped forward and raised his voice over the omnipresent whine of the ship's ventilators.

"Got a message from the colonel last night," the exec began. "A 'well done' on the practice landing yesterday. The movement inshore was expeditious. Units hit the beach in good order, with an aggressive spirit. Specific comments on Bravo Company: generally good, but battalion staff heard too much undisciplined chatter on the portable radios. In battle, reports have to be short, military, and to the point. You'll hear more from your noncoms, but in general, a good exercise.

"Today, I figure this is no news to you, we're slated for some well-deserved liberty. We'll be in Palermo for four days. For those who haven't seen the country on previous floats, you can have a good time here. But you can get really screwed up, too. The way to enjoy yourself ashore is to keep a few simple precautions in mind. . . ."

As he talked on, Givens stared at the back of Cutford's head. A rifle butt, he thought idly, would fit it so fine. Even the plastic Mattel toy shoulderpiece of the M-16 would fit so nice right behind the main gunner's chocolate-dark ear.

These six things doth the Lord hate. Yea, seven are an abomination unto him: a proud look, a lying tongue, and hands that shed innocent blood. An heart that deviseth wicked imaginations, feet that be swift in running to mischief. A false witness that speaketh lies, and he that soweth discord among brethren. . . .

His eyes drifted down to the lance corporal's hands. At attention, they rested curled against the seams of his utilities as if asleep, black-haired, pale-palmed, the index finger of the left hand nicotine-brown over brother-brown.

A good swing, and then the satisfying *chunk* as the rifle butt hit . . .

"This off-limits area extends from just beyond the railway station, the Estazione Ferroviaria. Under no conditions are military personnel permitted to cross into it. The Shore Patrol will point the limits of this area out to you, should this be necessary."

Ess-tossy-onay Fairy Veahria, Givens repeated in his mind. The exec sounded like a pansy.

No. That wasn't right. For a moment he felt scared. Thinking about hitting another marine—being disrespectful, even in his mind, to an officer—that wasn't him. His lips moved, calling for strength to resist the unrighteous. He was letting Cutford and Silky get to him. Make him like them, in their own different yet like images of power. So what if the exec knew some Italian. Maybe he could learn some himself. It had been easy enough to pick up a couple of words in Spanish at Rota. Hernandez said he sounded like a real "raza," whatever that was.

No, he had to discipline his thoughts. The exec was all right, for a officer. For *an* officer. Maybe, he thought guiltily, I better start listening up.

". . . Palermo has been a center of historical events and military campaigns for centuries. In A.D. 835 the Saracens captured the town, and held Sicily for two centuries, till Roger the Norman recaptured it. It was taken by Allied forces under General Patton in 1943, in the largest amphibious assault in history. . . ."

"Jee . . . sus," he heard Liebo mutter to his right, his round face outthrust so that Will could see him even with his eyes straight ahead. "Shut your fuckin' mouth, Dippy," came Sergeant Silkworth's rasping murmur down the line.

Where do they learn all that? Givens wondered. Was that college, too? Or did all the officers get briefed, before they hit a port? Read it out of some manual?

". . . And remember, as in any Catholic country, women are respected. Make no advances until you ascertain their status. A lot of the men here carry knives, and they know how to use them.

"That brings up one last point: politics. The Italian Communists are active here. They'd love to embarrass the Marine Corps and through us the United States. Don't be drawn into arguments. We don't want any international incidents, and we don't want any of our troops hurt, either.

"Any questions? . . . Top, take over and dismiss the men."

As the formation broke Givens let his knees sag for a moment. He looked around. The land was nearer, a hazy stroke of pastel across a blue-gray morning. The snickering sailors were gone from the crane. Cutford was talking to another brother. He looked dangerous, as he usually was after being subjected to an officer's lecturing. Will moved toward the rail to avoid hearing, to avoid being drawn in. His boots scuffed on the nonskid of the deck.

The ship was turning, the wind shifting to the starboard side, and as he reached the nets the land came suddenly into full view, much closer than he had thought. He dropped to sit, dangling his legs above the wake sixty feet below, and looked out.

Low, blue, the flattened hills were hazy and contrastless, curved in a sweep of sea and morning-pure sky. Other marines were looking on, saying little. One of them was Washman, clicking away with an Instamatic. Givens stared out. He was a long way from Carolina. For a moment he wished he had never come.

"Where you planning on going, Will?"

"Oh. Hey, Washout." He looked behind him to make sure Cutford was out of earshot, then turned back to the squad rifleman. "I guess, just ashore. You heard the stories Silky been telling. Be fun to see the town, wouldn't it?"

"Shit, yeah. I never been here, either. That off limits, that sounds like the place to go. 'Everything past the railway station.' We could spend all fucken four days there."

"We could go there for a little while, yeah," said Givens cautiously.

"And all the other stuff, too. The castles and the volcano and the mummies."

"*Mummies?*"

"Wa'n't you listening? Lieutenant said they buried 'em in a cave, dressed and standing up. Said they scared the piss out of him. Well, he didn't say 'piss.' But it's going to be on that tour they set up."

"Yeah. Sure. The tour." Givens paused, knowing that what he really wanted, every waking moment and most achingly at night, was forbidden. "Well—I guess it wouldn't hurt to go ashore, look around a little."

"I know one of the squids," said Washman, twisting his pimpled face nervously around the deck; he was afraid of Cutford, too. "One of the gunner's mates. We was talking about the mortars. He wanted a round of eighty-one and I told him no way, José; Butterbars counts them fuckers every time we open the ammo locker. But he said he been to Palermo lots of times. He's an old guy, thirty. I bet he'd tell us the places to hit."

"So let's go find him, man," said Will, thrusting his thumbs under his web belt and scowling. It was easy to act tough around the Washout.

"In your pack, man."

They found the gunner's mate coming out of the mess decks with a mug of coffee. He didn't seem to recognize Washman, but when they asked about town he nodded. They followed him up to the after three-inch mount and sat on a ready service locker. Washout borrowed his ball pen and got the essentials down on a torn-out page of his *Guidebook for Marines.*

The rest of the morning oozed by, slow as promotion, like all the time they spent on shipboard. He and Washman wandered up to the bridge and watched the coast draw clearer until a lookout chased them off. They wandered down to the first-class mess, attracted by the sound of a television, and were ordered to move along. They went by the ship's store, hoping for pogey bait, chocolate or gum, but it was closed. So after that there was nothing to do but go back to the berthing space. Two decks down into the hull, it was as hot and smelly as any cavern inhabited for months on end by two hundred prehistoric men. They sat at the card table and watched Dippy and Hernandez in their endless game of spades. Harner was there, sitting beside the Chicano rifleman, chain-smoking Marlboros like he always did; he never touched the cards, never kibitzed, volunteered nothing. He was the tallest in the squad and never complained, even on forced marches. Cutford was there, but he seemed to be on safe for the moment. Lying in his bunk, eyes closed, earphones over his stocking cap, he was nodding to his stereo. Silkworth, Liebo muttered, was in a meeting with the Top. A fly droned among the slowly tilting bunkframes, the drowsing men.

A little after lunch they heard the squids man up for sea detail. The squad played one more hand and then drifted off to their lockers. Givens pulled a set of fresh Charlies from the wrappers they had been stowed in since the States. Liebo dimpled his tie in the mirror by the hatch. Hernandez patted on cologne, and tropical flowers filled the compartment. Harner meditated in the head, his straight razor dangling in his hand, sucking silently at a bloody lip.

Givens checked himself in the polished glass. His garrison cap sat straight on short, wiry hair. The collar of his khaki shirt was straight with starch, his globe-and-anchors a dull and warlike black. He pinned his ribbons level with the deck, conscious of their paucity. Someday, he promised himself for the hundredth time, there would be more. A whole chestful. He bared his teeth at his image and wrinkled his nose, wishing it were not quite so wide, wishing he did not look quite so young—

"What the fuck you doin', Oreo?"

"Nothin', man." He moved aside as Cutford shouldered

his way into the mirror. "Uh . . . you goin' on libs, bro'?"

Cutford said nothing. He stared into the mirror, then shifted his narrow eyes to Will's. He's so much darker than I am, Givens thought.

"Jesus, you stink," said the corporal.

"That's Hernandez."

"Why don't you put some on, too?"

"I don't like the smell. It's too strong."

"Hey," said Cutford. "Dap, brother."

Givens dapped him unwillingly. He felt clumsy doing the rhythm. He missed one and Cutford sneered and turned back to the mirror, flipping out a comb. There were gray wires in his hair. "Oreo, you fucked-up ofay-lover, you can't even pass power right."

"Cutford, nobody goes for that power stuff anymore."

"That's what *they* been tellin' you. Where you think you're goin'?"

"Out on liberty, like everybody else."

" 'Like everybody else.' Yeah, that's just your tune, Oreo. You just want to be one of the boys." He accented the last word. "And where you plannin' to go on this sweet liberty the big man give you?"

"I don't know. Just go ashore, walk around a little."

"Who with?"

"Nobody. Just us pees in the squad."

"You referrin' to your swan friends, of course."

"The whole squad's goin', man." Will sounded plaintive even to himself. He looked around, hoping someone else needed the mirror; but the compartment was emptying, men pushing by them, stepping carefully up the ladder to keep their starched O.D. trousers from bagging at the knees. He wanted nothing more than to get away from this man, but he was part of the squad; the offer, at least, was a necessity. "Why don't you come with us?"

The corporal's face came closer. Givens dropped his eyes to his gold chain, the twisted-carrot trinket Cutford wore without explaining even under his uniform, even in the showers, and the invitation died on his lips.

"Private Givens. Will, baby." The corporal's voice became soft. "Listen. You don't need to go out with those
people. You don't need to suck up to them and buy them
beer. You don't need to snake their dirty whores in some
enlisted man's off-limits craphouse, then cover your ass
with that Jesus talk of yours. You're a black man, a black
king, every place but in your head, man."

"Get off my case, Cutford. We bunk with them and eat
with them and we're supposed to be ready to fight with
them. You're the main gunner, man. Why can't you figure
you got to live with them, too?"

"Fuck you, then, Oreo. Someday you're going to see the
light. Till then—"

He tensed, expecting violence, but the corporal disappeared from the mirror. He hadn't touched him, even.
When he was sure he was gone Will breathed out. He
removed his cap, ran his comb through the stubble again,
and ran up the ladder to the main deck.

From sixty feet up he could see all of Sicily. From the
pier back the city lay like a pastel carpet. Miles of buildings festered between the hills and spread beyond them.
Far inland a massive volcanic cone thrust upward like a
thunderhead. In the afternoon brightness of the Mediterranean, Palermo seemed endless, immense, the largest city
on the planet, and after weeks at sea or on barren maneuver areas the honking, dog-barking murmur of land, the
chuffing of a rusty tugboat, the rich smells of exhaust and
sewage and pasta were intoxicating. He joined ten score
other marines and a few sailors at the rail and leaned his
elbows on the warm metal, breathing deep. Silkworth was
right, he thought again. He had smelled it from far at sea;
had smelled it, stronger and deeper, all through the morning. Even the stink of the compartment, soap and ship,
starch and cologne had become part of it, natural, like the
perfume of a beautiful, unwashed woman, a naked woman
who spread her legs from hill to hill before him.

To ease his sudden excitement he leaned forward, looking down at the pier.

Below them, on the outstretched sterngate (the ship had moored stern to), sailors in dungarees shouted and jumped back. The gangway had broken loose. It tilted, balanced for an instant, and then slid gracefully into the brown murk at the foot of the pier. The marines groaned. The sailors stared stupidly into the water. A fish circled belly up in sluggish scum, drink cans, oily rainbows. A fat chief in whites came out from inside the well deck and began giving orders. The marines shouted suggestions. A couple of linehandlers, a policeman, and a priest in hot-looking black watched from the pier. The sailors fished cautiously off the sterngate. The grapnel snagged something, they hauled away together, and the end of the gangway crept up into view, dripping slime.

"Don't drop it again," Will shouted down, and beside him Washman laughed. "These friggin' squids kill me," he said. The priest caught a heaving line and the policeman and two linehandlers joined him on it. When the far end of the brow banged on the concrete, the chief ran across and began lashing it to a bollard.

"Let's head on out," said Hernandez, with a deep sigh of anticipation.

On the pier, free at last, they ranged themselves in swaggering line abreast. Past two passenger liners the quay ended at a modern-looking concrete building that as they neared it became flaking, prewar. Its walls flapped with posters in fading greens and reds. He looked back once. The *Spiegel Grove* looked small, moored among the liners; small and old, graceless and dirty. It had carried him in her guts for three months, and every minute of it he had hated her.

He did not look back again.

The six of them—Givens, Washman, Hernandez, Sergeant Silkworth, Liebo, and Harner—stopped by common accord at the first bar beyond the gate, on a cobbled street as full of diesel fumes as traffic. The proprietor grumbled at their dollars, but took them. After two or three beers

apiece to take the edge off they headed uphill at a more
leisurely pace. Silkworth declined to lead. He said he had
been drunk every time he'd been here and he could never
remember the way. They strolled uptown, conspicuous in
starched Charlies amid the thronging, swift-talking Sicilians. Givens stared open-mouthed at the shabby, crumbling   buildings,   the   mobile-junkyard   cars,   the
hammer-and-sickle posters six to every wall. He felt conscious of his uniform, his foreignness, his skin. He closed
up on Liebo and Silky and Washman, in the lead.

"Be careful of your watches," Harner said, startling
them all.

"Left here?" said Liebo, turning halfway around.
Washman pulled out his page and they studied it on a
corner, looking for an orientation point. Several boys offered to guide them. When the marines ordered them
away they left, slapping their arms in a gesture Will
thought picturesque. The smallest, a shaven-headed runt
of five or six, tagged after them, making motions for a
smoke. At last Harner gave in and tossed him a Marlboro.
Then he wanted a light.

"Aren't you a Wop, Dippy?"

"Fuck, no, man. Liebo's a good Portuguese name."

"Think we turn left here, huh?"

"Why didn't you get some street names from the
squid?"

"Let's ask this kid where the station is."

"Hey, man, where's the station? Railroad?"

"Compre'?"

"He don't talk English, man."

"The railroad, kid. Choo-choo. Ding, ding," said Liebo.
When the others laughed he reddened. "Hey, you fuckers
try to talk to him, then."

"Estacion-ay fairo-veree," said Will, on an impulse. The
boy brightened and pointed to the left. Harner gave him
another cigarette.

They turned left. "Pretty slick, there, Will," said the
sergeant. "Where you pick that up?"

"The exec said that at formation this morning."

"He did? I dint remember that. You must have a natural gift for languages, Private Givens."

"Ah, I just picked it up," said Will, pleased.

"Marlboro," said the boy. Harner looked at Silkworth, who shrugged, as if to say, if we don't some other guys will. He ain't our responsibility. He shook one more loose and held it out. The boy snatched the pack, his motion so quick he left Harner holding out his hand, and melted toward an alley. "Eh, fuck you, marines," he said.

"Jesus Christ," said Washman.

"They grow up fast back here," said Dippy.

"Maybe he's one of the sergeant's," said Washman. They laughed. "No, too goddamn polite," said Silky solemnly, and they laughed again, louder because it was Silkworth who said it.

"That must be the station."

"And there's the Shore Patrol," Liebo said. "Just like the man said. Fade, Sarge?"

"Stand easy," said Silkworth. "We're still legal. They can't touch us on this side of the line."

Harner pulled a spare pack from his sock and they lit up, standing on a corner, watching the two sailors roll back and forth in front of the station. They wore white bellbottoms and caps cocked forward, white belts slung low against weighted nightsticks, and blue brassards like mourning on their sleeves. They glanced at the marines, but made no move toward them. After several minutes they strolled on, past the station, and disappeared around a corner.

"Let's go," said Silkworth, flipping his butt to the pavement.

"They won't come back?"

"Not if they know what marines eat for lunch, Will."

Past the limit the streets looked just the same, or maybe a little narrower. They came to the T the gunner's mate had described and headed right. A little grocery was just where he had described it, and a bar, Judito's, was across from it, as he had said. Two women leaned against the entrance, looking toward them. "Here?" said Liebo, brushing at his shoulders, straightening his tie.

"No," said Silkworth. "I remember now. I went in there once on my first float. I didn't know nothing then. Those babes were all over me, back in this dark booth. Real jealous bitches. I didn't figure it out till I tried for a feel. Man! I like to shit. She had a bigger dick than mine. I was just a private then. One of them kissed me, too, before I caught on."

"Did he kiss good, Sergeant?"

"There was no goddamn difference, Dippy. None at all. That was what was so fucken weird about it."

Now the street became an alley. Their footsteps bounced off old stucco, off cobblestones strewn with trash, broken glass, a kid's doll. Givens thought: We've left Palermo. This was a place all to itself. Not even the junk-yard cars came by, only once in a while a battered, muf-flerless Vespa, piloted by boys in black jackets who did not look at them. Over their heads, outside shuttered windows, lines of clothing hung motionless in a dim cathedral light. A baby wailed somewhere, and tinny music beat time to their steps. He looked over his shoulder, and caught Washman doing the same thing. They grinned at each other uneasily.

"That's it," said Silky. "Lily's. Was that the place he told you guys about?"

"I think so, Sarge. He dint remember the name but he said—"

"Yeah, good steer. I been here before, too. It ain't cheap, but it's clean, and they don't rip you off. At least that's the way it was then. Must be four, five years ago now. Jesus. Here, it's this green door."

Will paused. He had not meant to come here. Walk around, see the city, that was all he had intended. He had not wanted to start drinking, but all the others had. He had promised himself not to participate in anything worse.

But he did not feel like waiting alone in the empty street. Not in this part of town.

He joined the others inside the door.

He had expected a stinking interior, but they had stepped into a garden. Real grass, trimmed and wet as if it had just been watered. Four wrought-iron chairs sat round a glass-topped table. In the middle of the lawn a blue-and-white Virgin stood in a grotto decorated with marbles and bits of mirror. He looked suspiciously at the statue. A Catholic country, the lieutenant had said.

"Hey. Nice," said Liebo.

Will had thought the walk was cement, but when he looked carefully it became mosaic, hundreds of square tiles, red and blue and white, glazed porcelain, set with care. Not a square was missing or even cracked. He felt awkward walking on it, even with polished shoes.

When he looked up the others had gone on ahead, and he hurried to catch up. At the end of the garden a stone stairway curved up to the second floor of a house, stucco like the outer wall, but unchipped and clean. Silky led them up it. On the porch he raised his hand to knock, then paused.

"You men armed?"

"What's that, Sarge?"

"You bring your shit?"

They looked at him blankly. After a moment he unbuttoned his blouse and reached inside, shaking his head. "Here, children," he said, and handed them out the flat packs of prophylactics, two each.

"Thank you, Sergeant," said Harner.

Silkworth knocked. The marines shuffled their feet and looked down at the garden, the statue; then the door swung open.

The Italian was old, white-haired, and unimpressed with them. He motioned them in wordlessly.

It looked like a living room. A dark television sat against the wall. Four rubber plants stood around it, as if it had been camouflaged. The old man shut the door and they became abashed, as if their grandfather had met them. "Who's he?" Liebo whispered. Silky shrugged.

He came back to them as they stood half at attention, and stepped up close to Will. Givens looked down at the opaque eyes, the pink scalp that showed through thin hair. The old man said nothing, just stood close for a moment and then moved to Liebo. When he came to Hernandez he looked up for the first time.

"You go," he said.

"What? Hey, why, man? I'm okay."

"He don't like the way you smell, Hernandez," said the sergeant.

"Well, so what?" The private took a step back, toward the wall. "I'm stayin', man."

"You leave," said the old man. "Or everybody goes. Sergeant, you tell him."

"He thinks you been drinking, Hernandez. Guess you bite the wiener. Don't wear so much cologne next time."

"Shit, man!" said Hernandez. He stared around at them belligerently, then seemed to wilt. "Okay, okay. You guys have a good time. Can I wait in the garden?"

"Sure," said the old man. "Just leave here."

"Here, man, hang on to my camera for me, will you?" said Washman.

"Okay now," said the old man. "Wait here. I get the girls."

"Oh, man," muttered Liebo. He shifted from leg to leg, looking toward the curtain at the far end of the room.

"Uh, I better go," said Givens then.

"What? We just got here, Will."

"No. I mean . . . I'm going to wait, too."

"You're okay. He passed you."

"It ain't that. I—"

"Come on," said Silkworth. "Don't get cold feet now, Givens. Just stay put."

He was about to protest, but something held him. He stared helplessly at the curtain. I should leave, he thought. I should leave now.

But he didn't. His knees began to tremble.

There were four girls in nightgowns. He was suddenly glad he'd had the beers at the pier. The fattest one picked out Silky at once. "Hey. I know you?"

"You know me," said Silkworth, grinning.

"You come for short time?" she asked him. "Twenty dollars, short time. For you, old customer, fifteen. You men pay me."

"This here is Lily." Silkworth grinned. "She wants the money now. Lil, you still got wine in back?"

"Sure. Got nice Chianti. All cold. You want some?"

"You bet," said Silkworth. He reached for his wallet. "And the same for my men, here."

"You bet."

It seemed to him that he had spent a long time in the blue bedroom, on the sagging, too-soft bed. But when he staggered out, with a headache from a bottle of wine on top of the beer, he found he had finished before the others.

He sat drained in one of the plastic chairs, waiting. Gradually it dawned on him that he should have stayed for seconds. He still had one of the rubbers in his sock. Lita had been nothing to write home about, but his last time had been too long before to remember. It was—no, it was even before they'd convoyed down to Morehead for onload, way back in April. He remembered now, through the alcohol haze, better than he could have sober. A chick he'd met in a dance place outside the LeJeune gate. He got up twice, half-minded to go back, but sat down again. The others would be out any minute.

No, that wasn't really it. He was afraid she might ask for another twenty dollars. He hadn't taken much cash ashore. He was still paying off a dead horse he'd drawn for his PFC drunk. And then, there was his secret. It was something he had never told the others, but he was saving money for school.

He slumped, studying the glossy toes of his shoes and wishing he'd had either more to drink, or less. He realized now, too late, how far he had fallen. He felt sick and sad. No, he thought, *There is none righteous, no, not one.*

At least she hadn't said anything about his color. Maybe Italians didn't care. She had smiled when he showed her the rubber. He wasn't taking any chances, not with all the scuttlebutt. But the Navy condoms were thick as fire hoses. You had to work, and work . . . he had to repent, cease following the way to damnation . . . his mind droned on like an uncoupled motor, fueled by alcohol.

A while later Washman came out, face flushed, and sat wordless beside him. They stared together at the dead television. "You make out okay?" Will asked him.

"She was awful fat. But I needed that bad, man."

"It isn't our fault. They keep us at sea too long."

"No shit, man. Any longer and I would of butt-fucked one of those whimpy squids. . . . You got your other one, Will?"

"Other what?"

"You know. Your rubber."

"Oh. No, I used 'em both."

"Me too. If I had another one I could go back."

They stared at the television and the potted plants. Will suddenly got up. "I'm going down and keep old Hernandez company."

"Yeah. Good idea."

They found the small marine squatting on the grass. They sat at one of the tables for half an hour before Silky and Liebo and Harner came down the stairs, their ties loose, laughing. Silkworth saw them and came over. "Well, is my squad satisfied? Bores clear?"

"Rounds complete, target destroyed, Sarge."

"Let's get something real to drink, then."

Suddenly noisy, caps canted and ties loosened like Sergeant Silkworth's, they ambled down the street. Liebo suggested Judito's, but after a couple of turns they discovered that they were lost. Silkworth seemed unworried. "The whole fucken Med's built on a slant," he told them.

"Any port in it, you get lost, just walk downhill and you'll hit water. It's real convenient when you're shit-faced."

"But we ain't drunk nothin' yet," said Harner.

"We'll get you screwed up as a sprayed roach, Kentucky Buck. How about that place on the corner, there?"

"With the commie posters all over it?"

"They're all over Italy, my man. Don't sweat it. Wops love marines."

There were a dozen men in shirtsleeves and black trousers outside the bar. They stared at them as they approached, taking their hands out of their pockets.

"Wait a minute," said Will, stopping. "This don't look right."

"It's a bar, fella. These guys are just waiting around for something to do." Silkworth seemed to be right; as he approached the door the loungers parted, glancing at one another. The other marines followed him. Just inside, though, the sergeant paused. Past him, in a smoky light, Givens saw a man speaking in front of a red flag, saw sweating faces turn. When he looked back the Sicilians were closing in.

"I think we just fucked up," muttered Liebo.

Givens never saw who swung first. Two men came for him, he was hammerlocked and punched. Hernandez was shouting in Spanish. The street staggered; there was a crunching sound, and he tasted bricks. Then combat training took over. He kicked out, hooked a man, and got halfway up before Harner tripped over him, knocking him down again. A Sicilian tried to run and he grabbed him around the waist and got a couple of shots to his back before he broke free.

A flurry of shoving, a sweaty face above him, the smell of garlic. He battled viciously now, hitting as hard as he could. A hand jerked him round and he found himself back to back with the others, facing a hostile but now wary ring of men. Two of them lay on the street. They were moving to retreat when Liebo said, "The Sarge. He's still in there."

They looked toward the tavern. The Italians, seeing them pause, moved in again. "Jesus," said Hernandez. "Will, go get him."

He took one step forward, and then the door opened and Silkworth came flying out. They pulled him into the circle. He looked undamaged, but confused.

"You better get out of here," said one of the Sicilians, in quite good English.

"We're going."

"Don't fuck with the Corps, buddy," shouted Washman.

"*Fuori, Americano.* Go on, get out."

"Come on, Sarge."

"My fucken cap's still in there."

"Come on, man," said Liebo. "There's a dozen of these bastards waiting to take us. I saw a knife."

They retreated in good order. As the range opened, the alley rang with shouts, but no one followed them. They rounded a corner as soon as they decently could. Will thought Silkworth looked strange without his uniform cap. Naked, more so probably than he had been back at the house. He took off his own and held it out. "You need it," said Silkworth, looking at it and then at him.

"Take it, Sarge. You got stripes to lose."

"Well, okay. Thanks, Will."

"Jesus, what was with those guys? All we wanted was a drink."

"I don't think they wanted to drink with us, Dippy."

"Yeah, I got that impression, too."

Considerably sobered, they took stock. Harner was unhurt, except for his pride; Hernandez had taken a shot to the crotch, and was walking doubled over. Silkworth was okay, but Liebo had a bad limp. Givens found that aside from a bloody nose he was all right. He held his handkerchief to it as they walked downhill. There was no Shore Patrol in sight at the station, and they did not stop till they reached a place Liebo had noticed on the other side. It was tiny, about ten feet frontage on the street, but inside was a spotless stainless-steel bar, an immense nickel cappucino machine, and two tables. They settled in with deep sighs, counting their money.

The barmaid added to their impression that everyone in Sicily spoke English and had cousins in Brooklyn. Looking at her as she bent over the beer tap, Givens wished again he had gone back for seconds.

It was funny. Growing up back in Carolina he had never dared look at a white girl. At LeJeune no one said anything, but somehow blood tended to stay with blood. Here, it was different again; it did not seem to matter, perhaps because they were all foreigners anyway.

Except, he thought, to nuts like Cutford.

The beers came and he drank his off in one go, realizing only now how much the fight had taken out of him. Thinking of the main gunner, probably still back in the compartment, listening to his tapes and reading *Soul on Ice,* made him mad again. "Man, you know that corporal of ours?" he said recklessly to Silkworth.

"What about him?"

"Nothing. But why doesn't he come out with us on libs?"

"He was in Nam," said the sergeant. "He might've got himself fucked up a little there. Not too many of them dudes left."

"So why is he only a E-4?"

"Cutford kind of has a e-motional problem." Silkworth lifted his beer in a slow way that said *let me think about how to say this.* "Now, that's his lookout, I figure. The Corps got no business inside a man's head, messing with his opinions. They tell you, treat everybody the same, but treating ain't the same as thinking. Know what I mean?"

He nodded. Silkworth finished the beer, called in another round, then went on, not looking at him. "Now, I don't mean things ain't improved. Hell, I remember when you didn't see a splib dude and a white guy out in town together. You did, they'd find one of 'em in an alley in the morning. You seem like a good head, Will, seem like to want to get along more than a lot of—more than some guys. But maybe outside the Corps, you don't like the Man, either. An' maybe old Moonshine Breath here wouldn't care to have you sniffing around his sister. I don't know. An' frankly I don't give a shit."

Harner smiled slowly at Will, but didn't say a word.

"Thing is, you and Buck here manage to get along in the squad, whatever you think about each other. Now Cutford—I don't know why, but he can't do that. He's a damn good soldier, don't get me wrong, but he just can't keep his mouth shut. That's why he's still a corporal.

"Why is he like that? I can't say. Maybe it was Nam, maybe it was where he grew up—or maybe he just turned mean one morning, like a Angel-of-Death pops up out of the ground. But there it is, and I don't think he's going to change anytime soon."

The six men sat in wrinkling uniforms, the marine edge of neatness gone, and drank beer. The sharpest thirst was off now, the dryness of the cruise broken, and they settled themselves to get slowly, thoroughly, permanently drunk. Silkworth switched back to wine, extolling its taste and cheapness to the rest of them. Buck Harner drank Jim Beam steadily, laying bills out on the table to pay for each double shot. The rest drank beer. Givens tilted his chair against the wall, nursing the long-necked frosted bottle, and looked out past the others to the window, to the street. Two Navy officers passed in short-sleeve whites, carrying briefcases. An Italian policeman, sauntering in the heat.

The bargirl brought a tray with little cookies, *amoretti* she called them, and they drank and talked idly through the late afternoon. About what teams would go to the playoffs this year, and what they would do when they got back to the States. Then they discussed the bargirl, and from there the conversation went back to Lily's, but only Liebo and Silkworth wanted to talk about that, so that didn't last. Then they talked about the last exercise, Valiant Javelin, and about one of the men in the platoon who had drunk all his water in the first two hours of the march, and how the second lieutenant had gotten his map coordinates wrong and took them east instead of north, and the fourth squad had to go around a mountain just to get back to their jump-off point, and then complete the march, which had been planned for a full day even if they hadn't gotten lost; and how the man had gone nuts from thirst, and that night went looking for the lieutenant with his Ka-bar. The end of the story was how the gunny had to jump him and hold him down until the medevac copter came. He was back in the States now. "Three months ahead of us, the bastard," Liebo grunted. "The screw-ups always have it easier. Ever notice that? Do your job right and they crap on you, but fuck up and you're money ahead."

"Yeah man," said Hernandez solemnly.

"Sarge, where we going after here?" Will asked Silkworth, noticing that the sergeant was looking gloomy again.

"Greece again."

"How long will that be for?"

"Couple weeks. Course, most of it we'll be at sea. Four five days ashore at Gythion, I guess." Silkworth stretched, rippling muscle beneath his ribbons. "You guys want to try someplace else?"

"What's wrong with here, man?" said Liebo.

"You all want to stay?"

"Good as anyplace."

"This Maria, she treats you nice." The girl behind the bar smiled to hear her name mentioned. "And you get to see that fantastic ass every time she bends over," Hernandez added, in a low voice.

"Cowboys like fat calves," said Harner deadpan.

It was dark when they left, reeling as if the street were *Spiegel*'s deck in a storm. They were going down the last street, the fine smell of the sea was growing beyond the city stink, when Will had to stop for a minute. He leaned against a storefront, waiting out the dizziness. He'd barf if he had to—Liebo already had—but a marine had to learn to hold his beer. He was telling himself this when he saw the guitar.

"Man, look at this six-string," he said to Washman.

"Nice. I like the pearly stuff there on the handle. You play guitar, Will?"

He stared at it. There on the narrow street, he seemed to smell, just for a moment, fresh-cut loblolly pine. "Oh . . . used to. I wonder how much it is."

"It's a pawnshop. Can't be that much. But it looks new."

"Yeah."

"You boys all right?" said Silkworth, not weaving very much as he came back to get them.

"Sure, Sarge. We're just going in here for a minute."

"We'll be down this alley. I got to piss so bad my socks are tight."

Inside the shop, amid racks of used shoes, cases of cheap watches and red-gold rings, he received the guitar from the hands of the owner. He turned it to examine the neck, then tucked it and tried a "G" chord. It was slack and he tuned it clumsily, feeling Washman's eyes on him. He brushed another chord from it, and it sounded good; it sounded real good. He swayed and caught himself against a rack. Records cascaded to the floor. "Sorry—I'm real sorry. Guess I must've—"

"You want? Thirty thousand lire."

"Thirty thousand—" but then slowly he figured the exchange rate, and it was not that bad; in fact, that was cheap for a good Gianelli. "Twenty thousand," he said thickly.

When Harner and Silkworth came in, the owner came down a few thousand. Then he stuck. "Think we can swing this," said Givens, and then found his wallet almost empty. Hell yes, he was saving his pay. What for? It didn't seem important now. "Washout—how about a loan? Ten more bucks would float it."

"I only got five, but you can have it."

"No, keep a couple for a last beer. Sarge, you got—"

"I got more balls than I got dollars," said Silkworth. "But got a pocketful of change here . . . lemme count."

Harner coughed up three bucks, and Hernandez produced the last, a beer-soggy, torn old bill that Silkworth handed to Will by its corner. He laid it all on the counter, then suddenly staggered back. The store twirled, his stomach prepared to abandon ship. He flung out a hand to brace himself, and pulled down a rack of shoes. Washman grabbed for them in midair and knocked over a bookcase. The owner began shouting and gesticulating.

"Let's clear out of here," said Silkworth, who had drunk more than any of the privates, but seemed unaffected, except that his eyes were glassy. He steered the suddenly inanimate Givens onto the street and leaned him against a lamppost. A ship's horn boomed out from the harbor as the sergeant examined the guitar, then handed it back. "Nice," he said. "But where you going to keep it? There ain't a lot of room in the troop space."

"Fin' someplace," said Will, with some difficulty. His face was going numb. "Maybe one of the squids'll keep it."

"They'll keep it all right. For good," said Silkworth.

And now the harbor, the bay, sparkling with the lights of anchored ships, opened out from the foot of the street. The pier stretched into darkness; laughter and rock from the bar mixed with a dance band on one of the liners. At the pier bar sailors and marines sat under Campari umbrellas, drinking wine and aperitifs. Two Shore Patrol, the men from the station, sat sullenly in front of Cokes. Fourth squad occupied the last empty table, and ordered beer. "My las' one," explained Washman, his hand missing the bottle by a full five inches. "I'm signed up for the cameo trip tomorrow."

"Yeah?"

"We're goin' right to where they make them. Say they're real cheap. Like to get one for my mom. You guys going?"

"No," said Liebo, holding his hand over his mouth.

" 'M broke," said Givens.

"I'm going back to Lily's," said Silkworth. A group of women walked past the tables and heads turned to follow them. When they went aboard the liner the marines lost interest; officer pussy. "I'm going to fuck 'em all, one at a time. Give you my profess'nal evaluation."

Will Givens lifted his glass. The green light shimmered through the dark liquid, turning cheap glass to sapphire, turning the drops of moisture to beads of cloudy jade. He knew he was drunk. But the dizziness was gone, backed off, and now he wanted the next drink and then the next after that, as much as the world held. He was with his buddies, and their color did not matter.

"The Corps," said Sergeant Silkworth solemnly, and they all, none of them seeing the necessity to add a word, raised their bottles and drank them down to the gurgling end.

4

Giardini, Sicily

CAPTAIN ISAAC SUNDSTROM, U.S. NAVY.
Pleased to meet you, sir."

"Honored to make your acquaintance, signore."

The commodore glanced around as he shook hands
with the chief of carabinieri. The office was disconcert-
ingly small. The plaster walls were cracked, and the chair
that he was shown to did not seem at all new or suitable
to his rank. In fact it was shabby. But he smiled nonetheless, and laid his white uniform cap, crusted with gold, on
the policeman's desk.

"A glass, Capitano?"

"Pardon me?"

"We have a fine local grape, 'Polypheme'—after the
Cyclops. Do you know the story of Ulysses?"

"I've always meant to read that," said Sundstrom.
"Well, it's early, but of course I'd like to sample the local
wine."

He checked his watch unobtrusively as the carabiniere
poured. Nine—not too bad. Good thing he'd gotten an
early start. But there was a limit, in the Med, to how soon
you could begin making calls. In fact, he had arrived at
the police station before the chief; he'd had to wait in the
car.

He leaned forward to accept the glass, smiling, but his
mind had moved on already to plan the rest of the morn-

ing. Fifteen minutes here, one drink, then on to see the mayor.

Ike Sundstrom knew many squadron commanders who disliked the time-honored, time-consuming ritual of paying calls. Some delegated the task to their commanding officers. But he enjoyed it; he felt he was good at it. And he knew Admiral "Smiling Tony" Roberts, Commander, Sixth Fleet, set store by such things. He tipped up the glass. "Excellent," he said. "I don't think I've ever tasted better. By the way, I brought along a little memento. I hope you'll do me the pleasure of accepting."

"How handsome! This is fine brass. I have a fine collection of these. It is the souvenir of your ship?"

"Of my squadron. I'm a commodore—in charge of a U.S. Navy task force."

"Commodore, eh? Of course, you are not just a ship's captain. Excuse, I do not know the American uniforms as I should." The carabiniere set the plaque aside and dusted his hands. "I have something for you as well, but it is rather large—when you leave. But, now, let us discuss business. Tell me, you have two ships in this port, that is correct? What is the length of your stay?"

"I planned for four days. Of course, there is always the possibility of change, but we're scheduled for three more days in your lovely town."

"I see. And how many in the liberty party?"

"I estimate six hundred a night."

"Sailors or marines?"

"Uh . . . I would estimate about three hundred would be marines."

"You will supply a shore patrol?"

"Ten men a night, based at the pier."

"Exactly the number I would have asked for. Well, I see no problem to mar your visit," said the chief of police. He glanced at the bottle, sighed, and put it away after offering Sundstrom another glass; the commodore declined, smiling. "Only four days, I don't know if the mayor will want

to arrange anything special . . . that will be up to him. You
will be calling on him?"

"This morning."

"Is there any other way in which I can assist you?"

"I would be happy, my friend, if one other thing were
understood between us," said Sundstrom, smiling. "If
there are any misunderstandings ashore, I hope you will
call me at once. If we can take care of things at our level,
not bother higher authority, it's much simpler for all concerned."

"I certainly understand. Well, please convey to the
mayor my respects. Thank you for stopping by, sir."

"My pleasure, sir."

They rose. Sundstrom gripped the policeman's hand
again, they both smiled officially, and the chief accompanied him down the stairs.

The gift turned out to be a huge wickered bottle of
Polypheme. "Put it in the trunk," said Isaac Sundstrom
to his orderly, when the Italian went back inside. "I can't
have the men see me drive around with a goddamn ton of
cheap wine in the backseat."

Ike Sundstrom did not value the smiles, the compliments,
the outward flourishes of protocol for their own sake.
They were valuable, not of themselves, but for their effec-
tiveness in communicating things that could not be communicated well, or sometimes at all, in words. Trust.
Worth. Respect. And above all, success. Every successful man he had ever served with, every officer who had
attained the broad gold stripes of admiral, had that in
common: a consciousness of appearances. Some were out-
standing technicians, some fine administrators, others
skilled politicians. They were all, he was the first to say,
fine men. But beyond that, they all knew very thoroughly
how to make themselves look good.

The Sundstroms were not an old Navy family. But neither were they Wisconsin sodbusters. His father had
owned a Hudson dealership in Eau Claire, but had died

in 1943; not in the war, but on a highway, leaving little after the loans were paid off. Isaac, the eldest, had to work his way through college. He had done this with dogged persistence for two years, and then discovered the Navy Reserve officer program. After that his only worry was grades. He was no scholar. But he was stubborn, and he applied himself; and he found that he liked the uniform, the way people looked at him as he walked across the campus on the way to drill.

He was unit commander his senior year.

He wanted to fly, but after a week in Pensacola his eyes gave out. He began seeing double. For a time he was on medical hold, then things cleared up; but still he was out of the flight program, for good.

He called his detailer long distance, and asked for destroyers.

He served in them for ten years, in the Pacific, and then was ordered to Washington as an aide to the Chief of Naval Personnel.

He had never thought about high rank till then. In those days the Pacific Fleet was a casual, rough outfit, still looking back to Midway and the Marianas, and hardly conscious of a larger Navy. It was at the Pentagon that he realized that he could be an admiral. He was in awe of them at first, these tall smooth men in crisp blues or khakis or whites. Academy, most of them, but not all. There was room in the postwar Navy for hardworking men, Annapolis or no, and he worked hard.

He did not like the Washington parties—he felt awkward at them, uncomfortable—but he made himself go. At one of them, he met the former Mary Hyatt, of Rockville. Widowed by Vietnam, she now worked in the Legislative Affairs office of DOD and owned a house in Alexandria. He adopted her daughter by the previous marriage, and they had two more children, both boys.

He went from there to engineering department head on a carrier, then to executive officer of an ammunition ship. A year later his commanding officer retired unexpectedly,

for reasons of health. Admiral Dorne was still at Personnel, and Commander Sundstrom made a long-distance
call.

He served as captain of the *Nitro* for two years, then
went back to the District on the staff of the Deputy Under-
secretary for Logistics. His next sea tour was a deep draft
command, of an oiler.

And then, even before he could have hoped for it, he
found in his traffic one day his orders as squadron commander, Amphibious Squadron Six. Not the choicest bil-
let for an ex-destroyerman, but a long step up nonetheless.
He had pondered it for weeks, worrying at the meat of
meaning in the spare phraseology of Navy orders. At last
he understood it. It meant that they were evaluating him,
grooming him for his stars. It was a test.

And they would be watching, waiting for him to fail.

Leaning back in the rear seat, Isaac I. Sundstrom
caught the glances of two Italians repairing their car on
the street. He straightened his back, put on a look of
concentration, and glanced down, as if he was studying
important documents.

He reflected comfortably that he was just forty-six years
old.

The mayor was out. He left his card with an assistant,
discussed garbage collection and fresh water for a few
minutes, then left. He considered going up to Taormina;
he remembered it as a pretty drive, but decided against it.
The day was wearing on and he had work to do.

"Fleet Landing," he said to the driver. "And step on it."

"Aye aye, sir."

The crew of the gig jumped up, ditching butts and
squaring away their caps as the blue Fiat, lights on, pulled
onto the pier. The orderly opened the door; the coxswain
held out his arm to steady the commodore as he stepped
aboard. He paused for a moment, looking around the
quay. A civilian was watching them. After a moment he
went over. "Going out to the ships?" he called.

Sundstrom evaluated the dark suit, the tie. "That's right. You're—?"

"American consul."

"Sure. Come aboard, I'm the man you're going out to see."

Sundstrom remembered the wine only when the driver, stonefaced, swung it down into the coxswain's arms. "Stow it below, sir?" said the sailor, equally expressionless.

"No, goddamn it," said Sundstrom, annoyed. "Dump it over the side."

"*Dump* it, sir?"

"You heard me, son."

The coxswain, the linehandlers, and the driver stared at the gurgling jug. When the last of the ruby flow had disappeared into the water, the commodore nodded.

He and the consul stood together in the stern as the gig backed out, then swung to seaward. The boat leapt forward, flag snapping in the wind, and they steadied themselves as it left the shelter of the bay and began to pitch, throwing spray. The engine was too loud for speech, and after a shouted word about the weather they stood silently together, watching the ship approach.

Sundstrom watched it with pride, touched with flashes of anger as he noted rust or dangling lines. *Guam* grew rapidly larger as they approached. Like a small carrier, he thought, appreciating the straight sweep of the flight deck, the warlike sheer of her sides. She rode easily to anchor, veering slowly to the wind. Two ready helicopters crouched high above the sea, forward of the island. His eye moved upward. Yes, she was flying the holiday ensign. It was not strictly in accordance with regulations, but he'd always felt that the bigger the flag, in a foreign port, the better they were accomplishing the public relations part of their mission.

He bent forward. He was unsure of diplomatic rank, but knew that consuls were important. "This is my flagship, sir," he shouted. "Coxswain, circle her once before you make the platform; let's show off a little."

"Aye, Commodore."

He showed the consul around the hangar and flight deck, and posed with him for a picture on the bridge. He stayed for lunch in Sundstrom's cabin, then left, pleading press of work. Sundstrom called the quarterdeck to let him have the gig. Alone, he relaxed for the first time that day.

The flag cabin was not large; but aboard ship, it was luxurious, almost a suite. There was an office-cum-living room, with a desk, chart table, leather couch, and several chairs. A door led to his quarters proper, a sitting room, bedroom, and attached bath. He showered, changed to khakis, allowed himself ten minutes on the couch, then called his steward for a cup of coffee and sat down to work.

Rota, Valencia, PHIBLEX; training anchorage for a week; Brindisi, Athens, Gythion, Thessalonika, Sicily, Valiant Javelin. It had been a full, busy deployment to date. MARG 2-2, his task force, had started sloppy. Exercises took too long and there were mistakes. He had corrected them. He felt that the squadron was shaping up, despite some of his captains' laziness or lack of willingness to impose discipline. In some cases he'd had to impose his own. That took time, time he needed for his own job; but then, he thought, no one had ever said command was an easy task.

A radioman knocked, entered, and laid the morning's message traffic before him. He read each one thoroughly, starting at the top of the stack and going down. Those he did not understand he scribbled on with a red felt-tip: *Chief of Staff: Check this out and report.* Three from COMSIXTHFLEET, Admiral Roberts, he laid aside for further study. Then he turned to his outgoing pile, messages and letters that had been prepared for his approval. He read these even more closely, lapsing into a scowl.

His staff, he thought, was lazy. They were satisfied with quick answers, off the top of their heads. They did not want to put in the time a real job required. But he would not let them get away with sloppy work. His pen slashed across the paper, asking questions, demanding references and clarifications. He tossed them back into the basket for revision, then reached again for the admiral's messages.

They were situation reports, secret, covering the entire Med. Particular attention was given to the larger than usual number of Soviet Fleet units in the east. He carried them to the chart table. There were seven ships off Kythera, a favorite anchorage for the Russians, and two more submarines than usual this time of year. Sundstrom wondered why. No use asking the intelligence officer, Byrne; he would indulge himself in his usual games, disguising his incompetence with sly generalities and effeminate mannerisms. The commodore's scowl deepened.

He reread the last message, about Cyprus, twice. He frowned at the map, gnawing at his lip. Cyprus . . . Turkey . . . the concentration of Soviet units . . . no, he was probably reading too much into it, worrying too much. If anything hot looked likely, Roberts would have them to sea at once.

But how much better it would look if, when he got that message, Ike Sundstrom could report that Task Force 61 was already underway.

But then, he couldn't take fright at every hint of trouble. If he did that, the MARG would never touch land at all. The whole eastern Mediterranean was a hotbed, like the Balkans in 1913. Lebanon was a running sore, the Persian Gulf a powder keg since the Iranian disaster. Turkey and Greece, ostensibly allies, were circling like wrestlers seeking an opening. A new Arab-Israeli war could happen anytime; Syria, heavily backed by the Soviet Union, was building up its forces once more. Libya and Iran, powerless against regular U.S. military forces, had resorted to funding terrorists, a cheap way to make war.

He sat and stared at the paper, gnawing his lip.

Isaac Sundstrom did not consider himself brilliant or creative. He was not a genius, a fire-eater, or a risk-taker.

So many nights, aboard the *Nitro,* he had lain awake sweating in his bunk after the officer of the deck called him, hoping he had made the right decision on a closing contact, waiting for the scream of the whistle; but his fitness reports had always mentioned his dependability. He was short, and that was a drawback. Most of the golden, the select, were tall men. But there was nothing a man could do about that but watch his posture, and of course his weight. He knew that his caution and thoroughness made enemies, as they had at the Bureau of Personnel, that there were people who cared less than he did for doing things the safe way. These people would make him look bad if they could.

But he was too close now to falter or even waver. The path was narrow, the ascent steep, and the competition keen. But he was still young. If iron determination, iron will, and tireless attention to detail counted for anything, Ike Sundstrom was sure he could make it.

The essential thing, he thought, *is never to make a mistake.*

5

Naples, Italy

WHEN WORD CAME DOWN AT LAST TO SE-
cure main engines something relaxed inside Kelly Wronowicz's chest. It was as if the dying whine of *Ault*'s
turbines, spinning down for the first time in two weeks,
was a part of himself shutting down.

He watched the throttleman spin the worn wheel with
one finger, cutting the invisible bloodstream of steam that
kept the old destroyer alive. The pressure gauge above his
head spun down to zero.

"Closed tight?"

"Yeah, Chief."

"Stewie, remember the jacking gear. We don't need no
bowed shafts. And I want lube oil temps below ninety
before you wrap up the watch down here."

"Aye."

"And take that leftover coffee. Dump it on the deckplates with some scouring powder and get Blaney to kai-
eye it down before he secures."

"Right, Chief."

When the jacking gear had been engaged and tested,
Wronowicz left the throttle board and walked aft through
the engineroom. To either side they loomed up, his
evaporators, his pumps, generators and reduction gears,
the steel-shining complexity of steam and cooling lines,
reach rods, wiring. He hardly noticed the hundred-degree

heat, the dank smell compounded of steam, lube oil, hot steel, and baked insulation. The walkway rang under his boots, slippery with condensation and oil, and his ear tuned without conscious thought from the slight off-pitch of number-one ship's service generator, to the hiss of steam through the gland exhausts of the air ejector (he would have to repack it soon, but not today, not today), to the gay shout of one of the watchstanders as he threw his log board onto its peg. Absently wiping his fingers, black with grease and soot, on a rag from his back pocket, he rubbed them over the casing of the low-pressure turbine. Around him, for the length of the engineroom, the grease-softened light of the fluorescents glowed off piping and ductwork, off hose reels, colored bottles of compressed gas and firefighting chemicals; off coils of emergency cable as thick as his hairy wrists. He paused at the ladder, looking back toward the throttle board. The top watch was making the last entries in the log, the lower level men were stowing their tools, oiling cans, rags, wrenches.

Machinist's Mate Chief Kelly Wronowicz looked over his kingdom, breathed one deep sigh, and went up the ladder toward the main deck.

By the time the mooring lines were fast, the ratguards rigged, "A" gang busy on the pier connecting water and telephone lines, Wronowicz was exhausted. Although he did not show it. He never showed weakness or exhaustion to the thirty roughnecks he bossed in *Ault*'s "M" Division, and especially not to the main propulsion assistant, Ensign Callin.

The chiefs' quarters was noisy with men showering and dressing, readying themselves for the first wild night in Naples. He peeled off his coveralls, noticing for the first time in days their smell, the grease and soot ground in so deep the ship's laundry had long ago given up on them, and sagged two hundred and twenty hairy pounds into his rack with a grunt. The mattress was soft, welcoming, and he felt that part of him that had relaxed with the shutdown ebb toward sleep. He wanted nothing more in the world. The last two weeks at sea—with materiel inspection, replacing a dozen failed flexitallic gaskets because Foster forgot he was driving a ship as old as he was, landing exercises, underway replenishment—had been hell. And Callin on him every minute, ignorant as a tick . . . he pulled his mind away from work. They were in port at last, and the machinery could cool into immobile metal, cool and shrink and rest. He rested too, and the whine of electric razors faded into a long-awaited unconsciousness.

"Hey, Kelly," said a voice. "Lieutenant Jay wants to see you out in the passageway."

Wronowicz turned over heavily in his bunk. "Whatever it is, tell him to grease it good and cram it up his ass.

"All right," he added, after a moment of silence. "I'm coming." Three deep breaths later he got up, pulled a pair of pants over his belly, centered the buckle, and went up into the chief's lounge.

The engineering officer was small and finely built. He was fresh off the bridge, in tailored trop whites, and gold glittered at his shoulders and on the cap he held under one arm. Wronowicz felt his glance at his gut, at the dark circles of sweat under the armpits of his T-shirt, but he knew Jay didn't really mind. If a snipe was clean he wasn't doing his job, and the lieutenant, despite his crispness on watch, got just as filthy when something needed doing down in the hole.

"You wanted me, sir?"

"Yeah, Chief. I can't find Mr. Callin. Some things have to be done before the department goes ashore." Jay glanced around the lounge; Wronowicz shrugged. That meant, in the shorthand of men who worked together every day, that Jay didn't want to say anything critical in front of the other chiefs, and that the machinist's mate didn't mind.

"What's that, sir?"

"Thing is, after the fueling, they didn't clean up right.

There's oil on the deck and handprints all over the bulkhead. The exec brought it to my attention."

"Yessir, I know about that. I figured the duty section could get it, sir," said Wronowicz. He wiped what remained of his hair back with one hand. "I hate to keep the snipes turned to when everybody else is walking off the brow, after the hours they've put in this last couple weeks."

"I do too," said Jay. "But we've been through this before, Chief. If they'd clean up after a job we wouldn't take this flak. I want the same people to clean it who were on station when it happened. And I want it done now."

"Aye aye, sir," he said, rubbing his belly sadly. Jay left.

"You look terrible, Kelly," said Chief Sullivan, coming out of the pantry with a cinnamon bun. He was already dressed for liberty in a loud Hawaiian shirt and seersucker slacks. "You said to stop by before we left . . . you sure you want to hit the beach tonight?"

"Yeah, I'll hit it," snapped Wronowicz. His sleep was wrecked now. "Just give me a couple minutes. I'll meet you on the pier."

"We'll be there."

He made it to a chair before his legs gave way. Two shots of Chief's Mess coffee, as much darker and more virulent than regular Navy coffee as that is to the weak stuff civilians brew, put strength back into his limbs. His heart began to beat. He felt mean again, as a chief should, and the lights got a little brighter.

One more cup, black, and then he went down to engineering berthing and collared Roberts and Smee, chewed them out, and sent them up to the refueling station. He took a quick shower and put on a fresh set of whites, cocking his cap in the mirror. He started out into the corridor; Callin was there, talking to one of the men. Wronowicz left by the other door, going through sick bay. He made sure that his men were at work; they were scrubbing away in their liberty clothes, their backs to the town, cursing him.

He sighed and walked on. Sullivan was waiting beside the after five-inch mount. They saluted the quarterdeck watch and clattered down the gangway; and then he was ashore, the wind cool with evening and the familiar strange scent of land, and all responsibility, all worry dropped away from him, and he was on liberty.

"Yeah," grunted Chief Wronowicz, stretching backward in the cramped front seat of the cab till his cap bent against the soiled roof. "Naples again, the asshole of the Mediterranean."

A molehill beside the chief's mountain, the little swarthy driver slid his eyes sideways. "Better put a lid on that," said "Unc" Blood, the quartermaster, wiggling his goatee from the backseat. "Remember, we're what's passing through."

Wronowicz grunted, then remembered a joke himself. "Yeah . . . reminds me of this guy, he can't get it up, right? His snake's on a Swiss vacation."

"Like your mind."

"Like your morals. Shut him up back there, bo's'n."

"Tell the joke," said Chief Sullivan mildly. "You half-Irish son of a bitch, tell the joke."

"So he goes to a doc, and the pill-pusher says to him, 'Mister, it sounds like what you need is more variety in your sex life.' 'Yeah?' says the guy. 'Like what do you mean? Another woman?' "

"The chief snipe makes these up as he goes along," Blood muttered to Sullivan. "That's why they take so long."

"Shut up, you turd. . . . 'Naw,' says the doctor, 'What you do is the same thing, but you do it different.'

" 'Like how?' says the guy.

" 'Well, you ever see two dogs goin' at it in the yard?' says the doc. 'Try it like that. See if it makes things more interesting.'

" 'I don't think my wife would go for that,' says the guy.

" 'Ah, give her a couple of drinks, I'll bet she would,'

says the doc. So the guy says he'll go home and try it."

"I think I heard this before, back in Sunday school," said Blood.

Wronowicz ignored him. "Anyway, the next day he comes back to the office. 'Did it work?' 'Not real good, Doc,' says the guy. 'She got drunk as hell, but she still wouldn't take her clothes off on the lawn.'"

The three chiefs grabbed suddenly for handholds as the driver braked, sending the taxi slewing. He leaned on the horn, his narrow face ferocious, cursing out the open window as traffic roared by, missing the cab by clearances that made his passengers flinch back.

"Jesus Christ," said Sullivan, rubbing his bald spot. "This bastard is going to kill us all." They shouted at the man, ordered him to drive on, but he ignored them, screaming at the driver ahead, who was looking back at them, making an occasional small gesture with his thumb. The other Neapolitan, a much younger man, looked cool and self-possessed.

Their driver became frenzied. Spittle flew onto the windshield. A truck rumbled by, missing their fender by inches, the horn loud but absurdly high. The cab surged forward, the driver jerked the wheel, screaming unintelligible maledictions, and the two men in back yelled at Wronowicz, "Grab the wheel! He's trying to ram the bastard!"

"Be damned if he isn't," said Wronowicz, regarding the little man with more favor. He put his big hand gently on the cabbie's chest and took the wheel, but before he could straighten, the Neapolitan released it with both hands and began to crawl out the window, screaming. The man in the car ahead looked back, grinning, and screwed his finger into his cheek. Before any of them could react, their driver was in the street, running, and they saw him reach into his pants and flick out a knife. The car ahead sped up and turned, and they heard him scream a last malevolent blasphemy as he doubled into a side street after it. The taxi slowed, jolting as someone behind hit it, and after his first astonishment Wronowicz hauled himself over into the vacant seat, where he huddled with his knees up to his face.

"Where the hell did he go?"

"Down one of those alleys."

"Well," said Wronowicz, "I guess we got ourselves a taxi. Where you birds want to go? Anyplace in town, two thousand lire." He winced as the gears ground, and clutched and threw it in again, his head cocked for the meshing; and then concentrated on the traffic, bending to peer out at the twisting streets, the churches, the pizzerias where sailors and marines sat, not together. The sky broke blue and strangely gay above the puce and pink apartments, new but shabby, the old women in black observing it all from their balconies like saints from a painted heaven. The stream of traffic came to a roundabout and he gunned the taxi rocking in tight circles around a crumbling fountain. The others cursed as, infected with the game, he cut suddenly across traffic toward an exit, scraping the fender of a Lancia. Wronowicz tossed his scraggy-bearded, wide-boned, madly blue-eyed face back and let out a shout of pleasure. His cap fell off and his thinning black hair sprang free. "Where to?" he roared again, the deep bass of his voice, the gaiety in it and release, filling the car; and the men behind him grinned, too.

"Let's get something to eat first," suggested Sullivan. "I'm going nuts for some linguine. That's the only good thing about this goddamn country."

"Wine," Blood said.

"Well, that's good too, yeah."

"Place up here I been to . . . there it is," said Wronowicz, slowing. "This look okay?"

"Sure."

"I been here before, too."

The three chiefs ordered and ate together with the complacence of old friends, though they had, in fact, not known each other long. Wronowicz was the longest aboard *Ault,* nearly three years; this was his second tour after picking up his anchors, which had come slow. Blood, the Mephistophelian quartermaster chief, had come aboard later, replacing a first-class who had displayed the poor judgment of smoking a bone while shooting evening stars one night.

Sullivan, the nearly bald boatswain, was brand-new this cruise. Things were not going well for him with the deck force. He was reputed not to be stern enough, unwilling or unable to kick ass the way a classic chief BM did; he looked in fact like someone's henpecked dad. Wronowicz, glancing at him, saw his hands shake as he lit a cigar after the gelati. Kelly Wronowicz was not insensitive, but before some human situations he was at a loss. A fractured piston ring in a compressor, loss of vacuum in a main condenser—yeah. Those he could handle. A man who slacked off, who was inefficient or ignorant, that he could handle.

Problems like Sullivan had, though . . . he rubbed at his beard, and his mind moved on. He had drunk almost a liter of wine with the linguine. Perhaps because of that, or the three cups of joe, he felt unwontedly keen about this night's liberty. Almost the way he had felt as a fireman deuce, so many years before it did not bear thinking about.

"How's things down in the hole, Kelly?" said Blood, breaking into his thoughts.

"Like always. Runnin' like a watch."

"No trouble with that new ensign?"

"Callin? He just needs straightening out. We're getting along," said Wronowicz. "Say. What you men feel like doing tonight?"

"I got no plans," said Sullivan mildly. "How about you?"

"Well," said Wronowicz, "I'd kind of like to pick up one of those Naples brass beds. The old lady was on me for one a couple of years back."

"Thought you were split up," said Blood, waggling his beard.

"When Wronowicz promises something it gets delivered. You heard from, uh, Sarah?"

"A letter," said Blood. "Oh. Picture of the new grandkid."

"Nice looking. Your first?" said Sullivan, examining the picture with genuine interest.

"Yep."

"I've got three. Two by my daughter, one by my oldest boy. How about you, Kelly?"

"How about me, what?"

"You got any kids?"

Wronowicz said, after a pause, "One."

"Oh, yeah? Got a picture?"

"Forget it, Sully," said Chief Blood. Sullivan looked to him, then back to Wronowicz, who was examining the dregs in his glass.

"Sure," he said. "Okay." He closed his wallet and put it away.

"How about we pick up the bed, then go to a place I know," said Blood, shoving his chair back. "You drink Jack Daniels, don't you, Kelly? And there's girls upstairs."

"That sounds good, Unc."

"Girls?" said Sullivan, looking from one of them to the other.

"Girls, yeah. You're a grandfather, you ought to know what split-tails are for."

"This may sound kind of funny to you boys," said Sullivan, "but this is my first time deployed. I came up through tugboats on the West Coast, San Diego. Aren't you afraid of . . . well, you get things from prostitutes, don't you?"

They stared at him. "You can, sure," said Blood.

"Well . . . what if you do? You don't want to take that home."

"Look," said Wronowicz, his voice rising a little, as it did when he explained to one of his firemen how to tear down a pump. "You ever heard of PCOD?"

"Pea-cod?"

"West Coast sailors . . . that's Pussy Cut-Off Date. At the beginning of a cruise you figure it takes forty days to cure you if you get the old, uh, scabulosis, or anything. Right? So you subtract that from the date you make home port. Add ten days for the symptoms to show; and that's PCOD. No screwing around after that. That way you're okay when you pull in to Pier Six and the old lady's there waving the flag for you."

"It sounds pretty cold-blooded to me," said Sullivan.

"You asked us, didn't you?" said Blood. "Say, what's the longest you was out, on those tugs?"

"Two weeks, to Hawaii."

"Try holding it for six months and then tell me about it."

By the time they finished dinner it was dusk. The taxi stood where they had left it. "Pile in," said Wronowicz. "Let's head up back in some of these alleys, see if there's any brass for sale."

"Good beds, huh?" said Sullivan. "They make 'em here?"

"Cast them right here in the city. Anybody hit you up for scrap yet? Any of the locals?"

"There was a guy on the pier wanted to talk about it. I told him to come back tomorrow."

"He's after brass. Shell cases, belaying pins from the signal bridge, turnbuckles off the lifelines, pipe fittings, anything. You got to watch them close if you let 'em aboard. One of 'em got the commissioning plaque off the *Belknap,* bolts and all. Okay, here we go."

The roads narrowed once they turned uphill, became cobbled streets dank with sewers, shops lit yellow in the falling darkness. Sausages and netted cheeses hung above mounds of grapes. Wizened men in suits raised glasses in a trattoria; women in shawls clustered around the door of a tiny church. The taxi snaked between walkers, dodged bicyclists; the way was too narrow for two cars abreast. At a corner a bersaglieri's head swung to follow them; Wronowicz stepped on the gas for several random turns. "Family neighborhood," said Blood after a time, from the rear seat. "You sure this is right?"

"It sure as shit is," said Wronowicz triumphantly. The taxi pulled to the curb, and the three of them piled out, clumsy from the wine and heavy food.

Alone in the dark windows, lit from far back in the building, three naked bedsteads gleamed copper-golden. They were identical, posts lathed into intricate knobs, the frames polished brass, or maybe only gilded. The light was too dim to tell, and the glass they peered through was cloudy with dust.

"Is it open?"

"Try the door."

"Locked."

"Closed."

"Too bad, Kelly. Have to come back tomorrow."

"Tomorrow, hell. I plan to be hung over and fucked out tomorrow. I couldn't even find this place again." He peered into the building for a moment more, then raised one immense hand and hammered at the door till glass rattled. "Hey! Anybody in there?"

"Jesus, take it easy," said Sullivan, looking back at the street. Several passersby had stopped to watch.

"Che cosè?"

"Who said that?"

"Up there. At the window."

They backed off and looked up. A woman was looking down at them. "We want the beds," Wronowicz called up. "Can we see them?"

"Come?"

"The beds! Beds!"

People laughed behind them. The woman frowned down at them for a moment more, then the window banged shut. "You're serious about this, aren't you?" said Blood.

"I told you, Wronowicz always delivers."

"Yeah, and I've heard ducks fartin' in the water before, too," said Blood; but he was smiling when the machinist's mate looked at him.

A light came on then, back in the store. A moment later the door jingled open, jarred on a chain, and without warning or premonition Kelly Wronowicz found himself looking into the most intense, most intimately wise eyes that he had faced in the peregrinations and permutations of forty-five years.

"*Sì,*" she said, looking at him, not at the others. He felt the wine reel in his head, only it was not the wine, and he reached a big hand to the window for support. It bent ever so slightly against his weight, readying itself to shatter.

"Kelly, you all right?" said Chief Sullivan, behind him.

He moved his hand to the frame, and looked away from her upturned face. It was an effort but he did it. "Yeah . . . hi. You mind the store? I mean, you work here?"

She nodded, her eyes darker than the dresses of the old women, deep as the strip of night above the unlighted street. He saw now, in the alternate scarlet and darkness from the taxi's flashers, that she was younger than he, but not by much. But the chin was firm as youth, the dark hair carefully wound, the housecoat held at the waist clean, and the swelling of bosom above that and the shadow below more than sufficient to bring the months at sea up thick in his belly. But it was more than that too, more than that.

For just a moment Chief Kelly Wronowicz, at home in a world of metal and men, felt afraid.

He pointed through the crack in the door, toward the beds, and she stared for a fraction of a moment; and then understood, nodded, and slid the chain free. The women outside tittered. She flipped a hand and spat a couple of words at them as the three chiefs filed inside. "Nice," said Blood, eyeing Wronowicz lewdly; and he did not mean the beds.

Conscious of her body close behind him, the big machinist ran his hands over the furniture. "Damn," he said.

"What's wrong, Kelly?"

"These look nice, but . . . listen." He rattled the frame, and the whole bed shook and squeaked. "Feels like they're made of sheet metal. No way this'll hold two people."

"It might, if they didn't move around much." Blood smirked.

"Shut up. She might understand English."

"She's old enough to know what beds are for, Kelly."

"Well, these are too flimsy." He turned to her, pitching his voice rough because of the other men, but when he met her eyes again, the silent understanding of her lips, he heard himself say shyly, "Uh . . . these all the beds you got, ma'am?"

She stared up at him. In the dim light from the back of the store he could see the individual strands of hair, each one incredibly fragile, but together dense as ebony. A strand curled along her neck, into the robe, and he could see where the fullness began, the breastbone etched by shadow. Seeing him wait, she smiled hesitantly and held up eight fingers.

"No. Not price. More beds?" He rejected the three in the window, pushing his hand away, then waved toward the back of the store. "Better beds. Strong. See?" He bared his arm, gripped his muscle, shook it. She furrowed her brow, looking at the tattoo, and then at him; then understood. Her face came alight again, and she motioned him to the back.

"Hey! Get away from that car!" Sullivan shouted, at the door.

"Trouble, Chief?"

"Kids. Tell you what, you go do your shopping, we'll stay out here and watch it."

"Yeah," said Blood, his beard elaborately innocent of guile or entendre. "You just come on out when you're finished."

Wronowicz looked after him. There were times when he liked Blood, and other times when he wanted to deck him. But then he heard her call something in liquid syllables from the dimness of the store, where piled furniture loomed in shadow like the monsters in the basement when you were a child. Light, yellow as Galliano, poured from a hidden bulb around her motionless figure, waiting for him, the housecoat draped opaque over firmnesses and softnesses already tangible in the anticipation of his trembling hands.

He forgot the others as he followed her up a flight of narrow stairs, the wear of years concave in the wooden steps; and looking up at her back as he climbed he could smell her, and the place itself: old wood, polish, obscure redolences of old perfumes, the deep ineradicable fragrance of olive oil seeped into walls for so many generations it is part of the wood. They reached the landing, where a huge old wardrobe stood, and she led him down a corridor and opened a door to him and gestured him in, standing aside.

"Yeah, this is what I wanted," breathed Wronowicz.

The bed was enormous. It was larger than a double, maybe a king-size, and it was old. The frame—it was real tin-rich brass; he could tell that even under decades of oxidation, careless coats of age-darkened varnish—was massive. Trying to shake it was like trying to shove the ship away from the pier with your hands. It dominated the room, and it was not until he stepped back, dusting his hands, that he saw the rest of it; the lofty, blackened ceiling; old plaster, flaked and spotted by water and years; an oak bureau, a washstand, for God's sake, with the same basin and pitcher he remembered dimly from his own grandmother's room, so long ago it hardly seemed like himself remembering it. He leaned to inspect a photograph. A woman holding flowers, a man seated before her with his hat on his knee; young in the tintype forever, but the high-collared dress, the buttoned shoes meant they, too, had joined the irrevocable past. Her parents? Grandparents, more likely. Had this been their bed?

He turned, to find her watching him silently, the light behind her from the hallway. He saw now that the housecoat was worn thin, that the darkness in her eyes was allied with worry. Alone? Yes. She was alone. And she needed money.

"How much?" he said, indicating the bed, hearing the eagerness and shame in his voice.

"One . . . one hund' dollari?" she whispered.

Too much, he told himself at once. And then thought, no, it's cheap. For a piece of scrapcast junk it was too much, but this was real. What would an antique like this be worth in the States? And, damn, she looked like she needed it.

"Okay," he grunted, and saw her face brighten, then fall as she looked at the bed; and then she lifted her head and smiled. He flipped out his wallet and went through the twenties. She took money like a child accepting candy, cupping her hands, and when he had given her all of it she counted it and thrust it into her robe and then, all at once, became businesslike. She stripped the bed, rolling the mattress off, and he held the headboard while she broke the rails free. "Let me do that," he said, but she ignored him. They stacked the headboard and baseboard in the corridor, and she closed the door.

For a moment they stood there, in the silence of the house. Then he took her by the shoulders. She looked up, and after a moment he found himself trembling, unable to move or even think before the vastness of her understanding, her certitude, her peace. And then her eyes closed, and he felt her yield to him without a word, without a motion, and her arms came up to hold him, too.

"Kelly! Kelly!"

He came back, feeling her move slightly in his arms, her breath sighing in his beard. He lifted his head from her hair and heard the voices in the street, the seesaw of a siren—

"Jesus," he whispered, and she caught her breath as he released her. He looked down at her, at her tremulous smile; and knew in that long moment that he would retain this the rest of his life, would yearn for this as long as he remembered. He would remember the room, the bed, the smells of olive and lavender; would live forever with the woman who looked up at him unsmiling, grave, and waiting. He had found this twice before in his life. Once, he had lost her, and once, he had married her; and both times it had not been her.

But now it was, and he was old enough to know that this was the last time.

And then the voices came again from below, calling him, and he reached for his cap as the banging began on the door.

He reached the stairway as Sullivan and Blood came running up it. "Hey. What's goin' on?"

"You done yet, damn it? We got cops up the ass out there."

"Cops?"

"They think we stole the taxi," Sullivan explained. His bald head was slicked with sudden sweat. "Is there another way out of here? We got the door locked but—"

The crash of glass from below finished his sentence. Wronowicz looked along the hallway. The balcony at the end . . . "Let's try out there," he said, pointing. "Hey! Wait a second!"

"What, Kelly?" said Blood, turning, the slender double doors already partly open. "There's a roof down here. I think we can make it."

"We'll make it with the goddamn bed. I just laid a hundred bucks out for that thing, and we're taking it with us."

"You got to be kidding."

"Grab, boy." Sullivan staggered back under the weight of the footboard; Wronowicz was reaching for the headboard when the first bersaglieri showed at the bottom of the stairs. One hand on the bed, he braced himself against the wall and sent the wardrobe sliding down the steps. It stopped halfway, stuck at the landing, and shouts came faintly from behind the heavy wood. "Take them a minute to get that stoppage free . . . let's go. Unc, get on down there, and I'll drop it down to you."

"I don't believe this," said Blood, but he disappeared over the casement. Sullivan followed him, struggling with the footboard, and a moment later brass clattered in the heavy music of bells on pavement as Wronowicz let the headboard and rails go. The shouting from below grew louder.

"Signore . . ."

He turned, half over the balcony. She stood in the corridor, leaning against the wall, her arms crossed on her breast. He expected her to reproach him, curse him, and waited for it; but she said nothing. Only her eyes spoke, with the same mysterious understanding that had penetrated him from the first instant they had met his; and he knew then that his leaving was wrong. He was not denying her. He was denying himself, turning away from the last chance at happiness his life would offer.

"I'll be back," he said, and meant it.

And he turned from her, hung from the balcony for a moment, judging the fall to the roof below, and let himself drop.

"You sure got dressed in a hurry, Kelly."

"What do you mean, Unc?"

"Nothing. Let's beat feet out of here."

"You got the idea, all right. Here, grab these rails. Sully, can you get—"

"Yeah, I got it. Let's go."

Staggering under the weight of the bed, the three chiefs pounded through darkened alleys, stumbling on the uneven cobbles, startling cats, kicking over trash cans, cursing at the night. And Kelly Wronowicz, machinist's mate chief, found that suddenly it was too much. His chest began to heave, and once he started they all began to chuckle and then laugh, then roar, staggering along, and then choke it off to a wheeze for lack of breath. But inside he was still laughing, filled with that inexplicable elation that justifies, when it comes, so much of life without joy, so much of duty.

And then he remembered her. That he had left her, and that he did not know who she was; widow; daughter; mother; where she lived; even her name. And he staggered, strong as he was, beneath the weight, stumbling on the ancient cobblestones; and his cry followed the dying sound of laughter, echoing in the silent streets of Napoli.

6

Taormina, Sicily

NODDING IN THE BUS THE NEXT MORN-
ing, watching the rising sun redden the sea below the coast
road, Lenson alternately yearned for coffee and nursed
resentment that he had to leave Susan and Nan so early.

And for so little reason. *Guam* herself was on four-
section liberty; only a quarter of her crew had to stay
aboard. Things were different for the commodore's staff.
Hogan had made it plain they were expected back aboard
every morning.

And we know where that order came from, he mused
with sleepy bitterness.

The launch back was full of hung over sailors, and
marines in even worse shape. It smelled of puke and piss
from the night before. He stood beside the helmsman,
scanning the roadstead carefully as they purred out. But
the trip was routine. Three miles out from Fleet Landing
they swung smoothly into the carrier's lee. At the last
moment the engine snarled into reverse and they slowed,
bumping alongside the boarding platform. The late-liberty
men watched blearily as he swung himself up the ladder
to the quarterdeck, looking across the bay.

It would be another bright day. Beyond the already
dazzling sea the land rose in greens and ochres. From the
coastal villages, windows flashed the new sun back out to
sea like signal lights. His eyes swept along it to the prom-

ontory. Yes, there was their hotel. Though he could not see their window he had a sudden warm picture of Susan, just as he had left her: breathing slow and still, one arm curled round the sleeping child, one brown shoulder showing above the sheets.

On the quarterdeck he came to attention facing the flag and nodded to the officer of the deck. "I report my return aboard, sir."

"Very well, sir."

He went straight to his stateroom and changed to fresh khakis. Sundstrom hated seeing his officers in civvies. He drew a mug of coffee from the wardroom pot and carried it up two decks to Flag Country.

Comphibron (Commander, Amphibious Squadron) Six Staff, sixteen officers and twenty enlisted men, were aboard, yet not of, the *Guam*.

A squadron no longer operated, as it had when Decatur scoured these seas for pirates, under the command of the senior captain. Instead, there was the Flag. Senior to the ship's captains, the commodore and his staff directed the operations of the entire Mediterranean Amphibious Ready Group, Task Force 61, when they were at sea. He promulgated the schedule of exercises. He set and maneuvered the formations they steamed in. He dealt with the NATO and host-country authorities. And in war—if war, or anything like it, ever came—he would lead them together into battle. In theory the Flag was mobile, but only the helicopter carrier had quarters that Sundstrom considered fitting to his rank. It was not a comfortable situation—there was friction between the ship's officers and the staff, who had to enforce the commodore's orders—but it was, like so many other things in the Navy, unavoidable and thus treated by all as just another pain in the ass.

Most of the staff were already waiting in SACC, the supporting arms coordination center, when Lenson went in. He took a seat at the rear, glancing as he did so at the map. The intel data from the last exercise had not yet been removed. Sundstrom liked such things scrubbed up without delay. He was about to call McQueen over when the chief staff officer came in and everyone stood up.

"Sit down, sit down," said Commander Hogan. He sat down himself, a lean, gray, avuncular man, and pulled out a pipe and a pack of Velvet. "Everyone getting along adequately ashore?"

"Fantastic," said Red Flasher instantly. He shifted in his chair, ready to elaborate, but the CSO just smiled and handed him a sheaf of paper.

"Your traffic, Red. I noticed you hadn't picked it up."

"Uh, not yet, no."

"Gentlemen, I want you all to read incoming messages before morning meetings. Otherwise we won't know what we're discussing."

The other officers nodded, and Lenson felt a touch of guilt. He resolved to get in earlier the next day.

"The commodore's ashore at the moment," Hogan went on, and suddenly the tension that had been in the room was gone. The men stretched; some of them lit cigarettes; Flasher took a sugared doughnut out of his hat and began to gnaw at it, dropping crumbs on his pants. "So I'll summarize what we have to do this morning, we'll get on it, and hopefully you can head for shore around noon. Dan, we have an inquiry from Sixth Fleet, something about ammunition. Please see if we have to respond. Stan, one of the LSTs needs some parts. Squadron Supply is here to help them out, so let's see what we can do. Mr. Byrne."

"Sir."

"Jack, you and I need to get together pretty soon on some of our intelligence requirements for Flaming Lance. And then there's this." He held out one of the red folders that meant Secret. "Just came in. Take a look at it, would you, and then see me."

"Will do."

Hogan glanced through the rest of his papers, made a few more comments, and then got up, heading back to his cabin. Flasher got up too, brushing crumbs to the deck, and made a face. Dan sent McQueen up to scrub the board, then went over to Byrne, who was standing with the folder open in his hand, looking puzzled and angry.

John Anson Byrne was the N-2. The squadron intelligence officer was dark, tall, and distinguished-looking. He kept a Florida tan current with nooners on the flight deck. Scuttlebutt had Harvard and money behind him somewhere, though Byrne only smiled at attempts to probe. He had a master's in international law, and Dan had been there when he had translated a flashing-light message between two Soviet destroyers. Passing Byrne's stateroom at night, Dan would see his face casual behind tinted aviator's glasses, staring into a book or scribbling onto yellow pads that he kept locked up along with the demolition charges for the crypto equipment. He must have hated Sundstrom; the commodore loathed him, and didn't hide it; but Byrne never remarked on that, either. Once, on the bridge, he had admitted to Dan that this assignment was a mistake for him. He'd been lined up as personal aide to Commander-in-Chief, Atlantic, but had turned it down for a sea tour. A lieutenant commander, next junior to Hogan, he still had the junior officers call him "Jack."

"What's it say, Jack?" Dan asked him. As he half-expected, Byrne slid the message into the red leather intel pouch he carried even as he glanced up.

"Nothing important. Warning order."

"For where? What's going on?"

"Whoa." The intel officer's smile creased handsome wrinkles around blue eyes. "The usual troubles—someplace east of here. I wouldn't worry, most of the time things quiet down again."

"Oh."

"Say, how's Susan? She was supposed to meet you here, wasn't she?"

Lenson smiled. Within the gray walls of the ship, the accustomed business of the day, her name had a sudden sweetness. "Yeah, she's here. So's Nan. We're up at the Piazza Vecchio, the stone mausoleum on top of the hill.

Why don't you come up tonight, have dinner with us or something?"

"Yes, perhaps I will," said Byrne politely, and Dan knew he wouldn't; but still he had remembered her name, asked about her. "I've got to go in and see the CSO, Dan. Excuse me, will you?"

"Sure, Jack."

He shot the bull for a few minutes with the others. Flasher, it seemed, had gotten entangled with a waitress. When the whole sad story had unwound itself he laughed, then strolled back toward his stateroom.

He began work with the message Hogan had handed him. It said, when he had tracked down the references, that duds had been reported in one lot of three-inch ammunition. COMSIXTHFLT, the headquarters commanding all U.S. ships in the Mediterranean, wanted an immediate inventory of the ammo TF 61 carried. He wondered about the urgency while he consulted his files and jotted out a reply.

The rest of his morning's work was routine. He read his traffic, then put an hour in on a tentative schedule for the next amphibious exercise, Flaming Lance. They would be heading east for that as soon as this port visit was over. Next he finished up a memo Sundstrom had requested on fire support during the Gythion exercise. Dan left plenty of room on his draft for changes. Sundstrom loved to hack things up, adding inanities and non sequiturs, and spreading plenty of flattery on anything likely to go up the chain of command. Just the sight of red ink—only "00," the commodore himself, was allowed to use it—sent Flasher into a rage.

When he was done with that he checked his watch. He might, if he moved out, make the noon boat. He checked his uniform in the mirror and rattled up the ladders toward the staff offices once again. If Sundstrom was ashore maybe the CSO would release the ammo report. Save everybody a lot of hassle. . . . He tapped at Hogan's door.

The commander looked up from an old *Navy Times.* "What can I do for you, Dan?"

He explained, and laid the form before Hogan. "So, since he's ashore, I thought you might sign it, sir."

The chief of staff chewed on his pipe, looking uncomfortable. "Is it urgent?"

"Priority, sir. I don't know why, but—"

"I'll take care of it," said Hogan, slotting it over his desk. "I'll give it to him when he comes back aboard. He said to expect him around noon, so it should go out a little after that. If there are changes, I'll handle it."

"Aye, sir."

"Anything else?"

"No—well, yes, sir. Request permission to go ashore."

"Caught up?"

"Yes sir."

"Go on, then. Tell Mrs. Lenson I said hello." Hogan smiled wearily. "Alicia says she's quite a feisty young lady. We'd like to have a drink with the two of you, if I can get ashore this trip."

"Thank you, sir."

He puzzled for a moment in the passageway. Obviously Hogan didn't want to release the message. In fact, now that he thought about it, he had not seen the chief staff officer sign a thing for at least a month, though his job was to handle the administrative load so that the commodore could spend his time preparing the task force to fight.

Conclusion: Sundstrom wouldn't let him. Lenson nodded to himself, contemplating what that might mean.

Dan tried hard to maintain the right attitude toward his seniors. That was just good leadership; mutter against them, and your own juniors will lose respect for you. But he had to admit that some of the things Sundstrom did were out of the ordinary. Like this. More and more, he insisted on handling all the detail work, the administrative stuff, and he nitpicked it to death. It was the latest evidence of his growing suspicion, his mistrust of others' competence and even their motives, that was cutting the officers of the squadron and staff off one by one from their commander.

It wasn't a good situation. But his mind's business with the item did not last more than a second, because just then two slow bells sounded over the announcing system. He had ten minutes before the next boat ashore. He tore down the ladder and through the passageways, flattening a seaman recruit against the bulkhead as he went by. In his stateroom he ripped free of his uniform, tossed on his civvies, and beat it for the gangway.

When he reached the quarterdeck, out of breath and feeling smothered in the tropic heat after the ship's air conditioning, he saw that Flasher had beaten him. The paunchy lieutenant was leaning against the rail, watching a gig angle in toward them. Dan shaded his eyes to look out at it, and then froze. He exchanged glances with Flasher.

"It's him, all right," said Red. "Quick, up here. He always goes down the starboard side."

"Right." The two junior officers faded behind a bulkhead, and watched as Commodore Isaac I. Sundstrom stepped from the launch to the ladder and hauled himself up, with deliberate dignity, toward the quarterdeck.

Simultaneously they realized that they were the only ones to have seen him approach. "Someone's going to catch it," breathed Flasher. "Hey! You! Officer of the deck!"

The ensign on duty swung around at the stage whisper. He followed Flasher's urgent finger, and his face suddenly matched his whites. The petty officer of the watch flicked switches on the 1MC, raised his hand to the ship's bell, but far, far too late.

Ike Sundstrom stepped aboard, smiling tightly. He had been standing behind another man, Colonel Haynes; that was why the OOD had missed him. But that was no excuse. In the engine spaces, in the troop berthing where marines sprawled still hung over, in offices and repair shops and through the cavernous hangar deck where the helicopters waited, the clang of the bell and "COMPHI-BRON SIX, ARRIVING" echoed through the ship; and the captain of the *Guam* started up from his desk to meet him, glanced out a porthole to see the launch already alongside, and covered his face with his hands.

On the quarterdeck the ensign saluted, anguish and fear in his boyish face. Sundstrom asked him his name, and nodded. In another man it might have been taken for amiability. He turned for a word with Haynes, then strolled forward along the starboard side. It was empty. The sailors who had been working there moments before had vanished, taking their tools and portable radios with them.

Sundstrom went up the Flag ladder and disappeared from sight. The ensign smiled helplessly at Flasher and Lenson, and then nodded to the petty officer. The final "bong" quivered away into the steel acreage of the ship.

"That chocolate-coated bastard," muttered Flasher. "That son of a bitch is a horse's ass, and that's all he is."

"Knock it off, Red, people can hear you."

"That's right, I forgot Mister Straight Arrow was with me. You really go for this bozo's style, huh?"

"I don't 'go for' him. But he's in charge. And we're his staff."

"Be realistic, Dan-o." Flasher looked, for once, as if he meant what he was saying. "This guy's a sundowner. He wants stars so bad, he'll leave a trail of bleeding bodies behind him to get there. You want to be one of them?"

Lenson didn't answer. After a moment Flasher continued. "Your problem, Dan, is you believe things are just the way they told you at the Boat School. Honor. Responsibility. Duty. Well, real life ain't that simple, boy."

"One jerk doesn't invalidate the concept, Red."

"Oh, forget it." Flasher turned away. "Let's get off this madhouse. I'm three drinks behind already today."

"You said it," said Lenson. And as he clattered down the ladder toward the waiting boat, tossing on the blue translucent sea, he had already left the ship, the commodore, and the entire Navy far behind.

Four days, Dan had told her that first evening; four days in Taormina, four days together.

She wanted every minute of it, and wanted every minute to be wonderful.

Sitting together in a taberna that evening, listening to violins, Nan beside them in a little chair the manager brought, it was for a while everything she had hoped for.

Susan leaned back in the delicate iron chair, toying with her second glass of wine.

They had so little time together. She had counted it up. Married four years; together four hundred days of that. Oh, he'd mentioned the separations before they were married. She remembered how she had thought it might be nice; time alone to pursue her own career. She hadn't realized how it would really be. How could she, when her father had been home with his briefcase every night of her childhood, dependable as a rock? And then Nan had come. She knew now what the Navy demanded. Six-month deployments, more months at sea for work-ups and exercises, and even when he was home, a seven-to-five working day and duty days aboard twice a week.

The Navy. At nineteen it had meant parades by the Severn, the Ring Dance, forbidden kisses along Stribling Walk. A romantic dream. It was different living it, trying to be a "Navy wife" (how she hated those words) when you were actually single, or worse; something like a legal separation, with visiting rights. Her dreams of a career had vanished; the grimy port cities the Navy based in were far from the action in archaeology. Oh, she stayed busy. Halfway to a master's, and substitute teaching, and of course her daughter. That helped time slip away when he wasn't there.

But she didn't want time to slip away. She was young, and she wanted life to be as she had dreamed it, romantic and beautiful. Or else professional and fulfilling; her dreams tugged her sometimes this way, sometimes that. So that now, living at least the romantic half of them, she smiled at him in the candlelight, and saw his smile grow, reflecting and then kindled by hers; and knew that to him, she was everything.

For tonight, anyway.

"Happy, Susan?"

She had been, but for some reason being asked if she was, irritated her. She felt her smile fade.

"Ooooo! Spaghetti!" said Nan, grabbing her silverware. Susan tucked her napkin back where it had fallen, and glanced at Dan.

"Good—just in time."

They plunged into fettuccine alla Romana, side dishes of more pasta, a meat course that she thought looked like flank steak from a squirrel. A little of the festive mood returned as he touched his glass to hers.

"Aren't you drinking?"

"Good grief, Dan, this is my third glass. What are you trying to do—seduce me?"

He glanced at Nan, who was ogling a passing waiter with wide brown eyes, noodles hanging from her mouth. "If I only had a chance."

"If you only did. But I'm married. At least I think so—my husband's been at sea so long I'm not sure anymore."

She regretted her remark instantly, but said nothing to repair it. The silence grew. At last he bit his lips and reached for the carafe. He poured more for both of them, topping the glasses till the wine trembled convex at the very lip.

"I can't do anything about that, Susan," he said at last.

"I know. I was being bitter. I'm sorry."

"Okay now?"

"Yes. Sure."

But that same taut silence kept coming back all through the wine, and what dancing afterward they could snatch before Nan got cranky. As they walked back to the hotel uphill past the shuttered shops, the scents of verbena and roses lying over the cobblestones like fog, he was wondering what to say, and she was trying to be cheerful. But she wasn't. Nan was whiny, tired, and the first order of business was to put her to bed. When she fell asleep at last, breathing raggedly out of a tear-swollen face, Susan dropped all trying, all effort, and slumped onto the bed. Too much wine had left her feeling dizzy and sad and conscious that she had eaten too much. When he lay down, the bed creaking, and put his hand on her breast she pushed it away. After a moment she got up and went to the window.

"Babe?" he said, behind her.

She didn't answer, looking out at the empty dark beyond the rippled antique glass. When she heard him get up she opened it and went out. The balcony was bare stone, but the climbing roses that seemed to infest Taormina wound over the walls, filling the airless night with sickening sweetness. She leaned down, holding tight to the balustrade, and heard from far below the sigh of waves.

"Oh," he said, beside her. "There's the ship."

It was true; they could see it now, out at the edge of the bay. "We couldn't see it from here yesterday," she said.

"Right, she's upped her anchor." His voice had changed, become evaluatory and professional; as if, Susan thought bitterly, she was not there at all. "She's got her running lights on . . . must be shifting anchorages."

"Forget the ship," she said. "You're away from the ship. We've got two more days away from the goddamned ship."

"Susan, come off it. Don't tell me you're not enjoying this, touring all over the Med. Lots of wives would kill for this."

"Screw them."

He didn't say anything else then. Afraid to, she thought. He's right. I feel dangerous right now.

And he was thinking, What is it? Why is she like this,

all of a sudden? I was looking forward to this so much
. . . it was so wonderful, last night. . . .

They made up somehow, clumsily. She did it against her
will, feeling forced to it by the shortness of their time
together. But she pushed the resentment down once more.
They were kissing at last, alone together above the sea,
when something buzzed inside the room.

"What's that?"

"I don't know . . . could it be the door?"

But when they went in they saw that it was the telephone. She picked it up, listened, then held it out.

"*Lieutenant* Lenson. It's for you."

"What? Who is it?" He took the instrument unwillingly, turning a little away from her. "Hello. Yes. Yes
sir."

She waited, her hand on his arm.

"Yes sir," he said again. "Now? I mean—tonight?"

"Yes sir." He hung up.

"What is it?"

"Jack Byrne. He called from the pier."

"How did he know we were here?"

"We have to leave a number when we stay ashore overnight. You know that, Susan." He stared at the phone for
a moment longer, then started buttoning his shirt.

"What's going on?"

"It's a general recall."

"You have to go back? When?"

"Right now. Jack says the launch is waiting at the pier.
Guam's underway at the mouth of the harbor, standing by
to get us back aboard."

"But wait." She felt the whole structure crumbling; she
was still dizzy from the wine. "Where are you going? For
how long? Will you be back in?"

"I don't know, babe."

"What does it mean? Is it a war, or what?" She felt
lightheaded, speaking words she was unable to connect to
any reality.

"I just told you all I know. I doubt it's serious. Probably

just a false alarm. Or Ike could be pulling it for drill. We'll probably be back in tomorrow morning."

"But what should I do? Should I wait?"

"I don't know," he said again, and she heard the pain in his voice. "Look . . . Mrs. Hogan and the other wives are down at the Naxos. Why don't you move down there with them, and as soon as we know what's going on, we'll get a message back to you."

"Wait. Wait, Dan."

Halfway to the door already, pulling on the one civilian coat he owned, he stopped when he felt her arms around him.

"Don't make a scene, Susan. I have to go. It's my duty."

"Duty! That doesn't mean you—just *take off,* and leave us here. You have duties to us too—"

"Susan, they know I got the message. And even if they didn't, I've got to be aboard that ship if she's going someplace."

"You don't *have* to."

"I do," he said quietly, taking her arms. "I do. That's what I'm here for."

She closed her eyes. It was useless arguing with him. Pain and love filled her in quick alternation with flashes of hatred.

"Hold me, at least, before you go."

They hugged in the darkened room. He felt her shoulders move; felt her hair brush his chin; lowered his head, feeling tears burn his eyes. Didn't she know there was nothing he wanted less to do in the world than leave her and Nan? Couldn't she know, without his having to say a word, that in spite of all he was, all he had promised, he wanted desperately to stay? But he knew he couldn't. It would be wrong for him to stay, not when the task force was sailing, and it was not fair for her to make it harder.

He opened his eyes and stepped back. "Babe . . . I'll get a message back as soon as I can."

"All right, Dan."

"Good-bye."

She did not answer. He touched her eyes gently with a finger. He had expected tears, but her eyes were dry.

She stood at the door for a long time after the lock snapped behind him. She was listening to the silence; the distant creak of floors; tick of an old clock; and from the window, soft in the airless night of Taormina, the ceaseless surge and whisper of the sea.

III

UNDERWAY

7
U.S.S. *Guam*

0300: UNDERWAY.
THE SHIP MOVED STEADILY THROUGH A dark swell, miles from land; but she was not awake. Three-quarters of her crew were dead in their bunks. Cradled, muttering lost in dreams, they curled unconscious as the unborn within the metal womb that carried them.

Like the pelagic sharks far below her keel, despite her sleep she swam and dimly knew. Deep in her boiler rooms sweating men labored between tornadoes of oil-fed flame. Her enginerooms were solid with sound, the shafts whirling blurs. Levels above, her senses fingered the darkness, sweeping the surface of the sea and the heart of a clouding sky. Specialists leaned over radarscopes and plots. In radio central the receivers and telctypes hummed and clattered. On her bridge men stared warily into the night, and the captain napped restlessly in his leather chair.

On the flag bridge, high above the black sweep of the helicopter deck, Lenson balanced his binoculars on the port coaming. The night wind combed his hair, drying the sweat from his forehead. He did not like night watches. He spun the focusing knob, setting it by touch, and lowered his face to peer into the absolute darkness of open sea under overcast.

Ahead, one point off the port bow, a single dim star rode steady, glittering distant. *Bowen,* their one remaining escort. She probed an elder realm than the sky, her sonars singing whalelike down into four thousand feet of black Mediterranean.

Lenson shifted his binoculars, blinking to clear tired eyes. Nothing else marred the invisible sea ahead. Even the huge objectives of the night glasses gathered only a faint gray where the sea broke and sky began. He shifted again, searching aft in bites along the barely visible horizon. There; a second light, low on the dark circle of heaving water . . . *Barnstable County.* He watched her for a few minutes, glanced at the amber face of a gyrocompass, and shifted the glasses once more.

A greenish, faraway spark under the immense dome of sky, the flat bowl of sea across which they crawled . . . *Charleston.* She was eight points back, abeam of *Guam,* the guide and axis of this moving circle of ships. She seemed distant, but the night-steaming plan was a sector formation, each ship roaming within a moving segment of arc, and her radar range was well within its outer edge.

He shifted. Far astern, the second LST, *Newport.* He studied her for a long time. Her range light seemed dim. Then it shone out; the ship had yawed, bringing some line or fitting out from between the glowing filament and his distant eye.

Lenson yawned. The binoculars dangled, their weight digging into his neck after three hours of watch. He turned from the windy night into the red-lit cave of the flag bridge, high in the island above the slow-rolling bulk of the assault carrier.

Instantly he was surrounded by a small world; the separate, silent, almost holy heart of a ship at sea, a pilothouse at night.

The flag bridge was thirty feet wide and twenty deep. Around the night-filled windows was a mass of equipment: radiotelephone handsets, gyrocompass repeaters, rudder-angle indicators, status boards, IC phones, all invisible except for pilot lights of red or dim blue. Clipboards and publications had been wedged into their cabling. To the left, under a faint red radiance, a chart table was folded out of the bulkhead. In the center of the bridge the green flicker of a radar repeater picked out the face of a man bending over it. To the right, against the after bulkhead, a sheet of Plexiglas covered with numbers glowed dim as a phosphene; another man stood motionless behind it, sound-powered headset clamped to his ears, a grease pencil tentative in his upraised hand. To the far right was another hatchway, open, but with only night and the rushing wind beyond.

Lenson paced the narrow aisle before the windows twice, then stopped at the repeater, leaning against it. A flash of white light came from a small room behind the bridge.

"Quartermaster, keep that curtain closed."

"Aye aye, sir."

He leaned without moving for a silent while. A maddeningly deliberate clock, lit amber, shaved thin slices from the night. Since World War II, some detached portion of his brain reflected, the Navy had patrolled this ancient Hell's Kitchen of the earth. He was the cop on the corner tonight. Did they sleep better at home, knowing these ships were here, that he stood nodding over a radarscope? He doubted it. But here they were just the same, obedient to their word.

"Everybody in station, Stan?" he asked suddenly.

Glazer glanced up. His face looked ascetic and gloomy in the verdigris glow of the scan. He stepped back to let Lenson dip his face to the night hood.

The fluorescent wand of the surface-search radar rotated tirelessly, sweeping across the dark glass that was, to his mind, the Central Med. Here and there were brief sparkles; sea return, the echo of peaking waves. But there were solid pips, too, fading slowly but returned to their hard brilliance moment after moment by the sweep of the scan. Glazer, the junior officer on watch, had drawn each ship's night-steaming sector on the scope with yellow grease pencil. One glance told Lenson that all units of the task force were in their assigned areas. To starboard, two bright pips showed the remainder of the formation; *Coronado; Spiegel Grove. Coronado* was at the far edge of her sector, but her captain believed in active patrolling. Every ship had her quirks, her individuality, even on so remote and inhuman a device as a radarscope.

One station was empty: *Ault*'s. In the hurry to get underway her captain had taken her across a shoal in the dark. She had reported no apparent damage, but still had hove to, to check out her bottom, once she was clear. She was coming up astern, but at reduced speed. He felt the gap the old destroyer left in their screen as a sheep must the absence of a shepherd.

His hand felt for the range dial, and turned it up.

Now the formation itself shrank to the center of the screen. It could be covered by a quarter. The beam swept out fifty miles or more, and he watched it scan around.

Far ahead, a blurry green smear flared and disappeared at the very limits of the radar's range. He stared at the blankness where it had been. Several sweeps later it painted again. He ratcheted the cursor for bearing and distance, marked it with the grease pencil, then lifted his head to look at the vertical plot. The messenger of the watch was stroking in characters, printing backward so the men in front could read. As he wrote he began to speak, his voice creeping into the silence, belonging there, like the muffled roar of the wind.

"CIC reports: Skunk "Oscar," bearing zero-three-two true, range forty-eight thousand. Course one-five-five, speed ten. Closest Point of Approach; one-one-five, four thousand yards; time to CPA, 0335."

"Very well," muttered Lenson.

"That him?" said Glazer, sidling over to peer past his shoulder.

"Yeah," he muttered, looking off into the darkness. The other ship, twenty-four miles distant, was headed south. Its closing rate, the algebraic sum of both ships' speeds, and its relative motion would take it across the bows of the formation and through it. It would pass *Guam,* at the center, two miles to starboard. That would take it between *Bowen* and *Barnstable County,* past the guide, into *Coronado*'s sector and then *Spiegel Grove*'s . . . if it didn't change course. If it was what he suspected, a merchantman or tanker bound for North Africa or Spain, it probably wouldn't. On the other hand, no naval officer trusted a merchant skipper to do the reasonable thing. The formation had the right of way in this situation, but the possibilities of miscalculation were too great, the consequences too terrible, to take any chances at all.

He had seen once what could happen. Sometimes, on night watches like this, he could still hear the screams on the wind.

For just a moment then, remembering, Lenson heard them. He closed his eyes, gripping the pelorus till his fingers cramped, then opened them, driving into them the dim glow of the instruments, the dim deckedge lights, the iron fact that he was on *Guam* and not another ship that lay now two miles beneath the gray rollers of the North Atlantic. Not now, he prayed. I'm on watch, I have to be alert. As if in answer the screaming waned, grew faint. He stared into the radarscope, breathing swift and shallow, hoping he would not be forced to live it all again.

Then, as the bow of an aircraft carrier took shape before his helplessly fixed eyes, he knew that he had lost.

Dan, left on the *Ryan*'s wing, had stood frozen, staring at what had a moment before been empty night. Something seventy feet high had suddenly created itself there, filling half the sky, its running lights burning steady, the cruel gleam of its bow wave sparkling against black. He gripped the splinter shield, unable to move or breathe. Behind him a cry of "Stand by for collision!" was followed instantly by the electric clang of the alarm.

The *Kennedy* hit them a hundred feet behind the bridge. The destroyer heeled, knocking him onto the gratings. A terrifying shriek of tearing steel succeeded the blow. The ship whipped and shuddered under him and he hugged the deck mindlessly, binoculars biting into his stomach. The lights of the carrier, penumbraed by mist, slid by high above him. A scream of yielding metal, a roar of escaping steam blotted out the drone of her horn. Something exploded aft, jolting the deck and lighting the sea like sudden daylight.

He scrambled up and was propelled by the lean of the deck into the pilothouse. He blinked flash from his eyes to find its familiarity changed into something new and terrible. The boatswain was shouting into the 1MC, but nothing was audible above the din. The chart table light flickered and went out, as did the binnacle and the pilots on all the radios. The captain was clinging to his chair, staring out the starboard hatch.

Dan fetched up against the helm and clung to it, looking out. The deckedge lights were still moving by above them, like a train on a high trestle. Then they were gone. The deck shuddered. Another explosion came from aft, a deep detonation that rattled the windows. The ship swayed back to vertical, then reeled to starboard with sickening ease. The deck took on a backward slant.

"Abandon ship," the boatswain was yelling into the mike. But it was dead.

"Knock that off," said Dan.

"Sir, we got to get off her—"

He ran to the port side. The carrier loomed abeam of them, a black cliff higher than their masttop. He craned aft over the splinter shield. Kerosene reeked the air. Flames were beginning to shoot up, with crackling rapid bangs, all along the asroc deck and down to the waterline. He saw a dark mass astern of them, not burning, but lit by the flames. It took a long time, two seconds perhaps, before he understood that it was the aft half of the *Ryan*.

When Dan turned back to the bridge he found the captain on the wing, looking aft. His pipe was still in his mouth. The OOD was with him, standing straight, both hands on his binoculars. "Abandon ship, sir?" Dan shouted above the rising roar of fire. The ship lurched again, settling, and the slant steepened.

"She never responded to the emergency bell," said Packer. His face was emotionless in the growing firelight.

"She's cut in two aft, Captain."

"All right. Do it. Get the order around the ship by word of mouth. Let's get as many off as we can."

Lenson found himself on the main deck. He did not recall the process of getting there. Men shoved past him. He could see their faces clearly now in the glare from aft. Naked from the waist up, a man threw his legs over the lines and dropped, running in the air. "Abandon ship," Dan shouted, fighting his way in the direction of the fire. He heard them repeating it as he left them.

The flames were coming up from the after deckhouse, licking swiftly forward. Their tips fluttered in the wind like bright pennants. He thought for a moment the metal itself was burning. The smoke was choking and he could feel the heat on his face.

He got abreast of the asroc launcher and then was forced back toward a hatch by smoke. Sailors pushed by him, going the wrong way. He shouted at them and grabbed their clothes but they tore away and went on. Lifejackets littered the deck, soft under his feet, like haunted houses where you pretend you are walking on bodies. The deck was bright as noon, lit by an immense soaring pyre, slanted by the wind, shedding sparks at its apex. The sea was burning behind it. He turned and looked upward at the bridge, expecting to see the captain still there. But the wing was empty.

Almost helplessly he turned again, like a moth in a forest fire, toward the mountain of flame. It occurred to him it was time he thought of abandoning. His assigned raft? No, it was in the heart of the fire. The bow would be best. He ran forward.

On the fo'c'sle a knot of sailors, moving with no particular hurry, were dumping lifejackets out of a locker. He selected one and began strapping it on. His hands were shaking. He tried the waterproof light pinned to the vest. It didn't work. Fortunately there were plenty of mae wests. He pulled two lights off them and stuck them in his pockets.

The bow was rising slowly. "You'd better get in the water," Dan said to the sailors. "If she goes down sudden she may suck us under. Jump in and swim clear."

"Aye aye, sir."

The men did not seem frightened, but neither did they move to obey. He picked up a lifejacket and threw it at one of them. "Get over the side," he said again, and waited, eyes on the man, till he began buckling it on.

He threw his legs over the lifeline and looked down.

The sea was black, with highlights of fire. Heads bobbed here and there, faces bright, looking strangely peaceful. His hands gripped the lifeline. He tried to make them let go but they would not. "Jesus," he said aloud, "I've got to get off this thing."

He cast a glance aft. More men, black cutouts against the brilliance, were leaping now. He saw one hit on his stomach and disappear. The firesound was enormous but cheerful, like a big bonfire at a picnic. Someone was screaming above it.

The lifeline was biting into them, but his fingers would not let go. He pleaded silently with them and suddenly, to his surprise, they released. He teetered for a moment on the sheer strake and then kicked away weakly and plunged feetfirst into the sea.

The impact burst breath from him and icy water filled his mouth. He clawed at the darkness but it was the life-jacket that brought him up. He bobbed, panting with the shock of cold. The side of the ship was an arm's-length away. A man hurtled over him and hit within spitting distance, sending cold spray into his face.

He began swimming then, starting instinctively with a dog paddle, then a crawl. The lifejacket dragged at him maddeningly. He swam as hard as he could for three dozen strokes and then was exhausted. He turned on his back and let the lifejacket hold him up and looked back at his ship.

Her forward half floated bow high, the deck listed toward him. She had moved. Still a little way left on her, then. From the forward stack aft a solid pyramid of white flame ran down along the sides, eating into the sea. Patches of inky darkness showed between the fires on the water. A few were still jumping and he saw one fat man in skivvy shorts standing calmly by the rail, looking out. Dan lifted his arm and turned the face of his watch to the flame. Only a few minutes had passed since the collision.

He became conscious now of the men around him. Some were shouting but most were quiet, tossed up and down by the four-foot seas. A few had turned on their lights. A sailor he did not recognize called out, "Think she'll float, Mr. Lenson?"

"Not much longer," Dan shouted back.

"She looks buoyant. Fire'll get her first."

"Maybe," he shouted.

Good God, the sea was cold. He kicked his feet a few times and the numbness retreated. He was still looking at the man, trying to recall who he was, when the *Ryan* exploded.

He was in a tunnel of flame. It roared up on both sides, choking him with smoke and heated air. He could not breathe. When he raised his hands he saw that they were black with oil.

A strange thing happened to him then. He was drifting in a sea of fire, but at the same time he could see the whole bright circle on the sea, the forward half of the ship capsized and burning, the aft section dark and almost gone. Around them he saw the tiny bobbing heads. But he saw it all from above. He was Dan Lenson and at the same time he was all the men drifting and crying out and the men trapped inside, hammering at steel in the dark. He saw through a tunnel of flame a place cool and at the same time bright as the fire. He moved upward through the fire and it did not burn, and the brightness increased, and he went through oblivion into a place of clean cool wind.

Dan stared rigidly into the radarscope. Not long had passed; the pip had moved only a fraction of an inch along its greased track. Was it over? He lifted his head. Yes. They grieved no longer on the wind, those ghosts.

The recurrence, brief as it was, decided him. He would take no more chances. Compressing his lips, he pressed a buzzer. Beside him Glazer laid out plotting paper and dividers and began checking the solution.

"Yuh," said a familiar voice in his ear. "Commodore. What is it?"

"Staff Watch Officer, sir, Lieutenant j.g. Lenson. We have an incoming contact."

"Let's have it," said Sundstrom, sounding more awake.

Lenson repeated the range and course data from memory. "We've got thirty minutes till she's inside *Bowen,* sir. I recommend bringing the formation left."

"What will that open it to?"

Lenson had to pause only for a second. Every conning officer learned to do relative motion problems in his head, to accuracies of five degrees and a couple of thousand yards. Two decks down Sundstrom, pulled from sleep, was doing the same thing. At least Dan hoped he was. "If we come left fifty degrees that will open her to seven thousand yards from the escort and twenty thousand from us, sir."

"What'll that do to *Coronado*?"

"He's at the outer edge of his sector. Should pass eight to ten thousand yards outboard of him."

"Do we have sea room to port? Any other contacts out there?"

"None on the scope, sir."

"Did you look?" Sundstrom's voice took on an edge.

"Yes sir, less than a minute ago. We're clear to the north."

"Okay then." The voice subsided into drowsiness again.

"Come left fifty. Keep an eye on him, Dan. Don't let him screw me up with some crazy course change."

"No sir."

"That's all I need, a goddamn collision, just when things are heating up."

"No sir," said Lenson promptly, but he felt a shiver nonetheless. He did not like that word, and he liked the worried whine in Sundstrom's voice even less. "I'll keep my eyes peeled, sir."

The receiver clicked in his ear. Lenson rattled it back into the holder and turned. "Stan—"

"I was listening. Here's the signal." Glazer flicked the red spot from his flashlight onto the plotting pad. "You want to put it over the net?"

"No. You do it. Good work."

He bent to the 'scope again, half his mind listening to Glazer on the radio, the other half watching the pip on its slow slide along the grease-penciled line toward them. Straight and true. He hadn't altered course yet. Probably hasn't even seen us, Dan thought. Got his scope set in close. His attention flicked out, to all the men on the ships around them, on bridges as dark and tense as theirs, listening at that moment to the supply officer's voice: calculating instantly in their minds how far that would put the contact, twenty or eighty thousand tons of knife-bowed metal rushing through the night, from their own hulls. "Stand by . . . execute," Glazer said, popping the button on the radiotelephone, and listened as each ship answered in turn.

"All units acknowledge, sir."

"Very well," said Lenson, watching the faint glow of the rudder angle indicator. Any minute now the men on the bridge above, *Guam*'s own bridge, would begin the turn . . . there. The rudder began to swing, faster and faster, then eased to a stop at left fifteen. Beneath their feet the ship heeled, first outward, then in. A pencil clattered to the deck.

"Check the port side," he said to Glazer.

"Right."

He went to starboard himself. He lifted his glasses long enough to see *Coronado*'s lights begin to swing, then glanced at the gyro repeater and set his elbows to the rail. Twenty miles range; a clear night despite the overcast, no haze. He might be able to pick her up. . . .

There she was. A dancing double star in the darkness, masthead and range almost in line. Too far for sidelights yet. The inbound merchantman seemed still oblivious of the seven ships that now were turning together north to clear her.

"All ships to port turning to port," said Glazer, at his side. "How long you going to hold them on this course?"

"Till this guy clears *Coronado*. Then we'll come back." Lenson let his binoculars drop, suddenly sleepy again now that the moment of action was over. He yawned, glancing at his watch. Another hour before their reliefs came up. "How about some coffee?" he asked Glazer.

"Saucers and all?"

"What?"

"Remember, *he* said no coffee on the bridge without saucers. Cup and saucer, from the wardroom."

"How many hands have we got, Stan? One roll and they'll be all over the deck. Send McQueen down for some of those Styrofoam cups."

"All right," said Glazer. He went back into the chartroom and Lenson relaxed, looking out to where the lights of the oncoming ship were visible now without the glasses.

Another night at sea. He had been afraid Ike would come up in his bathrobe and flipflops and start worrying. But tonight the old man had sounded bushed. Like all of us, Lenson thought, but he takes it worse. He was responsible, sure, but there were good men on the bridge of every ship; they had years of experience at sea, some of them more than the commodore; they could drive ships.

Tired, tired, tired . . . he stared down over the coaming, seventy feet down to the sea. Black, invisible save for the ripple of phosphorescence where the hull met water, it rushed past the ship like a subterranean river. A line of something rose to his mind . . . French class, the mids sitting row on row of dark uniforms. Apollinaire. *Sous le pont Mirabeau coule la Seine . . . et nos amours, faut-il qu'il m'en souvienne, La joie venait toujours après la peine. . . .*

Joy comes always, only, after pain. Yes, he was tired now from two days without sleep. The flap had started as soon as they cleared Italy. Messages to get out, steaming orders to write, the rendezvous with the other units of the MARG, dozens of pubs to break out and study furiously, goaded by Sundstrom's frantic orders. And they still did not know why they had gotten underway. Some of the officers thought it was Lebanon again, some Israel; Byrne, the only one apart from the commodore and possibly Hogan who knew what was going on, only smiled with his painful courtesy at their fishing. There was a lot of sea east of here, seven hundred miles of it, miles that slipped slowly under their keel hour by hour.

A lot of sea, a lot of beaches. If they had to put the marines ashore, there would be a hell of a lot to do, and not very much time to do it.

No, he thought. We won't be landing. This would be just another famous Navy steam-around-and-wait exercise. Cruise in circles, night-steam off some anonymous stretch of land, keeping clear of shipping that seemed to take for granted that a civilian had right of way. That was the drill for the Sixth Fleet when trouble started anywhere in the Med. But then one of the older ships would break down, or somebody would run low on fuel, and they would detach first one ship and then another for the run to port; and then one day the message would come, it's off, everything's settled down now, and they would turn and head back for Spain or Tunisia or Southern France.

And this time, Susan and Nan would be waiting there for him.

Après la peine . . .

He raised the binoculars to forestall the tightening in his

belly. But the image of her face close beneath his in the morning sunlight, of the smooth luxury of her, laid itself over the cold glitter of running lights on the waves.

La joie venait toujours . . .

"Here's your coffee, Mr. Lenson," said McQueen. "I didn't put anything in it."

"Thanks, Mac." He accepted the cup and sucked hot brew, moving into the shelter of the bridge, glancing at the gyro and then the radar. *Guam* had steadied up; all ships were still on station; the skunk was tracking down the new relative motion line. Glazer and McQueen were huddled over the chart table, updating the dead reckoning plot for the oncoming watch. The fathometer pinged sleepily through the open door to the chartroom, where racks of Coastal Pilots and hydrographic charts lay sheathed in red light. He checked his watch, estimating time to turn back to base course—he could do that without waking Sundstrom again, he decided.

La joie . . . when they came back in, weary from the days or weeks at sea, *she* would be waiting. The wives had an intelligence network that would shame the KGB. They would know where the ships would put in, almost before Sixth Fleet had decided. Sardinia, Mallorca, Piraeus, it didn't matter. There were hotels everywhere. Hotels and beds.

No, goddamn it, Lenson, you can't start thinking of that again. He paced around, reshelved the signal books, and glanced over Glazer's shoulder at the chart. The pencil line stretched out from the toe of Italy, reaching eastward past the open blue of the Ionian Sea, toward Crete. The island lay curled like a shrimp sixty miles north of them, the shallowing water inshore washed in lighter shades of blue and white. There the pencil line ended, hung in blue space.

Glazer felt his presence and turned his head. "Here we are," he said, putting his finger on a half-circle marked *0400 DR*. "But where the heck are we going?"

"Good question," said Lenson, glad of the opening for

talk. "Where would you like to go? Other than back to Taormina, I mean."

"Anyplace except Libya. Too many MIGs there for me."

"It's been pretty quiet there this year, since what's his face got the axe."

"Where's it hot?"

His eye traveled east, past the Libyan headlands into Egypt and the Sinai, past the scattered dots of the Dodecanese and Rhodes into a blue gulf. The eastern Med reached like a cupped hand between Asia Minor and Africa, the back of the hand Egypt, the outstretched fingers digging into the Middle East. And it was all their beat. They were the only American force prepared to move instantly, equipped to go ashore and stay. Aircraft could strike more quickly, but only to destroy. The Army could move in force, but it took months to gear up that sluggish machine. Only the Navy was ready now, marines and tanks and artillery, able with the guns of destroyers and air support from the carriers to land and hold ground.

And when you were ready, and the world knew it, most of the time the only action needed in a crisis was the sudden appearance of those gray ships offshore.

Somewhere east. Turkey? There had just been a coup there; a bellicose rightist government had taken power, but things seemed calm from the unclassified traffic he read every day on watch. The small countries, where strife never ended; Lebanon, Cyprus, Jordan? Or perhaps the Soviet clients, Syria, Iraq, the Palestinians. There were so many possibilities.

He put his finger on the coast. "I'd guess Lebanon again."

"Yeah? We haven't been there yet this float."

"Let's hope we don't go."

"Hey," said a new voice, behind the three of them, and Lenson turned. "Ready to relieve," said the round silhouette, not saluting.

He saluted back anyway. "Ready to be relieved. Hi, Red."

They went over the tactical situation, course and speed, the surface picture. "You'll want to come back to base course pretty soon," Dan finished.

"Yeah. I went out and looked around before I came in here. Oscar's the merchie off to starboard, green sidelight, right? Think I'll come back around soon as we relieve."

"Sounds good."

"What's *Ault* doing?"

"She's not on the scope yet."

"That's a hell of a note. You hear what happened?"

"She touched bottom getting underway, I heard."

"That's the short version." Flasher leaned a little closer. "Want the straight poop? What really happened was, when Foster—that's her CO—got our emergency sortie message, he came back and said he couldn't raise a local pilot that time of night, that it was a difficult channel out, and unless otherwise directed he was going to wait till first light. Well, Sundstrom went crazy; he was screaming around up here about how everybody wanted to make him look bad; he wanted to report the task force clear of land by dawn. He sent Foster back a direct order to get underway immediately. So he did, but in the dark he got out of the main channel and went over a mudbank at ten knots."

"Wow."

"You said it. But then, when her grounding report came in, Ike said to hold on to it."

"It hasn't been forwarded to Sixth Fleet?"

"Nope. It's sitting on his desk."

"Wow," said Dan again.

"Well, I got it," said Flasher a moment later, turning away to the radarscope. Lenson saluted again, feeling relieved; he was always nervous on watch, on some subliminal level. But now Flasher was on deck. No matter that he looked like a bum and saluted like a seagull with a busted wing, he was the best watch officer on the staff, competent and unflappable. As he headed for the ladder

Dan grinned suddenly in the darkness. Zero-four-hundred now, with staff quarters at seven; he could skip breakfast and get in a solid three hours in his rack. The thought was overpowering.

He reached for the door, knowing where the handle was just as he knew where all the instruments on the bridge were, by touch and not by sight, but even as he grasped it it turned under his hand. He stepped back, thinking it was another of the watch reliefs, and said, "Who's that?"

The man didn't answer, just shoved by him. "Hey," said Lenson, annoyed, turning to follow. "I said—"

"Take it easy, Dan," said Commodore Sundstrom.

Even in the dark Lenson could feel the silent shock of his presence run through the flag bridge. Glazer and McQueen, still briefing their reliefs around the chart table, straightened from their slouches. Cups disappeared in cleverly shielded prestidigitation. The messenger fitted himself behind the vertical plot with the instinctive dive of a rabbit. The drone of the gyros, hissing phones, the muffled roar of the wind took on a deeper tone without human voices. In the silence the commodore's footsteps were audible, scuffing across the slowly slanting tiles of the deck. "Dan—what is this? I want my bridge watch to have their heads up. Who's keeping an eye on the surface picture?"

"Sir—"

"What's happened to that contact you called me about? What course are we on now?"

Oh hell, thought Lenson, fear and rage gluing his feet to the deck. Just now, just when he was going off watch. "Zero-one-zero, sir. I—"

"Excuse me, Commodore," said Flasher's voice, coming from the darkness of the wing. "I've got the watch now, sir. The surface picture is as follows: Oscar, that was the contact you were called about, is abeam of *Coronado*, starboard-to-starboard passage. They're at a ten-thousand-yard CPA, and with your permission we'll come back to base course now."

Sundstrom ignored him. "Is that right, Dan?"

"Yes, sir."

"Where's the *Ault?*"

"She's still somewhere astern, sir."

"Christ." Sundstrom sounded both angry and afraid. "That stupid bastard . . . well, fortunately there was no harm done. He'll catch up with us. What about other contacts?"

"We have two skunks to the north, passing at over twelve miles. No visuals," Flasher told him.

"Dan?" Sundstrom said again.

"Uh, those were too far out to call you about, sir. I was just going off watch—"

"I understand. Well, I'd like to see you for a moment before you go below; we have some things to do . . . Mister Flasher! Let's stop wasting time. Get back to base course! We're losing ground every minute we spend heading north."

"Aye aye, sir," said Flasher happily, and picked up the phone.

"Let's go over here," said the commodore, his voice dropping. As they leaned over the papers he placed on the ruddy dimness of the chart table, Lenson saw that, contrary to his usual nighttime custom, he was in uniform; faded wash khaki trousers, tight at the waist; khaki shirt, sparkling with eagles at the collars but sweaty and wrinkled. Under the bagged, tired eyes, the heavy chin, gray hairs curled over a triangle of T-shirt. The other officers disappeared about their business, moving to darker areas of the bridge.

"Before you hit the hay, Dan, I have a job for you. You did a fine job on the Sardinia oporder. You seem to have a knack for moving out on things, more than my other officers." He pronounced the last three words with distaste. "So, though this is really the chief of staff's and ops officer's area of responsibility, I'd like you to take charge of it—just in case. I know you're bushed, but can you take this by the horns and get it over the finish line for me?"

"Uh . . . yes sir," Lenson said reluctantly. Writing an oporder could take weeks, but whenever Sundstrom wanted something he wanted it yesterday. He would be up the rest of the night, what little of it remained, and probably well into the next. Inevitably he would have to take shortcuts, make assumptions and guesses. Meanwhile the other officers, those whose job it was, would be sitting on their hands. Or worse, he thought bitterly, asleep. And then Ike would make changes, and be dissatisfied, and want it done over—

But even to think a complaint made him uneasy. Annapolis stamped the habit of obedience deep, far past logic. And didn't the fact that the commodore wanted a draft oporder mean something might really be up? "Sir," he said cautiously, "I'll need some information. Number of supporting units, to write the schedule of fires with—a map—"

"Of course. See the N-2 for those. And the oparea map—here."

Sundstrom slid it from its manila jacket under the scarlet light. Shielded by their bodies, it was hidden from the other men on watch. Lenson took the red folder hesitantly, flipped one corner of it back.

It was a 1:500,000 military map of Cyprus. He stared at the title with fatigue, then disbelief.

"Sir—"

"This is hush-hush, Dan," Sundstrom muttered. "Discuss it only with Byrne, and then only if you have to. I don't want people in this organization getting excited, riding off in all directions before we get the word to go. Thinking the problem through, and being ready for the worst case—being prepositioned, in an offensive aspect, when the need occurs—that's what makes a professional, in my book."

"Aye, sir," he said, refolding the map. He was still sleepy, but now he felt excited, too. Beside him Sundstrom seemed for a moment a commander with foresight. The commodore slid the packet across the chart table to him, and as he did so his eyes dropped. Lenson saw him examining the chart, and then his head jerked up.

"Mister Flasher!"

"Yessir!"

"Come here. Look at this mess." He laid his finger on a brown ring west of Pantelleria. "I gave specific orders that coffee wasn't to be brought on the bridge without a saucer. That's to prevent things like this—and just look!"

Flasher bent to look, his gut crowding Sundstrom away from the table. "Sorry, sir," he said, and reached for a pencil.

"What are you doing, Lieutenant?"

"Erasing it, sir."

Sundstrom stood rigid, his hand trembling on the chart table for a moment. The two officers waited. "Lieutenant Flasher," he said at last, "there will be no more coffee on my flag bridge. None at all!" Then, before either of them could speak, he turned away suddenly, into the darkness.

"Commodore's off the bridge," the messenger sang out.

"Christ, I'm sorry, Red. It's not Mac's fault. I told him to bring it up. I didn't think *he'd* be up here."

"Ah, forget it," said Red. "Excuse me. I got more important things to worry about than that crapola."

He moved to the radarscope and fell into conversation with his assistant. Lenson looked after him for a moment, thinking that this was just the kind of thing that could ruin a career when you were around Isaac I. Sundstrom: the kind of thing that he would pore over for months, and showcase in Flasher's next fitness report as "willful disregard of a plainly stated command policy." He was responsible for the coffee—for the ring on the chart—but Flasher hadn't said a thing, hadn't even left him an opening to accept the blame.

He wondered, and then recalled the oporder. He gathered up the chart and headed below. It would be a long day, this one, after a second sleepless night. He found lukewarm coffee on the deserted mess decks. In his stateroom he rubbed his eyes as he bent over the charts and timetables. Nothing would happen. He was certain of that. Still, he had to do his best.

Bent close to his desk, he worked silently on into the dawn.

8

U.S.S. *Spiegel Grove*

"ON YOUR FEET, SHITHEAD!"

Will Givens opened his eyes to another gray steel day. To the same words, the same tone, and the same voice that had torn his dreams to ribbons every morning since the beginning of the float.

"Roll out of that rack, Oreo. On deck! Day's too far along to let spittoon-faced niggers waste my time. Get your ass into the head."

A hand reached in between the bunk bars and shook him. He sat up, too fast, and the long, queasy, gut-tightening roll that had tormented his sleep all night long lightened him suddenly and his head banged into the framework of Liebo's rack, just above.

He had accepted, though he tried not to use, the omnipresent obscenity of the troop spaces. But now he thought: Cutford shouldn't use that word. Not even between the two of us.

He swung his legs out and dropped naked to the deck, glaring after Cutford's retreating back. "And get that fucken git-tar off your bunk frame," added the corporal, turning in mid-passage through the yawning postreveille stir of elbows and bony knees, hairy men momentarily without rank in their nakedness and their mutual need for a leak. "I like to caught my head on it. Ain't no room in a troop space for something that big."

"All right," Givens muttered. He had resolved during the long, half-nauseated periods of sleeplessness that night to not let Cutford bug him. He would just do what he said, let it slide off him and not bother him anymore. But it was already an effort, ninety seconds after his first moment of full consciousness. He trudged toward the head, made angrier by his inability to ignore the corporal's petty tyrannies.

The morning went on, though, and gradually his mood ebbed back into resignation as shipboard routine, the normal day for the three hundred embarked marines of the old landing ship's reinforced company, wore on in the grooves that three months in the Med had already cut deep. His utilities were a little dirtier, that was all; the ship's laundry was hopelessly behind; but for that it could have been yesterday, or the day before, or tomorrow. After finishing in the head he joined the line of hungry, morning-bleary men, all of them cursing the wait, and held his tray for the surly cooks to dish out what was left over after the sailors had eaten. He balanced his food against the slanting table and held a cup of tepid coffee in one hand so that an unforeseen roll wouldn't spill it; spooned down mushy grits and overcooked eggs, the stale hard sausage, and shoved the empty tray at another scowling peon in the scullery.

It was six-thirty.

Back in the compartment he lashed the guitar up into his bunk, changed into his one clean blouse for morning inspection, and dragged his way in line up four ladders to the helo deck. The marines clung to the handrail as the ship rolled, grabbing and cursing and stumbling against one another. The sky was gray, gray as the ship, and the sea a muted gray-blue, running strong. They formed up, muttering and blinking at the sky. Hernandez lurched past him, looking ill. "Another beautiful Marine Corps morning," he grunted to Givens.

"No shit."

The ship rolled heavily, and their ranks swayed drunk-

enly to it. The men half-listened to the top sergeant as he
read the plan of the day. They were watching the horizon
ahead for a squall, darkly expecting whoever ran the ship
to steer for one if it offered just to get them all wet. As if
sensing their mood, the officers kept their remarks short.
Givens watched Cutford's neck darken as they saluted and
strolled away, and felt the same way. *They* were going
back to the wardroom, to drink hot coffee and shoot the
shit with the Navy officers while the Top strolled through
the platoons, doling out shit details. Fourth platoon drew
a new watch bill, and he saw Cutford glancing around for
him. He got a noon-to-sixteen roving patrol, and was
pleased; he'd expected worse, maybe the graveyard shift.
Silkworth moved past, inspecting; a missing button here,
a scummy boot, unbloused trousers there. They stood at
attention in the reeling ranks, shivering as a sudden chill
breeze swept the open deck. By Christ, the men muttered
around him, they *were* going to get rained on; and then the
Top barked an order from up front and they broke, strag-
gling again into queues for the ladders down.

It was zero-seven-thirty.

He and Washman and Liebo went down together to the
tank deck, and waited as the armorer handed them out
their metal. Baseplate, the new issue, only twenty-eight
pounds heavy. Sight, in its black plastic case.

And the tube, his baby. Cradling its weight in his arms,
he inched his way back up the ladder to the troop space
and set up with the rest of the squad around their table.
Liebo and Hernandez laid out the cards for spades, and
Givens and Harner and Washman sat down with the
cleaning gear. This, Givens thought, is the high point of
the day. The thought dispirited him all over again.

As he got into it, though, his depression retreated. The
marines cleaned their weapons every day at sea. Silkworth
said it kept the salt air out of them, and though they
suspected that was bullshit, there was always something
nice about getting your hands on the gear. He leaned the
four-foot barrel securely in a corner of the compartment

and unpacked the gear box. Bore punch, reamer, swabs, a new pack of steel wool, the familiar green can of Oil, Preservative, Small Arms. The compartment quieted down as the men curled in bunks and chairs and began to disassemble rifles, machine guns, and sidearms. Liebo dealt the cards.

First of all, Givens thought, a nice coat of oil on the outside. He steel-wooled the twenty-four-hour-old preservative off the deep screw-threads down to bare steel. The can pinged as he tipped glistening yellow oil onto a rag and laid it on. He turned the mortar tube end over and squinted into the three-inch-wide barrel. Clean and gleaming. He scrubbed it out, feeling the slickness with physical pleasure against his fingertips, the slight roughness where the fins of the ten-pound shells had scraped going out in Sicily and Spain and LeJeune, and before that from dozens of deployments by marines long moved on, sergeants or mustang second looeys, or gone from the Corps. He liked to imagine the men who had done this before him, ministered to this same hunk of unfeeling metal, masculine in its length and power, feminine in its hollowness and texture. Had they cleaned this same barrel in Nam; it was old enough; in Cambodia; in Lebanon? Where were they now? Medal of Honor winners, shitbirds, psychos, congressmen, used-car salesmen . . . who knew the names and histories of the men who had scraped oil and powder soot from this same tube before him?

"Spades," said Hernandez. Liebo reached behind him and turned on his cassette, and the BeeGees hit the thick air of the compartment.

Reversing the barrel again, Givens set the bore punch up with a cloth swab and reamed it through. Beside him Washman hummed tonelessly over the baseplate. The patch came out clean. He poured on more oil and ran it through again and then set it aside. He put the allen wrench on the firing pin and broke it free, cleaned it, oiled it, screwed it carefully back and tightened it.

That was it. He was done for the morning. He looked at his watch. It was zero-eight-thirty.

"Now what?" said Washman, picking at a pimple on his chin. "Should we take it back, Will?"

"Naw. We can look busy better with it here. If we take it back Cutford'll just give us something else to do." Givens looked enviously at the two privates, deep in their cards, and then crossed to his bunk and stood beside it, looking at his guitar.

It lay lashed to the underside of Liebo's rack with shoestring, tempting him silently. His fingers itched for the smoothness of the pearl inlay, the thin hard steelness of the strings. He had taken it up to the fantail the evening before, and strummed it gently in the sun's lingering. There had been other men there, talking and smoking. But he didn't have to obey them, talk to them, be someone for them. Just for a moment, he could be the way he always felt, deep inside. Alone. Apart. Different.

He could be himself.

Willard Givens had picked up his first guitar at fourteen. The men at the lumberyard had handed him a cranky old flat-top his first day there, and waited. Just waited, their faces like flat stones, white and black, leaving the questioning and the discovery to the boy.

His mouth shaped an unconscious smile, remembering the country music. "Lucille." "Blue Suede Shoes." Fun, sometimes rowdy songs, the men had played them at breaks from the whining saw, sitting together on the fresh-cut planks, still sticky so that your overalls glued themselves to the smooth white pine. One would play a mouth organ, folding it into a gray-stubbled jaw like a chaw of tobacco. They would pass around a bottle sometimes, sometimes a wide-mouthed jar. He was too young for it, and the others, too, were sparing; if you got careless the big unshielded Cramer would pull off a thumb like a man pulling a splinter from a dog's paw.

And then sometimes an older man had taken it and picked mountain tunes, music that Will had known even then he would never hear again, unless he remembered it; and he had listened with his mouth open, his resiny fingers itching for that old handmade guitar, and known that it would never be like this again.

> *Once I had a girl on Rocky Top*
> *Half bear, the other half cat*
> *Wild as a mink and sweet as soda pop*
> *I still dream about that.*

He longed now to pick up the Gianelli and coax out those first few notes of "Steal Away." But no. That would be too much if the Top, or worse, one of the officers, decided to come through the compartment. Cards you could hide, but not a guitar. Instead he flipped back his mattress, then settled himself at the table, opening the book to where pencil and paper had been stuck in it. Hernandez dealt, and Liebo checked his hand, grabbing absentmindedly for the discard pile as it began to slide with a long heave of the ship. He glanced at Givens' lowered eyes.

"What you reading there, man?"

"Fuck book," said Hernandez.

"No. Just a schoolbook."

"That your engineering, Will?" Washman asked him.

"Yeah." He turned the book briefly to show Washout a page of graphs.

"You really understand that stuff? What kind of engineering is it?"

Washout's open-mouthed admiration made him feel good. "Naw," he said modestly. "I don't get half of what it says. This here is all about engines, how the heat gives you the power. Pretty heavy stuff. But someday I'll know how they work."

"Sure he will," said Hernandez. "Someday I'm going to be President, too."

"Maybe you could," said Will. "Why not?"

"Come on. I'm Chicano, man. You're no college-boy type yourself."

"I could go. They got that education bill for us."

Both Liebo and Hernandez lowered their cards at that one. "What the hell you talking about, man?" said Liebo. "You bein' real, Givens? It takes a shit-pot full of bucks to go to college. That little GI bill check won't cover diddley-squat."

"No, but I could save some."

"Save some from *what?*"

"Paychecks, Dippy. Remember, the money they give you every couple of weeks? The stuff you spend on liquor and women?"

"I know what a paycheck is," said Liebo. "An' I recall I wasn't the only one scarfing up a little nookie at Lily's the other day. But forget that. A private's pay don't hardly keep you in snacks and beer. If you got a car, too, that cleans your paycheck, man. You can't save any out of that."

"Save a couple bucks a month, that could add up. Over a four-year hitch you could come out with enough for the first year," said Will. They laughed. "Okay," he said, angry, looking down at the book again. "You asked me."

"Two," said Hernandez, returning to the cards, and Liebo dealt. Harner stared silently at the play. Washman cast about the compartment for awhile, glancing at Givens but not interrupting his pencil-chewing, and finally pulled himself up into his bunk. Their corner settled into silence for a time, varied by the creak of steel and the clatter of small objects across the deck as the ship began a series of heavy rolls, an old whore in the familiar embrace of the sea. The steam heaters clanked, and the hot air of the closed compartment banked itself against their braced bodies.

"Oreo!"

Oh, shit, thought Givens, and got the book under his mattress just as Cutford banged open the hatch. He filled the oblong opening perfectly, broad and high as the hatchway, his eyes darting suspiciously about the space.

"What you want, Cutford?"

"Goin' on a little expedition," said the corporal. Behind him two other black marines giggled and punched each other. "Know you gettin' bored back here with your swan pals, Oreo. We don't want you to forget who you are, you know. Come on, boy. Goin' to vary our diet a little."

"I'm cleanin' the mortar, Corporal."

"Fuck that," said Cutford, closing in on the four of them. He leaned forward over the table, which had miraculously bared itself of pasteboard; Hernandez and Liebo looked up at him innocent-faced, holding cleaning gear and pieces of their weapons. "Let's go, Givens. Warning you, man . . . not associatin' with your brothers, that might get you in a host of troubles."

Givens caught the shutter-click of Washman's scared glance, the slower, more judgmental regard of Harner, saw the careful way Liebo and Hernandez kept their eyes fixed on their hands. They wanted nothing to do with the corporal. Neither did he. But the irrevocable likeness of their skin meant that he had to respond somehow. He felt his thighs tighten against the underside of the table as the ship began another sickening coast. He abruptly loathed it all, the ship, the closed steel honeycomb of drones that was the world of marines afloat; but most of all, he hated Cutford. Hated his race-warped mind, hated anyone who saw them, him and the corporal, as the same, simply because of their tobacco-dark comradeship.

He was not like Cutford. He did not want to be like Cutford.

And yet, the corporal waited. . . .

"Okay, man," he said, lapsing into the accent the corporal had addressed him in. "Comin'. Washout, see the mortar gets checked back in."

"Sure, Will."

The two men with Cutford looked him over insolently as he followed the broad back out of the compartment. He

knew them: troublemakers from the second platoon, former noncoms. They had both been reduced in rate, for
what he did not know. Sleight, a bucktoothed twenty-
seven-year-old, was from New Orleans. Randy Jenkins, a
street-smart, heavy-lidded player from Harlem, was not
much older than he was. Neither welcomed him or offered
to dap. "Les' move, Oreo," said Cutford, turning, and the
corporal's heavy hand half-led, half-shoved him toward
the ladder down.

"Where we goin', man?"

"Like I said, goin' to improve our diet. Or do you like
that whitey shit they dish out in the mess lines?"

"It's better than I got back home."

"Shut up, Oreo. Get movin'."

The sounds of the troop compartment, the omnipresent
whine of the blowers died away as they wound down
ladder after ladder into the untenanted guts of the old
ship. The air was cooler, the bulkheads dirtier, the overhead lights flickering or burned out. They were below the
berthing areas, in the deep spaces where only the crew was
supposed to go. He glanced up from the bottom of the
ladder; the three faces stared down at him, closed, dark,
and hostile. "Where to now?" he asked the corporal.

"That passageway."

"We not supposed to be down here, man—"

"Shut up, Oreo. They got rovin' patrols. Might hear us.
Sleight, you got that key?"

"Here, man."

"Let's have her." Cutford matched the key to a stenciled number on a bulkhead, then led the way down a
darkened passageway. Their steps echoed against ex-
panded-metal cages, padlocked hatchways. He stopped at
the fourth door and checked the number again, then
looked back at them. "Randy . . . the ladder."

"Right. I got it."

"What's in there?" asked Givens, looking back to where
Jenkins lingered at the foot of the ladder, staring upward.

"Reefer space . . . yeah, it fits." The padlock clicked and

Cutford swung the hatch open a foot or two. Givens backed away as fog oozed out from the crack, bringing a chill breath of refrigeration. "Steaks," said the corporal, his eyes fixed on the blackness inside the half-opened door. "Go on, Oreo. Find us some steaks."

"Me?"

"You, boy. Motivate your black ass. Ought to be a light in there someplace."

"Cutford, I don't want any—"

Cutford pushed him in. He stumbled on the coaming, caught himself on a pipe, then jerked his hand away; it was scalding cold. Utter darkness surrounded him. The door stayed open, though, and he could see a little in the light from the passage. A square mass of boxes walled off one side of the compartment, hoared with translucent frost. "I can't see a thing," he whispered back, and the door yielded a little more light.

Steaks, steaks . . . he traced the words on the frost-webbed cardboard. PORK LOINS. FORMED POTATO FRIES. VEAL PATTIES. Sweat clammied under his thin skivvy shirt, the still air bit at his fingers as he brushed away icy webs.

PRECUT STEAKS. His fingernails scrabbled at the box. It was in solid, bound under layers of frozen meat. Got to unstack all these, he thought. And fast. It wouldn't take long to freeze in here, like a side of this meat. Help me, Jesus. He clawed the top layer down and stacked them quickly at the other side, knocking the wooden battens aside. Down here the roll of the ship was less, but from time to time it caught him off guard and he stumbled across the deck, weighted down with a heavy box. STEAKS. He wrenched it free. Did they want the whole thing, or just a couple for each man? He staggered toward the door.

"Cutford?"

"What, Oreo?" The corporal's whisper snapped through the chill air.

"I found some. How many you want?"

"Eight or ten. Can't take too many at a time or they'll

start missing 'em and change the lock. Hand 'em out, Oreo."

"Got a knife, man?"

"Here." A stainless Corps-issue pocketknife clattered to the deck. Givens scooped it up and sliced cardboard, narrowly missing his numb fingers, and pried at the mass of solidified flesh inside. The slabs came up unwillingly, peeling off from the block, and he thrust them out through the crack. "That enough?"

"Couple more . . . shit!"

"What is it?"

"Some asshole coming down the ladder. Keep quiet, man."

The hatch closed. He stood petrified in the dark, staring at where the door had been, a steak in one hand, the knife held blade outward in the other.

The low click of a padlock came through the steel from outside, followed by the sound of retreating boots; and then there was nothing but the slow chuckle of icy water through the piped walls, and the swift hiss of his breath. "Oh, man," he whispered. "Oh, *shit.*" Unconsciously his fingers bent the knife closed and slipped it into his pocket. He lowered the box and felt the steak back into it, folded the top closed, and sat down on it, still staring in the same direction; then got up again, shivering, and felt around the door for a switch. His searching fingers found nothing but cold metal. "Oh, shit, Cutford," he muttered again, and sat down on the box. With the door closed it seemed fifty degrees colder. He rubbed gooseflesh on his bare arms, and a shiver gripped him from feet to neck. His teeth began to chatter. If it had been a patrol . . . where would the three marines hide? What if a guard found them— what would they do? Jive him? Run? Or break his head and take off, trusting to the anonymity of green utilities and black faces?

Had there really been anyone on the ladder at all?

He hugged himself, shivering, and bent his ear to the freezing metal. Distant vibration of engines, the straining creak of a ship in a seaway . . . but no voices, no footsteps.

"Cutford," he whispered, "You wouldn't leave me here, would you?"

The cold ebbed into him, slowly, and the silence gave him back no answer at all.

"Rub his face," came the hurried whisper. "Jesus! The fucker feels cold as ice."

"Slap his face."

"Look at his fingers, man."

He got his eyes open in time to take a heavy blow to his cheek. The three faces above him sighed and looked at one another. "You there, man?" asked one of them.

"Yeah."

"Can you stand up? We can't stay here too long. That fucken patrol's gonna be comin' back."

"Yeah. I think." He climbed dizzily, four hands helping him. Cutford was standing off, looking up the ladderwell. He signaled impatiently to them to hurry. Givens could hardly feel his legs, and everything looked blanched and distant, as if he were seeing it from beneath a sheet of ice. "How long was I in there?" he whispered.

"Couple minutes."

"Near half an hour."

"I thought you—"

"Let's go," hissed the corporal. The two privates supported him toward the ladder. His legs sagged, but feeling was coming back. At the third ladder he shook off Jenkins and Sleight. Cutford, his back pockets bulging, climbed silently in front. They left the ladder before they got to troop level and went into a fan room. Cutford closed the door.

"Want a steak?"

"What?"

"I got mess kits, heat tabs, forks. You want a couple, Oreo? That's what we went down there for."

He imagined sizzling beef, and then realized what the

corporal had said. "You bastard, Cutford, I never wanted any steak. I almost froze to death!"

"We got you out. Cool it. These bulkheads real thin."

"I was in there half an hour! My hands are frozen!"

"You knew we'd be back," said the corporal. Squatting, pulling a pack from behind a pump cage, he began setting up a combat stove. "Didn't you, Givens? You trusted your brothers. Or did you think we were going to leave you down there in the reefer for the Man to find—like one of them ice creams on a stick, chocolate on the outside an' vanilla on the in?"

He smiled up at Givens, and the others began to chuckle. A lighter clicked, and the fan room filled with the smell of roasting meat. Will Givens hesitated, feeling still the weakness in his legs, and then he squatted, too.

With them, yet not looking at them, waiting for the steak, he squatted silently and hated them all.

Yet my face, he could not stop himself from thinking, seeing the four of them as if from outside, *my face is the same as theirs.*

9
U.S.S. *Guam*

COMMODORE ISAAC ICARUS SUNDSTROM, U.S. Navy, leaned back in his leather chair and took off his reading glasses. He rubbed his hand slowly over his eyes, then smoothed back graying hair. At least it's still thick, he thought abstractedly. You're not over the hill yet in that department.

He caught sight of his reflection in the bridge window. It was haggard. Defeated. It might be, the man seated before it thought, the face of an aging shoe clerk, a failed banker. . . .

He sat up instantly, throwing back his shoulders, enraged at himself. *What the hell are you mooning about? You're in command here!* he told himself. He had to maintain a positive attitude. That was key. That was the prime responsibility of a flag officer. He had to show every man, every day, that Task Force 61 was led by a Hard Charger, a True Professional, someone who would accept nothing less than perfection.

But after twenty-three years of charging hard, of fighting complacency and laziness and so many enemies . . . a man could be forgiven for getting tired sometimes.

His eyes strayed again to his reflection, then moved to a side view, his enigmatic image in the wing window. He straightened again in the chair and jutted his chin. Should lose some of this weight . . . but he looked all right, he was fit. Tired? Goddammit, and no wonder, he thought angrily. I'm doing the job of every man in this so-called staff. Not one of them could cut the mustard. Not one of them had his job in his hip pocket, the way he had when he was a junior officer in the Pacific.

The ship rolled, and he looked out at the sea again. Goddamn, he thought. I've got to stop agonizing over this. I'll give myself an ulcer.

But it was too important to leave to incompetents. Too important to the country, and to his career.

A day and a half out of Italy, two hundred miles from the nearest land, the Mediterranean was a dull and lonely blue under a late-morning overcast. A little after dawn, as he had ordered, the formation had closed in on *Guam,* except for *Bowen,* the frigate. She was relatively new, a capable ship, though short on guns compared to the older classes. Sundstrom wanted her well in the van, to give them warning of anything unexpected. She was a tiny dot now, far ahead, and he reached for his binoculars to check on her. Her silhouette caught at his throat. God, how he wished he was back in cans, the real Navy, and not stuck in amphibs like some second-rater . . . the other units were close in now, four to eight miles from the sector center. He could see them all plainly from where he sat. From his elevated chair he could look down, too, at the routine activity of a helicopter carrier's deck at sea.

It was maddeningly desultory. Two helos were on deck, with mechanics pottering around the landing gear. A few men were testing firehoses on one of the elevators, the canvas tubes firm and round under pressure. A platoon or two of marines—*Guam* carried eight hundred—were doing calisthenics aft. Their faint cadenced shout floated in from the open air. Aside from that, there seemed to be nothing much going on.

Ike Sundstrom did not like it when nothing was happening. He adjusted his glasses, bent his head again to the papers he was examining, and then lifted it. He stared around the bridge. Where the—where the hell was the watch officer? He twisted in his chair.

"Commander Byrne!"

"Sir," said the intelligence officer, coming up behind him.

"Where the hell were you hiding? Goddammit, I want an alert watch up here! I want you front and center with your eyes on the ball. Do you understand?"

"Yes sir," said Byrne. "I was looking at the vertical plot. *Bowen* is reporting a small contact, and it seems to be closing."

"How far out is it?"

"Still a long way, sir. I don't think we have it on our scope yet."

"I asked how far it was! They must have reported its range! I don't want to hear excuses, Mr. Byrne. I want performance! The flag bridge is no place to putter around *thinking.*"

Byrne had lowered his head under the shout. When the commodore paused, breathing hard, they looked at each other for a moment. Sundstrom could not see the man's eyes. Those ridiculous sunglasses—they masked his every expression. And where did he get that tan? He looked like he was fresh off the beach at Malibu. The intel officer's appearance, his attitude, his very existence irritated the commodore. It was all affectation, the upper-crust mannerisms, the Harvard accent. His father was the manager of a golf course. Sundstrom had checked.

"Get me the CSO," he said, turning away.

"Yes sir," Byrne said again, in that same smooth, supercilious tone. A moment later the commodore heard him call the messenger over.

"Mr. Byrne!"

"Sir."

"When I give you an order personally, I expect you to carry it out personally. *Do you understand me?*"

Byrne did not answer. He stood there.

"God damn you! Are you ignoring me?" Sundstrom

shouted. "I'm warning you—I demand respect from you, Byrne, and I'll get it! One way or another!"

"Aye aye, sir," said Byrne tightly. He turned from the enlisted man, who was staring at the two officers, and picked up the phone himself.

When Hogan came up, Sundstrom was deep in his paperwork again, breathing raggedly. The chief staff officer waited just behind his chair. At last the commodore noticed him, and swung around. "Good morning, sir," said Hogan.

"Where have you been all morning, Al? I don't think I've seen you on the bridge once since we got underway."

"Administrative matters, sir."

"Take that pipe out of your mouth when you talk to me. Administrative matters. Do any of those include training? I sure as hell don't see much of it going on. Have you put out a training schedule for this transit?"

"No sir, we got underway too quickly—"

"You've had almost two days since. I know for a fact that's enough time to make up a simple schedule. Goddammit, Al"—Sundstrom lowered his voice, with an effort—"We don't have as much steaming time deployed as we used to. This fuel situation is shooting our readiness to hell. If there's one thing I've learned in four months on this job, it's that you've got to keep these bastards on their toes. If we don't they'll forget everything, they'll go to pot. That's the nature of the beast. Do you understand me?"

"Yes sir, Commodore."

"I want my ships ready before the fact, not after the fact. I want this task group to be pre-positions in an offensive aspect when the need occurs, not milling around like a bunch of amateurs. That's the way the big boys play it. I report direct to Admiral Roberts, to COMSIXTH-FLEET, and I want him to know he's got a top-notch force out here, one he can depend on!"

"Yes, sir," said Hogan.

"Now. I want a training schedule for the next three days, and some thoughts on what to do if we stay at sea longer than that. I want signal drills, combat drills, and comm drills. I want each ship to go to general quarters for training as soon as possible. How long will it take you to get that on the street?"

"This afternoon, sir."

"Mr. Byrne! When will *Ault* catch up with the rest of us?"

"According to her last position report, late tonight, sir."

"Not good enough. He's just poking along. I want him here sooner than that. I want to pull a surprise battle problem tomorrow, the whole task force at once, get the bridge teams up to snuff on maneuvering, evasive action, antiair. And engineering, too, don't forget them; I want them practicing casualty control down in the holes. And I want it as soon as possible! Understand me?"

The CSO was writing in a small notebook. "Yes sir. You realize this will cut into maintenance time. Some of the ships were planning to pull pumps, and—"

"I know that, Al." Sundstrom cut him off. "I want normal maintenance to go on, of course. That goes without saying. Put that in the schedule, too. Now take that by the horns and march off with it. I want to see a draft message by thirteen-hundred."

Hogan's mouth twitched, but he finished writing and put the notebook away. "I'll get right on it, sir."

"Good."

"Was there anything else, sir?"

Sundstrom shook his head, and turned back to his papers. When he glanced up again the chief of staff was still there. He snatched his glasses off. "Well?"

"Sir, some of the men have been asking me whether we're going back to the Sicily-Italy area. They made reservations for hotels there, paid in advance; their wives are waiting. They need to know—"

The commodore forced himself to speak calmly. His stomach was tightening up. "I can't help that," he said, putting on his glasses again. "As far as I know we won't be back, but I don't want people getting the wrong idea and spreading rumors. Let's leave things as they are for now."

"Yes sir," said Hogan.

When he was gone Sundstrom studied his papers again, frowning and fighting the burning in his stomach. It was, he thought, typical of the kind of people the Fleet got these days. Everyone worrying about himself instead of the mission. It was the kind of mindset he had always hated. A family had no place in a life at sea. They were best left ashore, as he left his. On shore assignments it was better to be married; you looked more stable that way and the social things went more smoothly. But the sea was a man's world, a world of work and discipline, and there was no time to worry about anything else. Not if you wanted to do a good job. Not if you were a professional.

Musing, he gazed out at his ships. Gray, distant even in close formation, they pitched ponderously to the swell from the east. He glanced at the wind indicator. Ten knots. Not much of a breeze to be kicking up that sea. Could be bad weather ahead. Christ, that was all he needed.

He let the papers drop to his lap and leaned back, closing his eyes against the steady cloudlight.

COMSIXTHFLEET had been no help when he had called on the high-frequency net. He remembered the conversation with anxiety. Maybe he shouldn't have called at all, just waited for orders. Roberts had sounded annoyed. Cut your liberty period short? You'll have to use your own judgment about that, he had said. And when Sundstrom began to explain his reasons, about the warning order and the activity to the east, the admiral had cut him off before he'd begun. Granted, HF was not a secure means of communication. Anyone could have been listening. But still, to cut him short like that . . .

Sundstrom sat and worried, his eyes closed tight. Around him the bridge was deathly quiet. There was no talk, no idle chatter when the commodore was on the bridge.

The situation, he thought tightly, is becoming complex.

The turnover briefing at Rota had been a joke. The offgoing MARG commander was supposed to brief his relief thoroughly on the international situation. But Phibron Eight had been held over a month and Hacker had been hot to sail, so it had turned out a hurried conversation of an hour or two. Sundstrom had gained from it only a confused impression of impending trouble. (Which was, after all, chronically the situation in the eastern Med.) He'd had to piece his picture together from the daily secret sitreps and from Byrne's briefings . . . and he admitted he tended to cut those short; it was just too irritating to sit and listen to the man.

The warning order had alerted the MARG for Cyprus. Divided between Greek and Turk years before, both sides complained that the other was persecuting the minorities in their half of the island. It was possible, Sixthfleet intelligence thought, that rioting or even war could begin again.

But Cyprus was only one of the hot spots east of twenty degrees longitude. And possibly not the most dangerous. Libya, the bad boy of the Gulf of Sidra, was quiescent for the moment, digesting a coup. But it could become belligerent again at any time. Iran and Iraq were at war, but that seemed only to inflame their hostility to the U.S. Iran had stepped up its state-sponsored terrorism; two months before, in an action that had made world headlines, a team had killed an American general in Germany, had blown apart his armored Mercedes with an antitank mine planted in the roadway between his home and office. The Turks had caught the perpetrators between planes back to Teheran, and at the moment, Sundstrom hoped, they were hanging by their testicles in some Ankara dungeon.

Onward around the flaming littoral . . . Lebanon was tearing itself apart, faction battling faction in a labyrinthine bloodbath that Sundstrom, no matter how closely he read the reports, could never keep straight. Israel was on the alert after a series of guerrilla raids along the Jordanian border, suspected carried out by an especially rabid splinter of the PLO. No one seemed to know where they were based or what their goal, beyond killing people. Syria, the only country in the region officially allied with the USSR, was in another face-off with Israel along the Golan Heights. Syria, too, was involved in terrorism, and he had read somewhere about training camps there.

He could not make sense of it all; he had no idea which of a dozen crises was closest to blowing off the lid. Maybe the diplomats did, the politicians. Then again, maybe State was as lost as he was. Now, that was a depressing thought.

What would be best, he thought viciously, would be to let them all kill each other, and deal with whoever was left. But that was unrealistic. The Soviets would step into any power vacuum. If they could expel America from the Eastern Med, gain control of the oil from Arabia and the Gulf, oil that fueled Western Europe and Japan—Sundstrom shook his head. The prospect was too awful to contemplate for any length of time.

Anyway, he thought, that's not my problem. Not at the moment. At the moment he had to worry about the Americans and British in Cyprus. If fighting began they would have to be extracted, and immediately.

At any rate, he reflected wearily, he had made his decision. He had gotten the MARG underway. It had not been easy. No one was ready; they were all on stand-down and the captains complained, but it was safer. He knew the men wanted liberty, but that was secondary if there was something brewing. And the message had come in, in fact, only ten hours after *Guam* weighed anchor. Prepare to get underway, prepare for extended operations east of the toe of Italy. So he had not made a mistake after all.

Except of course—he rubbed his mouth—for that business with *Ault.* He half-suspected her captain had kissed that shoal on purpose, to make him, Sundstrom, look like a fool for ordering him out of port in the dark. Well, he wasn't going to fall for that. Of course you were supposed to report any time a ship touched ground, be it ever so lightly. But he saw no point in bothering Roberts with trivia if the destroyer was undamaged.

He resolved not to use the high-freq net again. The Admiral obviously didn't like subordinate commanders telling him what to do. He was worrying over this again, about the impression he had made, when someone cleared his throat beside the chair. He sat up, blinked, and shuffled the papers. "Yes. What is it now?"

It was Byrne, again. "Sir, *Bowen* has that contact in sight. Trawler-type, quite small."

"Yes? So?"

"Lots of antennas." Byrne pulled a book from under his arm. "We have a tentative identification. It's a Soviet flag."

"Oh, no. An AGI? An intelligence ship?"

"They think so, sir."

"And she's closing us?"

"Aimed right at the formation, sir."

Sundstrom stared out at the sea. After a moment Byrne closed the book and went away.

The AGI was small, all right, not much bigger than one of the landing craft. It was tiny, rusty, and wallowed like a toy boat in a tub with twins. But Byrne had been right. Its low pilothouse, aft of the open fishing deck, was thick with dish antennas and radio aerials. Sundstrom watched it through his glasses, cursing aloud as it closed slowly from ahead, made a wide turn, and settled comfortably into position six miles ahead of the main body, halfway between *Guam* and the lead frigate.

It was a tattletale. The Soviet Navy used them often, where a warship would be too conspicuous. They plodded along like pilot fish attached to a shark, keeping American formations in sight, reporting back position, electronic intelligence, and anything they could gather about maneuvering or tactics. The sailors called them "Snoopies."

And there was not a goddamn thing that he, Ike Sundstrom, could do about it. If the formation turned, the

tattletale would turn with it. If they tried to break away
at night, it had radar, too. And you couldn't harass it in
any way, send your ships in close or buzz it with a helo;
that was forbidden by the rules the two countries had
agreed on, to prevent collisions and their political consequences.

Damn the politics, Sundstrom said, but to himself. It's
the goddamned Russians behind it all anyway. We should
have nuked them back to bows and arrows when we could
get away with it.

At last the sight of it, steaming fat and happy along in
their midst, got to him. He swung heavily down from the
chair. "Mister Byrne!"

"Sir."

"Keep a sharp eye out. For a change. And find Lenson,
have him report to me on the double."

"Aye aye, Commodore."

He rang the steward for lunch in his cabin, then went into
the head. When he came out he found Lenson at parade
rest, stifling a yawn in the middle of the stateroom. Sundstrom was glad to see him. He was the one officer on his
staff who did not talk back, crack stupid jokes, or take
shortcuts. The mustache was silly, but that was his youth.
He was sober and industrious and deferential. Annapolis,
yes, but he had seen some less-than-stellar products of that
institution, too. He sat down at his desk and smiled.
"Hello, Dan."

"Good afternoon, Commodore."

"You look pretty run down. You ought to get some
sleep sometime."

"Yes sir," said Lenson expressionlessly. "Here's what I
have so far on that oporder, sir. I've been on it since I got
off watch, but there's a lot more to be done."

"I know, but good planning always pays off. Are these
the charts?"

"That's right."

"You haven't discussed this with the others?"

"Uh . . . I asked a couple of questions, sir. But that's all."

"Good." Sundstrom began to read the operation order. It was still new to him, this amphibious business. You did not land troops from destroyers. He rubbed his forehead, then pointed at the chart at random. "This dotted line. What's this?"

Lenson leaned over to see. Sundstrom liked this. The man did not answer off the top of his head; he thought first. After a moment he said, "That's the separation line between Red and Blue beaches, sir."

"Why is it there?"

"When the first and second waves go in, the boats tend to bunch up. That keeps them separated so they hit their assigned points together."

"I know that, Dan. Don't lecture me on the obvious! I mean, why is it *here.*"

"Because there's a straight line of bearing on this point of land, sir. We could use a radar beacon, but those boat radars aren't real dependable. This way the coxs'ns can steer by it without getting mixed-up."

"Good, good . . . now, when does the, uh, first wave hit?"

"H-hour's scheduled right at dawn, sir."

"Are you sure this time is right? Did you check it with the navigator?"

"No, sir, I calculated it out of the *Nautical Almanac.*"

"I'm sure you're right, but let's double-check it just the same."

"Aye, sir."

"And doing it right at dawn . . . we've done that in practice, too. Should we keep on doing it at dawn?"

"It's the standard time to hit a beach, sir."

"I know that, Dan, but maybe we should do it earlier. They'd be expecting us at dawn, wouldn't they?"

"If there was a dug-in defending force there, and they knew we were coming in, they might. But it wouldn't do them much good. The reason for hitting at dawn is to make it hard to aim, plus they're less alert then. I wouldn't try going in earlier, sir; it would be mass confusion if we got forty boats and LVTs out there milling around in the dark."

"Well, okay, I guess that makes sense. How about the helos? The gunfire support? I don't see anything in here about that."

"I'm going to work that next, Commodore."

Sundstrom glanced up. The j.g.'s face was intent, drawn, yet somehow detached. He looked tired. But when you were young, the commodore thought, you could take days of this. He felt a sudden lift of relief. The other officers were worthless, but with one or two like Lenson he might still pull off a successful landing, if it came to that.

"Well, let's get on that, then. We don't know when we might need to go. The upper echelons could pass us the ball anytime. When they do, I want to be ready to take it to the mat for a touchdown."

"Yes sir."

He leaned back, pushing the charts away, and watched Lenson straighten warily. Too bad, he thought, he was just a j.g. It got so goddamn lonely without anyone to talk to of his rank. There was Colonel Haynes, the chaplain, the doctor aboard, he could talk with them, but that was all. And after the first month they never came up to the bridge unless he called them. So strange that he, in charge of all these ships and men, spent most of his time alone. But that, too, was part of command.

The steward knocked and came in, steadying a covered lunch against the motion of the ship. Sundstrom debated for a moment asking Lenson to stay, but decided against it. Get the operation order ready, that was first priority. He stood up. Lenson finished rolling the charts. "That'll be all," Sundstrom said. "Please get the rest of it done as soon as possible for me, Dan."

"Aye aye, sir."

The steward uncovered the tray. Cottage cheese and

tuna salad, iced tea. His usual at sea. He sat down to eat, in a considerably better frame of mind than he had felt on the bridge.

And outside the door, Lenson turned a corner and nodded to Red Flasher. The operations officer fell in beside him.

"How'd it go?"

"Not so bad."

"How many stupid questions?"

"Oh, not too many," said Lenson. "Thanks for helping me, Red. I studied this at amphib school, but you forget a lot."

"Writing oporders isn't your job. It's mine. But it don't matter who gets the credit, as long as the job gets done."

"That's a real mature attitude, Red."

"I'm a real mature guy. Say, I checked on lunch. It sucks. I got a stock of Hersheys down in my stateroom. Let's get back on Appendix H."

"I guess it beats working for a living," said Lenson. "You think we'll really land there?"

"They don't pay lieutenants to think," said Flasher. "I leave that to the four-stripers and up."

Whistling, he headed for the ladder. Lenson paused a moment, looking back toward the commodore's stateroom, and then followed him down.

10
U.S.S. *Ault*

"SO YOU TELL ME," SAID BLOOD, POINT-
ing his beard in turn at each of the others over sloppy joes
and fries and black java circles that became ellipses as the
old destroyer paused at the crest of a sea, "why we scooted
out of Naples like a cat on fire. You don't think it means
anything? Bullcrap, Kelly. There's something going
down. Something big."

Wronowicz wiped his chin free of gravy and readied his
sandwich for another enormous bite. "Maybe," he
grunted.

"Maybe, hell. Tell me if I'm wrong, but—"

"You're wrong," said Chief Sullivan, lighting a cigar.

"Not *that* fast, dammit."

The others chuckled. The chief's mess, walled in by the
bow so that it narrowed both forward and downward, was
smaller but homier than the wardroom, more comfortable
than the crew's lounge. Now, at lunchtime, it smelled of
cigars and coffee and hot greasy food.

"No, I'm joking. Actually, seems to me Unc might be
right," said Sullivan, forking a last french fry. "Darn it,
I was counting on those four days in port. We got running
rust coming off the side scuppers. I don't think even the
exec knew we were getting underway till we got the word,
because he told me to—"

"They don't tell you shit," said Blood, meaning the

officers. "I'll tell you, if ignorance was bliss, all the chiefs on this ship would be one big blister. It's always the same: balls to the wall for some big event, then spend the next two weeks with your thumb up your ass."

Wronowicz grunted. He was not really listening to the words they bandied, though he appreciated the camaraderie. He was far away. He was in a cramped room high above the back streets of Naples. In the greasy air he longed for a subtler scent. He felt suspended, empty, and to fill the void he ate. He was surprised to find only stains on his undershirt remaining of the ground-beef sandwich. He stretched over the table for another.

"Whatever it is, I hope it don't interfere with the chief's initiation. Takes a lot of work to set up a good one."

"When's that, Sully?"

"Tomorrow night."

"The way they run this here peacetime Navy reminds me of the time I went over to Portsmouth Naval Hospital, few years ago," said the radioman senior chief, Chapman, a small man with an anachronistic pencil mustache and glasses; he was the oldest man aboard. "I had this high temperature, this pain in the side."

"Pain where?" said Blood.

"In the side. 'Bowel obstruction,' they called it on the ship. Anyway, they put me in bed, hook me up to this machine. Then the nurse calls the doctor in. He's a lieutenant. He looks at the machine and calls another doctor in. He's a commander. They call two more doctors in; they're both captains."

"What we got for dessert?" Wronowicz asked the messman.

"Cherr' pie, Chief."

"Bring it on."

"So they're all standing there with their mouths open, looking at the machine and then at me, and I'm looking back at them. Then this technician comes in. He looks at them and says, 'Hey, why you using this gear? Can't you see it's busted?' They wheel in another machine and it says my heart's okay." He leaned back and grinned.

"So what did they do?" said Sullivan.

"Ripped out my appendix."

"That's the goddamn most pointless, most asinine story I've ever heard in eighteen years in the Navy," whispered Blood to Wronowicz.

"Most what?"

"Never mind."

All right, said Wronowicz to himself, here goes. I don't feel like it; I feel like crawling into my rack with those two cool bottles of Smirnoff I brought back, but that's why I got to do it, because I don't feel like it. "I heard a good one couple weeks ago," he began heavily, shoving back his empty plate and reaching for the uncut pie. "Cowboy goes into this saloon—"

"Not another cowboy joke."

"—Goes into this saloon," Wronowicz continued, ignoring the interruption, "and there's a sign over the bar. 'Make our horse laugh and win fifty dollars.' So he asks the bartender, is this on the level? Bartender says sure, it's the white horse parked out front, just make it laugh and you win fifty bucks. So he leaves his drink and goes outside, and a couple seconds later this horse laugh comes through the door. Bartender goes outside, and the horse is laughing out loud, stomping its feet, about to roll over. He can't believe it, but he gives the cowboy the fifty."

Eight bells sounded. Several of the men slurped at their coffee and got up, but lingered at the door to listen.

"So a couple months later this same cowboy comes in from another drive, and there's a new sign over the bar. 'Make our horse cry, win a hundred dollars.' He looks at it for a while, then goes outside. Couple seconds later the sound of bawling comes through the door, and the bartender goes out. Big tears are rolling down the horse's cheeks.

" 'Do I win?' asks the cowboy.

" 'You sure do,' says the bartender, kind of teed off, because this is costing him money. He goes in and pays him, and then says, 'Say, generally I wouldn't ask, but you're the same guy made the horse laugh before, ain't you?'

" 'That's right,' says the cowboy.

" 'So tell me, how did you do it? Make him laugh, and then make him cry?'

" 'Easy,' says the cowboy. 'First time, I told him my cock was bigger than his was. The second time, I showed him.' "

Wronowicz leaned back as the other chiefs laughed, then shoved his chair away from the mess table. "Well, I got to get some work done today. That pie was real good, Manny."

"Thanks, Chief."

He dropped from the ladder into the clammy heat, the battering sound of number-one engineroom, with a feeling of relief. All day long he had been thinking of the woman, and he didn't like thinking about women. Oh, he'd done his best to forget. He had gotten through almost a fifth of bourbon before going back aboard at 0200 that morning. Then Callin had woken him an hour later with orders to light off, they were getting underway. . . . The joking in the chief's quarters helped too, but what he needed was work, to plunge himself into it with ferocity and absorption until he was no longer a man but just a pair of evaluating eyes, skilled greasy hands, a brain that thought only in microns and degrees and hundreds of pounds per square inch.

Now he was home. The engines and pumps and compressors slammed at his ears like a dozen jackhammers revising a four-lane highway. He punched the insulation over number-one cruising turbine, feeling it crackle and give under his fist, and made a mental note to get it replaced when they went alongside the tender. He braced himself on a pump casing as the ship rolled, and headed up onto the main deck again to cross to the after engine-room. He slammed the hatch behind him, rattled down slippery treads, and paused, breathing deep of the hurricane roaring down from the blowers. Steurnagel, the first-class machinist's mate, was standing in front of the throttleboard with his eyes soldered to the steam pressure gauge. *"What are we at?"* Wronowicz shouted, glancing at the RPM counter and then at the indicator.

"Just dropped back to eighteen knots, Chief."

"How's vacuum holding?"

"Low for the speed. Say, we got to get this damn stop valve packed again. It's drippin' right down the back of my neck."

"I'll put it on Santa's list. What are the bearings doing?" he said, thinking of the shafts, the screws, and the slight tremor he had felt down here when the *Ault,* saying her hurried farewell to Italy, had slid for a moment across the muddy bottom of the Bay of Naples.

"They're okay."

"The log here says a hundred and thirty degrees on the main port."

"Yeah, but it's steady."

"It was only running hundred, hundred and ten on the way over. Across the pond, I mean."

The throttleman considered. "I guess you're right," he said at last. "But I been watching it. It goes any higher, I'll give you a call."

"Okay. Just checking. Where's your messenger?"

"On rounds."

As if he'd heard, though of course nothing but a shout could penetrate the din of the engines, Blaney appeared at the top of the ladder from the lower level. Wronowicz felt instant anger. He was sure the nineteen-year-old fire-man—this was his first ship—was on something illegal half the time, and plain stupid the rest. Even the other E-2s played jokes on him, sent him to find ten yards of waterline, or grease for the relative bearings. His eyes looked normal today, though. Marijuana was not exactly everywhere, but Kelly knew it was used. Drugs aboard ship . . . what was his goddamn Navy coming to. . . .

And he was black. Wronowicz felt that he was as fair as the next man, but he had his private doubts. You couldn't say so anymore; he knew they were supposed to be equal and all, but it didn't stand to reason you could jerk them out of the jungle and expect them to understand complicated machinery. He snatched the logboard from an unresisting hand. "Stick your goddamn shirttail in," he said.

"What, Chief?" Blaney lifted one ear of his hearing protectors.

"Stick your shirttail in!"

"Sure, Chief."

"Stewie, keep these guys in uniform."

"Chief, it's a hundred and twenty down here. A T-shirt ought to keep the exec satisfied."

Privately Wronowicz didn't care if they walked around baby-naked with a hard-on, as long as the maintenance got done, but that wasn't the way Captain Foster wanted his ship run. "Don't give me any flareback, Steurnagel. Just do it."

"Whatever you say," said the petty officer, reaching a pack of Camels off the superheat gauge.

Wronowicz looked at the board for a minute more, then threw it back to Blaney. "I'll be in the logroom," he said. "Call me if anything changes."

"Okey doke, Chief."

DC Central, the engineering logroom, was empty except for a yeoman. Wronowicz grunted at him and then slid into his chair, reached into his box.

Paperwork. Callin had written him a memo on training . . . he stuffed that back and took out a stack of maintenance forms. Every repair or overhaul the ship did had to be written up and sent back to the States for analysis. Wronowicz was convinced they went straight into a dumpster behind the Navy Annex, but they had to be filled out by the book or you got a nastygram from the computer. He worked on them for a while, setting aside a dozen for incorporation into the tender work package. That would be getting hot soon; that is, if they were really going into port for repairs in three weeks. Why, he wondered, couldn't they set a schedule and keep to it? He had never been in the Med once where some flap hadn't come up, upsetting every plan he made.

He nursed the anger; it was better than regret. Too, the slightly elevated temperature on the port shaft kept nagging at his mind. After an hour of pushing the pencil he gave up, shoved the forms back into the desk, and went back below. Steurnagel was still on the job, head up. Thank Christ, he had a good first-class at least. "Any of your watch not busy?" he asked him.

"Blaney," said the throttleman, jerking his head backward, and Wronowicz turned and saw that the fireman was indeed sitting by the degaussing switchboard, doing nothing, looking as vacant and unconcerned as ever.

"How come *he* don't have anything to do?"

"He's been busy. He's on his break."

"Come on," Wronowicz said to Blaney. "I want to look at that port shaft."

"Sure, Chief," said the fireman happily.

Down in the lower level, near the vibrating stern, the two men stood on the catwalk, looking down at the spinning cylinder of the shaft. At eighteen knots, about half the destroyer's maximum speed, it was rotating a hundred and twenty-five times a minute, a foot-and-a-half-thick rod of alloy that carried power from the port engine and reduction gear back through the hull to the propeller. The port shaft was a quarter as long as the starboard, which led forward to number-one engine-room, and only a single bearing supported it between the hull and the gears.

Wronowicz knelt on the grating to get a better look. The bearing was a yard-wide ring of metal, set into the after watertight bulkhead. It had bolts so you could take it off to get to the bearing surface, a split ring lined to take the wear. He slid down into the bilge, hearing water splash as his boots hit the bottom of the hull, and put his hand gingerly to it. The bearing was warm, but not hot. The shaft whined steadily inches from his ear. A little louder? Maybe, maybe not. He turned his head till his ear was almost touching the spinning metal and squinted along its length. Every second or so a slight vibration wormed its way up it; he could see the spinning steel blur momentarily. So slightly, though, that it might have been there all along. It smelled all right, too. He checked the gauge. Hundred and thirty, just as the first-class had said.

"You been checkin' oil level on this?" he asked Blaney's open mouth, hovering over the edge of the grating.

"What, Chief?"

"I said, YOU BEEN CHECKING OIL ON THIS REGULAR?"

"Sure, Chief," said Blaney, grinning. Wronowicz looked up at him for a moment, spat into the bilges, and then hauled himself up. He walked back toward the throttleboard, noting with satisfaction that one of his third-class was hard at work overhauling a spare reducing valve, that two of the electricians were rewiring a controller. Things were going okay, after all. He decided to get a diver in Crete to check out the prop. A nicked blade could cause a vibration like that. There was a floating drydock there, or maybe they could replace it just with divers and a medium-lift crane; he had seen it done that way once. That would be a hell of a job, though.

Steurnagel was leaning in the same position, exhaling smoke and reading a paperback. He put it away quickly when Wronowicz came up.

"Secure that crap on watch or you'll be shitting shoelaces, Stewie."

"Aye aye, Chief."

"No bells, huh?"

"Haven't had a speed change since eleven-hundred."

The engine order telegraph pinged at that moment, and

their eyes jerked to it. Ahead full. "Shit," said the first-class, spinning the throttle open. "And they just took number-two boiler off the line."

"Oh yeah? Hey, I'm sick of playing mushroom down here. Call the boiler room. Tell 'em to stay with superheat for ten minutes more. I'm going up to the bridge."

"Okay, Chief."

"You're doing a good job. Just watch those bearing temps."

"Right, Chief."

Wronowicz emerged like a large badger from a scuttle by after officer's country. Halfway to the bridge, three decks up and two hundred feet forward of the engineroom, he remembered his head was bare. Muttering to himself, he went back to chief's quarters for his cap, then resumed his climb. Halfway up a dangling cable knocked it off his head. Wronowicz went down the ladder after it again, muttering a little louder. He stopped at the 01 level to catch his breath—it was a long way to drag his weight—and to tuck in his belly. His hands, filthy again, left black prints on his khakis, but he decided the brass would have to live with that. He squared his cap and went up the last few feet hand over hand.

Foster was on the bridge. He knew that even before he saw the captain's length, still in whites, slumped in his chair, his gold-encrusted cap tipped down over his face, unlit corncob drooping from his teeth. Wronowicz looked around the pilothouse, hoping for Lieutenant Jay, but aside from the enlisted men there was only the operations officer and Ensign Callin. Callin was standing dead amidships, gripping his binoculars and staring straight ahead. Wronowicz approached his division officer warily. He always felt uncertain on the bridge. Here the officers were in charge; everything was waxed and polished, clean and squared away, and most intimidating of all, quiet. He took a quick look out the windows, blinking in the cloudy light, but saw no other ships. Steaming alone, then. Good. But how long would it last?

"Mr. Callin?"

"Yes, sir," snapped Callin, turning. They were both startled. "Oh. What is it, Chief? Something wrong down below?"

"Oh, no sir. We just got your full bell. I wondered if you knew how long we'll be at this speed."

"Can't we handle it?"

"Of course we can handle it," said Wronowicz, thinking *What does he think we do down there? Play with ourselves?* "It's just that we had just took one boiler off the line and I wondered if we should bring it up again."

"I don't know," said the ensign, glancing toward where the captain, still slumped in his chair, had aimed his pipe in their direction. "Look, I'm busy. I got the conn right now. Maybe you just better bring it up anyway."

"It costs us more water that way. And fuel. If we're going to slow again in a little while—"

"Chief," said the captain.

Well, here we go, thought Wronowicz. He pulled his cap down a little more and swaggered over, putting his dirty hands behind him. "Yeah, Cap'n?"

"How's the plant holding up?"

"Pretty good, sir. Maybe a slight vibration in the port shaft. We could use some time alongside the tender, though. Getting some insulation dryout, and we need some gaskets replaced, and we got to get some more packing for the main feed pumps." He could feel Callin listening. Captain should be asking him this stuff, he thought. "We're using more turns than we should for the knots, though."

"How come?"

"We been out of the yard for over a year, Cap'n. Getting a lot of barnacles and crap on the bottom. It ain't the engines."

"I know that, Chief." Foster smiled and took his pipe out of his mouth. "You run a tight engineroom. Say, you mentioned the port shaft, vibration. Could that be a delayed result of the bottoming? Is there anything I ought to know?"

Wronowicz hesitated, choosing his words; you had to be so goddamn diplomatic up here, all this frigging gold braid. He decided the unvarnished truth would be easiest. "I don't know. I've been keeping an eye on all the bearings since Naples. I dint want to bother Ensign Callin, 'cause—"

"You better bother him," said the captain, but smiling. "You better bother the hell out of him. I want him to come out of that hole in a year the best goddamn snipe j.g. in the Fleet."

"Aye aye," said Wronowicz, grinning back.

"Mr. Callin, you hear that?"

"Yes, sir."

"Captain," said Wronowicz, "Are we going to be at this speed for a while? How long are we going to be out? I need to know to keep feed-water consumption down, stay off water hours as long as we can."

"Boy, that's a tough one," said Foster, biting his pipe and looking wry. "We're on our way now to catch up with the MARG. I wanted to take it easy, spare the plant, but CTF 61 just told us to move our rendezvous time up. You know we're on alert status now."

"Is that right, sir?" said Wronowicz innocently, although he, along with everyone else aboard, had been trading scuttlebutt about it all day. "Where's it for?"

"I don't know, Chief. Frankly, they haven't told me yet. To answer your question, I'd plan for full speed from now till we join up this afternoon, then slack back to ten or fifteen knots. For the long run, I can't say. We could be out here for a couple of weeks, or even longer."

"We'd have to refuel."

"I think you can leave arrangements for that to me and the squadron staff. All right?"

"Suits me, Cap'n."

"You're sure the port shaft is okay?"

"It's not perfect, but it should take flank speed, sir."

"For how long?"

Till it breaks, Wronowicz thought. How the hell should I know? Do I look like a goddamn gypsy? But aloud he only said, "I think it'll hold, sir. And we got a spare bearing aboard if that one craps out."

Foster nodded thoughtfully, and at last turned back to the sea. Wronowicz glanced at Callin; the ensign had his head buried in the radarscope. Taking that as dismissal, he left the officers to themselves and went down a level to the chartroom. Blood was there, fiddling with a complicated piece of radio gear.

"What's the good word, Unc?"

"Pussy. Spread the word."

"Funny," said Wronowicz. For some reason Blood's ribaldry did not amuse him today.

"What you doing up here, Kelly? Thought snipes got a nosebleed at high altitudes like this."

"Come up to figure how long we had before you ran us into Gibraltar."

"Not with this baby." Blood patted the chuckling machine affectionately. "Gives you a fix a minute, accurate to within a mile."

Wronowicz regarded it with suspicion. He distrusted anything you could not fix with a hammer. "Oh yeah? I always thought you used a Ouija board."

"Get out of here, Wronkoffsky. There are people on this ship got to work, you know."

"Tell me, Unc," said Wronowicz. "You ever get crabs in your eyebrows?"

"In my *eyebrows?* No."

"Lucky cocksucker."

"Get out of here, Wronowicz. Go polish the propellers, or something."

He escaped to the weather deck instead, aft of Mount 52, unwilling to go below again just yet. It was pleasant there, far above the waterline, in the light and wind. I don't come topside enough, he thought.

The rail was a steel balcony, swaying above the sea. Here the roar of the engines was a distant hum; the hollow crash of the bow wave was louder. It must be easy, he thought, standing your watches up here, to forget the oil-soaked bastards who labored like apprenticed devils far below. But the black gang made the ship go. They were the human energy turning the whirling shafts that drove this steel hive so smoothly over the face of the waves. . . .

The seas were coming from ahead, he saw, so that the bow dipped every few seconds, then lifted its head arrogantly again, like the bulls he had seen in Sevilla. He hoped they stayed on this course for a while. When they hit you from the beam these old destroyers rolled like pigs. They'd lost a couple of them in the Pacific in typhoons just from that, waves knocking them over so far the sea came down the stacks and doused the fires. He thought for a moment of going back to the chartroom, asking Blood what the weather looked like for the next few days, then decided not to. It would come whether he knew about it or not, and with this goddamn thing brewing—where the hell were they going anyway?—they would probably end up steaming around in the middle of a storm for weeks on end.

Callin came out on the wing, glanced down at him, but said nothing. He swept the horizon with his glasses and went back in. Wronowicz looked at the horizon, too. He saw nothing out there, only jaggedness, and then the blur of the edge of the world. Getting nearsighted, he thought. Have to start wearing glasses soon, like Chapman. The thought depressed him.

He leaned over the rail and watched the sea slide past. The white line of burble, where the smooth flow broke against the roughness of the hull. Stealing my power, he thought. Slowing me down. And the longer they stayed at sea the harder he would have to drive his engines to make thirty, then twenty-nine, then twenty-eight knots. . . .

Callin came out again, as he had known he would.

"Captain's been talking about holding general quarters this evening," he said. "Thought you might like to know. Get the men ready."

"They're ready for drills, sir." He watched the ensign hesitate, curious to see if his too-casual reply would provoke something. But this time it did not; Callin turned without saying anything more and went back inside. Wronowicz turned back to the sea.

Wronowicz, Callin, Foster, Jay, Steurnagel, even Blaney . . . he had a sudden unaccustomed image of the ship not as a ship, not as a mass of machinery with fire in its heart and electricity in its veins, but as a pyramid of men. The captain at its apex. Then the officers; then the chiefs, the ones who made it go. A multitude of hands, skilled and unskilled, adept and lazy, a cross section of the society that had built it in a shipyard noisy as the engineroom at speed. That had sent it here, to this far corner of the earth.

But to do what, in the end? To protect or punish whom? He read in the papers about arms shipments and wars, reprisals, juntas, international debt, and he did not understand what it was about, what it had to do with him. But somehow it did. For somehow he had helped send this machine and these men ten thousand miles, through pulling a lever every two years, like cranking his hopes and apprehensions into an engine-order telegraph so immense and ramified it took years to come up to speed or change its course.

He had no idea where they were going. But coming from the engine spaces as he did, everything down there logical, clear, laid out from the beginning in crackling blueprints, he had to believe that there was a good reason for it. The ship was machine, he and the others were men, but they were all parts of the larger machine that he himself had helped give motion and now maintained on its course forward to wherever those at the helm of state sent it.

Yeah. It had to make sense. Maybe not to Machinist's

Mate Chief Wronowicz, he thought, but to somebody. He hoped it made sense to somebody.

He started thinking about the woman again then, and shortly thereafter went below.

11

Nicosia, Cyprus

THE STREET WAS SOLID WITH SUNLIGHT
and the smoky fumes of diesel buses. Pedestrians and tiny
cars jostled shoulder to fender, making it hard to distinguish roadway from sidewalk. The bray of horns, the cries
of street vendors, pressed inward to her faintly through a
film of glass.

Susan Lenson hesitated in the air-conditioned cool of
the hotel lobby. Shouting, arguing, singing, the bright
swift life of the Mediterranean pulsed past, so foreign it
fascinated, but so intense that it daunted her.

She had not expected this. Moira Lieberman's letters
had been filled with scenery. The peach orchards of the
Solea Valley; the secluded charm of the hills, where she
was excavating a twelfth-century monastery. But that was
an hour to the west. Here in the capital, for all the charm
and solitude she could see, she and Nan could just as well
have stayed in Rome.

When she swung the door open the afternoon sun hit
her like a heated hammer. The air cut her breath off,
clotting like cotton behind her tongue. She unlocked the
car and looked back. The child was lagging back, looking
stubborn. She shielded her eyes and studied her daughter.

At three Nancy Lenson was sturdy and compact, her
brown eyes tarsier-solemn behind the glasses she had worn
for a year now. Her way of silently inspecting people

through them sometimes intimidated grown-ups. Her hair was the color of a chestnut horse, cut short except for a bang in front, and because of that and her stockiness—her mother worried sometimes about her weight—she had been mistaken more than once for a boy. She looked like one now, in the bib jeans and T-shirt Susan dressed her in for traveling. But today her solemnity was a scowl, and she looked drawn, her hair damp where it fell across her forehead.

"Bunny, are you feeling all right?"

"No," said the little girl.

"Don't you want to go? Come on, baby. Let's jump in the car."

"I don't wan' go anyplace. Can't we stay here? I want a Coke."

"Damn—darn it, get in the car, Nan." She reached for her daughter's arm, felt its heat as she bundled her into the blue Fiat she had rented at the airport. So hot . . . she paused to feel her daughter's forehead. Nan jerked away, whining, but she persisted, finally satisfying herself that though she was sweating it was only the sun. God, for her to get sick, that was all she needed. Already she half-regretted coming to the island.

But Cyprus had been so ruggedly lovely, from the air. . . .

She and Nan had arrived the day before, on an Air Greece flight out of Athens. It had finally become impossible to stay with the other wives. They meant well. But they were too—she searched for a word in place of "dull"—too conventional. Too safe.

And they were always *there.* There were five in their group, she and Alicia from the staff, the other three wives of the *Guam*'s middle-grade officers; and they were all older than she. For most of them this was their third or fourth trip to the Med, and they wanted to revisit the places they knew. They wanted to buy jewelry or lace or clothes, dicker for hours with shopkeepers, and eat. Nan was the only child, and although the other women praised

Susan for bringing her, she had the feeling that they thought she was wrong, that at some level they resented it.

There was no question that it was harder with her along. You had to watch her and cater to her, and Nan, though she was generally as good as you could expect a child of her age to be, didn't like strange foods (except for *gelati*). Susan had thought it all through months before, though. Nan would start kindergarten soon. This would be their only chance to travel for a long time, and she felt it would be good for both of them.

The other wives also made remarks about Susan's studying, and she, in turn, thought they were empty-headed. Oh, she knew that was unfair, they were all nice, but most of them did nothing but keep house, although Alicia was a librarian. They could share her fascination with cathedrals and museums; they liked to feel "arty" occasionally, but when she proposed renting a van and driving off to some obscure village in the hills to look at a dig they begged off. They would rather shop.

Well, now we can see something worthwhile, Susan thought. She crammed herself into the little Fiat and pulled out into traffic, trying to keep in mind that she had to do everything backward—you drove British-style on the left in Cyprus. Not to mention struggling with a street map at the same time.

"Mommy, *where* we going?"

"We have to get some money, Bunny, and mail a letter. Then we're going to see one of my old friends."

"Who?"

"Her name's Moira, dear. She's an archaeologist. You'll like her."

"Can we put the cold on, Mommy?"

"We don't have air conditioning in this car, baby. I'll turn on the fan."

It didn't work. A hundred bucks a week for this mousetrap, she thought viciously, and now this. She cranked down Nan's window and the child settled more or less satisfied, looking out the window at the cars, the streams of pedestrians. By the time Susan found the cross street she wanted, and squeezed into a parking space two blocks away from the American Embassy, she felt wilted; perspiration was soggy under her arms, beading on her face.

"Come on, darling. We'll walk a little."

"Want to stay here. It's too hot out."

"No. Somebody might steal you, Bunny."

She saw the frightened look cross her face, and thought: That was a terrific thing to say, Susan. Great, make her afraid of foreigners. "I was just joking. Nobody will hurt you. I just want you with me. Come on, dear."

"No."

No doubt about it, it was going to be a wonderful day. "Close that door," she snapped. "Stay close to me. Don't touch that puppy, you'll get dog spit all over your hands."

"Look, there's a man; he's got a gun—"

"He's just a policeman. Come on, Bunny."

The embassy was cool and dark, marbled peaceful after the noise and heat of the street. Thankfully, too, the line at the service desk was short. The teller was a dark Greek she only fleetingly thought attractive. "Do you change money here?" she asked him.

"Are you an American, ma'am?"

"Yes, I am. Susan Lenson. Are there any messages for me?"

"Just a moment . . . no, nothing at present."

She changed three hundred dollars to Cypriote pounds, big brown and blue notes, putting half in her purse and half in her jeans pocket, and handed over a letter for her parents.

"Do you have any maps of the island?"

"Where are you going, ma'am?"

"Near Kakopetria."

"The skiing is not good in the mountains now. You want to go to the beaches. Kyrenia was good once, but now the Turks are there. You want to go to Larnaca—"

"No. If I could have a map—"

"Is this your child?" said the man, reaching over the counter to pat Nan on the head. She looked up, suspicious.

"Yes."

"You're here alone? I would not advise going about the island by yourself. There are rumors."

"Rumors? About what?"

"It's said there may be trouble again. I don't know, it may be true. Now, you know, I go to Larnaca often. I have a small cottage there, on the sea. The beaches there are very good. Sunny, warm."

Ah, so it was the make. She should have recognized it long before this. "I have friends near Kakopetria. They're expecting me," she said sharply. "All I need is a map."

"A map, certainly you shall have a map. Here is one. You have a car? It's only an hour away . . . here is a fine map," said the man. "Have a pleasant trip, ma'am." As she turned away he was already saying to the woman behind her, "Good morning, miss. You're here alone?"

"Mommy, why did he pat me like that?"

"It's his job, dear."

"Why'd he ask if we were Amer'cans?"

Ah, Susan thought, she noticed. And how will you explain this one to your child, omniscient mother? Three generations now and we still must justify, still excuse our skin and our eyes. But we are so polite about it. To her surprise she heard herself say, "Because we're prettier than other Americans, Bunny."

They were her own mother's words, twenty years before.

"Come on. We have a long way to drive."

Once they were on the road out of the city, her mood, which had been edging from annoyed to dangerous, began to lighten. The scenery was fine. Past the airport, a few miles west of the capital, the fuss of new building sank back to scattered houses, and the road wound through open foothills, gradually climbing. She had to keep her eyes on the road, but Nan exclaimed over an orchard-filled valley, and a little later clamored for her mother to look

at the distant sea, blue and hazy. It was so pretty they had
to stop and take a picture. Long before she was tired they
stopped again in a little village for a cold drink. She had
lemonade and Nan was allowed a small cola. (Susan was
careful with her caffeine and sugar.) They sipped them on
a stone terrace under a shady arbor. Their waiter made
them taste the grapes—they were fat and tart—and tried
to tell them a story about them, but his English was very
bad. She tried her college French on him, but he only
looked puzzled. Nan laughed so hard at her mother that
she spilled her drink and started to cry.

"Don' worry, don' worry, I bring," said the waiter,
smiling, and brought them both fresh glasses. . . .

They rolled through Kakopetria in the middle of the
afternoon. It was a small town, high in the mountains,
which stood like Crusader castles above the shaded square
on every side. Susan thought she had never seen such a
lovely place. They asked directions of a bearded priest,
robed all in black despite the heat, and found the monastery west of town in the middle of an apple orchard.

The dig was deserted. She looked uphill—at school they
told you always to camp on a rise; it was more sanitary—
and saw the tents. The first one they stopped at was
Moira's.

Ten minutes later they were sitting in the midst of Real
Archaeology. At a camp table in her college roommate's
tent, sipping watered St. John Commandaria, she examined the potsherds and corroded crosses, each one neatly
labeled, that Moira Lieberman pulled excitely from rag
nests in biscuit tins. Her greatest treasure was a cork,
miraculously preserved for eight centuries in a patch of
dry sand. One end was still stained with ancient wine.
Susan passed it to Nan, who held it gingerly, not quite
understanding what it was, but knowing it was important.
"It's old, Bunny," she said. "Real old. From long, long
ago."

"Older than Grandma?"

"Older than your grandma's grandma's grandma," said

Moira, and they smiled at each other over the child's awed expression, her first intimation of the incredible span of years before her own existence.

Later, after a tour of the dig, they shared a camp supper with the chief of excavation, on sabbatical from Michigan; the Cypriote resident; and four grad students. When the stewed lamb and fava beans were gone, the cheese pie demolished, night had fallen like a mauve blanket over the mountains. The men built up the campfire and produced bottles in honor of the visitors. The talk was obviously secondary to the ouzo, and the two women soon drifted back to the tent. They sat on a cot, side by side, and Susan thought how much it was like college; how many nights she and this dumpy brilliant girl had spent sitting together, just like this, talking about their lives to come, the wonderful discoveries they would make. In some ways she had never been closer to another person, and it made her sad to think they had spent years apart.

"I've got to think of getting back to town pretty soon," she said at last. "We've had a wonderful time, Moira. I envy you this, your work . . . doing what we always dreamed of. By the way, are you sleeping with him?"

"With whom?"

"Professor Rentzey."

"Oh, good heavens, no."

"I didn't mean anything—"

"I know you didn't, Betts. No, it's one of the grad students. The tall boy, Michael Cook."

They laughed by the soft light of a kerosene lamp. "Betts"—she had almost forgotten her college nickname.

"But you don't have to go," Lieberman said then. "I don't want you to. I have an extra cot. Why don't you and Nan stay here?"

"Oh, Moira, I can't impose."

"Impose? Don't be an ass. I'd love to have you." Lieberman leaned back on the cot, looking serious. "You know, it would be ideal for you. You don't get to do much fieldwork, do you?"

"Are you kidding?"

"I guess that means no. But, Betts, why not? I could get Rentzey to give you part of the site. You can do ceramics; we have great trading pieces—you could do trading networks!"

"It would take so long."

"What else are you going to do?"

She felt trapped; worse, she felt guilty. Moira was right. It would be ideal; it would be a dream come true. Forget the textbooks, do real fieldwork. "But what would I do about Dan? I have to meet him, when they decide where they're going next. I can't just disappear."

Moira lowered her eyes. "It's your choice. I guess it would be rough for you out here, especially with Nan. . . ."

"I'd really like to," Susan said again. She tried to smile, to pass it off. "But we have our room back in Nicosia, all our things are there . . . we can visit you again . . . but I really think we'd better go back."

"Maybe you're right, at that. You know," and Moira looked into the dark beyond the open flaps of the tent, "the islanders are nice, but there's something else, some undercurrent. There's a lot of talk about the Turks."

"I heard something about that in the city, too. I thought it was just a pass. You mean there might be trouble?"

"I can't say. We have to be damn careful about the local politics. The man who owns this orchard, he comes around sometimes to watch us; he hates Muslims. Curses them. It's terrible, there's so much hate between them. And really they're not so different, to our eyes." Moira turned a piece of glazed ware, an ancient drinking cup, in her hands. "Anyway, it might be safer here. If anything happens, it'll start in the city. It always does."

"I'd stay, really, but Nan gets so cranky. I can't inflict her on everybody here. You don't know what it's like with a baby."

"She's not a baby. She's smart. And pretty. You're so lucky to have her, Betts."

"Oh, I know." Susan smiled, looking back toward the fire; Cook, his hair shining gold in the yellow light, was showing Nan how to coax hollow music from the mouth of a bottle. "It's a pain sometimes, but I love her. You should have children, Moira."

"Oh, Jesus, plenty of time for that. How's your husband? You know, I still remember the day you met him, when we went up on that bus. I was so jealous."

"Dan's all right. We have our problems. He's away so much. The Navy's like that. I can't say he didn't warn me."

"It must be rough, having him away. But you can cope, can't you?"

"I do, yes . . . somehow."

She parted the tent flaps, looking out toward the fire again. As she did so a puff of air made her shiver. It came from the east, several degrees cooler, a different wind than the hot, uncertain breeze that had prevailed all day. This was steady, calm and cold.

"Feels like rain," said Moira, close behind her. "The orchards can use that. It's been even drier than usual this summer. You know, Betts,"—her roommate put her arm around her, looking with her in the direction of the fire, the little girl, the circle of amused men—"I don't know if I should ask you this, but—"

"God, Moira, you know you can ask me anything. I may not answer you, but you can ask."

"It's like—when you're married, and your husband's away so much—don't you ever get horny?"

Susan had to laugh. Moira Lieberman—"the Ox" to everyone at Georgetown—had never been famous for reticence. But then her laughter faltered.

"You don't have to answer, like you said."

"No, it's all right. I was just thinking about it. It's so good when he's there. The being apart makes it like a honeymoon. If it wasn't for Nan we could spend weeks in bed. But when he isn't there—yeah, I get horny as hell."

"Do you ever think about other men?"

"Think? Sometimes, Moira. But that's all."

"And so you're happy? You really are?"

She hesitated then, for the barest fraction of a moment, looking toward the stakes, flickering in the firelight, that marked the careful rectilinear dissection of the dig. Her first love, the love of ancient things, the laborious, fascinating, ultimately impossible reconstruction of the past . . . "No, it's fine," she said at last. "I guess you can't have everything."

And she was grateful, somehow, that Moira did not remark on the pensive way she said it.

She began the drive back that night with more annoyance than trepidation. Nan was whiny, didn't want to leave, and her unusual behavior elicited an equal snappishness from her mother. There were tears from the backseat, where the bag of toys was, when at last they started down from the hills. But her annoyance melted as she concentrated on driving.

It was a task. The clouds that had come with the wind covered stars and moon, and there seemed to be as few lights now, late in the twentieth century, as there had been in the twelfth. Rain spattered briefly, then lifted, but the road remained only a pale winding among cliffs that shone like pavement in the weak headlights, and she had to concentrate to keep from mistaking one for the other. Shadows flew along before them, swept after the humming tires like black wings. When at last she turned onto the main road she gave a puff of relief. Only then did she wonder about Nan. She twisted to look into the rear seat, but only a flash of dark hair showed as Susan flicked the dome light on and off. She was curled up back there, asleep.

Leave her be, then . . . she turned back to the road. Mile by dark mile the island sped by, wind buffeting the tiny car.

The conversation with Moira had left her dissatisfied, on some deep level that she only vaguely understood.

What was it that had upset her? Her shortness with Nan had only partially been her daughter's fault.

Was it the invitation to the dig?

Had it been what the Ox had asked, about Dan? . . .

She was still wondering about it when her foot slammed down, sending her toward the windshield. The lights had loomed up suddenly as she came round a bend. Rain spattered the glass again, and she flicked on the wipers and peered forward, the car shuddering as wind lashed at the doors.

Trucks. They were turning out of a side road, down from somewhere in the hills; rolling slowly onto the highway that led inland, toward the capital. Two, and then several more; large canvas-covered vehicles with strange headlights. Then she realized that they were blackout headlights, and that the trucks were a military convoy. They wound slowly onto the rain-silvered highway, the growl of motors reaching her through the wind. They're headed east, she thought. East, toward the Turkish lines.

The last truck was towing an artillery piece. Its barrel turned toward her, directly in line with the little car, as the convoy gathered speed into the night. She sat frozen, holding the wheel, listening to their diminishing roar as the taillights dimmed into red blurs, dissolving in the rain.

That night, back at the hotel, Nan woke crying at three. She was feverish. Susan made tea, put cold cloths on her head, and then, when she finally went back to sleep, took out a book. She studied for a time, then got up, restless, and stood at the window. At last she opened it and stepped out onto the balcony that every hotel room in the Mediterranean seemed to have. She shivered in the wind, wrapping her robe more tightly about her, and looked out over the city.

At this hour, long before dawn, Nicosia was like a neglected cemetery. The buildings were grave markers, their bases whitened by the few streetlights, all their windows dark. The streets were empty. Several blocks away,

over a bus shed and a restaurant, a neon sign beamed out
CYPRUS AIRWAVES. Beyond that was a wider street, a few
palms and plane trees, and the pillared portico of the
Town Hall. Beyond the buildings she could make out
dimly the mound of the old city wall.

There are things to see here, she told herself. We won't
waste this time. But still the windy, waiting silence seemed
to echo something in her own heart, something lost and
afraid. She wished now she had stayed with Moira. They
would be asleep now in the tent, or lying awake telling
funny stories about college. But her next thought was of
Nan. It might be one of those waterborne diseases the
guidebooks warned about. If the fever held she would need
a doctor, and the capital, not the hills, was the place to find
one. So on balance, perhaps it was best that they had
returned. . . .

Something moved on the street, and she leaned over the
balcony, looking down.

It was a group of men, twenty or thirty of them, moving
along purposefully at a jog. They were carrying guns.
Police? Troops? So strange that they would be running
through the streets, at night.

Stranger than that, she realized suddenly, looking down
at their white shirts, dark hatless heads, was that none of
them was wearing a uniform.

That decided her. Armed men in the streets: That was
something more than rumor. That and the trucks . . . as
soon as it was light she would get Nan dressed, pack a bag,
and go . . . go where? To the embassy, of course. That
would be the safest place. And there might even be a
doctor there. She was not really worried about Nan—she
was healthy—but it wouldn't hurt to have her looked at.
And the man at the counter, no, his supervisor would be
better, perhaps could tell them now what was happening,
what everyone seemed to fear but not speak of, as if saying
its name would bring it on. She thought for a moment of
Dan, then dismissed it. He was far away. Always far away,
it seemed, when she needed him.

Well, that was the way things were for Navy wives. And much as you dislike the word, she thought, that is what you are. "Dependents," in the seemingly deliberate insult of military terminology . . . although she was feeling anything but dependent, and would see to it with all her strength that her daughter did not grow up to be.

She left the windows open and went back to the bed. Her daughter . . . she smoothed Nan's hair. It was hard sometimes to remember what it had been like before she had someone more important than herself to take care of, something more urgent than her own wishes. She'd been such a child herself when she'd married. Possibly, as her father joked sometimes, more than a little spoiled. She smiled to herself, her hand moving gently, and then the smile ebbed away.

She would do anything to keep her daughter safe.

She was picking up her book again, turning to sit down, when she heard distant gunfire. Her first feeling was incredulity. Her first action was to pick up the room telephone and dial the desk.

There was no answer.

That's it, she thought, all the fear galvanizing suddenly into resolve. To hell with waiting. We're going now.

Nan, bundled tight in two sweaters and the heaviest coat they had brought, did not cry or even whine in the elevator down. At two floors the lift jerked to a stop, the doors banged open, and more people crowded in, frightened-looking in hastily donned clothes. They seemed all to be foreigners—or non-Greeks, she corrected herself. Americans, British, an elderly couple with a small dog. When they reached the lobby she headed immediately for the desk, but there was no one there, no one at the switchboard. Carrying the single suitcase she had packed, she went next to the street entrance, and stared out. There were a few lights on now, in the storefronts, and knots of Cypriotes were gathering here and there on the street, looking east.

"We're going to the American Embassy," she said, to the lobby at large. "Does anyone need a ride?"

She took the old couple. Their name, the woman said, was Stanweis, and they were from New Jersey. The poodle's name was Ferdy. She bundled them into the backseat and headed south. Strangely, they seemed to be the only ones going anywhere. The Nicosians that they passed simply stood waiting, on the sidewalks or in front of their stores, watching them go by. She left the car on a side street, near where she had parked the day before, and they walked the last two blocks, Nan holding tightly and silently to her hand. Halfway there she remembered that she had left her camera in the car. She did not go back.

The embassy gates were open and lit. Two marines stood by them, looking self-conscious. They were unarmed. "Ma'am. Your passport?" said one, as she came up.

"Excuse me?"

"You're an American? We have orders to check."

"Of course I'm an American," she said. This was too much. "I was born in Washington. My husband's in the Navy. You can see I'm not Russian."

"We'll still have to see some ID, ma'am," the other marine said inflexibly. She showed him her dependent's card. As they went inside she heard the Stanweises begin to argue. They had left their passports at the hotel. She thought for a moment that she should go back, help them, but then looked at Nan. She looked so wan that Susan hurried on inside, wondering again about a doctor.

There were people already there. They stood around the counter, where another marine stood next to a civilian official; she was saying that conditions were unsettled; they couldn't say for certain what was happening; that everyone was welcome to stay, but that there wasn't much room. Susan could see that. People were already fencing off areas of the hallway with luggage and blankets. Walking down the corridor, she saw that several of the offices were open, with people sitting inside talking on telephones. She went back to the desk, noting that people were coming in steadily now through the gates. "Excuse me," she said to the woman. "My little girl is sick. Is there a doctor available?"

"A doctor? Not right now—we have a Greek nurse, but she won't be in till morning."

"Permit me," said someone behind her. She turned; it was the old man, Mr. Stanweis.

"I'm a doctor," he said. "Can I help?"

"Certainly," she said, and smiled. Bread on the waters . . .

A little later, she hastened to claim with their clothes and the suitcase the last few square feet of floor. She laid herself down next to Nan—"probably just a touch of flu," Stanweis had said—on the wool coat she had expected never to need in the Mediterranean. She was so tired. . . .

When she opened her eyes again, later, she realized she had dozed off. The hallway lights had dimmed; Nan was asleep, snuffling a little as she dreamed.

Lying there, Susan Lenson mused drowsily on the thick walls . . . the guards out front . . . the impregnable, invisible, inviolate shield of the American flag. For the first time that day she felt secure. The marble floor was hard, but as she drifted off, she thought it was lovelier than the softest bed.

Nothing, was her last thought, can touch us here.

And outside, gunfire rattled distant in the Cypriote night.

IV

THE READY

12
U.S.S. *Guam*

FIVE HUNDRED MILES TO THE WEST DAN
Lenson raised his head suddenly from his desk. He recalled neither nodding off to sleep, nor what had just awakened him. He blinked blurrily at his watch. Fifteen minutes . . . was that all that he'd been out? . . .

He was holding his time-distance ruler, trying to recall what he'd been calculating on it, when the phone on the bulkhead buzzed again. At the far side of the darkened stateroom a horizontal figure stirred, flinging up an arm in unconscious protest. He grabbed for the handset. "Lieutenant Lenson."

"Dan?"

"Speaking."

"Good morning. Are you going to relieve me? It's ten minutes past."

He looked at his watch again, registering time rather than duration. Ten past four. Where had the night gone? He had poured it all into the scribbled sheets that covered the desk, into planning for something that would in all likelihood never happen. And now it was time for watch again. "I'm sorry, Commander . . . I mean, Jack. I got to working here and forgot the time."

"I understand. You'll be up soon, then?"

"Yes sir, right away."

"Take your time. Just wanted to check."

He snapped the phone into its rack and slumped, closing his eyes. Three days now without sleep. His face felt wooden, his skin numb, and the coffee he drank by the dozen cups a watch seemed to have no effect anymore. Watch, and work, and watch . . . then being saddled by Sundstrom with this stupid operation order on top of everything else. He pushed the mass of paper into the desk and locked it, then got up, staggering with a roll, to pull his flashlight and jacket and cap off the bottom bunk.

Her picture. He hesitated for a moment, torn between her shadowed eyes and the need to relieve the man who waited for him topside. He imagined her somewhere behind them, she and Nan breathing close and soft in some hotel room in Italy or Greece. At this moment, this moment.

If I was there, he thought, I would not wake them. I would lie softly down beside her, and in the morning, wake them with tea and kisses, equal distribution, each to each.

Yet he was here. Christ, he thought, testing the flashlight with a stab of his thumb. How much longer could this go on?

Until it ends, he thought. Or until something snaps.

And if anything does . . . it can't be me, he thought. His lips tightened. Not after last time.

His hand crept up to touch his shoulder.

It was not quite dark when he got topside. Though it was still well before dawn, there was enough gray to the east for him to distinguish bow from sea. He checked the running lights around them as he climbed the last few steps to the flag bridge. The formation had altered during the night, ships shifting position around the fixed axis of the *Guam*. They seemed closer, too, as if the amphibs had drawn together for protection during the long passage. Only Snoopy, the Soviet trawler, had maintained his station, plodding ahead at the same range and bearing he had occupied at sunset.

Jack Byrne was leaning in a corner of the wing, staring back over the quarter. "Morning, Jack," he said.

"Hi, Dan." When the N-2 turned, his tanned face looked naked without the sunglasses. "You fit and eager to take it?"

"You want a straight answer to that? I'm bushed."

"Up all night again?"

"The commodore's oporder."

"My sympathies." The intel officer didn't sound like he meant it. Yawning, he went through the litany of watch relief: course, speed, formation, contacts. *Ault* had joined up and was in a screen station ahead. That made two escorts with them now. At last Byrne bent, fishing a message board from the bridge safe. "And, got a pass-along to you from Lieutenant Flasher. Let's see, I think I can do it verbatim: 'Double-nuts wants the ops type to have the traffic memorized when he gets up. Seeing as how he's doing my job, I might as well leave that to Sundstrom, junior.' "

"Who?"

"You, boy, you."

"Red said that? Jack, this isn't my idea. *He* ordered me to do it. It's kind of unfair to—"

"I know, I know. Forget it. We're all on edge." Byrne yawned again, and snapped his mouth shut. He looked bewildered for just a moment. "Anyway, this is going to be a busy day. Formation battle problem is scheduled to begin on our signal around nine. Drills from there to thirteen hundred, then each ship has its own individual sked of damage control and engineering casualty-control training."

"We got a copy up here?"

"Taped to the bulkhead." Byrne pointed. "Middle of the general quarters, we'll be passing TF 60. Be warned."

"America?"

"The big birdfarm herself. You'll see in the traffic, they'll pass north of us. We're not supposed to interact, but with Ike in charge I'm sure that will be subject to change."

"Uh huh," said Lenson, thinking of it with resigned dread. Funny, though, that Byrne should say something like that . . . he had never heard him criticize the commodore, even indirectly, before. On edge, sure, just like Flasher . . . "Anything else?"

"That should be enough to keep you occupied. I'm headed for the rack. Get in a couple hours before the fun starts. Are you ready to relieve?"

"I got it," said Lenson. He no longer bothered to salute. As he strolled into the bridge, walking uphill against a roll, he nodded to Stan Glazer and folded back the red cover on the ops file.

The blue mimeographs were black under the red light of the chart table. Yeah, he thought, Flasher's right; *he* always wants to be briefed first thing when he wakes up. It made no difference that the commodore was awakened anyway for any message Priority or above. It was as if he was afraid he would forget something important, or, more likely, Lenson thought, that it just made him feel important to be briefed, like an admiral. And if I'm up here, and he wants me to do Red's job, then he'll probably expect me to brief him.

Shit, he thought. He glanced round the bridge. For the moment it was quiet. Glazer had his head up; the only surface contact was several miles to the south and opening. He rubbed his forehead and lowered his eyes again to the messages.

Weather . . . getting worse. Fleet Central reported winds twenty-two knots and rising, barometer dropping. Units east of twenty-seven degrees longitude were warned to prepare for heavy weather. He memorized the numbers and went on. Couple of well-dones for the Indian Ocean battle group. They were well clear of this flap; he envied them. Some supply messages. Transfer orders for the captain of the *Barnstable County,* effective next month. Commodore'll want to know that, he thought. He flipped on. Unclassified, confidential . . . a Secret marking caught his eye. Soviet naval movements.

Well now, he thought, and began to read.

Thirty units in the Med, twenty percent over normal for this time of year. Why? No answer. Two of their newest destroyers, big as a U.S. cruiser and better armed, had just been reported in the Aegean, transiting south at high speed. Their sea legs were shorter, but once in the Med that hardly mattered. The Black Sea Fleet's time on station in the Med was doubled or tripled by the repair and refueling facilities in Syria and Libya. Syria, allied by treaty with the USSR, had a full-fledged operating base for them at Baniyas.

He had seen the Russians. No one sailing these waters could miss them. Their lean lines, bristling with topside armament and electronics, looked deadlier than corresponding U.S. classes. They were faster; they cut through NATO formations from astern, passing the cruisers and cans, their gas turbines whining wasplike across the water as they creamed by. They passed close enough for you to see the men on their bridges, watching you with binoculars just as you were watching them; staring at each other across the sea, like looking into a mirror at a strangely altered and unknowable image of yourself. Oh, he knew they were no supermen. They spent less time at sea than the Americans and British; the ships were cramped and the men poorly trained, and part of the reason they had so many weapons and sensors was that they crapped out more often than Western gear did.

But they would be no pushover, if it came to the test. Certainly they could take the MARG out in a matter of minutes, if they caught them unescorted and away from air cover. Lenson thought of the three-inch popguns the amphibs carried. Not much of a contest there.

"Permission to relieve the lookouts, sir."

"Yeah. Go ahead."

He flipped through the rest of the messages, found the one on the carrier group, and took it over to the chart. In the growing light he examined the pencil marks where Byrne had plotted their track. Carrier headed west, MARG east; he was surprised to see a full thirty miles separation at the point of closest passage. Why had Jack even mentioned it? There was plenty to keep them occupied steaming just as they were.

"Anything interesting?" said Stan Glazer, looking enviously at the board. "I never get to see that thing."

"Hey, Stan, it's secret. The commodore catches you looking at it, *both* our asses are grass."

Glazer looked disappointed. He turned away and raised his glasses again. Dan tossed the board back in the bridge safe, swung it shut, and sighed. He'd thought, late the night before, that he'd never want the stuff again, but now he thirsted for coffee. Thirsted for the impossible . . . if Sundstrom smelled another drop of joe on the bridge after his interdict, Dan knew, there would be a shitstorm that would make Fleet Weather blanch.

God damn it . . . he checked the radar, the vertical plot, the gyro, out of habit. The wind indicator and barometer he scrutinized carefully, but as yet they showed normal readings. His attention shifted back to his internal state. His feet hurt already, and he hadn't been on them thirty minutes yet . . . he felt half-asleep.

Reaching up, he slapped his face twice, hard, and went out on the wing for a dose of fresh air.

Morning, at sea.

Though it was not yet sunrise, the sky was already red beyond scattered clouds. Flaming, though the fire was still hidden behind the rim of sea that lay like a heated saw-blade across their bow, cutting the mass of the flight deck, still black as night. The cough of a starter came from somewhere aft; the ready helo was checking out its engines. The wind, over thirty knots when you added the ship's speed to the prevailing breeze, was cool and blustery, and he drank it with gratitude. Sleep retreated a step. The eastern sea threw back the sky's tints, scarlet and gold, not flashing yet but glowing, like molten glass. The last minutes before dawn; just a little too late for morning stars . . . thinking of that, he glanced upward. The ship's navigator was standing on the wing above, fitting his sextant back into its wooden box. A snatch of talk drifted down on the wind: "Deneb . . . just got her . . . sixty percent cloud cover."

He leaned back and his gaze dropped once more, as it always did, to the ever-changing, never-changing sea. Below the overhang of flight deck it surged in five-to-seven-foot crests, each wave rising and falling in the dim light like a life all in itself, complete and perfect and individual and then gone, but rising again instantly in another form. He watched, his mind empty. The ship drove through them, vibrating, powerful, intent, and his eyes drifted aft to follow them as they dropped astern. Aft of the helicopter deck the sky was still tinted enough with night so that as he looked astern he could see the darkness, fleeing away behind them along the terminator of earth. The masthead and sidelights of the *Barnstable County* twinkled far astern.

Glazer came out. "When's sunrise, Stan? You know?" Lenson asked him.

"Oh-five-twenty-seven local. Another ten or twelve minutes."

"Less than that. Looks to me like the upper limb's about there."

"Well, we're moving east. I didn't allow for that. That would make it earlier—earlier? Yeah."

"Here she comes," said Lenson.

They stood on the wing together and watched the sun rise. It began with a more brilliant glow at one point of a line of sea that up to then had grown uniformly lighter. The glow shimmered, intensified, and then, suddenly, an ovaled blob of molten gold winked on like an ignited flare.

The waves marched under it. Too small to be the sun, the luminous oval jiggled and shimmered, suspended in the air for a long moment, and then drained downward into the sea.

The sun came into view. It was a flat gold edge, bigger than it should be, but not as bright as it would be later in the day. Now it was the shining rim of an unmilled coin, and he could follow its creep upward with unprotected eyes. You never actually saw the sun rise ashore, he thought. There were too many hills, trees, buildings in the way; it was already flaming steady when you caught it for the first time. A seaman, though, could see the birth of a new sun each day. He could see it move, minute by minute, almost second by second; watch its slow ticking upward, the powerful lunge of the chariot into the sky. Already, in the two or three minutes they had watched, half the disc had freed itself of the sea.

"Think we'll see the green flash?" suggested Glazer, beside him. He sounded skeptical.

"Maybe."

"You believe in it?"

"Sure," said Lenson. "It's pretty clear today, aside from the clouds. Why not?"

"I think it's a put-on. Like the mail buoy."

"Go look in Bowditch. It's in there," said Dan, ending the discussion pretty effectively, he thought. He raised his binoculars. If the fabled flash, the concentration of green light as the rays passed just above the rim of sea, actually happened, he wanted to see it.

Through the binoculars the disc loomed huge, painfully bright, though as yet too filtered by passage through atmosphere to be dangerous. He could see sunspots and a few wisps of haze or cloud between him and the sphere. The disc was three-quarters up. The glasses increased its speed, made it race upward, looming like a detonation, a terrific fireball. He studied its lower edge. Each wave, miles away yet still distinct, etched itself plainly against the brilliance, tiny and perfect.

The sun's rounded belly emerged from the sea, shimmering and trembling, yet connected to it still by a glowing tail. The shining umbilical elongated, and then, decisively, snapped away from the horizon into a perfect disc. It was day.

"Nope," said Glazer, disappointed.

"You'll see it sometime. It's not as rare as they say."

"If I stay in that long."

"Yeah, well," said Lenson. He knew what Glazer meant. Being at sea—you loved that; action—that would be all right, if it happened. It was the bullshit that went before, the flaps and flails and paperwork and most of all Sundstrom, that got to you after awhile.

"NOW REVEILLE, REVEILLE," said the ship's announcing system a few minutes later, startling them both. Lenson glanced at his watch; 0600, on the dot. "ALL HANDS HEAVE OUT AND TRICE UP. SET MATERIAL CONDITION YOKE THROUGHOUT THE SHIP. SMOKING LAMP IS LIGHTED IN ALL BERTHING SPACES. NOW REVEILLE."

"Now for it," he muttered. Right on cue, the commodore's buzzer went off. At the same time, the flag radioman came up to him, holding out the message board. "Just a minute," he told him, picking up the phone. "Flag bridge, Lieutenant Lenson, sir."

"Good morning, Dan," said the voice, so familiar it pursued him even in his dreams. "What's going on up there? I haven't been called all night."

"No contacts, sir." He gave the commodore what he wanted; all the data; Sundstrom kept interrupting him, asking him to repeat things. He wanted to know about the weather, and the barometer, what the Soviet trawler had been doing all night, whether *Ault* was in station, whether the carrier was on the scope yet, and a dozen other things. Lenson told him.

"You're sure there's nothing else? Nothing about the situation up ahead?"

"Nothing in the traffic, sir." Beside him, the radioman tried to give him the message board again; he covered the phone with his hand. "What the hell do you want?"

"Got an immediate, sir."

"Well, wait a goddamn minute. I'm talking to the commodore."

"How did the night exercises go?" Sundstrom asked him. "What were the reports like from the ships?"

"Uh, they didn't make any, sir. Would you like me to go out on pri-CI, ask them—"

"No, no, forget it. It's too late now." He heard Sundstrom's exasperated sigh. "You've got to keep an audit trail on these things, Dan. To me, this is basic. If you don't check up on these guys, stay perched on their backs at all times, they just won't perform. That's what it's all about, in a nutshell."

"Yes sir," said Lenson.

"Well, keep me informed. I'll be up to the bridge in a little while."

"Yes sir," said Lenson again. The commodore hung up. He hung up too, and took the message board. "Now what the hell is this that's so important?"

"Immediate from Sixth Fleet," said the radioman.

Lenson flipped back the cover. The sunlight was pouring in through the bridge windows now, brushing a film of gold over every instrument, every surface. For this one moment every day the worn paint on the bulkheads glowed, metal glowed; the tired faces of Glazer, McQueen, the other men on watch took on form and brilliance, became deeper and more real. He rubbed his eyes, feeling weak and hungry, and began reading. There was a long list of addressees, then the text. Two or three paragraphs.

The Turkish fleet was at sea.

Reported sortie from the base at Izmir, observed by a British patrol plane out of Crete. Several destroyers, a couple of what looked like troop transports. Headed south. There were more details, but he barely registered them.

This was not routine.

It made no difference that he had been working all night on the oporder. It had been remote, a contingency plan. Guns, aircraft, marines wading ashore . . . they had existed only in his mind, as a mathematical exercise. There was so much at sea that was done just in case, done on the off-chance, that to know suddenly and for sure that something was going to happen gave him a strange feeling. It wasn't power. He had no power. Even Sundstrom, "Comphibron SIX Actual," was only an instrument, like the ships around them, something to be moved about a vast blue chessboard for some distant, unclear, and to them almost irrelevant end. It was different . . . like going into combat for the first time.

And what had Byrne said about a battle problem this morning? His mind was going fuzzy . . . he initialed the SDO box on the message, told the radioman to get the board below to the commodore immediately without really thinking about it. It was automatic, like the slewing around of a gun mount under remote guidance. He was not really there.

He was in Cyprus, waiting for the Turks.

He was an Anatolian soldier, sick with his first experience of the open sea, clinging to the rail and watching the coast of Asia fade into blue distance.

He was a section of once-peaceful city, jumping under the impact of shells.

He was holding Susan, in the moment of surrender and forgetfulness of self, the moment of release. . . .

"What's the matter, Dan?" said Glazer, looking up from the scope. "You look kind of pale."

"It's for real," said Lenson, and looked around the bridge. It looked so peaceful in the sunlight; the way it had always looked, for weeks and months and years of steaming through the Med, the Atlantic, the Caribbean. But now it was different, all of it.

"What?"

"That message." He swallowed, and ran his hand over sun-gilded steel. "I think this time, we're going to be playing for keeps."

13

U.S.S. *Spiegel Grove*

"YOUR TARGET—SPLASH, TO PORT OF THE wake."

"Left, left left—*on*!"

"Range, four hundred and opening."

Bravo Company was firing for practice from the fantail. Cutford's face, dark and closed-off under the lip of a steel helmet, hunched itself into the sight of the mortar. Sweat gleamed and trickled down the back of his neck. "Left more," he barked, then "Pull two bags—two—ready—"

Behind him the team jerked into sudden furious activity behind the sky-slanted barrel. Hernandez spun the lid from a green plastic tube and slid out a shell. His fingers ripped at the foot-long cylinder. He threw the detached packets to the deck, away from the muzzle, and thrusted the readied round at Givens. Givens hefted it to the sunlight, checking the powder and fuze, hooked his finger in the pin and yanked it free; pulled free the retaining clamp; balanced the round poised, his eyes on the main gunner. "Half-load," he shouted, as loud as he could. Cutford jerked away from the eyepiece and pulled off the sight, cradled it to his chest.

"Fire."

Will opened his hand. The round left his glove and began to slide, scraping down into the tube like fingernails down a wall, and he ducked his face for the baseplate, thinking hunchback, clapping his hands over his ears under his helmet.

Ploong. Part cork pulled from a bottle, part the toll of a gigantic bell, the muzzle blast banged his helmet awry and slapped his face. He bobbed up, grabbing the next round, and then froze. The others had their heads back, eyes high to the sky over the helo deck, watching as, far and small, the finned dot halted. They said in mortar school that you could only see that from two places: where you launched, or (God help you) where the nine-and-a-half-pound 81 mm high-explosive projectile was about to land.

They gazed upward through a long hot ear-ringing instant. Far below the suspended projectile the sea gleamed and heaved in silvery silence, bright with sun under briefly parting cumulae. Half a thousand yards out from the old ship a gray splash of smoke and water was dying back into it, the spotting round second squad had just fired, and which they were using now as target for live-fire drill. The whirling dot hung suspended, a black star, and they watched for the whole aching instant that it took to decide for sea or sky.

It decided, and began to fall. They lost it, but a moment later it reappeared in an abrupt vertical plume of dirty foam and smoke, well short in range of the first. The detonation, sea-muffled, tickled their ringing eardrums.

"Ready again?" Sergeant Silkworth said, squatting down beside Cutford, who had removed a hand from the sight to wipe sweat from his cheek. It was hot and still on the open deck. The wind had dropped early that morning and now the intense, almost African heat was wringing sweat from them under the heavy utility jackets. "That last was a little short."

"Fucken tub was pitching," grunted Cutford, screwing his eye once more into the sight. "Crazy fucken drill, shootin' into the water . . . ready! Right, right, down down down *fire!*"

The *blanngg* this time was louder, smacking him on the

head like an angry teacher. He lifted his head to see the
projectile dwelling high, too high. Like the black angel, he
thought, the one they said came at the moment of death;
and this angel, too, hesitated, looking down for the man
whose name she carried, and then winked off as it gathered
speed.

It was so simple, he thought, as he did each time they
fired the mortar. Beautiful in its simplicity. The mortar
was nothing but a steel tube, closed at the bottom. There
was not a moving part in it, nothing to foul or jam. You
dropped in the shell, gravity took it down to impact on the
fixed pin, and the bags of powder carried on the round
itself fired and propelled it up, out, in a long curve toward
what you never thought of as men but only as a target. He
was remembering the parabolas in the physics book when
the plume leapt upward, far beyond the others, out on the
rolling smooth horizon; and his helmet bonged as Cutford's gloved fist came off it. "Oreo, you fucken lunatic!
What the fuck you dreamin' about? That fucken shell—
neither of you shitheads touched the charge!"

"You didn't say to, Cutford!"

"No order, Private, then it's the same setting as before,"
Silkworth shouted, equally loud, into his opposite ear.
Givens felt suddenly excited, sexually aroused. The shouting noncoms, Washman's scared acned face, the firing-
range stink of burnt propellant, all woke him into a sudden
sense that he was here, he was alive, all this was real. Then
Silkworth cuffed his helmet and he grabbed for the next
round out of the pile of opened tubings, snarling, twisted
off two of the waxed cotton bags himself, not waiting for
the ammo handler, and poised it trembling above the
mouth of the mortar. Along the deck the lieutenant yelled,
"Get those rounds out there, Silkworth!" and Cutford laid
his cheek to the sight and Harner twisted the elevation
knob and Givens heard the command and shoved the
round down, hit the gritty hot steel of the deck; the air
banged. "Forget watching it, dickhead!" screamed Silkworth in his ear. "That's the gunner's job. Do yours and

we'll get hits." Hernandez thrust another round into his hands, smooth metal, the yellow-striped olive drab of live explosive, a ten-pound egg finned like a fat arrow. A machine gun stuttered from behind him, farther along the deck, rattling cases out from the smoking receiver as the riflemen took their turns at familiarization firing.

"Right . . . down . . . fire!"

Blangg.

"Fire!"

The mortar tolled again. As each round went out, the baseplate, thirty pounds of cast iron, leaped up an inch from its cushion of sandbags.

Another stutter from the 7.62 sewed sound into the hot air of the afterdeck. "Rounds complete," bawled Silkworth in the lieutenant's direction. "Permission to fire small arms, sir?"

"Go ahead, Sergeant. One magazine apiece. Get your men aft of the safety line before you issue ammo."

"Aye, sir."

The riflemen unslung their weapons, their faces lighting, and ducked under the line roped across the deck to join the squad that was already aiming with care and futility at a fifty-five-gallon drum bobbing back in the slow wake of the ship. Will looked across at Cutford. The corporal was drawing his pistol, the only hand weapon the mortarmen carried. He drew his, too and accepted a half-full box of ball from the armorer, who was hovering behind the firing line with his Mickey Mouse ears bulky atop a shaven head. Givens' fingers trembled as he jammed rounds between the sharp lips of the magazine, and then he stepped to the deckedge, let the slide bang forward, and began to squeeze off slugs. After the mortar the pistol made a puny crack, like a child whacking a cheap drum. The riflemen fired, spewing tinkling brass out across the deck, where it rolled slowly with the ship, drifting up against the footknockers. Cutford fired rapidly, the automatic kicking up into the sky at each shot, his eyes squeezed so tight Givens wondered how he could see. The machine gunners cried out to each other, cursing at a jam, and flipped up feed mechanisms, slapped in a new belt. A faulty cartridge glittered end over end to disappear into the sea. Blue powder haze drifted over the churning wake, red arches of tracer burning holes into it. The armorer, eyes on the lieutenant, furtively passed out more ammunition as the clamor slackened and men glanced back, their rifles smoking empty.

"CEASE FIRE AFT," came over the deck loudspeakers. "CEASE FIRE AFT. ALL MARINE CORPS PERSONNEL LAY FORWARD TO THE CRANE AREA."

"Get back, men, back," shouted the lieutenant.

"Fucken butterbars," Cutford said, out loud.

Forward on the ship, two decks above them, Givens saw the squids lean forward on their metal bucket seats. The twin slim barrels of the ship's guns pivoted suddenly toward him, serpent-swift, the ringing of an electric bell accompanied by a prolonged clanking of mechanism. A sailor silhouetted himself against a cloud, lifting a pointed round, slamming it down into a hopper.

"Get back, you stupid scumbags," the Top shouted.

The big gun fired, incredibly loud, first one barrel, then the other, and then the first again in a continuous blast of sound and orange fire. Brown smoke blotted out the whole port side and blew down on them, cordite smell and fluttering bits of paper filler like holiday confetti. The gun clanked and banged and fired, BLAM . . . BLAM . . . BLAM . . . BLAM. The noise slammed at his ears, sucked air from his lungs, and far aft the sea around the untouched drum erupted in black smoke and boiling spray.

"Shit," shouted Washman, beside him, his narrow, red-splotched face intense. "Shoot that fucker! That's the kind of gun the Corps ought to have."

"You want to hump it ashore, Washout?"

"They better save some of that shit. We might need it."

"This tub is packed with the stuff. And them destroyers carry more. Bigger, too—five-inch."

Still enthusiastic, they carried their hot weapons back belowdecks when the firing was over. "We ought to fire this sucker more often," Washman said, rolling the baseplate to a halt against the bulkhead like a mechanic with a spare tire. "Even at sea—there's something gets you about firing a mortar. A lot more than a rifle. But an eighty-one—"

"Quit playing with that, Washout. It's a weapon, not a toy."

"Yeah, I know. Will—" he paused, the elation ebbing from his face, replaced by a worried frown that Givens, remembering Palermo, thought he had seen before, at Lucy's—"You think—well, you hear what the guys been saying. You think we might have to—you think we might go ashore?"

"Heck, I don't know, Washout. Captain don't keep me abreast of things like he should."

"Yeah, he should tell us more, keep us up-to-date," Washman agreed eagerly, missing the sarcasm. "But, geez—what about it? You think we'll go in on, what did Cutford say, Cyprus?"

"We might. Maybe that's why they held the shoot, get us up to speed a little." Givens broke the firing pin free and set to work cleaning it. This time there was reason to it, dirt and soot stained the rag as he scrubbed. Just six rounds, but the bore punch came out black, and he turned the rag and ran it through twice more before he was satisfied and tipped oil onto the cloth and wiped it down.

"You think they'd shoot at us?" Washman asked him. "Where the hell is Cyprus, anyway? What do they talk there?"

"It's an island," said Givens. "Out in the middle of the Med. Paul went there. They speak Greek."

"Greek, huh? Paul—Paul who?"

"Saint Paul."

"You heard," said Sergeant Silkworth, stopping by the card table, "about the Greek boy?"

"What Greek boy, Sarge?" said Washman, his mouth open, swabbing away at his baseplate.

"The one who left home. He didn't like the way he was being reared."

"Oh yeah. Pretty good, Sarge," said Washman.

"But he come back later."

"Why's that?"

"He couldn't leave his brothers behind. Okay, listen up. You troopers got half an hour to get squared away and get that gear stowed. Then we got school call."

"School call, Sergeant?" Givens asked him.

"Yeah. Whole company's going to be there."

"What on, Sergeant?"

"You'll know when I do," said Silkworth, and went on, stopping to talk to one of the second-platoon sergeants out by the ladderwell. They talked in low tones, but the two privates caught one word clear. It was "contingency."

"What's that mean, Will?"

"I don't know, Washout. Maybe we're going to get ashore this float after all."

The worried look returned to Washman's face, and he bent it to the baseplate and scrubbed away, saying nothing more.

The school call turned out to be that most familiar thing, beside boredom, and waiting, in life as they had come to know it aboard ship, on this long and aimless float: an anticlimax. The men had not known what to expect, but they had expected something. Some hot scoop from the exec; a rumor from the Top; anything that might give them some idea of what was happening out there, somewhere beyond the rolling horizon, even in what direction it lay they did not know. When the assistant company commander strolled in and they bolted upright into attention, they thought this was it.

Instead, they got a lecture.

"First thing we gathered you here to talk about," the senior lieutenant began, after they had settled again to the hard deck, padding it with rolled shirts or lifejackets from a rack or even just their hands, "was a couple of things the ship's captain has been passing on to us. We're their guests here, you know, and when we're aboard here he acts as our CO.

"So it pays us to keep them happy.

"The first thing is cleanliness. Not personal cleanliness—I know you all are doing the best you can considering the shortage of fresh water—but cleanliness of the ship. This is our home, and we've got to keep it clean. There've been too many butts found around, in the passageways, in the urinals, even up on the signal bridge. The Navy says they don't throw butts on the deck, it must be the marines."

The troops groaned. He said quickly, "Maybe it is, maybe it isn't. But I want you all to know that cleanliness has got to be a habit, a way of life, here aboard the *Spiegel Grove.* That begins in the troop spaces, and goes wherever you go in the ship. . . ."

The lieutenant droned on, and the men listened, lolling around the deck, most of them somewhere else inside their heads. The older troops had heard it all on floats before, knew that no matter how often they policed up, every piece of crap the squids found would be blamed on them. To the sailors the embarked marines were cargo, not unlike carrying a herd of cattle battened down in their pens below deck, and the marines returned their contempt with interest. They insulted each other and stole from each other, fought when they were ashore, and only the officers, who had to eat in the wardroom, repeated the fiction that they were all in the same service. The marines knew they were not in the Navy. Bunch of damned pussies in candy-assed sailor suits. Behind their hands the corporals yawned, winking sarcastically at one another.

". . . That said, I'm going to turn you over to the Top for the afternoon lecture. Sergeant Bayerholt."

"Small-unit tactics," bawled the Top, and the men relaxed again. Book drill. This they had all, even the boots, heard dozens of times before through long dozing afternoons. They could have predicted each of the sergeant's sentences as he talked in a steady hoarse shout, going through it all, line by line, as if he had memorized it somewhere back in the years and it had never changed a syllable. Fire-team formations, skirmishing lines, hand signals and how to pass them along. Digging entrenchments. Camouflage. Movements, contact, conduct of battle, consolidation and reorganization. Givens, his head tilted back against a reel of hose, stared up at the maze of pipes and sprinklers and lights that lined the overhead like stenciled filigree.

He was thinking about his guitar.

The skill was coming back. His fingers remembered it like the scars in his dark-lined palms remembered the timber hooks. He had never thought much about music before. It was the books that had fascinated him with their abstruseness, their logic, the hints they held of a wider, fuller life. But now that had changed. It was not that he no longer cared about engineering. He did, he wanted to be an educated man. But music was different. He couldn't tell what fascinated him about it, but there it was.

His fingers moved against the rough fabric of his blouse, strumming out an inaudible chord, and he blinked sightlessly at the overhead.

". . . And last, remember your gas mask. Take care of it like you take care of your piece. You men carry rubbers? Think of your mask that way. If you need it, you'll need it quick, and you won't be able to borrow your buddy's, 'cause he'll be using his."

They laughed dutifully, then quieted as Bayerholt turned the lecture back to the officer. His first words made them sit up.

"As you may have heard," said the lieutenant, "there's been some trouble recently in Cyprus."

Ha, Will thought. The scuttlebutt was right.

"I won't go into the politics. It's pretty confused, like

it is in most countries around the Med. There've been outbreaks of violence for a lot of years.

"Normally, the U.S. tries not to get involved. We deal with it by diplomacy, try to influence the winners and keep them off whoever lost. But two factors complicate the situation here.

"The first thing is, with the Soviet Fleet as strong in the Eastern Med now as ours, it's even more important that we, with our allies, keep things calm. The Russians like nothing more than trouble. Then they have an excuse to step in, either directly or, more likely, by means of the internal political organizations they maintain in all the littoral countries. Terrorism and destabilization is in their interest, and against ours.

"The second problem is that there are something like two thousand dependents and civilians there. Both Americans and British. There's a big tourist trade, and commercial interests, as well as the diplomatic personnel. In case of unrest, we become responsible for guaranteeing that those people are in a safe location, or for getting them out safely if the local authorities lose control or turn against us.

"There's not a lot more to say at this point." The lieutenant looked around at them. "Reports coming out are confused, as I said. Things like this happen all the time in the Med, that's why we maintain a presence here. Most of the time they straighten themselves out and we aren't needed. We don't want to show force unless the time comes—that's just as bad as no force at all—and that's why we cleared out of Italy and are well out to sea. We want to stand by, stay at the ready. There are no plans to do anything for now; but if those people ashore need help they'll need it fast, and that means us.

"That's all. Take charge and dismiss the men, Sergeant."

"Comp'ny. Ten-SHUT! Dismissed."

As they crowded out Givens saw Cutford for the first time. The black corporal, just ahead of him, looked pensive. For a moment he was tempted to catch up with him, say something, but then he remembered the freezer; his terror at being locked up, abandoned. What do I have to say to him? he thought. Nothing. And him to me? He'd just tell me to shut up. He'd just call me Oreo.

Oreo.

He did not care, did not think, about faraway conflicts. His conflict was here, every day.

He hungered for the touch of strings, and went below.

14
Nicosia, Cyprus

She struggled in the grip of the sea. Above her glimmered light, but so faint and far she knew she would never reach it. Not burdened as she was. But still she grasped Nan tighter, and with her free hand clawed upward.

The sea, crushing, invading . . . she tried to cry out. But it poured into her open mouth, choking her scream, strangling them both. . . .

Susan woke. Her free arm was tangled in the blanket someone had thrown over her in the night. A dream. But the pain was real; she was sore as she came up from sleep. The marble floor had impressed itself into her bones. Then she realized that it was not discomfort that had awakened her, nor the dream. It was a hand on her shoulder, and she opened her eyes.

"I'm sorry, it's not much," muttered the young woman apologetically, holding out the tray as she bent over her. "We're not equipped for so many people. There're blankets, water, but not much in the way of supplies."

"Thank you, this will be fine, Miss Freed," she said, looking from cookies and toast to the official's tired smile. She had probably been up all night, checking in refugees. Susan wasn't hungry, but thinking of Nan she took a few of the wafers. "It was good of you to think of breakfast."

"We'll have something hot soon, tea or coffee. How's your little girl?"

She glanced at her daughter. Nan lay curled into her mother's coat, face shadowed against the morning light by a sleeve. "She's still resting. She looks better, I think . . . maybe the fever will break today."

"Do you think she'll want to eat? We have a limited amount of cereal back in the staff kitchen. Bring her back when she wakes up and we'll fix that and some powdered milk."

"Thanks very much, we will," said Susan. She looked after the woman as she picked her way between the blankets and luggage and the people who dozed or chatted in low voices, holding her tray awkwardly aloft. It had been nice of her. But what she really wanted was to go back to the hotel, poach herself under scalding water, then crawl onto a mattress for about twelve hours.

Unfortunately, Susan, that doesn't seem to be possible just yet, she thought. But maybe tonight it will be. Maybe it was a mistake, minor rioting . . . perhaps the local police would have it straightened out.

She sat up carefully to avoid disturbing Nan. Rubbing her eyes, she saw that the refugee group had grown during the night. The stone floor was covered with blankets and clothing, leaving not a square inch more of space, and those who had come late sat against the walls, watching those who slept with thinly concealed envy.

"Coffee!" yelped someone, and she saw that near the counter one of the marines was easing down a pot. Steam rose from it as he broke open a roll of paper cups. Susan gave Nan a last glance—she was still, breathing in the shallow rhythm of sleep—and got up to join the line that formed. People stood silent, cups in their hands, waiting. An old lady smiled at her. "Good morning," she said.

"Oh . . . good morning, Mrs. Stanweis."

And "Good morning," someone else said, and then, standing there, the smell of coffee getting stronger as the line shuffled forward, they began chatting. It made the whole morning different; all at once it was almost like Monday at the office, as if they bumped into one another in the American Embassy in Nicosia, Cyprus, every day.

"Did you get any sleep?"

"Some. That floor's pretty hard."

"Are they still shooting?" asked a man.

"I heard some a little while ago . . . the marines won't let us go out. They locked the gates."

"Who is it? What have you heard?" Dr. Stanweis asked the guard, who was standing by the coffeemaker, arms behind his back.

"Uh, I'm not sure, sir. But things are pretty tense out there. There were crowds in the streets when I came in from watch, a little while ago."

"Cookies and toast! You'd think they'd have more than that in an embassy . . . don't you have any cream to go with this, Sergeant?"

"I'll see what I can do, sir."

Susan half-listened to the chatter, saying little. Some of the people, she saw, were frightened; others cool. Mrs. Stanweis approached her as she stepped away, balancing two cups, one of them, Nan's, syrupy with sugar. She supposed the caffeine would be all right, considering the circumstances.

"Mrs. Lendman, how nice you look this morning. I don't see how you do it. How are you? How is your little girl?"

The old woman was bright-faced despite the hour, despite the circumstances. Ferdy, cradled in her arms, looked sullen, and snarled when Susan tried to pet him. She jerked her hand back. "It's Lenson, Mrs. Stanweis. Susan Lenson. She's sleeping, thank you."

"Did the aspirin help?"

"Yes, thank you! I think they're helping her fever."

"I'm just glad I had a few in my bag. Leon always says there's nothing better. And he's been practicing for forty years. The young doctors, they all say there's no one left like him in all of southern New Jersey—"

When she got back to their place Nan was awake, sitting

up and looking around. She looked hot and confused, and coughed as her mother set the cup beside her.

"Mommy, where are we? I had such *funny* dreams—"

"I know, Bunny. Everybody has those when they're sick. Don't wipe your nose with your sleeve, use this tissue. Look, cookies for breakfast! And you can drink coffee this morning, just like Daddy does."

"Don't *like* coffee."

"There's sugar in it, baby, try it. And this nice lady is Mrs. Stanweis; she gave us the aspirin for you last night."

"Hullo," Nan said unwillingly.

"Hello, Nancy. Do you remember Ferdy Dog? Ferdy, this is Nancy, she's a pretty little girl, say hello."

The dog growled. Nan glanced at her mother, then buried her face in her T-shirt top. "She's shy around animals," Susan was saying, embarrassed, when a jovial voice caught their attention.

"Good morning, all! I'm Fred Persinger, the American ambassador here. If you'll give me your attention for a few minutes—"

The ambassador was not a short man, but his shape gave one that impression; he was almost round, with a round head, a round chin. He was wearing blue slacks and a white golf shirt, so casual looking that Susan felt concerned. Did he understand how serious this could be? He smiled as he stood by the desk, waiting for the murmur to quiet, but his eyes gave the impression that he had been required to smile so long at so many people that a smile was all there was left; that he would crack a joke and slap a back on the way over the brink. He raised a hand, smiling, and then one of the marines stood up behind him, looking grim, and the crowd quieted.

"I know this isn't a political rally back in Philadelphia, but it sure looks like one!" He paused for his laugh, and drew a few nervous chuckles.

"Well, folks, I hate to say welcome, considering the circumstances, but welcome. There does seem to be some confusion out there about who owns this island, but right here you'll be safe. So we'll just sit tight for a day or so, till they sort it out, and then we'll head for the airport and all go on about our business." He pronounced it "bid-ness." "As you can see, we're not known for our hotel accommodations—but that just makes us try harder! If there's anything we can do for your comfort, please ask Ms. Freed—she's my assistant, this attractive young lady—or one of my aides."

"Mr. Persinger?" Mrs. Stanweis fluttered her hand.

"Yes, ma'am," said the ambassador, bending forward at the waist.

"Will we be able to send telegrams? I'd like my family to know where I am."

"You sure can. We have facilities for that, we're in touch with Washington right now. I'm sure Ms. Freed can take you down there in the basement and get a little message out. Yes. In back—?"

It was a short man with a grizzled brush-cut. "Ambassador, Joe Bunch, here. I'm a veteran, Korea. If that crowd turns ugly—can we hold them off? I noticed our gate guards aren't armed."

"Glad you asked that, sir. No, this building isn't designed to be defended. Few U.S. missions are. We feel since both sides are our friends, we won't need to worry about defense. We can close ourselves off from the street, we have an iron gate for that, and there are always the local police in case of trouble. No sir, I think that'll be sufficient."

"Are you sure? The embassy in—"

"You have a point there, Joe, and I'm going to look into it this very morning, that's a promise," said Persinger smoothly, and went on. Susan had to admire the way he shunted the man aside, leaving him still standing but with nothing left to say. "Any other questions? No? Then, thank you, and I'll be about my business."

His pep talk over, the ambassador disappeared back into his offices. But his attempt to calm them had made her nervous again. When Nan had finished her hot drink she drifted up past the desk, wanting to see these gates for herself. At night, coming in, she hadn't noticed them.

An iron gate? she thought, when she stood behind it, looking out past the back of a silent guard. They were light metal, filigreed like a New Orleans balcony; compared to the stone walls into which they were set they seemed flimsy. The marines who stood by them, on the other hand, looked as rough and heavy as the walls, and for that she was glad.

A current of cool air came through the bars. She glanced back into the hallway. Smoke-hazed, filled with people, it seemed cramped, almost fetid, although she knew it was not; no one had been there more than a day. But it was a bit close, and the air from outside was fresh, smelling of rain. She moved the last few feet to the gate. One of the guards glanced back at her; he grinned. "Getting tired of indoors?"

"Yeah, a little." She leaned her head against iron, against the smoothness of many coats of black enamel. The metal was thin, but she was grateful for whatever protection it offered.

She looked into a deserted street. The roadway glistened with rain, and there was still mist in the air. The unaccustomed cold made her shiver. Above the buildings she could see the gray underbellies of clouds, seeming to scrape the tops of the hotels. A storm, yes, the weather was turning mean; the orchards would get their rain, and more wind than they wanted. How wet it is, she thought. I thought it was supposed to be dry here.

She was about to turn back to Nan when one of the guards straightened and stepped up to the gate, looking out.

"What is it, Corporal?"

"People coming, Sergeant."

"Locals?"

"No, don't think so—"

They were Americans, ten or a dozen of them; she couldn't see whether they had driven up or walked; they were just there suddenly. The younger marine—the corporal—talked to them through the gate for a few minutes. The discussion became heated, with ID cards and drivers' licenses thrust through the openwork. When he finally drew back the bolt, the gate opened inward to a press of bodies. He had time for only a brief glimpse at IDs. One of them shouldered past Susan, a dark man, dropping his passport back into a sport coat; their eyes met briefly, then he was past, inside. The next face Susan saw was Moira's, and her friend saw her at the same time. They met with a tight hug, and she could feel Moira's dampness, her shivering.

"Betts! I'm so glad you made it here. Is Nan with you?"

"You bet she is." Susan held her roommate at arm's length, studying the bruise that marred the Ox's perfect complexion. "I figured you'd stay at the digs, out of the way! What happened to your face?"

"It's turned bad out there," said the archaeologist, looking back into the crowd that pressed still against the gate; the guards had regained control, were letting them through one by one now. "Michael! I'll be inside, with Susan here.—Yeah, even in the hills. They won't talk to us anymore, and the man who owned the land ordered us off. I don't know why . . . on the way back, some people tried to stop our car, and there was a fight. Anyway, the airport's closed, so we decided it would be best to come here."

"I'm glad you did. But I hope you brought something to eat."

"Uh-oh." Moira winced. "Food problems?"

"Looks like there might be. There are a lot of people here."

"Yeah, I see that. Well, we didn't bring much to eat, but does wine count?"

Susan had to laugh. "It's certainly a plus."

Cook, Moira's grad student, had a small radio. They lay around on Susan's blanket and listened to it through the morning. They could hear Turkish being spoken, but none of them knew it, so they stayed with the Greek stations, and later found a British Forces broadcast in English. Both sources agreed that tension was building hourly along the line of demarcation. The British said that a move forward was imminent. The Greek-speaking stations agreed, but added, in strident accents, that if an advance beyond the cease-fire line began, the army and people would resist, and that Athens, the mother country, would not stand back this time.

"I don't get it," said Susan. "Why would the Turks attack? They already have half the island, and only about a third of the Cypriotes are Turkish."

"It's all for show," said Moira. "Why do men make wars, anyway? To prove they have balls."

"I think it's a little more serious than that," said Michael, opening his mouth in Susan's presence for almost the first time. He had a gentle smile, long, sun-bleached hair that fell over his forehead and sprang up in a cowlick, and she liked him immediately. "Probably the new Turkish leadership. They want something to unify the country, and they're generals—war is a natural. Don't forget, this island's only fifty miles from Asia. The Turks owned it for a long time. It goes back and forth. Our bad luck to be here when it's happening again."

"Not everybody seems to take it as fatalistically as you do," said Susan. She nodded at the radio, where a speaker was holding forth on blood, fire, and resistance to the last bullet.

"It's their home," said Moira, and changed the subject, looking at Nan, who was sitting up, looking sleepy. "And how's my niece doing? Feeling better this morning, huh?"

"Hi, Moy-ra!" Nancy shrieked. "Mikey! Where's your bottle?"

"We've got to empty one first," grinned Michael, patting his clinking knapsack.

* * *

There was very little for lunch. Canned soup, a few more cookies, and that seemed to be the end of the embassy's supply. She took Nan back to the kitchen for the promised cereal, but it was gone. Someone else's child, there were three or four others among the families camped in the crowded hall.

The afternoon wore on much like the morning. They hung above the radio, their sole source of news, until Nancy, growing costive, demanded they turn it off. Susan was glad enough to comply. After a while her daughter napped, and Michael brought out a pack of cards. They played whist and passed one of his bottles of *rodakino* around through the afternoon and on into dusk. It was too sweet, and she only sipped at it. The corridor darkened gradually, and around the four of them as they played the other people prepared for sleep. Ms. Freed came out to snap on the lights, but nothing happened. The power had gone off sometime during the afternoon.

It was a little after that, as if the gradual withdrawal of day was a cue, that the far-off shooting began again. Susan suspended a hand rich with royalty—it was almost too dark to distinguish jack from queen—as they turned to the courtyard windows to listen. More shots, drifting, it seemed, above the low roofs and into the open windows on the wind; and then, closer, the sound of shouting.

"A real *Kristallnacht*," said Moira softly. She shuddered.

"Riots?"

"Not that harmless." The archaeologist was biting her lip, looking at the falling darkness outside the windows. "It's going to be bad. I can't say Moslems are my favorite people, but I wouldn't want to be one tonight in Nicosia."

"They'll kill them?"

"At least beat them, burn their houses and shops. There aren't many here anymore. Most of them went to live on the eastern side of the island. But there were a few that stayed. They had homes here, too."

They listened somberly, each imagining him or herself at the mercy of a crowd like that.

They tried to go back to cards, but Susan could not concentrate. She found herself still listening, and from time to time she heard the sounds of guns again. And then shouts.

"Jeez, they're getting closer, aren't they?" said Moira.

"Maybe it's the wind," said Michael, but as they suspended play again to listen Susan felt sweat trickle along her forehead. They were closer, all right. Maybe on the next street over—

Something flickered at the corner of a window.

"I can't take this." Michael jumped up, upsetting the bottle; sticky wine gushed over the blanket. "Oh, hell. Moira, can you get this? I've got to see what's going on. I'm going up to the gate."

"Be careful, Mike."

"Sure."

He left. Moira mopped at the stain with a tissue, gave up, and tipped the bottle back for the last swallow. "Jeez," she said again. "You don't think they'd bother us, do you, Betts? These people don't have anything against Americans that I know of."

"You're the expert here, not me," said Susan; but she was thinking, *and what about the people who tried to stop you on the road, Moira? The ones who gave you that bruise?*

The shouting beat at their ears again, louder, the sound of a dangerous surf. Looking toward the courtyard windows, Susan felt the pasteboards tremble in her hands. Fear? Yes. She was afraid. It had been growing all afternoon, since she had seen the gates.

Perhaps the embassy, the shelter of the flag, was not inviolate.

The flicker was stronger now.

Michael returned. He pushed his hair back. "Everything's cool out front," he said. "A crowd went by there awhile back, but they didn't seem to notice the embassy. Or care. The shouting's coming from down the street."

"Man, that's good news. But what's with the fire?"

"It looks like part of the city's burning."

It was then, for the first time, that Susan was sure something bad was going to happen. She knew it all at once, deep inside, and reached out to shake Nan awake, pulling her daughter into her arms.

"Calm. Please stay calm," someone was shouting. "We have everything under control. No one has any reason to disturb us. Please, you're quite safe here." It was Persinger, the ambassador; his bald head shone in the light of a portable lantern at the counter. From outside the flames grew brighter, flickering through the windows and into the corridor.

Above his voice, above the whispering of the refugees, came another spatter of shots. Five of them, spaced out, almost like a signal. They were close, just outside, and around her she heard the muttering stop and then rise again, louder. In front of them, like a scene lit for the stage, the sweat-shining face of the ambassador gleamed in the firelight as his mouth smiled and talked on.

The two marines who had been off watch came running from the offices, carrying rifles. They slowed as they came abreast of Persinger, looking at him for direction, but he simply waved them on, toward the gate. As she hugged Nan, watching, Susan saw the ambassador's face change as he looked after them. The smile faded, flickered back up, and then left his face. Without it he looked blank and slightly surprised. He pulled his coat down and sucked in his belly. He rubbed his mouth, glancing back at the people who had filled his once-cool and peaceful post. Then he nodded slightly, the first thing she had seen him do that seemed to be done for himself, not for the observation and consumption of others.

He turned and went with short bouncy strides after the marines. Behind him she saw the dark man she'd noted earlier rise from a seat along the wall and follow him toward the gate.

Michael got up, too. "Where do you think you're going?" said Moira instantly.

"See if I can help."

"That's their job. They—"

"There's only a few guys to hold the fort. One more might make a difference. Stay here with them." He, too, moved into the flickering darkness, toward the shouting.

"Are they coming in here, Mommy?"

"No, Bunny. Don't worry, Mikey and the soldiers will stop them."

"Who is it out there? Bad men?"

She looked down at her daughter's frightened eyes, and smoothed with her hand the drops of moisture at the edges of her forehead. Bad? She hardly knew how to answer . . . she had never, reading the papers back home, really thought of attacking an American embassy as bad. It was only natural, the outcome of a policy that supported any oppressive regime, any dictator, so long as he claimed to oppose Communism. She had thought it a form of popular justice.

But could you feel the same way, when you were one of the frightened people inside?

And how did you explain the difference between war, and dissent, protest, justified revolt to a child? Good and bad . . . that was a child's distinction. In this night an enemy identified himself by the primeval differences, language, race, even appearance. "I don't know, Nan," she said at last. "I don't know who they are or what they want."

"Will they hurt us?"

"No, of course they wouldn't," Susan said; but she wished there was someone who could tell her that with all the conviction of an adult to a three-year-old.

Several minutes passed. Huddled in the near-dark, the refugees waited. Susan felt helpless. It enraged her. Give *me* a rifle, let *me* stand at the gate . . . then she thought of Nan. No, her place was with her daughter.

If only Dan was here . . .

The shouting came again, louder. She couldn't make out words. The flickering light of torches or street fires wavered redly against the courtyard windows. Huddled back in the corridor, behind a hundred other frightened civilians, she and Nan could only hear what happened. They couldn't see the gate, but they could hear the shouting that came again and again, louder, then the shattering of glass and a closer glow of fire, a stink of oil and flame.

The front window burst in, paving rocks skidding into the crowded women and children, glass opening in a glittering bloom like a lake under raindrops. Nan screamed, and Susan held her tight against her heart, shielding her child with her body. The hall flickered, paved with shadows, and it was like—the thought came to her from somewhere—a medieval play; all dark save for the flamelit foreground, the shouting, the silent or weeping spectators.

A moment later there came a burst of gunfire, so loud and close it seemed to come from within the embassy itself.

Please, not to us, she prayed blindly. At that moment a textbook image had come to her, the layers of charred ash and bone at Knossos, Troy, Mycenae. How many mothers had held their children like this as battle raged at citadel gates, moments before defeat and death.

God, no, not to us. Not to me and my child.

She was hugging Nan, as much to comfort herself as the child, when another stutter of shots came, not from outside, but past the counter. The refugees gasped. She caught Mrs. Stanweis' eye. The two old people sat close together, and the woman was hugging her dog, just as she was hugging Nan.

Another shot went off, a single one this time, and she heard many voices shouting. There was a sharp explosion, not loud, but cracking like a whip. A yielding, high-pitched screech succeeded it, like a truck grinding a motorcyclist into shreds of leather and flesh, and then the clang of metal on stone. It could only be the gates, torn free of the walls, ringing on the pavement outside.

Ms. Freed came running back, white-faced. "What is it?" "What's going on?" They reached up to stop her, to ask her questions.

"Don't—let me by! There's a man with a gun—he's shot a guard, and—" She turned in mid-run. "This way, and—Doctor, can you help the ambassador, *please?*"

"Oh, my God," said Moira.

It was Persinger. Michael was half-carrying him. His round head was rolled forward on his chest.

"What was he doing out there?"

"Probably making a speech," said Moira. Susan turned on her, ready to cry out, but then she saw that she was serious. Yes, she thought. The smiling man probably had done just that: tried to reason with a mob.

Behind Persinger and Cook a rifle came into view. It was being pointed by a small man dressed in nondescript dark trousers and stained short-sleeved shirt. His teeth were very bad. They stared at him as he threaded silently among them, his eyes darting restlessly here and there, but principally on the two who staggered ahead.

Behind them, like an actor emerging into limelight, someone else stepped into the firelit hall of the embassy. Susan saw him clearly. He was no more than twenty-five, in jeans and an open-collared white shirt under a sport coat. With a shock she recognized the man who had shoved by her at the gate. A rag of green cloth bound his arm. For a moment she thought he was wounded, but when he raised the short-barreled weapon he carried in that hand she realized that it was a marking, some kind of impromptu uniform. He was looking over his shoulder toward the gate, where the shouting went on. Turned, balanced, the weapon raised high, he looked heroic. She felt a thrill mix with the fear she felt not for herself, but for her child.

Nan, though—she glanced down—had stopped crying, and stared now with wide eyes, unblinking. It was the same rapt expression she wore when she watched television.

The man with the rifle gestured toward the gate, calling out. There was too much sound; she could not make it out . . . in answer six or seven more of them ran into the hall and stopped, looking at the people on the floor. Some of them carried strange-looking pistols, some the short rifles, and one brandished what looked like a grenade. For a moment the two groups seemed frozen, facing each other; both uncertain, perhaps both afraid.

The leader waved them forward, and the men moved in among them. They held their weapons ready, looking down at the people who crouched away. Neither side spoke. The refugees were silent. The intruders were silent too, their faces angry and frightened at the same time. From time to time they reached down to pull apart a bundle of clothes, perhaps searching for arms. Michael spat in Greek at one who picked up his knapsack. He looked surprised, but finally shrugged and put it down.

But their eyes, and Susan's, kept going back to the first man, the one who held the rifle and directed the others. He stood with his head thrown back, black hair tumbling over his ears. He was thin, imperious, fierce-looking. He alone of all of them seemed to know what to do. And then, for the first time, she saw his eyes straight on, and knew why. They were fixed and wide and black, and utterly determined. They made her think of John Brown.

More men stumbled in, making perhaps a dozen in all; the last three he waved back to the gate. The language came from deep in his chest, the very sound of it fierce and strange. She caught a few of the words: *"Irjah la wourd . . . Bara wala dakh'el."*

"Who are they?" she hissed to Moira.

"I don't know. That's not Greek. He's posting a guard," Moira whispered. "That's good—I think."

"What? Moira, *who are these people?*" she whispered, feeling the uncontrollable quiver in her throat.

"Terrorists."

"Tell me something I don't know! Where are they from? What do they *want?*"

"I'm not sure yet . . . Turkish Cypriotes, maybe leftists . . . but that didn't sound like Turkish, either. Anyway, what's the difference? They've got guns and we don't."

"*Skhot'!*" said one of the men threateningly, and they all understood that; be quiet.

She was quiet; she and Nan, and Michael and Moira, and all the refugees, were quiet, and watched and waited. Sooner or later, they would find out what he wanted, this fiery young man who directed the others as if they were peasants. And then they would know what had to be endured. Until then they did not know whether to fear little or much, whether what he planned was harmless to them, or might mean great harm.

She wondered, then, what had happened to the guards at the gate.

"Mommy?" Nan's face was pressed to her breast; she could feel the heat of her whisper.

"Go to sleep, Bunny."

"Will that man hurt us?"

"I don't know, Bunny."

"Will he stay here?"

"I don't know."

"Where's Daddy? I want Daddy."

"Daddy's not here, baby."

"But I *want* him." She began to cry, and Susan, frightened, tried to stop her. At last she muffled the child's face against her chest. When she released her Nan sobbed for breath, looking scared. "Mommy—you *hurted* me—"

"I'm sorry, Bunny, but you've *got* to keep quiet," she whispered urgently. "Please, *please* don't cry now. Go to sleep, darling love. Better just go to sleep."

At that moment there were shouts from the rear of the building. Suddenly two of the men emerged from the office area. They were pushing a pale American in a gray suit whom she had not seen before. An embassy ID swung at his pocket. He stumbled along with blood on his face and a shattered pair of glasses hanging off his ears.

"*Houweh i'jahreb yezhab la barra.*"

"Mau'to!"

By the tone it was an order. And they acted on it. They forced the official down to his knees. He made no resistance, as if he knew this would be his fate, as if he accepted it.

Susan stared, her mind empty, stripped to observation and horror. The gun came down smoothly, fitted against the pale forehead without haste or hesitation. Against flesh and bone it made a muffled bang, and liquid flew from the back of the head and pattered against the wall.

"Bismallahi rahmani rahim!" said the tall man. "Listen to me, you people. I want everyone to stay seated. Do not move! Do not attempt escape. This man"—he prodded the gray bundle at his feet with the muzzle of his weapon—"was attempting escape. Penalty was death. Penalty for disobeying of any my orders is death. Until I choose to tell you our plans for you, you will wait. There will be no moving and no talk."

Susan smoothed her hand over her daughter's hair. She had not thought to hide it from her. It had happened too quickly, too casually, for her to realize what it was until it was too late. Now she saw her terror. No, darling, she cried deep in her heart. Don't fear. I'm afraid, but let me fear for us both. Because if you do, daughter, it will last you and mark you your life long.

Nan closed her eyes. Susan smoothed their lids, so tiny, so delicate, with her lips. Did she understand? She felt the small heart thudding against her own, fast, so fast. . . .

The men stood around the walls, guns dangling. She watched them, head lowered, masking rage and fear with the same blankness she saw the other women wearing. One of them bent to a confiscated cigarette, and the flare of the match lit their faces for an instant. They were alert, hostile, foreign, and she could not tell what was in their minds. They waited. Across their features flickered the light of the distant flames, dancing in fierce liberation in the streets.

15

U.S.S. *Guam*

The sail is a living thing, struggling for freedom in the sunlight, in the hard smooth wind.

"Stand by to come about," he calls.

"Aye yi, Daddy!" The child, laughing, scrambles for the opposite side of the little daysailer. The woman flips free the sheet.

"Ready," she says.

"Helm's a-lee!" He swings the tiller and hauls in on the main. The boat begins to turn. The boom comes across, all three of them ducking. The jib cracks and shudders as they meet the wind, then tautens as the woman hauls in on the sheet.

"Nicely done, crew."

"Thanks, Captain Bligh," says the woman, laughing. She is dark as a Polynesian; she tans that way every summer, in one afternoon. The sun, dropping toward the hills, outlines her breast under thin cotton.

And he thinks then: This is all I want from life. To be here, with these two, to be with them and make them happy. He points the little boat at the sun and suddenly, for just a moment, feels his whole chest fill with joy. On impulse he leans down to her lips. They are warm and salty and open, and his free hand drops till it brushes the inside of her thighs.

"Not here," she murmurs. "Nan."

"Isn't this how she got started?"

"Maybe," she whispers. "I forget." In the bow, oblivious to her parents, the child dips her hand into the sea, watching awed as it sparkles through her grasp. The cutoff khakis her father wears have holes in them, and her mother's hand finds one of them. "Oh, I remember now. It was something in here. . . ."

A hard set of knuckles dug into his ribs, just above his belt, and he started upright in the chair. "What the hell!"

"Better keep your head up, Dan," said Commander Hogan mildly. "We'll start the briefing in a minute, soon as the commodore gets here."

"Uh, yes sir," said Lenson to the chief of staff. "Thanks," he muttered to Flasher, who sprawled beside him in the supporting-arms center, his shirt unbuttoned to mid-chest. Flasher nodded heavily. He looked tired, like the rest of the men who waited. Most were from the staff, but there was a sprinkling of marine officers, Colonel Haynes' men, and the commanding officers from the other ships of TF 61, who had arrived that morning by helicopter.

"Attention on deck!" shouted someone, and the officers and enlisted leaped to their feet.

Commodore Isaac I. Sundstrom paused in the doorway, his face closed and secret. He lingered for a moment, as if unconscious of those who waited for him, then nodded frostily to Haynes and to his captains, in the front row. Crossing the room, he took the center front seat, which had been left empty. His steward was right behind him with a gold-rimmed china coffee cup and saucer.

"Carry on, gentlemen," Sundstrom grunted. "Mr. Byrne, let's get this show on the road. I'm sure not everyone here has as much time to waste as you seem to."

"Yes sir," said Jack Byrne, getting up. His tone took no notice of the commodore's taunt. He looked drawn, eyes hollow behind the aviator glasses, but his uniform was fresh and starched, as if he had just taken it out of a drycleaner's bag ashore. Lenson wondered how he did it.

Byrne paused for a moment before an easel, prompting an impatient cough from Sundstrom, and then flipped back the cover to show the first page.

It was a map of Cyprus. A ripple of interest moved over the assembled men; even Flasher stopped yawning and craned forward to see.

"Good morning, Commodore, Colonel Haynes, gentlemen.

"As you know, Task Force 61, the Mediterranean Amphibious Ready Group, with MAU 32 embarked, has been ordered to proceed to the Eastern Med and hold itself in readiness for landing operations. This intelligence presentation, with an overall Secret classification, will brief you on the situation around the eastern littoral, and especially Cyprus. After it, Lieutenant (j.g.) Lenson will present an overview of the operation order he has prepared."

"Come on, Commander," Sundstrom broke in. "Cut the Pentagonese. Just tell us what's going on."

"Yes sir . . . As most of you know, political unrest has been longstanding between the majority of the Cypriote islanders, who are of Greek origin and language, and a sizable Turkish minority. At present, the island is partitioned between the two." He extended a pointer to trace a cease-fire line.

"Tensions have recently risen again. In general, the Greeks have behaved with restraint, but the new military government of Hassan Raschid needs a crusade to unite the country.

"Our position is delicate. As NATO partner of both countries, we've tried to keep out of the quarrel. This has made Allied forces, based in the British facilities in the Akrotiri Peninsula, particular targets of both Cypriote and Turkish protests."

"Tell us about Nicosia," said Sundstrom. "Damn it, I don't give a crap about this political stuff. Let's get to the point."

Lenson blinked, hauling himself upright in the chair again. He was having trouble keeping his eyes open. "Yes, sir," Byrne was saying. "Let me make one other point, though. The Turks have been reinforcing quietly up to now, but Sixth Fleet Intelligence feels that the sailing reported this morning from Izmir could constitute a major attack. There's no evidence yet that the Greeks know about it, but when they do Athens might also mobilize. That could lead to a sticky situation for us. TF 61 would be right in the middle."

No one said anything. After a moment, Byrne went on. "All right, our reason for being here: a possible rescue attempt."

Lenson rubbed his face, trying to concentrate. He'd planned for a relatively peaceful evacuation. Rescue? This was something new.

"When the rioting began, there were in the neighborhood of fifteen hundred American and British tourists, students, and retired personnel on the island. Most of them got out by air or headed for Akrotiri. However, because of the suddenness of the trouble, a sizable number were trapped in the diplomatic compound in Nicosia."

His pointer rapped the capital. "Until early this morning, State hoped to barricade the embassy and wait out the rioting. At about 0200 today, however, the U.S. Embassy in Nicosia was attacked and seized. We have word that the ambassador was killed."

"Holy smoke," said Flasher, beside him. Lenson, startled into alertness, glanced at Sundstrom. The commodore knew. His face did not move a muscle. After that initial murmur the room was quiet, intent on Byrne and on the news.

"After that message all comms with the embassy were lost. We have a report as of 1000, though, that an undetermined number of Americans, tourists and diplomatic personnel, are being held by the group that took the embassy."

"Wait a minute, Jack. Who are they? The attackers?" asked Hogan.

"We're not sure yet."

"No guesses?"

"Guesses, but no facts yet." Byrne nodded at the chart. "I don't need to tell you this changes things. The local army and police are occupied with their own problems. What this comes down to is that we may be the only force available to go in and get those people out. The administration probably feels—"

"Don't bother to speculate, Mr. Byrne." Sundstrom's voice was sharp. "There are some real pros on the Sixth Fleet staff to take care of that. I know that for a fact. Some of them are my personal friends."

"Yes sir." Byrne sighed almost inaudibly and flipped a page. "I might mention one other item from this morning's traffic. That's Lebanon. The month-old cease fire between the Maronites and the Shiites was broken last night with a four-hour bombardment of the Christian sectors of Beirut. The Shiite militia used T-54 tanks and Soviet-supplied multiple-rocket launchers. The Maronites immediately returned fire. Approximately a hundred civilians have been killed so far. Prospects for the truce appear—"

"Mr. Byrne. I'm sure it's regrettable, but what bearing does Beirut have on Cyprus?"

"Well, indirect, Commodore, but one might speculate—"

"I ordered you once to can your goddamned speculations! Facts, mister, that's all I want out of you!"

Byrne sighed again, and began briefing on the Cypriote militia. Lenson felt his eyelids drift downward. It was news, it was exciting, but after three sleepless days—or was it four?—he was out of it. His mouth was dry with fatigue, and sitting here like this, listening, he seemed to tack moment by moment between waking and dream. The boundary line was so fine it was only by digging his knees into the desk that he could be sure he was really awake.

"There's just one more point to bring up," said Byrne, turning the final page to show several ship silhouettes. "It might be important. It's this: There's not much difference between the Greek and Turkish ships and ours. We've supplied destroyers and electronic gear to both sides. If shooting starts, we're going to be right in the middle, without a clear means of identifying ourselves, and that could be hairy." The intel officer paused. "All right, that's the briefing. Any questions?"

The commodore lowered his head and sipped coffee, ignoring him.

"Yes—Captain Fourchetti?"

"How about the Soviets, Jack? We know they're interested—Snoopy's still with us. Where are they; what are they going to be doing while we're steaming around at the ready out here; and what will they do if we go in?"

"All good questions." Byrne addressed them at length, but Dan got just two things out of it; there were plenty of Russians around, and nobody knew what they had in mind. As the N-2 droned on, his eyelids sagged closed again.

He was thinking of her again. As she had been, not in Taormina, but the first time he'd entered her, in her father's borrowed MG. For perhaps a second, dreamlike, he relived it all. When they were done he'd looked across at her, seeing perspiration glowing like satin between her breasts, in the shadow of her thighs.

It's strange, he thought, sitting there in the midst of the other men. When I remember our making love I never think of what it feels like. I love the feel of her, but that's not what I think about when I re-create part of her with my own hands in the shower. Instead I recall the expression of her face, the words she says, the way she looks in the moonlight or the light of bedroom or hotel room, her body under dresses or sheets or in jeans. . . .

I need her, he thought. She's the one thing that keeps me sane in this crazy outfit. At times, looking up at her picture on this endless cruise, he caught himself almost praying to her. He wanted her so much . . . but at least she was safe. The airports would be closed in Greece; she would have to settle into a hotel there with the other wives, but she and Nan would be all right.

His eyes slid closed again. He remembered again the car, the way they had snuggled together; the way she had taken care of him, given him the pleasure, made him—

"Mr. Lenson," said Byrne again.

"Yes, Jack?"

"We're waiting."

He flinched guiltily. Byrne had finished his briefing, and it was his turn. All the men in SACC were looking at him; the commodore twisted round in his chair, looking annoyed.

"Sorry, sir," he said. And with a red face, holding his notes in front of his belt buckle to hide the evidence of his daydreaming, he walked to the front of the compartment to begin.

As usual, Sundstrom had plenty of changes to make. Dan had expected him to concentrate on the changes required by a raid, instead of a peaceful evacuation. But he had few questions on the technical aspects: communications, logistics, tactics. He seemed to be leaving those to Dan. What he didn't like were cosmetic things, such as the code name for the operation, "Urgent Lesson," even though it was the next one on the list of NATO names. "Makes us sound like slow students," he said, frowning. "Make it 'Urgent Lightning.'" And there were more. So many that, trudging back to his stateroom after the meeting was over, Lenson resigned himself to another night of battling sleep.

But at least this time there was a reason, a possibility they might be needed.

After a wordless lunch of cheese sandwiches, grits, and bug juice—he wasn't hungry, but food seemed to compensate a little for not sleeping—he went up to the bridge at 1230, just in time to catch the first Soviet overflight.

It was disreputable panic. He stood to the side of the pilothouse, listening to Sundstrom scream. The commodore was livid. The first notice he'd had of the swept-

winged Bear, flying low to the west of the formation, had
been a shout from one of the lookouts. He wanted the CIC
officer on the flag bridge, and when the ensign showed up,
already white-faced, and Captain Fourchetti with him,
looking glum, subjected them both to a twenty-minute
dressing down, complete with references to their fitness
reports. The staff officers, embarrassed, looked away, out
to sea. When it was over, the two officers gone below and
Sundstrom slumped exhausted in his leather chair, Dan
went up to Red Flasher and saluted. "Ready to relieve
you, sir."

"And goddamned ready to be relieved," muttered
Flasher. "He's been up here since the briefing; he even ate
here. Like a goddamned cat in heat. Much more of this
and I'm going overboard, swim ashore for a drink."

"Just a minute, I'll get my flippers."

When Flasher had gone below he glanced toward the
chair. The commodore was motionless. He checked the
chart. They had finally reached it: the ready station, where
COMSIXTHFLT had directed them to stand by and
await orders. The force was in a circular formation, slowly
steaming on a southerly course . . . he turned, instantly
alert, as Sundstrom muttered something.

"Excuse me, sir?"

"Nothing, Dan, nothing . . ." The commodore stirred
in his seat, glancing out to the far horizon where the
aircraft, its check complete, was tail to them, headed back
to Libya or Syria or Sevastopol. He was turning back to
the chart when Sundstrom sat up abruptly. Uh-oh, he
thought. It was going to be a long watch.

"Dan . . . did you see what they did to me? That ensign,
and that Italian brownshoe?"

Fourchetti was an aviator, assigned to *Guam* as his
obligatory deep-draft command before carrier assignment.
It was a sin that Sundstrom, for some reason of his own,
apparently could not forgive. Dan phrased his response
carefully. "Sir, they've been having glitches in the air-

search radar. There's a casualty report out on it. I think they—"

"No, no, no, no. Not you too, Dan. I've got a bellyful of excuses. Not picking up an incoming bogey—that's unforgivable. They could see him on the surface search, I know that. Christ, he was low enough. They're just goofing off down there, that's all. They're not taking this seriously. But they've got to learn."

"Yes sir," said Lenson.

"Hand me that microphone."

"Aye, sir."

He went out to the starboard wing as Sundstrom's voice boomed out over the ship.

"THIS IS THE COMMODORE SPEAKING. LET ME HAVE A FEW MINUTES OF YOUR TIME, PLEASE.

"A FEW MINUTES AGO THIS SHIP, THIS FORMATION, WAS OVERFLOWN BY A RUSSIAN BOMBER. WE HAD NO WARNING, NO ONE DETECTED IT. EVERYBODY ABOARD THIS SHIP WAS ASLEEP AT THE SWITCH!"

Lenson watched men look up at him from the flight deck. They looked at each other, and then up again. The 1MC clicked off, then on again. Everyone on the ship could hear Sundstrom's angry breathing.

"THIS IS NOT GOING TO HAPPEN AGAIN, NOT ON MY WATCH! I WANT EVERYONE ON THIS SHIP TO REALIZE THAT WE ARE NOW IN DANGEROUS WATERS. WE COULD BE ATTACKED AT ANY TIME. THERE'S NO EXCUSE ANYMORE FOR SLACKING OFF, FOR SITTING AROUND DRINKING COFFEE WHILE WE'RE OUT HERE. FROM HERE ON IN I WANT THIS SHIP RUN LIKE A NAVY VESSEL, LIKE A COMBAT UNIT, WHICH IT IS *SUPPOSED* TO BE.

"I WILL ACCEPT NO MORE EXCUSES AND NO MORE SUBSTANDARD, LACKLUSTER PERFORMANCE FROM ANY MEMBER OF THE

CREW, FROM THE CAPTAIN ON DOWN! THIS IS
MY FLAGSHIP, AND WE WILL DETECT AIR-
CRAFT AND SURFACE ATTACKERS FIRST AND
BE READY TO TAKE THEM UNDER FIRE ON A
MOMENT'S NOTICE. I WANT YOU ALL TO UN-
DERSTAND THIS AND ACT ACCORDINGLY."

When the 1MC clicked off he went inside. Sundstrom
was leaning back in his leather chair, smiling as if it hurt
him. He handed Dan the mike. "Hang that up for me,
Dan. There. That ought to wake the bastards up a little,
eh?"

"Yes sir," said Lenson, keeping his voice flat and businesslike.

"Dan, I realize you have the watch, but you're the only
one I can trust not to screw this up. Write me out a
message to the other units of the task force, saying the
same thing. Make it strong. I want this on the record."

"Yes sir," said Lenson unwillingly, and looked at
Glazer behind the chair. The supply officer made a cretin
face. Lenson made one back, went to the chart table, and
pulled out a message blank.

Sundstrom stayed on the bridge, but fortunately there
were no more flaps. The message, with several more sar-
casms red-penciled in, went out by flashing light to the rest
of the MARG. Toward 1400 the commodore fell asleep,
snoring in the big leather chair, his feet on one of the radio
handsets. Lenson and everyone else on watch went around
on tiptoe. At 1410, though, a voice message came in from
Coronado. A routine report, but it awakened him. He sat
there quiet for a few minutes, then: "Dan."

"Yes, sir."

"What did you think of that battle problem yesterday?"

"Uh . . . I thought it went okay, sir. We had the aircraft-
tracking exercise Commander Hogan made up, and then
we had the—"

"It sure didn't do the job, did it? Goddammit, I told
Hogan to get these people trained. I can't trust anybody
anymore . . . Dan, let's wake them up a little."

"Sir—it's the middle of the working day. Everybody will be—"

"Goddamn it, Dan. Don't let that attitude infect you, too. I expect better from an Academy man. They can work at night, like I do. Let's go. Battle stations, the whole formation. Right now!"

With a heavy heart, he picked up the handset.

The surprise drill went rather well at first, Dan thought. As the bell shrilled, the flight deck filled with running men. The ready helos coughed into life. The staff officers and enlisted arrived panting from the run up from staterooms and offices. Gear lockers rattled open. McQueen tossed helmets, life preservers, masks, and pistols to reaching hands. The windows slammed closed, hatches banged to, sweating men dogged them tight. Lenson buckled on the heavy steel helmet stenciled "Staff Watch Officer" as the 3"/50 mount below the bridge began to hum and clank; the gun crew was feeding rounds into the revolving magazines. Flasher and Byrne and Hogan crowded into the narrow bridge, making twelve men all told, leaving hardly enough room to reach for a pencil. He saw Red settling the lifejacket on his belly; it protruded nearly a foot. His battle station was staff watch officer, but neither of them said anything; Lenson kept the deck. Flasher looked carefully around the bridge, over the coaming at the decks below, then lifted his binoculars for a sweep of the formation.

Lenson followed suit. The other ships were buttoning up, too. He could see men running, guns swinging as the crews tested the drive and elevation motors, then settling into the Ready Antiair position. He looked around at the grim battle-ready faces, and felt his fatigue lift on a wave of excitement.

This was how it should be, he thought. No matter that Sundstrom had his faults. He was still their commander. No matter that they had been at sea so long, that their ships were old and their equipment obsolete, that they worried constantly about breakdowns and spare parts. The amphibious Navy was used to being the orphans of the fleet. Their crews weren't the hand-picked men of the submarine force, or gung-ho marines, or spit-and-polish cruisermen, cocky and loudly proud of it. And maybe the officers, some of them, were not the sharpest-looking or best-connected. They were amphib sailors, the "Gator Freighters"; but they knew their unglamorous business; and they were ready now, awaiting whatever orders came. He felt the pride come to him in that moment. *Guam,* and every other ship in the Mediterranean Amphibious Ready Group, was cleared for battle.

"Flagship report yet?" Flasher asked him.

"Yeah. They're manned."

"That was quick."

"Chief Staff Officer!" said the commodore, from his chair.

"Yes sir."

"Have all units reported manned and ready?"

"Just a moment, sir." Hogan lunged for the PRITAC.

"No, goddammit. Why don't they report? I want them to report."

"Yes sir."

"Let's see if they're on their toes this afternoon. Dan! Let's come around to two-seven-zero."

"Just the *Guam,* sir?"

"No, goddammit! Use your head! You think I want a collision out here? Bring the whole formation around."

"Aye, sir." He scrambled for the radio.

"*Charleston* reports, manned and ready," Glazer sang out.

"*Bowen,* manned and ready."

"*Newport,* manned and ready."

"*Barnstable County, Ault, Coronado, Spiegel Grove* report manned and ready, Commodore."

"Very well," muttered Sundstrom, holding up his arm to examine his watch, but saying nothing more.

The ship shuddered, leaning into the turn. Fourchetti

was bringing it around with full rudder, Lenson saw. Below, on the flight deck, crews scrambled to shove extra blocks beneath the helicopters as the deck tilted. The gun mount below clanked as the crew fed rounds to the breech.

"Are we clear?" Sundstrom asked the bridge in general.

"All units coming around, sir," shouted Glazer from the starboard wing. Lenson turned guiltily to port, but Hogan was already out there. He held up his thumb through the closed hatch window.

"All clear to port, sir," Lenson bawled.

"Quickdraw," said Sundstrom.

"Sir?"

"I said, Exercise Quickdraw! It's a standing exercise, goddammit—'On receipt of signal, all units fire three rounds of inert ammunition on a clear bearing.' Put it out, right now!"

Dan was still holding the handset. "All units, November Zulu," he shouted automatically into it, "This is November Zulu. Immediate execute: Exercise Quickdraw. I say again, immediate execute, Exercise Quickdraw. Stand by—"

"Belay that!" shouted Flasher suddenly.

"What—"

"Belay it! Disregard! *Now!*"

"What the devil—" said Sundstrom.

Lenson hesitated for a fraction of a second, looking at Flasher and then Sundstrom, then said tightly into the handset, "Disregard. I say again, disregard this transmission. Out."

"Just what the hell are you doing?" shouted Sundstrom, regaining himself. Except for his voice, the crowded bridge was silent. "Lieutenant Flasher, since when—"

"Quickdraw is a destroyer exercise, sir," Flasher said, speaking rapidly, moving up near the commodore's chair. "Most of these amphibs have never heard of it. But some of them have, and they'll start to shoot."

"So? The rest of them will catch on. We've got to—"

"Sir. Look out at the mount."

Sundstrom stared at Flasher for a moment, then bent forward to look through the window, down toward the 01 level. He watched the crew for a moment. "What? I don't see—"

"Look at the shells, sir."

"The *shells?*"

"They loaded with live rounds."

Sundstrom did not speak.

"They think this is for real, sir," Flasher muttered, almost into the commodore's ear. Sundstrom was still looking down. "They think we're under attack. I'll bet every tube on every ship has live antiaircraft rounds in the breech. If we all start firing, somebody's going to get hit."

Sundstrom looked down for a moment more. The bridge was absolutely quiet. And Lenson watched the struggle plain on his face, the anger and humiliation.

"Belay that order," the commodore said.

"Aye aye sir," said Lenson. His finger pressed the "send" button for a moment, by reflex, but he did not lift it to his lips.

"Have all units clear their guns."

"Aye aye, sir." He lifted the handset again, feeling a wave of near sickness. He could see, looking down over the coaming, the green-and-yellow noses of the antiaircraft ammunition. Flasher was right. Proximity-fuzed live rounds, at random bearings, the ships this close together . . .

And off their beam, well within range, men on the bridge of the Russian trawler studied them through binoculars, impassive and intent.

They stayed at GQ for a long time after that. Sundstrom was subdued. No one else said anything beyond the most routine of reports, and those in hushed voices. The time for evening meal came and went. At 1800 the commodore sent down for a tray. When his steward came up he ate it sitting in his chair, regarding the choppy horizon with an impassive expression. The officers stood about as if afraid to move, afraid to speak. At last he called Lenson over. "Yes sir," Dan said, straightening to a tired attention, looking at the remains of a bacon-lettuce-and-tomato sandwich.

"Dan, I think you got a little carried away on that message you wrote for me. I let it go out as is, but it was a little too purple, if you know what I mean."

"Yes sir."

"Anyway, we got results. They know now I mean business up here. We'll stay at GQ for a while, get the men used to their stations. This was a good idea, to call them away without warning. When I play the game, I like to play it to the hilt. That's the way professionals operate. But we don't want to overdo any aspect of the problem. Do we?"

"No sir."

"Where's Commander Hogan?"

"Out on the port wing, sir."

"What's he doing out there?"

"Uh—I'll find out, sir." The old Naval Academy response.

"Get him in here."

"Aye aye, sir."

He listened to the conversation. Sundstrom wanted a beefed-up watch. He wanted officers on both wings of the flag bridge with binoculars, since the lookouts on the ships were worthless. He wanted a staff officer in CIC at all times to oversee the operators on the air-search radars. They were just putting in the time, they weren't bearing down, they were goof-offs and Captain Fourchetti wasn't supervising them. So his staff would.

"We have a full watch bill, sir," he heard Hogan saying.

"I don't give a damn about that! You saw how he let that Russki make me look silly. This is too important to let some ensign drop the ball on us."

"I agree with that, sir, but the point is we only have so many men. We'd have to go to port and starboard watches on the bridge—"

"Don't bother me with the details. Just do it. If my staff can't cut the mustard, get some of those helo pilots out of the wardroom. They just sit down there with coffee cups in their hands all day. Christ, Bill, do I have to reinvent the wheel for you every day?"

"No, sir."

"I'm not just out here to prove a point, my friend. I'm not gilding any lilies here. We are entering a multithreat environment, and I demand positive control."

"Yes sir," said Hogan.

Lenson stood just behind the chair, watching the back of Sundstrom's head as he talked. For just a moment, looking at the graying hair, he imagined . . . No. He shut his mind off before it betrayed him into something terrible.

"Well, I'm going below. I've been up here since midnight." He dismissed Hogan with a flip of his hand, glanced back. "Think you can handle things for me, Dan?"

"Yes sir."

The commodore swung himself down from the chair, grunting. As soon as the door swung shut behind him the crowded mass of men breathed out. The bridge suddenly seemed wider. Byrne sat down on a switch box, rubbing his knees. Flasher pushed back his helmet and wiped his forehead. Lenson opened his mouth, about to comment, but he caught the tight expression on the chief staff officer's face and closed it again. After a moment Hogan went below too, and he shoved his own helmet back and leaned into the radar repeater with a sigh. No one said anything for a few seconds.

"Good times, huh?" said Glazer.

"It's no goddamn joke," said Flasher. His face was white. He patted his uniform pockets. "This guy's dangerous."

"That was a nice save with the guns, Red."

"Yeah, right on the money."

"MacInroe would never have done that," said the operations officer. He found gum in his back pocket and wadded three sticks of it into his mouth.

"MacInroe?" said Glazer.

"The commodore before Double-Nuts. Left before you came aboard. He was no hand-holder; he'd tear you a new asshole if you fucked up; but he knew what he was doing. This guy . . . he's a fucking idiot. We got to watch this one real close."

Looking at their faces, seeing the despondency and choked rage—these were lieutenants, lieutenant-commanders, reduced now to being wing lookouts, a seaman recruit's job—Lenson felt he ought to say something. There had to be a reason for the way Sundstrom acted. But nothing came to mind. It was Jack Byrne who said at last, "Well, you know he's got a lot on his mind."

"Jesus, I should hope so," said Flasher.

"Serious," said Byrne. He straightened, adjusting the dirty lifejacket with a little movement of distaste. "Sure, he went overboard there, but basically I think he's right."

"Come on, Jack. He craps on you more than any of us. What's right about that?"

"I'm not referring to that. I mean the tactical situation. Actually, he's not taking enough precautions. Or not the right ones. We could use some air cover, for example. I think we ought to get ready for things to heat up real fast around here."

Flasher bared his teeth, and seemed about to speak when a metallic voice said, "Flag bridge, bridge."

"I got it," said Lenson, reaching for the intercom. "Flag bridge, aye."

"Is the commodore down there?"

"No. He's gone below."

"Oh." He recognized Fourchetti's voice. "Well . . . all right if I secure from general quarters now? I got a lot of work to get done on those helos. If we're not doing anything, I'd like to secure my men."

"Commodore didn't say to, sir."

"Well, look, Mr. Lenson—"

"That's what he said, sir," said Lenson savagely, thinking Why do I have to get in the middle, a lieutenant junior grade; let the four-stripers fight this one out. I'm just carrying out orders. "He wants the men to get used to their battle stations."

"My men spend all day working at their battle stations, Mr. Lenson," the captain said frigidly.

"Yes sir."

"I'll give him a call."

"Yes sir." The captain rang off. A minute or two later the 1MC spoke: "NOW SECURE FROM GENERAL QUARTERS. SET THE NORMAL UNDERWAY WATCH. ON DECK, SECTION THREE."

"They're still in three sections," muttered McQueen. Lenson turned to look at the petty officer, but he had already bent to his charts again, his back rigid.

'Dan, how about we secure, too?"

"No, goddammit, Red. We're not part of the ship. We work for him. We'll stay at GQ here till he secures us himself."

He felt like an asshole, saying it, but that was the way it worked. Here in Comphibron Six, under Isaac I. Sundstrom. Resenting their resentment, his own bitterness and fatigue, he stared out, over the choppy gray sea, toward the distant line of an approaching squall. Somewhere out there were men in ships, putting out to battle.

He wished with all his heart that he was one of them.

16
U.S.S. *Ault*

DEEP IN THE SHIP, SO DEEP THERE WAS nothing below him but a skin of metal and then the sea, Kelly Wronowicz braced himself against the steel web that held up the roaring engines.

The ship rolled, and he held on grimly. Around his boots black stinking water streamed sluggishly from one side of the bilges to the other. A work light, a naked bulb at the end of a cord, dangled out at a crazy angle as the *Ault* hung at the end of her roll. When she came back the slime reversed its course, like a tide. It swirled around the men who kneeled and lay beneath the deckplates, made them slip and curse as they crawled forward, scattering handfuls of detergent ahead of them over the scummy steel of the bilges.

"Over here," said Wronowicz, wriggling between the engine mounts toward the farthest corner of the void. "Under the main condenser, here. We got to get this too, guys."

"Sure, Chief."

"We got it covered. Go on back up to the mess."

"Yeah, we'll take care of it, Chief," grinned Blaney.

Prone under the torn-up gratings, his belly against the sea-cold steel of the bottom, Wronowicz said nothing. Smee and Polack and Blaney were working late this evening. So was he—six hours of general quarters had bitched a whole work day. Now, in the dirtiest, oldest coveralls the engineering department had, their faces smeared with the used oil and crud here at the lowest point of the ship, where all the leaks and emptyings of tanks and engines and pumps collected, the three men were cleaning the bilges. It was a dirty job, back-breaking, stifling in the heat and sound of the running engineroom, done in darkness and fetor.

Just for that reason, he felt he owed it to them to share it, at least for a while. "Scrub it in good now," he said. "Use the big brushes first. Save the little ones for the angle iron. I don't want to see nothin' but red paint when I come back after you hose down."

"Sure, Chief," Blaney grinned, his teeth shining in the dark of the voids. The two other firemen worked silently, or cursed. Wronowicz understood that; cleaning bilges was the least favorite job in the engineroom, probably in the ship, possibly in the Navy. He had done his share of it. But Blaney neither cursed nor complained. He was scrubbing ferociously at the underside of a stringer, flat on his back in muck blacker than his face, humming as if he enjoyed sweating for hours under conditions any sane civilian would walk away from.

Wronowicz wondered darkly what he was on.

When they were well at work, forcing the gritty Navy bilge cleaner deep into the weld seams and steel angles, he hauled himself up through an access and stamped his boots on the deckplates. They left black imprints, as if he had been wading in tar. He wiped them off with a rag—no use tracking it all over the ship—and dragged his arm over his forehead. It did no good, and he saw that his arm was dripping, too. It was well over a hundred ten, maybe a hundred twenty in the space. The engines tore at his ears. He retrieved his cap from where it hung on a valve, cocked it back on his head. He glanced at his watch and went forward, absently checking each gauge he passed, to the oil king's shack.

"Evening, Joe."

"Oh. Hullo, Chief Wronowicz. How you doing tonight?"

"Okay. How's the fuel situation look?"

The second-class boiler technician waved at the racks of glass bottles lining the bulkheads of the tiny room, hardly larger than an apartment closet. Lit from behind, they glowed amber and yellow. Each fuel sample had been drawn that day from one of the tanks that lined the hull. "I'm about half done . . . we got some algal contamination in one of the wing tanks. The stuff left over from the Caribbean. I figure we better use it pretty soon."

"Better switch tomorrow. Use it all."

"Then saltwater ballast? Word is this weather's going to turn Billy Hell."

"I hate to do that. A shot of water in the fuel can ruin your whole day. I still don't know how long we'll be out here."

"Well, we'll keep her steaming somehow."

"You got that right. Well, I'll be in chief's quarters for the rest of the evening. Going to initiate that first-class radarman tonight."

"Yeah, I seen him going around in his diapers." The BT grinned. "What goes on at those things, anyway?"

"That's a deep dark secret. You'll find out, five-six years from now."

"No way," said the man, grinning.

"Yeah, I know: sob story number eight, how you're gonna get out, get a fat civvie job waxing floors."

"You said it. Think I'm gonna re-up on this crappy tub?"

They grinned at each other, and Wronowicz left. As he climbed the ladder the evening routine of the ship echoed through the corridors. "NOW TAPS, TAPS, LIGHTS OUT. KEEP SILENCE ABOUT THE DECKS. THE SMOKING LAMP IS OUT IN ALL BERTHING SPACES." Upward, past the mess decks, the smells of ham and fried potatoes lingering from evening chow, a few sailors arguing sleepily over a hand of five-card stud while the compartment slanted under them . . . the unceasing whir hum and murmur of a ship, sleepy and low, the world changing from white to red around him as a petty officer flicked a switch. The ship surrounded him, enclosed him, carried him through the unseen darkness of the sea, gliding over fathomless miles of dark bottom, and he smiled to himself, anticipating the evening.

The chief's mess was full. The XO was there, the department heads, and Lieutenant Morton, the operations officer. It was one of his radarmen (no, "operations specialists"—but to Kelly they were still radarmen) who was pinning on the anchor tonight.

First, though, he had to be initiated.

Wronowicz found a seat next to the court, joking with the men beside him. At the baize-covered mess table Chief Chapman presided in a black robe; his glasses gleamed under a wig of cotton batting. Two other chiefs, the recorder and the prosecutor, sat at either side, and an immense pewter pitcher and two tumblers waited at their elbows. Behind a curtain Wronowicz could see the other implements of trial, and his grin grew wider. Yes, it was going to be a good initiation.

"Is the court ready?" Chapman asked, when the room had settled down.

"The court is ready."

"Is Captain Foster coming down?"

"He's on the bridge," said the XO. "He's going to try to come down later."

"Very good . . . Bailiff, bring in the accused."

Operations Specialist First Rogelio appeared in handcuffs, carrying his offense log linked to them on a chain. His bare belly bulged over too-small diapers. Aside from that, and a large crow-and-stripes tattooed on his chest in magic marker, he was naked. Lieutenant Morton got up and stood rather uncertainly beside him, facing the court. They both looked apprehensive, willing to laugh, but uncertain whether they should.

Certainly Chapman's scowl did not encourage it. "This

court is convened," he growled. "Bailiff, read the charges."

"First. That OS First B.T. Rogelio did say to a certain chief aboard the *Charleston,* while on liberty in Barcelona, that the chiefs aboard this vessel were a six-pack of shit-heads."

The audience groaned. Chapman looked aloof. "Accused, how do you plead?" he asked the first-class.

Morton stepped forward. "Chief—"

"Your honor," said the bailiff menacingly.

"Uh . . . your honor, my client wishes to state—"

"Shut up," said the judge.

"Sir—"

"He's guilty. I can see it in his fat face. Put down that he pleads guilty."

"He pleads innocent—"

"The truth serum," muttered the prosecutor.

"Yes, administer the truth serum. To counsel, too. He looks just as dishonest as this guilty bastard."

When both Rogelio and Morton had swilled down a tumbler, quickly replenished from the pitcher by the prosecutor, the trial resumed. "Second charge," grunted Chapman.

"That the accused did attempt to enter the chief petty officer's berthing area, and was discovered lying in the rack of one of the senior chiefs aboard this vessel, stating that he was 'trying it out'—"

"Hang him!"

"Shoot him and throw him off the fantail!"

"Bailiff, silence these yelping mongrels . . . does the accused want to try to worm his way out of this one?"

"Sir, my client never—"

"Is he saying I'm a liar?" roared Wronowicz, jumping up. "I'll rip his yellow guts out and eat them for midrats!"

"Is counsel accusing Chief Wronowicz of fabricating this charge?" Chapman asked Morton sweetly.

"No, but—"

"Would counsel like some more truth serum?"

"Counsel would not," said Morton, swallowing. He looked yellow himself, both from the steady roll of the ship and the tumbler of tabasco sauce, cooking oil, and raw eggs.

"The verdict is guilty. Also, counsel is assessed twenty dollars for insulting the witness. Pay the prosecutor. Next charge."

"That accused stated in CIC that, having passed the tests for chief and being recommended by his officers, to whom he sucks up shamelessly, especially to the XO, a notorious duck-fucker and nose-picker, he expects to be admitted to the rank of chief petty officer in the United States Navy."

"Dismissed," Chapman stated. "Obvious insanity. Any more charges, prosecutor?"

"A whole bagful, not worth wasting the time of the honorable judge," said the prosecutor, slamming shut the log.

"We agree . . . we will now proceed to the tests. Blindfold the accused."

Two more raw eggs seeped down from under the blindfold. Rogelio started to giggle. "Is the accused laughing at this court?" Chapman screamed.

"No, sir. It's hiccups," said Morton.

"More truth serum for this lying shyster!"

"Yes sir."

"And another twenty dollars fine. Bring out the first test."

The board was eight feet long, with mouse traps nailed to it. The chiefs set it a foot off the deck, on firebrick, and hoisted Rogelio to one end. "The accused will note that he is standing on The Plank," the prosecutor intoned. "The way is narrow and adorned with bear traps. If you slide your foot forward you'll feel one. Just to show you they're armed. . . ." The prosecutor tripped the first trap with a stick, and the naked man jerked his bare foot backward, almost falling off the plank.

"Proceed," said Chapman.

Rogelio edged forward blindly, balancing himself against the roll of the ship, and lifted his foot for the first step. He came up on the second trap, missed it, and the prosecutor tripped it closed with a snap. He took another step, another, learning to slide his toes forward until he felt the edge of the mouse trap, then lifting his foot over in a bold step. He came to the end, teetered, then jumped down. The chiefs were dead silent.

"The accused has passed the first test. Prosecutor, bring on the Bed of Glass."

An aluminum tray was duly produced, and shaken back and forth as audible witness that it was full of jagged shards. "Every piece of glassware broken on the mess decks this year is in that tray. The accused will mount the chair."

"I am now placing the Bed of Glass beneath you," the prosecutor explained. Rogelio nodded the blindfold. "You will now call on one of those whose ranks you aspire to join, to properly place the tray."

"Chief . . . Wronowicz?" said the radarman.

Wronowicz hustled forward, grinning. He rattled the tray loudly in front of the chair, made as if he was setting it down, and silently switched it with the other tray the prosecutor as silently handed over. "Ready," he said to Rogelio. "Safe as houses when you're with Wronowicz. Jump right down, straight in front of the chair."

"I . . . do I got to?"

"Nope," said Chapman promptly. "This is the one test that's voluntary. In case the worst happens, we have the Doc standing by. 'Course, if you elect not to take it, you call the whole thing off . . ."

"Okay," said Rogelio. They could see him bite his lip. "Here goes." He stepped off the chair, and a gruesome crunch filled the room. Rogelio tore his blindfold off and stared down at his feet. He lifted one. It was covered with broken potato chips.

"For this next, and last trial, the blindfold will be removed. Attach the Device."

The Device was a length of ninethread line, tossed over
a sturdy pipe in the overhead. One end led through the
lifting pad of a generator casing, and Chief Sullivan
grunted as he hoisted it above his head. Rogelio paled as
Chief Blood, looking his most sadistic, tied a slip knot and
made the other end fast around his balls.

"Hey!"

"Is the accused ready?"

"No! Hey, wait—"

"Corpsman, stand by—*let 'er go!*"

Sullivan dropped the casing and jumped back. It plum-
meted downward, the line twanged taut, and the pipe
came out of the overhead, trailing string and masking
tape, and followed the casing to the deck with a terrific
crash. The room broke into cheers, and Chapman got up
to clap a relieved-looking radarman on the back. "Fine
performance," he said, smiling. "Prosecutor, bring out
Chief Rogelio's anchors."

Rogelio's smile vanished as he saw the plate. It was
filled with dogshit, a coiled heap of it six inches high.
"You'll have to eat a lot of this when you wear khakis,"
Chapman said. "Might as well get used to it now. Go on,
your anchors are in there. No, don't use your hands."

When he held his smeared face up at last, the gold
anchors gleaming in his teeth, the other chiefs broke from
their seats to surround him, clapping him on the back and
wiping chocolate icing from his face with a towel. They
brought out his uniform and he dropped his diapers for
skivvies and then khakis, and the XO and the senior chief
pinned on the gleaming new insignia of an E-7. Chapman
stepped back, letting the audience applaud, then held up
an imperious hand. The room quieted.

"Chief Rogelio, during the course of this day you have
suffered indignities and experienced humiliation. This you
accomplished with rare good grace, and I now believe it
fitting to explain why we did this.

"There was no intent, and no desire, to demean or insult
you.

"It was done to show you that your entire life changed today. More will be expected of you; more will be demanded. You have not merely been promoted a pay grade. You have joined an exclusive fraternity.

"Its privileges, and its responsibilities, do not appear in print. They exist because Navy chiefs for two hundred years before you have accepted responsibility beyond the call of their assignments.

"You were humiliated to prove that humiliation cannot mar you. Bear humiliations and accolades alike with the same dignity and good grace you bore them with today.

"We take a deep and sincere pleasure in clasping your hand, and accepting you as one of us."

With that, the ceremony ended. Wronowicz shook the new chief's hand as the gathering broke up, then strolled thoughtfully back into the scullery for a glass of ice water.

He found himself, more and more these days, musing over things after any kind of ceremony—and the Navy had quite a few, from the oath when you first enlisted to the Service for Burial at Sea. When he was younger, he thought they were a load of baloney; now that his hair was thinning, he realized that a lot of things that he had thought were baloney weren't.

It was like that with the initiation, he thought. Chapman had summed it up pretty well, but there were some things you could say better without words. As a chief you had to walk in the dark sometimes and trust your luck. You had to rely on your fellow chiefs. You had to lay it all on the line sometimes, with the officers or with your men, risk losing your rank or else deny what that rank was all about. And yeah, you did have to eat crap sometimes, and it wasn't always chocolate. It was all part of being a chief. Like the oath said, the chiefs were the Navy, after all.

Yeah, it was all real symbolic. He brought the glass out into the lounge with him, wishing it was bourbon, and settled in with Blood and Sullivan and Chapman for a quick game before bed. Blood dealt, his satyr's beard close over the table as cards fluttered through the tilting air of the lounge.

"Rough tonight," said Sullivan mildly. "Unc, what we got coming?"

"My kind of weather," grinned Blood. "Whitecaps in your coffee cups. Got a semitropical heading up from Africa; it'll pass us close aboard. Five-card stud, deuces. What do you say . . . how'd you like the initiation?"

"Real good. You ran it real well, Pop."

Old Chief Chapman made a face. "Not like what we had in the old days. Quonset Point, once, we had a winter initiation. Got a tumbler of booze in each of them, stripped 'em, marched 'em out onto this fresh-water lake and went ice fishin'."

"Christ," said Sullivan.

"Wasn't too bad, we only lost one guy's pecker."

"You jerks going to ante up, or what?" said Blood.

"Did somebody just turn on a forced draft blower?"

"Up yours."

"Ten."

"Yup."

"Gimme three."

"Two cards."

"Real el crappo hand."

"So anyway," said Wronowicz, chilling his tongue on a deep draught of water, "d'ja hear the one about the Jewish princess, got herself a gold diaphragm?"

"Why's that?"

"So's her men would all come into money."

"Uh-huh."

"Raise you ten."

"Shit!"

"Pass."

"Yeah," said Blood, squinting at his hand, then reaching into his pocket for a cigar. "You guys want one? . . . Sully?"

"Sure."

"That reminds me of the one about this guy goes into

a bar. He's dressed in a tux, got this flashy blonde on his arm. He makes like he's this big shot, tells the bartender, 'Bring me a bottle of good wine. Got any Chateau Lepew, 1937?' 'Wait a minute—I think we might,' says the barhop. He goes down into the cellar and comes up a couple minutes later with this old, dusty bottle with spiderwebs all over it. Pass."

"Pass."

"Raise you a quarter."

"Son of a bitch."

Blood lit the cigar. "So the guy smells the cork, and makes a big production out of tasting it. Then he says, 'There's something wrong here. This isn't a '37. I think it's a '38.' So the bartender wipes the dust off with his elbow, and sure enough, there on the label it says 1938. 'Gee,' he says, 'sorry. I'll go get you the '37.' And he goes back down in the cellar."

"You look like a movie star with that cigar, Unc," said Sullivan.

"Yeah?"

"Yeah, like Lassie taking a shit," said Chapman. He giggled. "Sorry, Sully, I heard it a long time ago."

"Back on the *Maine,* I'll bet," said Blood.

"Like you're always saying to me, tell the goddamn joke," said Wronowicz.

"Bartender comes up with another bottle, the guy tries it, says 'No, that's a '36.' He cleans off the label, sure enough it says 1936. He shakes his head, goes down again, comes back up. This time he checks the label first, and the guy in the tux tastes it, nods, says 'Yeah, that's it. 1937.'

"Meanwhile, there's this old warrant sitting at the bar, drunk as shit, watching it all and muttering to himself. After a while he calls the bartender over and says 'Gimme a wineglass.' The bartender gives it to him, and he turns around there at the bar and pisses it full. Then he calls over to the civilian, 'Hey! Taste this stuff,' and slides it down the bar to him.

"The guy takes one sip and sprays it all over the bar. 'That's urine!' he says.

" 'Sure,' says the warrant, 'it's piss. But tell me: How old am I?' "

The four chiefs laughed. Chapman took the pot and scooped it in, putting it in his empty cup to keep it from sliding over the table as the destroyer rolled. "Your deal," said Sullivan to Wronowicz.

"Boston. Seven cards, three up, nothing wild. Unc, that must be the same warrant that went into a bar one day with three of his pals."

"Sounds like him so far, yeah."

"They sit in the back for a while, then the warrant comes up to the bar and orders a beer. The bartender is this big ugly guy—"

"Sounds like you, Kelly."

"Shut up. With a busted nose. Mean-looking. The warrant watches him polishing the bar, and finally he says, 'Say. You a betting man, Shorty?'

" 'Sometimes,' says the barkeep.

" 'I'll bet you a buck I can bite my eye,' says the warrant.

" 'Bite your *eye?* You're on,' says the barkeep. So the warrant reaches up, takes out his glass eye, and bites it and puts it back. The big guy shakes his head, pays him a dollar. The warrant sits for a while, drinking, then says, 'Say. Want to make another bet?'

" 'What is it this time?' says the bartender. Now he's suspicious, see."

"Good cards at last," said Sullivan, his face lighting up. "Raise four bits."

"In."

"Forget it."

"See you and another two bits, too."

"Heavy betting," said Chapman.

" 'Bet you five bucks I can bite my other eye,' says the warrant."

"His *other* eye?" said Sullivan.

"Yeah. So the bartender says, 'Now, wait a minute. You didn't come in here with no dog. Sure, it's a stupid bet, but I'll take it.' He puts down a five, and then the warrant takes out his false teeth, bites his other eye, and puts them back in."

"Ha. Good one," said Blood, and it was unclear whether he meant his hand or the story.

"The big guy's kind of mad, but he goes back to polishing the bar. The warrant sits for a while, then he says, 'Tell you what—I hate to see a man lose twice. One more bet. Bet you I can piss a beer bottle full while it's sliding down the counter, without spilling a drop.'

" 'There's no way you can do that,' says the barkeep.

" 'Ten bucks says I can.'

" 'I can't pass this one up,' says the barkeep. So he takes an empty bottle, the warrant unzips his fly and hauls his dick out, and the barkeep skates it down the bar. The warrant runs along the bar, pissing like a horse, and it goes all over the bar. He doesn't get drop one in the bottle. 'You stupid shit,' says the big guy, laughing his ass off. 'Pay up.' So the warrant pays up, and starts to leave. 'Wait a minute,' says the barkeep. 'You knew you couldn't do that. Didn't you?'

" 'Yeah, I guess so,' says the warrant.

" 'So you just dropped ten bucks. How come?'

" 'Well,' says the warrant, 'you're right. But, see, I bet my pals there in back a hundred bucks that I could piss all over your bar and make you laugh about it.' "

Their laughter was interrupted by the drone of a foghorn, muffled by the many decks between them and the mast, but still distinct. They saw Blood stiffen. "You got to go up?" said Sullivan.

"Nah. Captain's up there, and the navigator. It's probably just a squall." He relaxed, but still chewed at the cigar, which had gone out. "Your deal, Pop."

Chapman dealt. "Singapore," he said.

"What the fuck is that?"

"You'll see . . . picked it up in Havana. You ever been to Havana? No, you boys are all too young."

"Jesus, yes," said Wronowicz. "You pick up anything else in Havana?"

"Oh yeah." Chapman chuckled. "That was one wide-open port . . . you boys think the Med is wild, you ought to of seen the hair shows on Calle Punta."

"I was to a dog and pony once, in Tijuana," contributed Sullivan, and they looked at him.

"Kid stuff . . . they had this dame on Punta Street, used to pick up coins with her twat. Guys would throw them up on stage, she'd kind of squat down, wiggle around, and stand up with it there, no hands. Damnedest thing you ever saw. So one time," Chapman giggled, "this motormac I was with, I was a third-class then, he got out a silver dollar, and we heated it up with our Zippos and tossed it up on stage. God-*damn!* You never heard such a ruckus."

"How the hell old are you, anyway, Pop?" Blood asked him.

"I'm so old," said Chapman, giggling over the cards, "I was tyin' square knots before you got the pins out of your diapers. I'm so old that squeezin' into a parking space satisfies me sexually. I'm so old I remember before they had crappers."

"Come off it," said Wronowicz.

"Serious . . . in the old Navy they didn't have none of these porcelain thrones. You sat in a line over a trough, just a steady stream of seawater goin' under you. It was the goddamn funniest thing . . ."

"Funny?" said Sullivan, tossing one of his last coins into the pot.

"Yeah, ever so often some smartass on the end would wad up some toilet paper, light it, and float it on down the line. Scorch everybody's butt, they'd pop up and scream one after the other . . . jeep carrier once I was on, they had an avgas leak in the piping system, contaminated the firemains; guy threw his butt into the trough and it exploded, killed two weather-guessers and a reserve lieutenant commander."

The three younger chiefs looked at Chapman, undecided whether to laugh or believe him, and his wizened poker face—it seemed almost as old as the sea itself—gave them no clue at all. "Shit," said Wronowicz at last. "Let's play some cards, here. You and your goddamn sea stories. Next you'll be telling us you were a plankowner on the Ark. Cut the friggin' cards, it's your deal, Sully."

"This better turn out. I'm 'bout broke."

"I got the next watch anyway," said Blood, fanning out his cards. "This is the last hand for me. Yeah . . . yeah. Kelly, you ever get back to that babe in Naples?"

"No," said Wronowicz shortly. He wished Blood hadn't mentioned her; he had hardly thought about her all day.

"Some piece . . . I thought those goddamn bersagleers had us."

"Where'd you put the bed, Kelly?"

"Lashed it down in one of the fan rooms."

"Gimme three."

"Two."

"Think I'll stick with these, crummy as they are."

"Yeah, I had me a redhot shack-up a few years ago in Newport," Blood mused. "Secretary at the ninety-day-wonder school there. Thirty-six-inch bust, chokies big as silver dollars . . . nipples as big as your thumb. Tell a dirty joke, get her excited, you could see them pop right up under her dress. She was right-handed. The right one always went first; then the left one, and you knew she was ready. Crummy face but great boobs, and I'm your basic tit man. She loved to take it aboard, too, but there was one problem."

"What was that?" said Chapman.

"She smelled. It was like northern herring after a week in the sun. We used to go out bicycling, and it got so bad I had to stay upwind of her."

Sullivan looked uncomfortable. "Jesus," he muttered.

"What's wrong, Sully?"

"Nothing, nothing."

"Yeah, she liked it, all right. I bet she had more sailors aboard than the U.S.S. *Independence*. Most guys was only good for maybe three times for her, though. But she had the old wide-on for me and no lie. She even said she was in love with me."

The table was quiet for a moment as the chiefs concentrated on their cards. "Why didn't you tell her?" grunted Wronowicz.

"Tell her what?"

"Tell her she smelled. She could've fixed that."

"Hell," said Blood, grinning, "then some officer would've moved in. Talk about lube jobs! We'd go into the head in the acey-deucey club and she'd haul out my—"

"She loved you, you asshole. What did you do when you were finished with her, walk away?"

"Hey, what else could I do when the old lady arrived? I was married, man. See, here's the way I see it. You got to grab every piece of it you can get. It might be your best, and it might be your last. Like you did with that cunt in Naples—"

"Shut up, you fuckhead," said Wronowicz, standing up. Something vicious rose in his chest. He slammed his fists down on the table, scattering the cards, and leaned over the astonished quartermaster like an avalanche. Confused feelings struggled in him, the urge to smash in the squinty eyes, the pointed, too-neat beard. Wronowicz didn't understand why; he didn't have the right words, though he had words, plenty of them, all obscene. But that was part of what enraged him, the relentless obscenity. He held his fists on the table with sheer will, and he and Blood stared at each other, the other two chiefs scrambling up from the sliding pile of cards and chips.

"Kelly, take it easy—"

"Cool it, Kelly. He's just telling a story."

"Yeah? Well, I don't want to hear another story out of him for this whole fuckin' cruise," Wronowicz said, looking down at Blood. The quartermaster slid back in his chair. The other chiefs moved unobtrusively behind the machinist, ready to grab him, but he did not move. Instead he held Blood's eyes until they fell to the cards and then he turned and walked heavily down to chiefs' berthing, listening to his heart thud in pace with his footsteps.

Dangerous, he thought. Doc told me, blood pressure. Ah, to hell with it. He threw himself into his bunk, rocking the partition, and stared at the overhead, listening to himself pant.

What the hell is wrong with me?

It was a foreign thought, frightening, from somewhere outside of him, and he pushed it away. He lay there for a few minutes, waiting for his pulse to still, and then got up in the darkened compartment and went to his locker. Back in the bunk, curtain drawn, he uncapped the fifth and took a deep drink of warm vodka. It fumed his throat like grease stripper, and he coughed and coughed and then took another long swallow and capped the bottle and snuggled it beside him, next to the bulkhead. Callin might come in, or Jay. . . . Fuck 'em if they do, he thought savagely. That fucking Blood. He took another drink, his gut warming to it, and reminded himself that he had only that bottle and one other to last God knew how long, till they made port again, and with this Cyprus horseshit that could be weeks.

You shouldn't've lost your temper, he told himself. But as he thought of it he got mad again, and cursed half-aloud there in the bunk till his mind went silent, emptied finally of words, and he lay still, lifting the bottle from time to time and listening to the distant foghorn.

"Chief."

"Yuh," he grunted, rolling over. Something hard and rounded under him . . . he rubbed his face and squinted at his watch. It was zero-two-hundred.

"Chief Wronowicz." A hoarse whisper, half-familiar. The curtain slid aside and he saw Ensign Callin's face, red in the darken-ship lights. He closed his eyes, opened them, but his division officer was still there.

"Sir?"

"We need you down in the hole, Chief."

"You got the watch, don't you?" he said, and then a bad feeling came over him. Callin wouldn't be here unless something was wrong. He wasn't officially qualified yet, but he could handle most of the ordinary emergencies by now. So it must be serious. He swung his legs out, rolling the bottle back so the officer couldn't see it. Good thing it was vodka, couldn't smell it on his breath. "What's wrong?"

"We're not sure. Mr. Jay wants you down right away."

". . . goddamn boots . . ."

Number-two engineroom was oddly quiet to him, though to an outsider it would still have been an unbearable storm of sound. Following Callin down the after ladder, he knew it was the port shaft. That bearing, he thought, but Steurnagel and Lieutenant Jay and two of the firemen were standing beside the engine. "What is it?" he asked the first-class, coming up to them.

"Vibration," shouted Steurnagel. "Started all of a sudden. We cut to half rpm but it got worse. I told the bridge we had to shut down the port shaft."

"Yeah, good work. That bearing—"

"It ain't the shaft bearing, Chief. It's still runnin' warm, but that ain't it."

"Oh yeah?" said Wronowicz.

Lieutenant Jay came back around the engine casing, a flashlight in his hand. He was in khaki trousers and a T-shirt, already greasy. They must've got him up too, Wronowicz thought. "Any idea what it is?" he asked the chief, brushing a lock of blond hair off his forehead and leaving a black mark.

"I just got here, sir. We'll probably have to turn her over a few times, see what it was."

"Let's do it," said Jay. "Captain wants this cleared up

ASAP. We're in formation now; if we have to slow we'll drop back."

"You guys know anything?" Wronowicz asked the oilers.

"I seen it shaking," said one man.

"Where?"

"Here." He pointed to where the steel thickness of the shaft, immobile now, entered the reduction gear.

"What's the problem?"

It was the XO, looking angry. Wronowicz stared at him. He seemed out of place in the engineroom; he seldom went there, spending most of his time in the administrative offices. "What is it?" he said again, looking at Jay and Callin.

"We're trying to find out now, sir."

"Let's get it fixed. We have commitments to meet."

"Aye, sir."

Wronowicz ignored the officers, gnawed at his beard for a moment, then turned to the first-class. "Keep an eye on me," he said. "Unlock the shaft when I nod. Lock her up again when I wave my arm."

"You want steam?"

"No, just let everything spin on the prop."

"Right."

Wronowicz waited, watching the huge steel casing that housed the massive gear. The three turbines (high pressure, low pressure, and cruising) of the main engine fed power to it through short shafts, and the complex of machinery took their thousands of rpm and geared it down to drive the screw, fifty feet behind them. Now the first-class, at the throttleboard, brought up astern steam pressure till he could disengage the jacking-gear lock. As he lowered pressure again the shaft eased slowly into motion. As it blurred Wronowicz saw it start to jump. A high squeal tore at his ears. "Shut it down!" he screamed, waving his arm, and immediately it slowed, turning from a blur into a spinning line of metal. The lock went in with a jolt, making the men around it jump back.

"What's wrong?" said the XO.

"Shit," said Wronowicz, staring at the gear.

"I said—"

"The chief's figuring it out," said Jay, a little too sharply. The XO shot him a glance and then stood silent, looking at Wronowicz. They all looked at Wronowicz.

"It's the reduction gear," he said.

"Oh, Jesus," said Jay.

"The gear," said Callin, as if he understood what they were talking about.

"Yeah," said Wronowicz, staring at the thing. He was still slightly drunk, somewhere back in his head, but it had long ago left his memory. Now he was totally here in the engineroom, inside the ten-by-twenty-foot padlocked cover of the gearbox, past steel and lube oil and into the meshing of intricate metal, the sliding biting transmission of power, so smooth and dependable it was usually unthought of by anyone at all. "It wasn't the line bearing that went. I was watching that. It's like a pivot, though; the stress gets transmitted, and it went into the reduction gear. I figure we got a wiped bearing in there somewhere."

"Well, let's get it fixed," said the XO.

"It ain't that simple, sir," said Wronowicz. "We'd have to figure out which gear it is, get the load off it, then take out the bearing and replace it. The metal inside it rides on is gone."

The five men were standing there, looking at the reduction gear, when a clatter of feet came from the ladder. They turned. The gold-braided cap bobbed downward, glittered under fluorescent light, vanished behind the throttleboard, and then Captain Foster came up to them, pipe clenched in his teeth. "How long am I going to be at half power?" he asked.

"The chief was just saying that's not the problem, sir," said Jay.

"Well, what *is* the problem?"

"We don't have any spares for the reduction-gear bearings, sir," said Wronowicz.

"No *spares?*"

"No sir."

"Why the devil don't we have spares?"

"They aren't in our allowance, Captain," said Jay.

"Why not?"

"They don't break down that often, sir," said Wronowicz. "If we carried an extra for everything, we'd have
another goddamn ship aboard. And there's another problem."

"What's that?"

"We're not allowed to go into this gear, Cap'n."

"Who says?"

"Navy Regs, sir. This is a shipyard job."

The captain stared at the gear, at the shaft, at the engines, at the XO, very briefly, and then turned to Jay.
"Can I talk to you, Phil?" he said.

"Certainly, sir."

The officers went forward. Steurnagel came up, wiping
his hands on a piece of rag, and Wronowicz motioned at
the gear. "Which one you figure it is?" he said. "You guys,
get your heads in here and listen. You're gonna need to
know this someday."

"Uh . . . I don't know."

"Think. We got three turbines and one shaft. Are the
turbines jumping around?"

"No."

"Then which one is it?"

"The shaft bearing?"

"Or one of the pinion bearings inside the gear, yeah. So
how would we figure which one it is?"

"Uh . . ." The petty officer thought about it. "Take up
on the shaft so it doesn't bear, and then engage the engine?"

"That's good, but it'd take too long. No, I'll show you
how to find the bad one with a screwdriver. By sound.
Then we'll pull it for a look."

"Oh. Yeah."

Jay came back and squatted beside them. He looked

somber. He was as dirty as any of them now, but the uncrossable gulf of rank made them wait for him to speak. "Okay," he said. "Here's the picture. Captain Foster says we got to get the port shaft back on the line, just as soon as we can. If it's against the regs to open her up, he says he's the one that'll swing, not you."

"Jesus, sir, without parts how the hell—"

"I don't care," said Jay sharply. "You get me? Captain says it doesn't matter if we wreck the engines, over the long run. Tomorrow, or the day after, the task force may be ordered to assault a defended beach. You understand? It's a combat situation. We got to go in with them, to protect the amphibs. Then we got to patrol close in to the beach, to provide gunfire support if the grunts get in a jam ashore. To make it there with the rest we'll need both shafts and every knot you can give us. We can limp back after that; we can go into the yard in Gibraltar; we'll worry about that later. But we *got* to have both shafts."

"This bearing won't take it, sir," said Wronowicz. "That's the God's honest truth."

"Then you got to jury-rig it so it will," said Jay. "You're the chief machinist's mate. We'll give you all the help you need, but it's got to be done."

Staring at the gear, Wronowicz saw it in his mind's eye in all its complexity. It had been machined in a shop clean as an operating room, fitted by craftsmen with calipers and years of experience in their trade. The steel was the best American industry could make, each square inch alloyed to take thirty thousand horsepower for a billion revolutions. They were so dependable that the faraway experts who studied his maintenance reports had decided he didn't even need spares for them.

But everything failed sometime. He knew that. He was a machinist. Everything made of metal, everything that carried hydraulic fluid or electricity, everything made of flesh, everything that existed in time; they all failed, given enough years, enough stress. And that time had come, now, for something inside his ship; and it was for this night that the Navy had trained him and fed him and paid him and carried him a dozen times around the world.

"Chief?" said Jay.

"Yes sir," said Wronowicz, taking a deep breath. "We'll get right to work."

17

U.S.S. *Guam*

IN THE DARKNESS STEEL CRIED ALOUD, twisted by the immense force of the sea. A helicopter carrier was a big ship, but its very weight made it flex, deform, as the waves heaved and tore at its flanks.

The man lay awake, listening to the torment that came clearly through the metal to his ear. Rough weather, he thought. And getting worse. It was dark around him, as if the lightless ship, groaning in the implacable embrace of the sea, was already settling four thousand feet into the endless night below.

He raised his hand, half-expecting the rough underside of a lid above his head. When it encountered nothing he let it fall back to the bunk. He swiveled his eyes to the luminous dial of a chronometer, and forgot Poe.

It was almost midnight. Almost the magic instant when today became yesterday, tomorrow today.

When I was a child . . .

The thought came from nowhere, from the maelstrom of fancy and doubt that had filled his mind since he lay down. The man who lay in the dark did not often remember his childhood. But now, alone, he let a corner of that carefully wrapped past unfold.

As a child he had waited for midnight, lying in his bunk bed with his older brother. It was the mark of adulthood, to stay up, and though their dad had ordered them to bed they could still, boylike, defy him by staying awake. They were determined to. And when, by the light of a toy flashlight, he had seen the hands join, he had whispered to his brother; but his only reply was a snore.

Only Ike Sundstrom had kept his eyes open. To see, sliding across their ceiling, the headlights of the Hudson as his father drove off for the last time.

Now, in the darkened stateroom, far at sea, he wished his brother were there. Or his wife. Anyone . . . anyone, that he might not be so alone.

He turned over impatiently and fluffed his pillow for the dozenth time. Damn it, he thought, I knew this would be a bad night. He had never been able to sleep before important tests, interviews, or decisions. The steward had brought him milk, then been sent back to the pantry for a piece of pie. He didn't need the calories, but he couldn't sleep when he was hungry. Now he felt full.

But that was not what kept him awake.

His mind milled on like the wooden ducks one saw on the lawns of suburbs, beating the wind with their wings but going nowhere. It would not cease. All that night it had imagined difficulties, problems, conspiracies, accidents. Then it elaborated intricate plans to deal with each one. To some extent he enjoyed this. He believed that thinking through problems before they arose made you readier to deal with them. But now he was deadly tired, he wanted to rest and forget, and his mind would not let him. Despite his will it circled back again and again, like a faulty torpedo, to two things. One, the impending action. And two, the treachery and incompetence that surrounded him.

This whole day has been an object lesson, he thought angrily, in how not to run a task force. At every turn Hogan, that clock-puncher, had obstructed him, as he had through the entire cruise. The chief staff officer's job was to make the commodore's easier, to act as an alter ego. Instead Hogan obtruded difficulties at every turn. He was always whining about the men, about maintenance, about his sacred "routine."

Sundstrom closed his fists in the dark. The man had no conception of what real leadership meant. If everything ran by routine, why was there a squadron commander at all? No, his job was to *upset* routine, to jolt people into seeing their own error and carelessness, and to ready them for battle. That was what Sixth Fleet and the CINC expected, and that, by Christ, was what Ike Sundstrom was going to give them: a responsive, detail-oriented team, ready to do whatever needed doing. If he let the Hogan-types handle it, they would be caught with their pants down, every time—just as they had when the Soviet patrol plane showed up.

Another stab of memory made him writhe under the sheets. The debacle that afternoon. First, their reaction had been incredibly slow. In the Pacific his destroyer had been buttoned up and ready for battle in seven minutes. These unwieldy amphibious ships took ten, twelve, fourteen minutes to report. He couldn't believe it was that much more complicated for them. In three months of drills he had tried to hammer the time down, with only indifferent success. In that respect, today hadn't been bad—what was it, ten minutes for the whole formation? That was progress, anyway.

But the biggest problem was not his commanding officers. They were lackluster, that was certain. Sometimes he wondered if that was why he had been ordered here, to whip a slack organization back into shape. At other times he suspected that it was an exile, contrived by his enemies at the Bureau to hamstring his chances for making flag. But they were not the main problem. The main problem was his staff.

Worthless was too kind a word for them. He'd realized that the minute he stepped aboard, four months before. MacInroe had let them go to pot, indulged them, and when he expected them to perform or face the consequences they reacted with resentment and what amounted almost to sabotage. The N-2, Byrne, was a fool, full of fancy phrases and quick only at avoiding real work. A limp-wrist type. The supply officer, Glazer, was too young to know the ropes. The engineering officer was a nonentity. Lenson . . . a possible exception; if he had a few more years under his belt, they might do something together. As it was, the operations officer was poisoning him with his slack attitude.

It was Flasher who had humiliated him in front of the whole task group that afternoon. Sundstrom grimaced at a pang above his navel. That was what made it maddening: It looked as if he had been wrong and the fat lieutenant right. It was not his fault; it was the fault of the gunnery officers on the ships; they had panicked and loaded with live ammo. That was evident. But even Lenson had stared at him, after canceling the order to fire, as if he was in the wrong.

He lay in the dark, eyes open, and his mind spun in tight circles of rage and humiliation. Over and over he retraced the day, ending always with the moment when his own staffer had countermanded his order, and the others had gone along.

That must not happen again.

At last, it seemed like hours later, his anger ebbed, and he drifted toward sleep.

The phone buzzed. He slammed his knuckles on the steel fixture getting it free. "Commodore," he snarled. "What is it?"

"Staff watch officer, sir. Sir, we have a crossing merchant vessel, range thirty thousand, no sidelights. Course is one-two-zero, six knots. Closest approach will be—"

"What's our course?"

"We came to westerly leg at 0130, Commodore; we're on two-seven-zero."

"Go on."

"Closest point of approach will be two thousand yards

astern of *Bowen,* at 0210. Recommend turning the formation right to three-two-zero, that will clear—"

"Wait a minute," Sundstrom said. Sitting up, alone in the dark, he passed his hand over a sweat-slick forehead. The ship creaked and vibrated as a trough passed beneath. He tried to visualize the sea, courses and speeds, but it had deserted him. He could not recall the course of the incoming ship. "Wait . . . wait . . . oh, negative," he said. "How far ahead of us is the escort?"

"Ten thousand yards, sir."

"What is that goddamned AGI doing?"

"Snoopy's still in his usual station, sir, four thousand yards ahead of us."

"Maintain base course. Tell *Bowen* to maneuver independently to avoid," he said. "Maybe we'll get lucky and this guy will hit the Russian."

"Aye, sir." The receiver clicked. Sundstrom replaced it and lay back, sweating. His hands curled tightly into the sheets.

This was useless. He was not going to sleep. Work? He had worked all day, but it was all there was left in the end. He swung his legs to the deck and shoved his feet into slippers. He turned on the light over his desk and sat, pulling a chart toward him.

He had studied it briefly the day before, after Lenson had brought in the first draft oporder. He had doubted, then, that it would amount to anything. Now, with the twin shocks of the Turkish sortie and the embassy seizure, the probability of Urgent Lightning being executed was growing by the hour.

The thought made his stomach tighten again. Carry out an amphibious landing . . . he'd practiced, but he felt all too little confidence. Either in his own skills, or in those of his staff.

He sat at the desk, listening to the cries of the ship, and tried to imagine how the situation looked to Roberts, and above him CINCUSNAVEUR, and above him the CNO,

the Secretary of the Navy . . . and higher; a decision like
this would go all the way up the line. A long hostage crisis
was out of the question. This administration couldn't af-
ford it, not now, with the elections warming up. It had too
many bad echoes. If it wasn't resolved quickly by the local
authorities there would be enormous pressure to move in,
and fast.

Sundstrom propped his chin on his hands and stared at
the chart. There were only two ways to get troops into the
Eastern Med. One was by air. If he was in charge he would
consider the 101st Airborne, based in Germany. The
range was too great for helos, but a conventional parachute jump from transport planes would be the fastest way
to put a force on the ground. Drawbacks to that . . . he
pulled down the Navy-issue atlas and measured miles
clumsily with his fingers. No, damn it, the range made air
assault marginal. One-way, maybe, but not even that if the
southern rim allies refused refueling facilities. And in this
case, they might.

There would be political drawbacks to an airborne landing, too. He couldn't remember the last time one had been
carried out, other than in Vietnam. It had an unpleasant
flavor of war, that was sure.

The other possibility was the MARG.

He imagined himself sitting in the War Room, judging
alternatives. In favor of the Ready Group: They were on
station; they had mobility and light armor and helicopters.
Again in favor, there was plenty of precedent. The Sixth
Fleet had gone ashore dozens of times, all the way from
police operations up to near wartime situations. It was
almost routine, and the press was used to it. The fact that
the troops were sea-supported guaranteed their transience
in a way that the Army and Air Force, with their penchant
for giant supply depots and bases ashore, could not. Send
in the Marines . . . it had a solid ring to it. This was just
the kind of operation the Corps was designed to do.

The trouble is, he thought, the Task Force just isn't
strong enough.

One Marine Amphibious Unit was too small for a full-force intervention, even facing Third World armies. Their weapons were too light. Two thousand men with a handful of armor might be adequate for an unopposed landing as a peacekeeping detachment, or at most a coastal raid. With two-carrier air cover they might even hold a stretch of beach against counterattack for a few days. But it was not an invasion force, not at all.

All true . . . but looking at it objectively, Sundstrom had a nasty feeling that it might happen. Roberts might pin the rose on him. If he did, he hoped that at least one aircraft-carrier battle group came along with it.

Sixth Fleet's attitude worried him. The contretemps about getting underway from Italy had been a bad precedent. He did not know Roberts as well as he pretended. (If he was honest, he doubted if the admiral remembered him: They had met only once, at a Navy League dinner in Alexandria.) Without air cover, the MARG could find itself in real trouble.

And the big question, lurking in the back of his mind and he had no doubt in Roberts' as well, was the Soviets. Their Mediterranean fleet, like a rogue queen on a chessboard, inhibited the use of American force. Especially now, with the inexplicable increase. Some day, if this continued, the Sixth Fleet would attempt intervention in support of America's allies, and the Russians, moving in support of theirs, would say, very quietly, "Check."

The thought made him shiver. He had no idea what would happen then. He pulled his bathrobe around him, adjusted the lamp, and bent to the map, trying to see it objectively, tactically, as the commander of an amphibious task force should see a beach.

The best landing areas were on the southern coast. Lenson had recommended Larnaca. Sundstrom found it in the southeast, on a shallow bay. Behind a wide stretch of beach the land was flat for ten miles, then began a slow rise. The principal road ran back and forth across a hill range. Not too bad, maybe . . . the alternative was a road to the west, cutting across country. Still, it would be worth keeping in mind.

Christ, he thought, but which one is better? The direct one—but any enemy would expect them to use that. The indirect one, but—

For a moment he considered calling Haynes. The colonel knew land fighting; he knew terrain and the capabilities of his troops. Nominally the task-force commander was in charge of all aspects of an assault, but Sundstrom had no idea what marines did ashore. He trusted Haynes, so far anyway. His hand hovered near the phone, then dropped to the desk. He would get to him first thing in the morning.

His mind moved off the map, into the blue that ringed the green and tan of the island. That was another world, and another set of worries. Could he get the MAU ashore, if he got the word to go? The weather worried him. The seas were building, barometer still dropping at last report, and Fleet Weather was not optimistic about an early clearing. The rain and wind he did not care about, except as they impacted helo operations. The rough part would be carrying out a landing in heavy surf. He might still be a tyro at this amphib work, but the exercises had taught him how critical surf conditions were in those all-important first hours. The LCM-6s, LCM-8s, LVTs, and LCUs all had different characteristics. Each step downward in size increased their vulnerability to broach and capsize. At the same time, if he sent in only the largest craft the movement ashore would be intolerably slow—days instead of hours.

And once they started ashore, he'd be committed. A landing could not stop halfway. He would have to continue, even if the weather degenerated beyond the safe point.

Another worry occurred to him. Byrne. What had he meant in the briefing today, bringing up Lebanon? He almost wished he had let him go on. But no, he thought, that was rambling, just hot air, just ostentation. The man had nothing to offer.

No, there was no way to solve this in advance. He would have to ad-hoc it. He hated doing that, postponing the planning process. He hated to depend on things he could not influence—weather, the orders of higher authority, the decisions of unknown men ashore. On the whim of chance. Once the operation began he would have to make decisions in seconds, without adequate information, without proper staff support.

Yet he, the commander, would still be responsible for success or failure, measured by a yardstick of human lives.

Ike Sundstrom had never enjoyed responsibility. He had heard those above him, the golden ones, say they enjoyed it. He did not believe them. He had never found it other than a worry and a burden. Fortunately, up to now he had always found someone above him more than willing to assume it for him. For that was the way of the bureaucracy the peacetime Navy had become.

He switched off the lights and climbed back into the bunk. Lying in the darkness, he wondered if he should reach for the telephone. The corpsman could bring him something to make him sleep.

But then it would be all over the ship the next morning. No. He did not intend giving *them* ammunition like that. He would be cautious; he would keep himself in check. No more snap decisions, like the Quickdraw mistake. He had to bear down, concentrate, and lead. He had to make up for all the inefficiency, the slackness, the plotting against him. He had to do it alone.

My head is on the block, he thought.

He saw himself midway on a ladder reaching from obscurity to power. He had climbed it tenaciously and without joy for over twenty years, without love, without laughter. He had never laughed at the idea of a career. It would take all he had, and all he could do. He knew that. He accepted that.

But I'm scared.

Commodore Isaac I. Sundstrom turned on his side, anchoring himself against the roll with an outstretched arm. Staring into the darkness, he waited rigidly for the dawn.

V

THE STORM

18

U.S.S. *Guam*

DURING THE NIGHT THE WIND IN-
creased. Dawn broke gray and lifeless, gradually il-
luminating lowering clouds over a ragged formation. Task
Force 61 was no longer a unit, a uniform, compact body
of steel. Instead it was scattered individuals, each struggling to maintain course into twenty-foot seas.

The rain that lashed at his face was surprisingly cold.
Wind snapped at the collar of his foul-weather jacket as
Lenson, on *Guam*'s bridge wing, raised his glasses to
search for *Barnstable County*. He found her at last, far
astern. Smallest of the amphibious ships, built shallow-
draft for beaching, the LST was making heavy weather.
From twelve thousand yards away he shivered to see her
horned bow dip as if to gore an oncoming sea. It boarded
green and leapt foaming along her foredeck, shooting
spray high as her bridge. But then she lifted, shaking off
the water, and his heart rose too as she steadied herself for
the next line of seas that marched in from the east.

He hunched to mop water from his binoculars, and
looked next for *Bowen*. The frigate was hidden for long
seconds by the swells but at last he caught her, tossing a
wavering streamer of white as she rose on a crest. It would
be no fun aboard her, either. His attention moved round
the ragged ring of warships. *Coronado* was riding well, her
higher freeboard keeping her decks dry save for rain. *New-*

port, making as heavy a time of it as her sister LST. *Charleston* and *Spiegel Grove* both looked good. The attack transport moved behind the trailing skirts of a squall as he watched, and a few minutes later the wail of her foghorn came faintly across the wind.

He turned, and searched the horizon astern for *Ault,* their crippled duckling. Captain Foster had reported the propulsion casualty at 0330. Sundstrom had reluctantly given him permission to slow as necessary for repairs. Since the MARG was simply maintaining station, running legs west and east while waiting for orders, they would find her again on the next westerly course, later in the day.

As he had expected, she wasn't in sight. Christ, he thought, I hope she catches back up; we'll need those six guns if we go in . . . something else about her absence gnawed at his mind. Something else was missing too . . . he made another quick sweep, identified all the ships. But still the feeling nagged. He rubbed salt spray into morning stubble, hard, and the sting woke him a little. He tried to squeeze whatever it was out of his brain. Nothing came. Coffee . . . he wanted caffeine with all his soul, but with the commodore in the state he was in he didn't dare send a petty officer below. No, he had to stay awake by pure will, and frequent trips to the wing to lash his face with cold spray.

Was it possible, in seas like this, that they would be ordered to land? He felt divided between eagerness and fear. The eagerness, because this was their reason for being: to put the troops ashore. The fear because they would have to do it under so many handicaps. The sea. The impending war. And of course, Sundstrom.

But if we do, and pull it off, he thought, that would be a coup for everyone involved. Maybe even wipe out the stain of the *Ryan.* He felt guilty thinking of it that way. But there it was, and it was why he'd volunteered for sea duty again after the disaster.

Nodding into the wind, he slid off into remembrance of

a warm bed, warm sheets, the softness of a loving body. . . .

"Lieutenant," said Stan Glazer, from the wing door.

"Yuh!" He opened his eyes behind the eyepieces, frightened at himself; he had almost been asleep.

"You better get in here. They're calling us on HF."

He jumped for the hatch that Glazer held open against the roll. He had never used the red phone before. The high-frequency command net was for FLASH-precedence traffic, where seconds counted. A speaker above his head made it audible to everyone on the bridge. As he wiped sea from his face and picked up the handset, the distant whine of atmospheric static sent a thrill along his spine.

"Denver George, Denver George, this is True Dream, True Dream. Over."

"True Dream, this is Denver George, over," he said rapidly. To Glazer he muttered, "Stan, get the commodore up here right away. And Flasher, too."

"Right."

"This is True Dream Actual," said the distant voice, calm over the hiss and scream. *"Is Denver George Actual on this net?"*

"Denver George Actual on the way up, sir. Over."

"Will stand by for him. True Dream out."

"Denver George out," said Lenson, but at that moment Sundstrom took the handset from him. He had come up from behind, fast and noiseless in stocking feet.

"True—what is it?" he said.

"True Dream, sir. We're Denver George."

"I know that!—True Dream, this is Denver George Actual. Hello, Tony!"

"Hello, Ike," said the distant voice. *"Can you copy me all right?"*

"Loud and clear, Admiral," said Sundstrom. His demeanor had changed the moment he picked up the handset, his voice going crisp, his back straightening. Behind him, Lenson smiled at Red Flasher, who was tucking his shirt around his gut. He looked like he had just rolled out of his rack. Flasher nodded back, but for once he didn't grin.

"I'll make this brief, Ike, because there's a message en route, but I wanted to get you the word as fast as I could. Two developments. First, we've got some word from the authorities in Nicosia. About the hostages. They're being moved."

"Oh shit," muttered Flasher.

Sundstrom shot him a look of mortal warning. "Moved, Admiral?" he said into the handset.

"Right. We have a tentative ident on the terrorists as a PLO splinter."

"Uh-oh."

"Uh oh is right. They've demanded a plane. TWA or El Al. They want it at 0800. So they may be out of Cyprus before you can land."

"What's their destination, sir?"

"They won't say, Ike, but the jet they want could get them to Teheran. Or any place in the Med, basically. I'm putting up a radar bird to track it. We'll know when they set down. But for the moment, all I can say is, keep it hard; we may need you fast, or we may not need you at all."

"Understood, sir, and I want to assure you that TF 61 is ready now."

"Good . . . also, we've got names on the hostages. Mixed bag, U.S., Brits. One's a military dependent, appears to be one of your men. I forget the name, but it's in the message that's going out to you now."

"Yes sir."

"Okay. Second development: This weather is putting a crimp in our reconnaissance assets, but we've spotted the Turkish invasion force. They've jogged south, a little over a hundred miles northeast of your last reported position."

"Yes sir," said Sundstrom, and Lenson watched his head hunch into his shoulders.

"What's your heading, Ike?"

"Zero-nine-zero, sir."

"How are the seas? Can you get your formation around?"

"State four, bow on. I think I can get them around, though."

"Good. Open the Turks as far as you can while staying within range of your original objective."

"Aye, sir."

A sudden roar of water beat against the windows. The squall. Lenson missed the next few words as he flicked on the wipers. They flailed against the rain, motors whining. For a moment the glass cleared; he saw *Coronado* lifting her stern far ahead, and then the world dissolved again into a solid wall of rain.

"We don't anticipate your meeting them. Our guess is they'll turn north again shortly for a landing near Famagusta. What we're worried about here, though, is the Greek air force. They may try for a strike. And the Turkish air may be out trying to preempt."

It could be war, all right, Lenson thought. Between two NATO allies. They had clashed before. And with the ships of the task force, and the hostages, caught squarely in the middle.

Sundstrom seemed to be thinking the same thing. "Can you give us air cover, Tony?" he was asking.

"I'm trying, Ike, but basically we want to keep the heavies out of this," said the distant voice. Lenson caught the implication: *America* and her nuclear-powered escorts were too valuable to risk. *"Consider this a Warning Yellow, threat axis three-zero-zero. I want your units ready to defend themselves, Commodore. A direct flight path from the Greek airfields to the Turkish force passes right over you. A mistake in identification could have serious consequences."*

"I understand," said Sundstrom. "You know, sir, we have only one escort with us. That's not much in the way of air defense."

"One? My plot shows you have two. Bowen and Ault."

"Yes sir. Well, Admiral, *Ault*'s reported some engine trouble. She may not be able to keep up with us."

"What's wrong with her? Well, never mind, I'll look at the casualty report. I'll try to get you cover. Maybe the Air Force has something available. If you see aircraft don't get panicky. They may be ours. If they're not, rules of engagement follow in hard copy."

And Lenson, leaning against the rain-smeared scope, felt fear stir beneath the weariness. No air cover. He could read that behind the admiral's half-promises. At this range Air Force fighters would be able to stay half an hour, no more. Hardly worth sending. They were on their own.

"Any questions, Commodore?"

"One, Admiral," said Sundstrom. "If they don't leave the island—or if they land somewhere within range—do you plan to send us in?"

"We're in touch with the War Room, Ike," said the distant voice, taking on its own hard edge. A crackle of static sounded like gunfire, as if it were the distant admiral who was on the front line, and not the swaying, rain-lashed ships. *"We're getting guidance direct from the top on this one. I'll let you know. Meanwhile, stand by. True Dream, out."*

"Denver George, out," said Sundstrom, and let up on the button. His arm sagged, holding the handset, and Lenson took it from his hand and hung it up. The commodore looked out forward for a moment, over the rainswept gray and painted circles of the flight deck, to where *Barnstable County* rolled like a pig in mud on the horizon. The squall had cleared as abruptly as it had begun, fallen astern. But they would meet it again as soon as they turned.

The squall . . . Dan wished suddenly for a real storm, a hurricane, an engulfment. The blanket of cloud and rain was suddenly comforting. Rain would give them *some* cover.

"Jesus Christ," Sundstrom said, to no one in particular.

"Sir?" said Flasher. "Any orders?"

"They're going to leave me dangling out here," said Sundstrom, his voice low. "Jesus Christ! Tony's going to let me go down the drain. It'll be the *Pueblo* all over again!"

"Want us to come around, sir?" said Lenson. "He said—"

"I heard him, goddamnit," said Sundstrom, the uncertainty instantly replaced by anger. "Are you trying to tell me my job, too? Well, forget it. Roberts wants to see me fumble; you all want to see me drop the ball. Well, I've got the bubble; I've been in deeper kimchee than you can imagine and come up smelling like a rose. Let's get these people around, right now!"

"Aye, sir."

The ships acknowledged the order by radio, doubt in their voices. One by one, waiting for lulls, they put their helms over and came about. Lenson watched *Newport* hesitate, waiting for a heavy sea to pass, and then lean into the turn. She was three-quarters of the way through it when a secondary system caught her on the quarter and pooped her. Green water foamed and spumed along her exposed deck, as if she were sinking stern first. Through the binoculars he could see the aft lookout running for shelter, jerking his phone cord behind him. The little ship hesitated, as if deciding whether to broach; then diesel exhaust burst from her funnels and she straightened, taking the next sea from directly astern. For a moment, staring out at her, he almost remembered the thing he had sensed at dawn; but as he groped for it the memory slipped back into the fog of fatigue. A spatter of rain blurred the little ship from sight.

"Goddamn weather," said the commodore, watching her too. "How they can expect us to land in this is beyond me. Well, maybe we'll get lucky and those bastards will fly to Iran."

Lenson stared at him. He couldn't believe the man had said that. That would mean another humiliating crisis, one that could drag on and on . . . "Commodore," he said then, remembering, "hadn't we better get the word out? About the readiness condition?"

"Of course, Dan. I told you that already. Antiair Warning Yellow, and all units at Condition One."

"General quarters, sir?"

"That's what I said. Right now."

"Sir, we don't need—Yellow doesn't require—"

He saw the coming anger on Sundstrom's face, and said quickly, forestalling it, "Aye, sir. General quarters," and reached for the handset.

They spent the rest of the morning at GQ. At noon Sundstrom grudgingly gave permission for Flasher to take over the watch. Lenson paused aft of the bridge, bracing himself. *Guam*'s motion was different on this heading. With the seas astern she heaved herself up with each wave, digging her bow into the troughs like a man scooping hard ice cream. When it steadied for a moment he slid down the ladder.

In the supporting arms center McQueen and Byrne and Glazer were slumped in their chairs, eyes closed. The N-2 turned his head as Lenson dogged the hatch behind him.

"Hey, Jack," he said.

"Dan."

"What's wrong?" Something in the way Byrne stared at him made him pause for a moment inside the door.

"Oh. Nothing . . . what's going on topside? We don't belong down here. We're ninety miles offshore."

"I know that, and you know that, Jack, but *he* doesn't. He's got the whole formation standing to."

"What for? Oh—the Greek Air Force. But why are we manned up in *SACC*? We can't do any good down here," said Glazer.

"Brilliant deduction," said Lenson. He dropped into his chair and reached for his headset, too tired to argue.

Cyprus covered the bulkhead in front of him, red and yellow and brown, writhing with roads, indented with bays. His eye went directly to the southern coast.

McQueen had taped in the beach blowup, and he had drawn in approach lanes and drop points himself the night before. Now, he thought bitterly, it was all wasted. Where would these faceless terrorists take their victims next? The ship tilted in a corkscrew, and a handset clattered to the deck.

"Jack—you get all the hot gouge the same time Sundstrom does. Have you heard anything more about the embassy?"

"Well, a little." Byrne pulled off his aviator glasses and rubbed his eyes. Again Dan caught that hesitation, as if the intel officer was stalling to think through his words. "They're moving out, all right. Might even be for the best. There's a lot of firing reported from the city. The UN peacekeeping team pulled out last night; New York felt they were too small to be effective anymore."

"Anything about the hostages?"

"Ah . . . nothing new. Just that there's about a hundred of them, mostly U.S. and British."

"Who's holding them, sir?" asked McQueen.

"That we don't know yet, exactly," said Byrne, rubbing the bridge of his long nose and sounding very tired, "though we can guess from their demands."

"What do they want?"

"The usual stuff . . . remember the guys the Turks caught heading home after the bombing in Germany? They want them released. So it's probably the same group. They're covert; we don't know too much about them, other than that their leader, guy who calls himself 'the Majd,' was implicated in the synagogue massacre in London last year. But it's terrorist theater, standard procedure: The point is less to actually achieve a stated goal than to humiliate us, demonstrate our impotence, delaminate us from our allies, et cetera."

Once again, Lenson was glad Susan and Nan were safe back in Athens. "You think we'll release them? The prisoners?" he asked Byrne.

"They aren't ours, they're the Turks'. We can't do a

thing but ask them. And they don't play patty-cake with bad guys. Those are tough bastards, Dan. I've seen them execute their own crewmen. Firing squads, on the fantails of their ships. They hold this little religious service, they shoot the guy, he falls overboard. That's it. Not a lot of concern for what the other ships in formation think about it. No, I don't think we're going to talk the Turks out of much. Plus, they're tied up in Cyprus now—oh, it's masterly timing."

"You think we should have put the MAU ashore, then?" asked Glazer.

"If we could have done it that would have been the best way," said the N-2. "But I guess it's a missed chance. We'll be twisting in the wind for months on this one."

"SACC, flag bridge," said the squawk box, in Sundstrom's voice. "Dan, are you down there?"

"Yes sir."

"Let's get some drills going, as long as you're on station. Bring the other ships up on the net, get some comm drills going. I want us to be on stream, ready for any eventuality."

"Aye aye, sir," said Lenson. The intercom clicked off. The other officers glanced at each other, rolling their eyes. He ignored them, pulling out a call for fire form. They could laugh, they could be sarcastic, even—in spite of one of the oldest rules in the Navy—in front of an enlisted man.

He would not. He would do his duty, despite fatigue, despite everything. No matter how silly or meaningless things seemed to him, he had to believe that Sundstrom knew what he was doing, that he was right. It did not matter, he told himself fiercely, what he or anyone thought of their commander. Because in the last analysis, if there was not obedience, and respect as well, then this ship, and this squadron, and the Navy, were lost.

Suddenly his pen stopped moving. He sat up.

"Dan? What is it?"

"I just remembered."

"What?"

"That tattletale," he said. "The Russian. Snoopy."

"What about him?"

"He's gone. He left the formation during the night."

"What's that mean, sir?" said McQueen.

"Nothing," said Lenson slowly, staring at the map. "Nothing . . . I hope. Come on, let's start the drill."

19

Nicosia, Cyprus

THEY WOKE HER AT DAWN, FOR NO REA-
son Susan could see. With the others she sat through the
morning, huddled, waiting. None of them knew for what.
The men, whoever they were, who owned them now
leaned with guns casual in their arms as umbrellas, smoking, eyes restless. Outside the shattered windows the drizzle drifted down steadily from clouds low-flying as
pigeons, gray as lead.

She held Nan close, and did not dare to wonder what
lay ahead.

At a little past ten they were motioned up from the floor
and roughly instructed. Outside. Single file. One piece of
hand luggage, no talking. She wondered why, but only
briefly. One man—the Korea vet, she remembered—at-
tempted to object. No word was said to him in reply; he
was simply clubbed toward the exit. After that the hostages got up swiftly, all at once.

As she filed obediently through the shattered gates of
the embassy she pulled Nan close, hiding her face from
what lay in the dripping rosebushes. Someone had thrown
a blanket over the younger marine, but the sergeant lay
rigid in dress blues, his face upturned. Rain pooled in the
hollows of the opened eyes, ran down the cheeks to drip
in the grass.

"Go on! Over street." "Move, or we shoot!" The shouts

hurried them, like whips, along a gauntlet. They clattered into the street between two ragged lines of guards. One of them, shirt clinging translucent wet to his chest, shoved Ms. Freed savagely ahead of him. Shallow puddles of dirty water dotted the roadway. The wind drove ripples across them like miniature oceans. On one shore a red-and-white Lucky Strike package, empty and crumpled, lay hard aground. When the blanket fluttered, Susan caught sight of a dark wrist. The corporal had been black. She bent over her daughter, glancing fearfully toward the nearest terrorist.

"Nan? Are you all right?"

"Cold, Mommy . . ."

She searched the upturned face. Her cheeks were too red, her eyes blurry with fever. It wasn't imagination. Nan was worse this morning. Maybe it wasn't flu, despite what Stanweis said. She wondered how much medicine the old man really remembered.

If she got wet and cold now, even flu could turn into . . . she hated to think. Where were they going? Nan needed warmth and food and sleep. Where were these people taking them? Didn't anyone know that this was happening?

"Where are the police?" she whispered fiercely.

Moira, just behind them, was holding the pulpy remains of a Greek-language newspaper over her head. She looked pale and frightened. "I don't know, Betts," she said, her voice pitched under the aural cover of the rain. "Probably waiting for the Turks."

Of course. She had forgotten the impending invasion. But the takeover of an American embassy could not be overlooked, even at the edge of that abyss. "Somebody has to know what's going on here," she whispered.

"I don't," said Michael.

"I mean, outside of us. Somebody's got to be thinking about what to do, how to get us away from . . . *them.*"

She flicked her eyes past Moira and went silent. Arms folded over his rifle, shirt open to his waist, a young man watched them go by. He looked no older than sixteen. His eyes were both wary and repelled, as if those who passed carried some disfiguring disease. The green armband was dark with rain. A knife was thrust into his belt. He was only a boy . . . but it must have been just so, Susan thought suddenly, that the blond young fanatics of the SS had regarded those they called subhuman. They passed him and she whispered again, "Don't you think so? They can't just let them *do* this."

"I think Persinger might have got a message off, just before they came in the gate," said Michael. He seemed about to say more, but just then one of the guards, as they plowed by him through a puddle, reached out suddenly for the radio.

Cook grabbed for it, but too late. Plastic shattered, and the pieces subsided back into dirty water. Cook stared at the Palestinian for a moment—this one was short, ugly, and thirtyish, with crooked teeth and a crazy smile—and then reached out. He had his hands on him when Moira pulled him back by his shirt, putting him off balance. The man smiled even more then and stepped into him and stroked him to the roadway with the automatic pistol he carried. The sound of steel on bone was just like a baseball bat connecting.

"Michael!"

"Oh, mommy, he hit Mikey!"

For a moment she could not move. It was the first time she had seen a man strike another like this, not caring if he killed. For a moment she seemed to go far away. Then she came back, called by her daughter's cry. But the world was different now, and something in her, too, had changed.

"Help me get him up, Susan! Damn you," Moira spat at the small man. He stood watching, grinning down at Nan, but keeping the pistol pointed at Cook. Behind him two other terrorists stepped up, their faces closed.

"Majd say no radios," the small man said, still grinning.

Susan set Nan down and reached for Michael. A thread

of blood showed at his ear. The women got the archaeologist out of the water and up on their shoulders. He stood, with an effort, and tried to push their hands away.

"I'm okay, you don't have to drag me . . . he just got me down for a minute." He waggled his head.

"You're bleeding."

"Har*rach!*" said one of *them,* moving forward.

"Let's go," muttered Moira. She wrapped Cook's arm around her shoulders. "Come on."

"Mommy, carry me. It's cold," whined Nancy, putting up her arms to be carried. With a wrench of her heart Susan saw how small she was, standing in the empty street, armed men around her.

The small guard reached out then. "You have pretty girl," he said. Presumably he meant only to pat her head, but Susan bent hastily, scooped her up and backed away, watching craziness well up in his eyes. Her heart began to thud, but after a moment he turned away, laughing with the others.

"Michael, you sure you're okay? You're all wet—"

"Yeah." He glanced back, eyes narrow. The collar of his shirt was turning pink, blood mixed with rain. "That snaggletoothed little sucker sure hits hard."

They were headed, it seemed, across the square, and again she wondered why they were being moved. If, as seemed most likely, they were being held as hostages, why should the terrorists move them? Wouldn't there be more symbolic value, for whatever point these people were trying to make, in holding them in the American Embassy?

The leader, the young one . . . he had ordered it. He . . . what had the guard called him? "Majd." That was it.

At that moment she saw him. He was standing to the side of the line of march, with three swarthy, mustached men. Rifle slung over his back, hair slicked wetly over his forehead, he was smoking a cigarette and listening gloomily to one of them. As she watched, he nodded, once, took a last puff, and flicked the butt toward the passing Americans. He looked off, toward the embassy.

She glanced back too, to see the last of the hostages filing out. When they were clear two of the guards lingered by the gate. As she watched, one pulled a bundle from his shirt, bent, then threw a piece of cloth over the twisted ironwork. A flag, red and green. Then, to her amazement, the other aimed a camera. The first posed, grinning, his weapon at port arms. Then they rejoined the rest.

She was wondering about that when they came out onto the main plaza, and saw the buses.

And the police. There weren't many. A handful of men in khaki, sitting in open vehicles in the drizzle, about two hundred yards away. They were faced on her side of the square by four of the terrorists, bareheaded, wet, and armed. The file of Americans turned as they came into the open, away from the motionless soldiers, and headed for the buses. The guards kept them to a slow walk. It was as if they were being displayed.

In the distant gray, behind the police cordon, she caught the slow pan of a lens.

The buses were silver-and-blue Mercedes, new. The same ones that had been waiting, diesels idling, to ferry Japanese and German tourists around the island, when she and Nan had arrived at the Nicosia airport. Now their route signs said, cheerily, PRIVATE PARTY.

As they came abreast of the police, still distant, she noticed the terrorists move closer to the Americans, pointing their weapons at their heads. It was done without words, visually, but the message was unmistakable. Keep back, they were telling the police. Do as we say. Or these people die.

She felt ice touch her spine. They weren't being held in secret. People outside knew. But they couldn't help.

No one could help.

The plane was a three-engine jet. Beyond that she could not tell, nor did she much care. But she was briefly heartened to see the big red letters gleaming shiny-wet on the vertical tail. TWA. At least, she thought, it should fly all right.

They were herded aboard quickly, single file, forced to run across the tarmac. The drizzle broke long enough for her to see the mountains to the west.

"So long, Cyprus," muttered Moira as they bent at the top of the ramp.

The interior was a madhouse. Screaming, the terrorists (now, she wondered, were they hijackers, too?) shoved their way through the aisles, pushing men and women into seats with the butts of their rifles. She half-sat, was half-thrust into a seat midway along the fuselage, right side, just aft of the wing. She held Nan on her lap. Moira was two seats back, Freed a few forward of her; she'd lost sight of the others. The seat beside her was empty and she wondered why. She found out when one of *them* sat down beside her. He was one she hadn't encountered yet, a rotund fellow with quite a bit of stubble. She knew immediately he had been doing some sweating. By no means pleasant company, but he neither struck anyone for the time being nor gave Nan more than a single uninterested glance.

They sat on the ground for about half an hour. Midway through that the seated passengers heard voices raised from the flight compartment. At last two men in blue uniforms came down the aisle, still arguing, and being shoved by the Majd himself. He spoke in English, as he had the night before, and this time she caught a slight British intonation.

He jerked open the hatch and shoved them out. One pilot almost fell, saving himself only with a grab for the ramp handrail. "And tell them we want others within five minutes!" he shouted after them.

Ah, she thought, imagine the headlines in *Time*: PLO DEMANDS BETTER-QUALIFIED CREWS. "Latest from embattled Nicosia is word of a safety initiative by terrorist leaders—"

Get a grip on yourself, Susan.

When the new pilots (this time in lighter blue and looking more frightened than the first pair: Turkish? she wondered) came aboard there was more palaver. At last the door to the cockpit closed. Susan glanced the length of the passenger compartment. There must be no more than a dozen of *them,* she thought then. No room for more than three in the cockpit, and she could count eight spaced along the aisle. They had reserved seats for themselves, but most were still standing, scanning the ranks of heads and filling the air of the compartment (still unventilated) with cigarette smog.

The announcement system came on at last, and simultaneously with it the engines began to whine. Through her window she caught a glimpse of a man in coveralls pulling away a cable. Yellow trucks trundled back. "THIS IS CAPTAIN SPEAKING," it began.

Then came a yelp. A crackle, and then the voice resumed.

"WE WILL BE HAVING ABOUT A ONE HOUR OF FLIGHT EN ROUTE TO THE DESTINATION. THE LEADER HERE TELLS ME YOU WILL NOT BE BEING HARMED UNLESS YOU MAKE THE NOISE OR MOVEMENT. UNDERSTAND? NO THE NOISE, NO THE MOVEMENT, VERY GOOD.

"WE WILL BE TAKING OFF SHORTLY."

But, she thought then, for where? She glanced at the man sitting beside her. Then she lowered her head again.

For the first fifteen minutes their flight was smooth. She held Nan's head against her breast and smoothed her hair, over and over. Beneath the wing Nicosia dropped away and then vanished, dissolved into mist. The mountains dropped away. Then all was white, as if they were flying through milk. Long minutes later the plane emerged from a zone of turbulence into sudden brightness and blue sky. Below them cumulus bloomed like vast lush flowers in instant, brilliant splendor, and then began slowly rolling back toward the tail.

An hour, she thought, cuddling Nan. Where can we go in that long? These planes made something over five hundred miles an hour, she knew that. Moira might be able to guess; Michael seemed to know things, but her own ideas of distance in this part of the world were sketchy. Besides, she didn't even know the direction they were headed in.

She decided she had so much to wish for now, she might as well wish for a compass, too.

One of the men came down the aisle, his arms laden with Pepsi-Cola and grenades. He handed a dew-beaded blue and white can to the man beside her. Her seatmate pulled the tab with his teeth and sucked at it noisily. She was hungry—none of them had eaten since the toast and coffee the previous morning—and was growing thirsty, too. Yet she dared not speak. He seems human, she thought, watching his reflection in her window. For the second time that morning she felt a flash of hope.

It disappeared again when the identification check began. The tall man appeared and stood quietly by the first-class compartment, watching as his men moved slowly down the aisles row by row. Most of the passengers had blue U.S. passports, a few United Kingdom, lion and unicorn stamped in gold. Susan readied hers, then began to sweat. Did it say anywhere in there . . . holding it low by her thigh she paged through it. No, there was nothing about the military in it—

Their vaccination certificate! From the base dispensary. She worked it cautiously from beneath its paper clip with small movements of her fingers and slipped it under the seat cushion. After a moment's thought she opened her purse, pretended to be rummaging. The man beside her glanced at it, then away when she pulled out a chapstick. She thought for a crazy moment of offering it, then was afraid he might take offense. If she did, or if she didn't? At last she did not. While he was looking away she found and hid her dependent's ID card as well.

She sat back then, shaken, but feeling safer. If they

searched her thoroughly they would find something, a receipt from the commissary, a credit union card . . . but if they search us all, she thought, it will take them hours. We should be down by then.

I am Susan Lenson, housewife. My husband is an insurance salesman, or no, what would they like better—

Ahead of her they came to Ms. Freed. It was the boy, the youngest one, who was checking the right row of seats. The passport she held up to him was red. Susan saw it shaking in her hand.

The boy snatched it from her, and Susan saw his eyes widen. He called in Arabic to the others. They converged on Freed, three of them, and jerked her up from her seat. Over the whisper of the engines she could hear them clearly.

"Red passport. You CIA?"

"No. State Department. I'm just—"

"Yes, CIA. You admit now."

Susan caught a glimpse of her face. It was white as the clouds. One of the men jerked her hands into the air, holding them crossed at the wrists. Another—she saw it was the one with bad teeth—ran his hands over her clothes, under them. With an exclamation he pulled out a package, ripped it apart. It contained several chocolate bars. Thrown contemptuously to the floor, they were trampled gradually to brown pulp as the interrogation proceeded.

Freed did not struggle. They shouted at her, slapped her face, but she responded in the same low trembling voice. One of them hit her in the stomach and Susan caught her breath, feeling the blow in her own.

When the snaggletoothed man put his pistol to her head, the Majd held out his hand, palm down. There was a quick spatter of conversation among them, almost in whispers. At last they left, shoving her back into the seat. She bent there, head downward, and Susan heard her quietly using an airsick bag.

A moment later they came back and led Freed forward.

The curtains of the first-class section fell shut behind her. From the far side, a few minutes later, she saw Mr. and Mrs. Stanweis being pushed forward as well.

Susan stared out the porthole, holding Nan between her and the outer skin of the plane. Above the sunlit convexities the blue sky was empty. At long intervals the heavy cover would thin, and she glimpsed for just a moment something shiny and vast far below, like tinfoil crumpled and then resmoothed.

The sea. But it too was empty. For a moment, craning backward to watch the brilliance slide over it again, she wished for something else up here. For other planes. She imagined them riding alongside, escorting them, reassurance if not protection. Did no one know where they were? Where they were going? Or did anyone care?

Numbly she reached for the seat pocket and took out the ditching instructions. For a long time she stared at the overwing exit sign. It was only a reach away for her, two red handles that led to the outside. To death, here, far above the clouds. She fantasized holding those trip levers half-open, threatening their captors with sudden decompression unless they surrendered their weapons.

Behind her she heard them begin to question Moira Lieberman.

Later Nan began to wriggle. When Susan looked at her, she whispered shamefacedly that she had to pee.

"Can't you hold it, Bunny?"

"*Been* holding it." Nan would not meet her eyes.

She felt helpless. There were no containers, and she did not dare draw attention by asking to use the toilet. Nor had anyone else so far in the flight. At last Susan held her as she urinated over the edge of the seat, on the carpet. She had just set her back up and drawn up her jeans when there was a sudden jolt, not loud, but sharp. It seemed to come from forward, though she could not see past the curtain. But a moment after there were yells, then a strange acrid stench seeping back, tanging the air.

The plane tilted down, and people began to scream.

"Silent!" shouted the man beside her. He tripped his belt and got half to his feet, waving his rifle threateningly. Susan wrapped her arms around Nan, unthinking reflex, as the slant steepened and then, all at once, the plane seemed to slide off of one wing. They've shot us down, the idiots, she thought, frozen with terror.

From her window she looked straight down into the clouds.

The youngest guard came running down the slanting aisle, screaming something. His face was livid. The smell grew stronger, and she saw a curl of blue smoke grope out of the ventilators.

"Mommy, my ears hurt."

"Swallow, baby." She held her daughter close, rubbed her throat. Suddenly, then, the terror left her. She knew they were going to die here, now, in the next few seconds. Nan, she thought. If I could have saved you I would. My life, nothing. I would give it for you. I'm sorry. We should have stayed with the rest—

"I love you, Bunny," she whispered into her child's ear. "You were always good."

The world went dim, and she blinked for a moment before understanding: they'd entered the overcast. White, blank, the window glowed like a snow-filled television screen. The lights flickered. She felt pressure in her ears, swallowed again. The plane suddenly rolled wing over wing, juddered, and then gave a savage buck. Around her people screamed. The terrorist beside her was knocked to the floor. His rifle skidded away under the seat. She stared out the window, holding her daughter tight.

The cloud cleared, and she saw below them sea, and then, instantaneously afterward, land. Low, bare hills, dun-brown. A huddled village, fields. They flashed by, so close she could see goats on the hillsides.

The nose came up a little, and then a little more.

The lights went out. The plane reeled, digging the belt painfully into her stomach. The sign at the front of the cabin winked on and off redly, a picture of a buckle closing, over and over.

"PREPARE FOR LANDING," said the cabin speaker. "I TRY TO LAND—PREPARE—SEAT BACKS UPRIGHT—"

The plane staggered down from the sky. She watched the hillsides grow. Now she could see scrub, no, it was in rows, a man with a donkey, both of them looking up, lines of olive trees. They flashed over a parked truck and a group of women in black, carrying bundles; over a pond with drinking cattle; then the hills rose again, the engines bellowed outside the aluminum walls, and the earth rushed up to meet them.

The plane slammed down, the wheels shrieking. She felt it reject the earth, leap upward, then slam down harder. Dust flew up from the carpet. The engines roared. Deceleration pulled at the child in her arms and she wrapped herself tightly around her. Nan whimpered, deep in her throat, but did not cry out.

If we land safely, Susan thought then, I'm not going to be afraid of anything that happens after that.

The engines screamed in reverse thrust. She glanced out, but brown dust veiled vision. On the floor the man who had fallen scrabbled between her legs for his rifle, dragged himself up by the seat-back. He glared around, looking frightened.

"WE ARE LANDED," stated the intercom. "PLEASE TO STAY AT YOUR SEATS."

Someone else spoke then, rapidly, in the language she had to assume was Arabic. The plane slowed, jolted as if it had run over something, and the brakes squealed.

They stopped, rocking slightly from side to side.

The engines wound down. Beside her the chubby one slung his rifle and leaned forward. He struggled with the handles for a long moment, and then the window popped and fell outward, banging on the wing. She saw the other terrorists working at the forward and aft exits, and a moment later there was a whoosh and she saw something orange unroll downward. When it began to inflate she realized it was the emergency slide.

"Up! Move forward."

"PASSENGERS WILL GO TO THE STATION FOR EMERGENCY DEPLANE," said the pilot in his strange English.

Suddenly everyone in the compartment was on his feet. The terrorists shouted, clubbed here and there, and restored some measure of order. But still she was shoved and battered as she dragged Nan into the aisle. The forward exit, or over the wing? It was solved for her by the press of people. Like toothpaste in a tube she was squeezed forward. When they reached the hatch she had eyes only for the smooth plastic. She seated Nan between her legs, squatted, and tobogganed downward to a rough contact with the ground.

When she got up, the snaggletoothed man was pointing his pistol at them. He did not waste words, only motioned to his left. She jumped to her feet, not bothering to brush her clothes off, and snatched up the baby. Carrying her, not noticing the weight, she followed the others at a near-run around the plane.

They were in the desert.

Nothing around them but the bare brown hills, low, weather-worn. And sand. Where had they landed? On open desert—but no, there was asphalt under her feet, cracked and faded to gray, but still a strip of sorts—

They rounded the wing, and she saw the buildings. A small group, one low, two others, behind it, taller. They looked lonely against the empty hills.

The knot of hostages came to a halt a hundred yards from the jetliner. Two of the men motioned them down with gun barrels. She squatted on the hot tarmac and looked back. The plane squatted too, two of its tires shredded, all of them smoking. Otherwise it looked unharmed. From the rear exit people were still tumbling out. She looked forward, and a fine sweat broke on her as she saw that they had stopped a hundred feet short of the end of the strip. Beyond that was bare sand.

We're down, she thought numbly. Alive. Beyond that, for the moment, she could not think at all.

Two guards waited by the portico of the central building, the tallest, five stories high. As they neared it she saw that it was ornate, old, not a glass-and-concrete box. Two lions of black stone flanked the entranceway.

Moving up in the world, Susan, part of her said tentatively. But no humor came through the strange paralysis she had felt since seeing Cook struck down that morning.

The lobby was deserted. The interior, decorated in pale blue, was dark, the chandeliers unlighted. It looked almost new, unused, yet the curtains drooped dusty and faded as if abandoned for years. What must have been a souvenir shop was dark, iron grating drawn across its glass. The desk was empty. Wires dangled from an unlit switchboard. A key lay on the dusty marble of a desk. It was as if ghosts had lived here, and vanished as quickly and completely as ghosts do with the coming of the sun.

The elevators didn't work. The hostages stood crowded together in the hot, still air of the lobby, surrounded by armed men, until the tall man came. He began shouting angry orders. Not ten feet away, she had a chance to observe him.

The man they called the Majd was young, yes, but older than she had thought the night before. Twenty-five? No more than twenty-eight. With a sleepless night and black stubble his romantic picturesqueness had faded, but his motions were still brisk, commanding, electric. The eye sought him like the focal point of a painting. Someone objected; he swung to face him, moving closer to speak, and she realized with a small surprise that he was nearsighted.

He seemed to be placing his men at ground level. The hostages would be on the second and third floors. Ah, she thought. So escape would be more difficult. Not that she had given it even a passing thought. So far there had been no chance, especially with Nan.

Seeing what had happened to Persinger, to the employee in the gray suit, to the two marines—and the unhurried, brutal way they had interrogated Freed—she did not feel like being the first to try.

So now they were installed—she and Moira, Michael and Nan—in a double on the third floor. The room, like the lobby, had been long abandoned. A rag of a dress hung in the closet, a razor lay rusted to the sink. The bed was a bare mattress. She wondered who had been here and where they had gone. The door was open, so that a man patrolling the corridor could see in, but for the moment they were alone.

She did not know whether their condition had improved with the flight. It was slightly more comfortable, but she did not know where they were, even what country they were in. She did not know what fate awaited them. Most fearsome of all, she did not know what was in the dark man's mind.

But I've got to be cheerful, she thought, looking at Nan. Got to keep smiling, if only for her. "I'm glad as hell they didn't take you, too," she said to Moira.

"Take me?"

"The people they picked out. Freed, and the Stanweises—a few others—I was afraid—?"

"They asked me if I was Jewish."

"And you—" she hesitated, uncertain just how to phrase it.

"What do you think? I said no. They fell for it." The Ox's heavy eyebrows bent. "At least, for the time being."

"I'm glad you're both with us," Susan said. "Now, if only we had something to eat—"

"Don't *remind* me! God, I'm dying of hunger. But . . . at least we know they know what's happened."

"*They*, Moira?"

"The World. The cameras! Didn't you see them?"

"I saw them. What good will they do?"

"You have me there, Betts."

"I hope they can figure out what this guy, this Majd, wants," put in Michael. "If even he knows."

"You don't think he does?"

"I wonder. You know, I get the feeling this isn't going quite as planned."

"What?"

Michael paced the room, probing the lump that was rising over his ear. "I think they had a bunch of people who got through the gates, all right, and took the embassy, all right; but then found themselves upstaged by a real war. So then this Majd character decides to move us where he can get more coverage, or maybe where things are safer for him. And then—well, I don't know whether he planned to land here, or whether we were forced down."

"You don't think this is, like, where they come from? Their base, or something?"

"Have you seen anyone else?" Cook went to the window and leaned against it, looking out. There was a balcony, but they had been told to keep the windows closed, not to go out. He tapped his knuckles on the glass. "Whup! Company."

"Who?"

"An armored car, I think. And some jeeps. On the far side of that hill. Waiting."

"What for?"

"Well, what do you want them to do? Tear gas, like they used on Jimmy Cagney? We'll all bite the dust if they try that. And more—" he paused and his face darkened. "They might be out of the same bag as these guys."

"What do you mean?"

"Do you know where we are?"

"No, dear. Do you?"

"I always feel skittish when she starts calling me pet names," Cook grinned to Susan. "No, seriously, Moira, I'm pretty sure we flew east. That would mean we're in Syria or Lebanon. Maybe Jordan."

"Not Iran?"

"Weren't in the air long enough."

"Mommy, I'm hot," said Nan suddenly.

Susan shivered. "Let's not talk about it now," she said to Cook.

In the bathroom the taps turned, but there was no answering rush of water. She stared briefly at a useless bidet. "Damn," she whispered. She'd been content to be thirsty on the plane, no need to piss, but now she visualized a long iced tea with longing. Better yet, a tall gin and tonic. With lime.

A few minutes later she bent over Nan with a hand towel. She'd had to use what remained in the tank. She sponged her throat, cheeks, forehead, feeling the fever through the cloth. She held the aspirin bottle to the light. Only five remained, and some broken fragments at the bottom.

"Come on, honey, take this. Here's some water."

"I don't feel so good, Mommy."

"Mommy knows, darling." Her helplessness and fear made her hands shake as she held the hotel glass to Nan's lips. *Dear God,* she thought suddenly, coming a little out of numbness into despair so sharp she saw why her mind had walled it off. *Dear God, what is going to happen to us?* Someone in her head chattered on as she watched her daughter drink, hoping the water was clean, that it would cool and not harm her. In the Med you couldn't trust it . . . no, that was not her thought. That was what the other Navy wives had said. That was the reason, ostensibly, some of them drank nothing but wine.

Yet after all they, whom she had scorned, had been proven the wiser. They'd distrusted change, stayed on their worn path of tours and shopping. A sudden rush of terror and regret clogged her throat, made her hands tremble as she wrung out the cloth. If only she'd stayed with them! The Athens airport was closed, the radio had said. But Alicia and the others would be free, aside from that, free and safe, safe, safe.

But she hadn't been satisfied. *She* had wanted adventure. Not even alone, but with a three-year-old.

Nan pushed away the glass, spilling it on her T-shirt. Susan caught it, saving the last swallow. "Don't want it," the child said. "Want something to eat."

"There isn't anything right now, baby. Tell you what . . . let's take a nap. You and me. Aren't you sleepy?"

"But I'm hungry." Nan began to cry, sobbing into the cloth of her shirt. Susan tried to soothe her, feeling like crying herself. Moira and Michael stood across the room, watching, holding hands.

At last she lay down beside her child, stroking her head over and over, her eyes on the open door.

20
U.S.S. *Guam*

LENSON WAS ON THE FLAG BRIDGE
again at thirteen hundred, an hour past noon, when *Bowen*
reported incoming bogeys on her radar.

Bogeys—unidentified aircraft. Dan jolted awake instantly from his daydreams. "This is it, pal," he croaked
to Glazer, who was staring at him open-mouthed. His own
lips were suddenly dry. He keyed the air-warning handset
with one hand, acknowledging the transmission, as he
picked up Primary Tactical with the other. "All units
November Kilo," he said rapidly, "unidentified aircraft
inbound, two-niner-zero true. Air warning Red. I say
again, bogeys inbound, sector delta, Air warning Red. All
units keep guns tight pending orders. Control on Air Defense Net Bravo."

He clicked off Pritac, not waiting for their responses,
and hit the squawk box. "Bridge, flag bridge, you copy?
Ready on chaff and electronic countermeasures?"

"Bridge aye," said the intercom. At the same instant
the alarm began to bong. "GENERAL QUARTERS,
GENERAL QUARTERS. THIS IS NOT A DRILL.
AIR ATTACK INCOMING. ALL HANDS MAN
YOUR BATTLE STATIONS. SET MATERIAL CON-
DITION ZEBRA THROUGHOUT THE SHIP." In
the background he could hear Captain Fourchetti shout-
ing orders.

"Stan. Crank the commodore. Call Flasher and Hogan and get all stations manned up ASAP."

"Right."

He felt something hard behind him; it was McQueen, holding out the steel helmet. Perhaps an anachronism, but it felt good, settling heavy, shuttering his skull. He shifted his gas mask and life vest to his hip, bent to check that his socks were rolled over his trousers and that his collar was buttoned tight against flash burns. All this World War Two stuff, he thought. We should have some kind of protective suit, at least ballistic vests.

The bridge manned up fast. More people crowded in by the moment. He looked around for Sundstrom, but he was not yet there.

"There they are," said Glazer suddenly. His voice sounded thick.

"Where?" Dan craned into the windows, searching low clouds. Rain squalls—low mist to the east, the seas cresting in long runs, spume blowing off them as they broke—

"No, on the scope. They must be low fliers, all right. Three pips breaking off a big group to the north of us."

"Report 'em," he was saying, when at that moment the position report came in from the frigate. As their escort, and the only ship with halfway-modern radar and weapons, *Bowen*'s commanding officer had taken over defense of the formation at the first contact with incoming aircraft. Now he was broadcasting range, bearing, and target data, helping the amphibs slew their 3″/50 batteries toward the approaching aircraft.

"Why's he giving orders? Who is that? I'm in tactical command here. I'm the commander of this task force!"

"Yes sir, you are," said Lenson quickly, turning to where the middle-aged man stood, his uniform wrinkled, his eyes bleared. It was good someone could sleep, he thought jealously. "He's taken over as Force Air Defense Coordinator, sir. It's standard procedure, re our oporder. You still retain firing authority, though."

"Firing authority?" repeated the commodore. "The rules of engagement—but Sixth Fleet hasn't sent those to me yet; he said he would, but he hasn't—"

A spatter of rain hit the windscreens and was instantly whipped away by the wipers. "Fifteen thousand yards," sang out Glazer from the 'scope. A shiver swept the men, packed close together, enclosed by steel, or rather its illusion; the amphibs were unarmored. The planes were closing faster than Dan anticipated. Supersonic, he thought. Modern jets. He felt his guts ease under the life vest.

"We have missile lock-on," crackled the radio. *"Interrogative weapons tight."*

"Should we give the frigate a fire order, sir?"

"No, goddammit, no!" shouted Sundstrom, making a violent motion of negation. "Tony said he'd try to get us some Air Force cover. This might be them. I don't want to fire until we have a positive identification. What about IFF? Electronic identification?"

"They'll all squawk NATO friendly," said Flasher, from behind them. "Greek, Turkish, or ours. That won't tell us a thing."

"Will they answer a radio call?"

"We don't know their frequencies, sir."

"We'll have to wait till we see them, then," said Sundstrom tentatively. He moved toward the hatchway.

"November Kilo, interrogative orders," the frigate asked again. He sounds so cool, Lenson thought. So unhurried. I might be too, if I were aboard her. She was built to shoot back. Smaller, more maneuverable, with a good gun and missiles. The thin-skinned amphibs, though, would be helpless before a determined attack. He looked at Sundstrom, waiting for orders. The commodore looked back at him, very briefly, and he saw indecision in his eyes.

"Dan."

"Sir?"

"Without rules of engagement, we'll have to wait until we're fired on. Even if these are Greeks."

"That's right, sir. They're still our allies."

"We have to wait, don't we? Am I right?" He looked around the bridge. "Mr. Flasher? Do you concur?"

"I guess so, sir."

"Send 'hold your fire,' " said the commodore.

"All units November Kilo: weapons tight until specific word." He repeated the message, authenticated it, and signed off.

"Three miles," said Glazer, his voice high. "Closing fast, with a rapid right bearing rate."

"Where are my lookouts? I ordered lookouts on the wings!" shouted Sundstrom. Hogan started, then undogged the port hatch, moving with clumsy rapidity. A blast of wind and spray came in as he ducked out. Lenson caught the door as the ship rolled, held it open, looking out toward the northwest.

It was only a glance, half a second out of a lifetime, but he knew he would always remember the way the sea looked that day, how the sky leaned close above the jagged tops of the waves. It printed itself clearer and surer on his mind than film could record. No film could recall the way the wind slapped spray from the sea and whirled it above the waves, rattling against the hull like thrown shot. No film could remember the cold, colder than thermometer could register. No camera could catch the intense crystal clarity of life, the colors gray, gray; gray-silver sea, dark sky, gray hulls of ships, small and lonely distant. Gray rain, sleeting down like a taupe curtain between *Guam* and *Coronado*. Abruptly he was glad for the rain, and then cursed it. It offered no concealment. Without visual identification the task force couldn't fire. But the planes would have better radar, more modern weapons . . .

"D'you see them, Dan?"

"Not yet, sir—there they are!"

Hogan pointed at the same instant. Three specks, frighteningly close, moving low and fast from left to right beyond the crazily rolling *Barnstable*. He riveted his eyes to them, afraid to raise his binoculars. At this range you could lose something that small in a moment, you could look away for an instant and they would disappear. Fighters, but he couldn't tell the type. They vanished into the overcast, but not before he had seen them bank, veering in the direction of the formation.

He turned, to find the commodore beside him. The rain was dark on his khaki uniform, and beads of water dotted his face. He stared into the mist, blinking rapidly.

"Orders, sir?"

"What, Dan?"

"Do you have any orders, Commodore?"

"You've got the deck, don't you? Do I have to tell you people everything?"

Lenson looked at him for a long moment, then pushed by into the bridge.

"Stan. To all units: radar-illuminate and lock on incoming bogeys. Load, but hold fire until we pass the word."

"Got it."

"Red, on the CIC-to-CIC net, have everybody get their electronics up. I want everything radiating. Radar, radio, fire control, the whole schmeir. If they've got sensors on those bogeys I want them to know we're American."

"It might not matter," said Byrne. "Most of the Turkish Navy is ex-U.S. They'll have the same signatures."

"Well, at least we'll be able to track them. Sir—permission to hoist a battle ensign? They could see that better—"

"Goddammit, yes," said Sundstrom. "Right now."

The roar came then directly above the ship, a rolling blast that rattled Plexiglas in its frames and made all the men duck. Lenson ran to starboard in time to catch the yellow-blue flare of the afterburner as the fighter pointed itself upward from the pass. The forward gun mount trained around after it, but far behind, too slow to keep up. This time his eye caught the familiar stub wing: an F-16, built in the U.S., but from rain and speed he couldn't see the insignia. The Air Force flew Falcons. But so did the

Greeks, and the Turks too, for that matter. There was just no way to tell.

It's that way for them too, he thought with sudden horror. They can't tell who we are. They're going too fast, the visibility's bad. If they're Greek they're looking for ships, the Turkish invasion fleet. But they're land-based pilots; they probably can't tell an oiler from a surfaced submarine, much less—

The fighter shrank as it opened, turning, its momentum taking it far out from the task force. It almost disappeared, winking on and off at the limit of sight. Then it became a dot again, head on, and he saw the other two joining above and behind it.

They dropped suddenly to just above the gray-green crests, no higher than the bridge. He knew then that this was a firing run. He glanced back. Sundstrom met his eyes for a moment, then dropped his gaze and shook his head slightly. Knowing it was not enough.

They had to wait until they were fired on.

And then they were. The sound came faintly across the water, a popping rattle mixed with the rising howl of engines. He saw flashes, streamers of pale smoke from the wings, and jerked his head round; but as his mouth came open Flasher was already barking, "Batteries released! Shoot the sons of bitches!"

"Fire," said the commodore a moment too late. Dan stared out as the fighters roared directly over them, dreadfully close. They banked left, the first run complete, and were erased instantly by a low bank of cloud. "Make sure the destroyer gets that word—"

"*Bowen!*" Flasher was already shouting into the handset, forgetting, or not bothering with, the call signs. "D'you copy my weapons free? Answer up, damn it!"

"*Copy,*" said a voice from the frigate. One word.

"Flag bridge, bridge," said the squawk box. Fourchetti's voice. "We have radar lock-on with the aft three-inch mounts. They're closing again—almost in range—"

His voice was blotted out in a sudden chorus of high-pitched bangs from aft. Between the detonations the rattle of machine guns swelled to a roar and then cut off as the planes appeared overhead. The forward mount, fifty feet down, fired suddenly, creating twin balls of bright orange flame as big as the bridge. Each flash was succeeded by gray-black smoke and a bellow of sound that shook the steel fabric of the island.

The aircraft flashed by like silver sabers, a hundred yards on the bow The guns whined around, trying to follow but far behind, twin barrels spewing alternate balls of fire thirty feet across. Empty brass arced upward from the breeches, somersaulting through smoky air with incredible slowness, and clanged into the decks. The guns fell silent as the barrels trained into the superstructure. The bow mount fired last, four spaced rounds after the rapidly dwindling planes. Lenson imagined the shells hurtling after the jets, closing at first, then slowing, dropping, ripping at last into the sea. Choking smoke blew in through the open hatchway. ". . . Hits?" said the commodore, turning for the bridge wing, where Hogan stood with binoculars to his eyes.

"Sir. Don't go out there. They'll be back."

"I think we hit one, goddammit!"

"Not a chance. Those old three-inch were thirty degrees behind them when they went over," said Flasher.

"Maybe the frigate'll do better," said Lenson.

"*Somebody* better do something, and quick. Or we're going to have some dead sailors here."

Dan thought for a furious moment, calculating lead angle, found he lacked data. He pulled a phone from the bulkhead and snapped its switch to *Guam*'s fire-control circuit. "Guns!"

A faint, tinny voice answered. "Here."

"Flag bridge. Were you on those babies?"

"Not a chance. Our max target speed is five hundred. Radar'll keep up, but these old three-inch can't train fast enough."

"Commodore," said Dan. "They're flying too fast for a director solution."

But when he turned to Sundstrom he saw that he was staring, lips slightly parted, out over the sea. He hesitated this time only a second. There was one answer left, though it was not in the book. He picked up the Pritac handset and wet his lips.

"All ships with three-inch: Listen up! Target speed's too high for director control. Shift from radar track to visual. Lay a barrage and make them fly through it. I say again, shift to visual track, barrage fire, all guns, estimate range five thousand. November Zulu out."

A different, deeper explosion came from outside, making his stomach jump. It was from the ship, a shock transmitted through her steel body before it reached their ears. Lenson craned out the window, and saw it, down on the flight deck. A mass of fuel-fed flame, a litter of twisted metal igniting into magnesium glare. Men ran, some away, others, dragging hoses, toward it. One of the helicopters. As he watched another began to burn. "HIT BRAVO," said the metal voice of the announcing system. "HIT ON FLIGHT DECK—REPAIR FIVE PROVIDE—"

"Air support," said the commodore. They turned to look at him. Helmet unbuckled, collar awry, he leaned against the coaming of the starboard hatch, the climbing smoke black behind him. "We've got to have some goddamn air support, or we're all going straight to the bottom. But they're not going to pin the rose on me for this debacle. Get me Tony, right now."

"Sir?"

"High frequency . . ." He made an impatient gesture for the handset. "Goddammit . . . what's our call sign—"

Flasher told him.

". . . This is Denver George. We're under attack. Repeat, under attack. About a dozen fighters, type unknown. Request air support instantly. Tony, do you read me? I need air support! I've got six ships out here in a storm and we're helpless . . . do you hear me . . ."

"Sir," said Flasher, putting his hand on Sundstrom's arm. The commodore shook him off. "Goddammit, Tony, I say again—"

The ether crackled, far off. *"Denver George, this is True Dream. Say again your last transmission."*

"We're under air attack! Aren't you listening? Is Tony there? Uh, Dream Actual?"

"No, sir." The voice was young, but still as distant as the ionosphere that broke and reflected his words. *"I'll relay that to him. TF 61 under air attack. Requesting air support. Out."*

Sundstrom stared at the handset for a long moment. Slowly it slipped downward, out of his hands. It hung motionless for a moment at the end of its cord, then picked up the roll of the ship and began to swing.

"You all heard that," he whispered.

"Inbound," shouted Hogan, from the port wing, and they all ducked again, facing to port. Lenson keyed the squawk box but then saw the rudder indicator already pointing to hard left. Fourchetti's boys were awake. Bow on fewer guns would bear, but *Guam* would present a smaller target. The clamor of the guns resumed, an ear-splitting barking that shook the flag bridge and filtered smoke and powder fumes through the closed windows. Lenson found himself on the deck, clinging to the base of the radar repeater, hugging its reassuring solidity.

Out of our league, he thought blindly. His breath squeezed from his lungs. Helpless. Not a goddamn thing to do but hang on and take it.

But they were fighting back. The three-inch were old guns, designed to shoot down prop-driven kamikazes, and their radar control was obsolete; but there were plenty of them aboard, and each barrel dumped forty-five shells a minute into the sky. He raised his head, inch by inch, and was rewarded with the sight of gunflashes from the *Barnstable County*. The landing ship had closed up instinctively to two thousand yards, and was matching the flagship's turn; she pouring it on, too, to the targets that to her were crossing her stern, heading for the *Guam*. He hoped they weren't too fighting crazy to let go their triggers when their checksights filled with the gray bulk of the helicopter carrier.

The aircraft popped up, suddenly, two of them—why two?—just above a green-gray sea that crashed into the bow, jolting the ship and sending the men on the bridge staggering. Blossoms of yellow fire, perfect rings of smoke, whipped past him on an icy wind . . . muzzle flashes from the leading edge of wings, the gaping mouths of air intakes, the cutting brilliance of aluminum. They bored inward, inexorable, invulnerable, growing like nightmares in his tranced sight. A whiplash of sound shattered a window and traversed the width of the flag bridge. He ducked, but did not drop, and thus caught for a fleeting moment the bent, anonymous helmet of a man in one of those cockpits, pitiless and merciless, or pitiful and merciful, there was no way of telling. You did not face your killer in modern war, just as he had no time to see those he destroyed. Instead you took cover, hid, if there was any hiding, and fought back with any means, any means that you had.

"*Bowen* reports a splash."

His ears were ringing. "What did you say, Stan?"

"One bogey in the water . . ." Glazer held up his hand as he listened. "Fired two Sparrow missiles; second one connected. Flamer. Parachute. Pilot's in the water ten thousand yards to starboard of the force. Should we, uh . . . should we send out a chopper?"

"Wise up, Stan."

"Sorry."

"Sir? Commodore?"

Alone of them all, Sundstrom was still standing, his head bent against the arm of his chair. At Lenson's words he lifted it and stared at him. Belatedly he saw what the commodore had been looking at: a jagged hole through the brown leather, just at chest level. He could see the bulkhead through it, and the oblong hole in the starboard side the round had made going out.

"What?"

"Any orders, sir?"

"We're firing back, aren't we? Can you think of anything else to do?"

"Uh . . . no sir."

"Then don't keep bothering me for orders, goddammit, just do what has to be done. Thank God we never gave these people nukes."

"Jesus, amen to that," said Flasher, under his breath. He winked at Glazer, and then reached into his foul-weather jacket. Lenson expected a Hershey with almonds, but instead he came out with one, two, three red rubber balls.

Kneeling there, he started juggling, hiding it with his bulk from Sundstrom, who was looking anxiously upward. Lenson stared.

"Where are they now?" the commodore muttered, and Dan jerked his eyes away from Flasher. *Bowen* came over the net just then with a report. "November Zulu, this is Juliet Romeo. Two remaining bogeys have cleared the Missile Defense Zone, heading three-one-five."

"Sir, they're outbound."

"Expended their ordnance . . . goddammit, let's get some damage reports," said Sundstrom, rushing out to the wing. "I can't tell what to do without info. Get on that net, Dan! Right now!"

"Aye, sir." The commodore grated his nerves like sandpaper, but Lenson was still too excited to care. Could it really be over? He jotted down reports as they came in. *Coronado* had fragment damage, two casualties, investigating. *Guam* had lost two helos from strafing, taken fragment damage, and had four men wounded. *Charleston* and *Newport* were untouched. *Spiegel Grove* had a fire in her superstructure and heavy damage from aircraft cannon, but no casualties. *Ault* had been out of the action entirely. He had worried about leaving her astern, but she'd made out like a bandit; the fighters had never seen her.

The remaining ship, *Barnstable County,* had not been so lucky. One of the Falcons had carried rockets. Most had gone high, their aim perhaps upset by the barrage, but at least two had bored into the forecastle and exploded inside the ship. The causeways were a wreck. Even worse news was that the bow ramp was damaged and jammed. Fortunately, the heavy seas were helping them fight the fire. Her commanding officer was down directing the DC team in person right now, the OOD reported. Staring out the open hatch, past Sundstrom's back, Lenson could see smoke whipping back on the wind from the LST's forward deck, could see men moving about, dragging hoses.

He rogered for the reports, signed off, and went out to the wing. Sundstrom listened gloomily, staring over the coaming as a foam truck gushed white over the blazing aircraft. "Goddamn," he said, as Lenson finished. "They clobbered us. *Barnstable* has twenty amtracs aboard. If we can't get those ashore, a landing won't have much chance."

"I don't think we did so badly, sir. Half a dozen wounded, and no major damage. It could have been a lot worse. All that three-inch in the air—we couldn't aim it worth a shit, but I bet it made them think twice about making another pass. And *Bowen* got one!"

"Men can be replaced. Those causeways and amtracs can't. Two helos out—that cuts our air-landing capability, too."

"Yes sir."

Sundstrom rubbed his face. Now that it was over, Lenson saw that the commodore was trembling. He felt pretty shaky himself, come to think of it.

"No, Dan, this was a debacle. We should have been able to shoot down all three of those bastards. They were right down on the water. And we should have had air cover. If we'd had a couple of F-14s they'd never have attacked us. It was a debacle." He struck his fist slowly on the steel.

Lenson began to shake. He looked at the commodore, then out at the sea. He turned silently for the bridge.

"Dan," the commodore called after him, "I want our ships to stay at GQ. Those guys could be back any time."

"Yes sir," said Lenson. It was all he could do to say it.

They found out later that afternoon what a debacle it had truly been. Not for them, but for others.

Coronado reported the first drifter, and requested instructions. Sundstrom agonized over it for five minutes, then ordered her to maintain course and speed. He was afraid of submarines. Then there were more, the escort reported "many many," and when the officers went out to the bridge wing they saw them. Heaving on the seas far ahead, they grew as the ship throbbed forward; became white specks, drifting bales, and then, last of all, dead men. They slipped quietly past, face down, most in muddy-colored trousers and white T-shirts, a few naked. *Guam*'s crew stared down at them from the flight deck, quiet as the bloated bodies, unwilling to speak. One had long hair, and the wind ruffled it as he rolled at the crest of an oil-slicked wave to face upward, one arm outflung as if imploring aid. The arm ended in no hand. There was no blood on any of them. The sea had taken it.

The squawk box sounded, and Lenson reached down to answer it, still looking over the side.

"Flag bridge, bridge. What do you make of them?"

"I guess that big gaggle of bogeys to the north found their Turks, Captain."

"Maybe. I'd like to heave to, pick one up for identification."

"Aye, Cap'n."

"Who is that?"

"Lieutenant Lenson, Captain."

"Oh. Is the commodore there?"

"No sir, he's below eating his dinner. Ah—" Dan hesitated. "Why don't you just go ahead and do it, Captain?"

"Good point," Fourchetti said. "Bridge out."

One of the radiomen came up with a priority message. Lenson glanced at it, saw that it was about the embassy hostages. Their commandeered airliner had landed, in Syria. It interested him at the moment very little, and he sent the man down to the commodore's sea cabin.

Suddenly there was nothing to do. He leaned against the window and watched the damage-control teams working. A tractor was clearing the burnt-out helo over the side. It teetered on the brink, as if reluctant to leave, then gave way and toppled into space. A splash, a spreading cloud of white foam on gray sea, and it was gone. A roar from overhead made him glance up. Theirs; the two fighters from the *America.* When they had vectored in, half an hour before, he'd been angry at their lateness. Now, looking at the men in the water, he was glad they were there.

The commodore's phone buzzed. Oh, Jesus, he thought, and picked it up. "Yes sir."

"Who's that? Lenson?"

"Yes sir."

"Good. Dan, did you read this message?"

"Uh, glanced at it, sir."

"What do you think?"

Think? He tried to. "Uh, Syria . . ."

"The coordinates they give for the abandoned airstrip. What does that mean to you?"

Still holding the phone, he crossed to the chart. Measured roughly, with his fingers spread. "Uh, that'll be just north of the Lebanese border, east of—"

"Goddammit, Dan, I know that. I can read a map! But look how far inland it is."

"Oh. Not that far."

"Not that goddamn far at all. Dan, I think it's still possible we could be sent in."

"Into *Syria?*" He could hardly believe what he heard. It was as if Sundstrom had proposed landing in East Germany.

They were both silent for a moment. Lenson stared at the chart. It did look tempting. Only thirty miles or so overland direct from the beach. But no, he remembered what Byrne had said—Soviet client, Soviet naval base, hell of a well-equipped army—

"Maybe not," the commodore muttered into his ear. "But I want to be ready, damn it. Those are our orders. What would we have to do?"

The fatigue had fallen back a bit, and he thought more rapidly now. "Well," he said, "that coast is only a hundred miles east of us . . . we could make that pretty quick. They know we're here though, they could track us as soon as we started to move." An idea woke and moved around back in his mind.

"Could we be ready?"

He had the answer to that all right. "I don't know, sir."

Reaching for the idea, prodding it forward into daylight.

"Maybe we ought to head in that direction, anyway, just in case—"

"Not as a group," said Dan then.

"What's that?"

"Sir, if anyone expects us to get the MAU ashore there in one piece, it's got to be done fast as hell, and it's got to be a surprise. Otherwise there'll be a division of tanks waiting for them on the beach. I think we ought to disperse."

To his surprise Sundstrom did not dismiss it immediately. Instead he said, "Disperse—you mean break up the task force?"

"Yes sir. This overcast, plus the air attack—if we split up they'll think we've lost some ships, we're hurt bad, we're just milling around. Even if that AGI's still around he'll only find one of us."

"I don't know, Dan. Say we scatter and head east. Then what?"

"Well, I guess we wait for orders."

"But if somebody gets lost, they're not used to navigating on their own—"

Sundstrom had several more nitpicking reservations. Dan answered each in turn, feeling increasingly weary.

There wasn't much chance of it anyway. At last the commodore hung up and he stood motionless for a moment, feeling weak. Then he reached for the signal book. Disperse, steer various courses east, rendezvous point to follow—he flipped pages listlessly.

Fourchetti came up again on the squawk box a few minutes later, reporting pickup complete. He felt the ship shudder as the screws bit in. He hit the intercom.

"Bridge aye."

"Flag bridge again. Captain—you get any ID off him?"

"Who?"

"Your drifter."

"Oh. No. I can't even tell if he's Greek or Turk. In fact . . . he looks just like one of our sailors."

That suddenly, out of nowhere, his body dropped away, like a stone through air. He leaned his weight into the radar console, his head bending into it. Not in acquiescence; he was simply unable any longer to support himself. The ship reeled under his feet. Nausea . . . he struggled to lift his head, feeling the blackness of the deep sea come up in waves through his legs.

"Dan, you all right?"

"Yeah. Just tired."

"Sit down for a minute. I'll take over."

"No, I'm okay."

"This is Big Red, I got the deck," said Flasher loudly. To Lenson he said, "Look, go on below. Hit the sack for half an hour. How long you been up, anyway?"

"I forget."

"Lay your butt below, man. You won't be any good if you're falling down."

"I'm supposed to be on—"

"So he makes a stink, I ordered you below. My ass, not yours. Don't worry so much, you're getting like him."

"That's below the belt, Red. But okay." He breathed deep a few times, felt the darkness edge back; enough at least for him to stagger to the bridge ladder. But at its head he turned back. "Red—the order to scatter—"

"I was listening. It's a good tactic."

"What?"

"I said, it's a good idea. Damned good. Wish I'd thought of it."

"You think so?" Dan grinned through the faintness.

"Yeah. Go on down. I'll call him again, maybe get Haynes to call him, argue him into it."

He got below somehow, but in his stateroom paused at the bunk frame, breathing hard. He felt weak. He rested for a moment, waited for the ship to roll, and kicked himself up. Or halfway up. He hung on the edge, steel biting his wrists, and slipped back. Still no good. He needed will, energy, something more than his drained mind could force from the exhausted knot of carbon compounds that crouched six feet below its rest.

He visualized a face. Pudgy and worried, suspicious and self-protective. And worst of all, indecisive. The energy came then, the hate, and he launched himself upward with his last strength, into his rack.

There was time for one look at her picture before he closed his eyes. He stared upward at it, his breath coming shallow. The nausea and fatigue, like acid etching away the unessential, made him see clearly something he had never dared to admit before.

He did not belong here.

It was not Sundstrom, at least not him alone. Foolishness and incompetence existed as much, he told himself, in any profession—although the power a commander wielded at sea made it harder to bear. It was simpler than that. It was wrong because he was away from them. But he was bound, both by law, obligation, and by his own choice. The sea, the clean, uncomplicated life of orders and men . . . he loved it. He always had and he always would.

But not as much as he loved his family.

Shore duty, then? He was due it after three tours at sea. But the sea was where a smudged career could be made white again, where advancement was won, where a line officer, an Annapolis man, belonged. Ashore . . . there was only one way to go ashore for good.

His mind backed away from the thought. It was too final, too frightening, worse to face than the flash of wings.

21
Ash Shummari, Syria

SHE WAS HALF ASLEEP—HUNGER MADE
her drowsy—when her dreams were penetrated by a
scuffle, a scraping noise, and a moan.

Things were so pleasant in dreams. She struggled to stay
where she was, aware in some redoubt of consciousness
that it was better than what she was returning to. But that
suspicion made her aware that she was dreaming; and
with it the sleep-world unraveled, and she found, looking
back, that she had already crossed into waking. She rolled
over and snaked out her arms without opening her eyes.

Nan wasn't there.

The mattress creaked as she sat up. The wan light of an
overcast dusk filtered through closed shutters, over Moira
and Michael, who had twined themselves together fully
clothed on the floor. Their hoarse breathing, Moira's familiar snore, were more ominous, somehow, than silence.

"Nan?" she murmured.

She got up sluggishly, feeling and smelling her own
sodden staleness, and looked into the connecting bath.
The watercloset lid, a shelf of heavy porcelain, lay where
she had moved it, reflecting the watershimmer from inside
the tank. Nan was not using it. Susan remembered how
welcome that achievement had been. But then she felt
alarmed. She went quickly to the door, but paused on the
threshold. They had been told not to go out. The guard

on this floor had made that plain with gestures. They were to stay in their assigned rooms.

She thrust her head into the corridor, surveying it from end to end with one swift turn of her eyes. It was empty. She took a breath, remembering. *Punishment for disobeying any of my orders is death.* She glanced back once more into the room, making certain the child was not there. Well, she thought then, if they catch me I will explain. I was looking for my child. They'll understand. Wouldn't they?

They would have to. She had no choice.

Her bare feet were soundless on the carpet. She passed open doors, looking in. The other hostages did not look out as she passed. Many were asleep. A few talked in subdued voices, or stared out their windows. One couple was telling fortunes, the Tarot spread between them over the bare ticking of their bed.

She began to feel frightened.

At the next room she paused. When the occupants looked up she said quickly, "Excuse me. Did a little girl come in here to you, or go past your door? A little girl with dark hair and glasses?"

They shook their heads, too surprised to speak.

She asked at several more rooms. No one had seen a child. The fear grew inside her. It was as if cotton stuffed her throat, turned her mouth dry and wadded the used air inside her lungs. She went on, walking more rapidly. At last the rooms were empty, but still doors gaped ahead along a corridor that disappeared dreamlike into hot and airless gloom.

When her feet whispered between the silent walls she realized she was running. Her breath roared in her ears. Where could Nan be? Where was their guard? Room after room rushed by. The hallway turned, grew darker. It was a submarine dimness, dusky blue, and from somewhere the memory came of another time she had felt this same terrible and growing fear: deep beneath the sea, her hands tearing desperately at the resisting dark for a small body.

But no, that had been a dream, and this was real. Then another bend, and she was running hard, sobbing aloud, her hair slapping her back. There was a humming ahead; light, voices, people . . . she had circled the floor and returned to her own room. But now people stood in the hallway; there was a swell of excited talk.

From outside, clearly audible through the opened windows, came a new sound, a distant thunder.

She didn't stop to listen. Sobbing, she pushed at the people who turned at her approach, fell back from her, reached out half-heartedly as if to help or stop her. One woman murmured something to another. For a moment Susan refused to make sense of the words; they seemed meaningless, as incomprehensible as the Arabic of their captors. Then she did.

"Poor woman. She's lost her child . . ."

She stopped dead in the hallway, put her fists to her mouth, and screamed.

From down the corridor, somewhere, came a faint answering cry.

"Nan?" she screamed again. *"Nan!"*

Michael's hand closed on her arm. "Betts. Get hold! Was that her?"

"Oh, God, I think it was! Did you hear her?"

"Where's the guard? Anybody see him?" Cook asked the other hostages. They moved back, several shaking their heads.

"Come on," said Moira.

When they opened the closed door they saw the two of them together. It was the short one, the man Michael called "Snaggletooth." Nan sat across from him, on a blanket he had spread across the bed.

"How you?" he said, turning his grin to the door. Lazily, he tossed aside a scrap of cloth and reached for the pistol he had laid aside.

The archaeologist was moving, but Susan was faster. She thrust him against the still-opening door and was on the man with her fists. Screaming, but there were no words to it. Nancy, still crying, crawled across the bed, away from the adults.

"Okay, let him up," she heard Michael say. Over the guard's shoulder she saw him pick up the pistol. "Get back. Get away from him, Susan!"

There was more shouting behind them in the hall, a great deal more. She ignored it, she ignored Cook. She had her hands on one of them at last. Grappling close, her teeth searching for a hold, she gasped as his decaying breath seared her face. He was strong but an animal in her, stronger than she, had been unleashed. His face tore under her fingernails and she panted and dug in again. He screamed and tried to roll; she got in a knee, drove it in again, and then hit him in the face backhanded, dragging her ring across flesh. She could feel it tear. The breath went out of him with a grunt and he doubled and rolled away and fell to the worn carpet on the far side of the bed.

"Shoot him," she said, backing away and wiping her hands on her shorts. They left bloody streaks. "Do it. Do it now, Michael!"

The terrorist lay motionless. Facing a gun instead of holding one, he had melted, too hurt or too frightened to move. Blood ran from his cheeks and dripped from his open mouth onto the carpet. Susan circled around him to the corner where Nan huddled, her arms over her eyes. She bent and pulled her up. The little girl whimpered once, then wrapped herself round her mother.

Susan turned then, holding her, to face him. Something far back in her mind had drawn her lips into a primeval rictus. There was no man or husband to protect them now. She was the mother alone with her child. And like any animal that guards its young she would bite, she would claw, she would kill if anyone touched her child again, regardless of the risk or cost to herself. And now she wanted this man's life. "Michael—give it here. I'll do it." She reached for the pistol.

"Khal'lis haydeh," said a voice behind her.

The small man's expression changed. He scrabbled

backward on the floor, a retreating crab, till he fetched up against the wall. His extremity of terror was not for her, she saw, or even for Cook. Susan turned.

It was the dark man, the leader, the one they called the Majd. The one she had seen in firelight, leading his men in the ferocity of attack. Now he stood still in the doorway, surrounded by silence and heat. Black hair fell over his forehead, damp-looking, over opaque eyes. The automatic rifle—she had never yet seen him without it—he held at his waist, pointed at the three of them.

"Put it down," he said to Cook. "I will deal justice here."

She saw the archaeologist measuring the odds. "Michael, don't," she murmured.

"You'll see that this man is punished?" Cook said.

"If I decide."

"What does that mean?"

"It means no bargains! I do not punish *for* you or make promises *to* you. Put down the gun or all in this room will die."

His voice was iron, and the catch on the weapon snapped as it went off safe. When he moved a step to the side she saw that several others, also armed, stood behind him at the door. More of them came running up the stairwell. *"Ha'ded,"* he said, and they lifted their weapons. "Put it down *now!* My next word orders them to fire."

Cook held the pistol pointed at the seated man, who was holding himself and groaning, for a moment longer. Then he tossed it on the bed. It bounced once on the dirty ticking and lay still, and Susan saw again how ugly guns were.

"There, good," said the Majd.

He rubbed his fingers slowly along the stock of the rifle; and then his eyes swung to hers. His hand stopped. They looked straight at each other, gaze into gaze.

Too long, a part of her mind told her. This means

something different here. Drop your eyes *now*—look away—

But she couldn't.

Some eyes, when you met them for the first time, were flat and foreign. Others were friendly, there was that spark that passes instantaneous and warm, not a shutter-flicker long, and you know that you have found a friend.

These eyes were soft as obsidian and friendly as the eyes of serpents. They were warm as some icy-flowing limestone sinkhole lost to the sun for a million years. Not so much hostile as inhumanly detached, inhumanly determined, they locked into hers like a bayonet onto a rifle across ten feet of space, across a room filled with frightened people.

It was no more than half a second, but it felt as long as years. With a sob, she drew her fist to her mouth. Only when Nan began to cry, beside her, could she drag her eyes away and look down.

The Majd spoke angrily in their language to the huddled man. He scrambled up quickly, holding his genitals in one hand and his face with the other, and ran crablike toward the door. The Majd spoke sharply again, one word, and he turned back hurriedly. He did not look at the leader, but as he passed her and reached out to retrieve the gun she saw his eyes glitter briefly at her, feral and enraged in the bloody mask.

When he went out again Susan exhaled raggedly. She had expected some punishment. At least, to see him disarmed. But it hadn't happened. He was dangerous now. He would wait and watch for his chance, for his revenge on her, on Michael, perhaps even on Nan.

That was when she realized, fully, where she was, and under whose power.

When the small man was gone the leader let his rifle sag. With a graceful motion he leaned it by the doorway, flashing a glance to one of the men behind him. He came into the room and knelt beside her where she held Nan. Susan tightened her grip, but he only put out his hand and smoothed the child's forehead. He was slighter close up than Susan had expected. She smelled tobacco. She expected Nan to draw back, but the child stared upward at him, her mouth open.

She feels it too, Susan thought. . . .

"Put his shirt back on," he ordered. She hastened to comply. He brought his face close to Nan's. "Did the man hurt you, boy?"

"She's too frightened to talk. But I think we came in time. He only scared her. And she's been sick."

"Oh, she is a girl . . . she has been sick long?"

His voice was direct, hard, though he had tried to gentle it. It stirred something on the back of her neck. She remembered the marines. Faces turned upward, sightless, rainwater smoothing their cheeks like tears. She saw that again, and at the same moment she smelled him as he bent closer to Nan. This time she huddled back, into Susan's arms. Susan moved instinctively to protect her.

"No. Don't touch her. Leave us alone."

"Do you have medicine for her?"

"Medicine! Don't make me laugh." The question made her forget her fear, made her angry all over again. "We don't even have food. Or water. As you know well."

"I'm sorry. We were not prepared to make you comfortable," he said, and smiled.

She almost gasped. His whole face had changed. There was such cheerfulness in it, such life, that her own lips moved in unconscious imitation. Nan opened her eyes and laughed a little.

"You're a pretty little girl. And your mother, too, is most attractive. You say," he went on, lifting his eyes to hers, "she is ill. I see that for myself. Fever, yes, it is plain in her eyes. You tell me what she needs. We are not animals. Some of us have children, too. Say it, we will try to get it."

"Food. A doctor. Water. And some privacy."

He made a wry face. "Some of those are easy, some are not . . . *Daouk!*" He fired Arabic at one of the men at the door, who nodded halfway through, then disappeared. The Majd turned to her. "We will have some food here soon, probably after dark. Something to drink we will get for you now."

"Thank you," she said. Hearing the stiffness in her voice, the fear transmuted into suspicion, she found herself wondering *Why do I sound like that? So angry?*

Then she remembered. The smile, the pretense of caring meant nothing. They were prisoners, and this was the man who kept them here. Who had murdered, and was no doubt at that moment threatening to kill again if his demands were ignored.

He had turned to the others while she was thinking this. "You are comfortable?" he was asking Michael.

"Comfortable enough," said Cook warily.

"I'd like to ask you something, though," said Moira.

The Majd looked at her, and Susan saw him narrow his eyes as if to see better.

"—If I'm permitted."

"I am listening."

"You're the leader—the one they call the Majd."

"That is what they call me, yes. I am the *za'im*—the one who leads. My full name, Hanna Abu Harisah." He said it carefully, slowly, as if to give them time to memorize it. The "r" he pronounced hard, like a "d."

"I see. What we want to know is, what's going on? What's that noise outside?"

His eyebrows lifted. "You don't recognize it? No, you grew up in peace. It is artillery. Cannons. It is Christians killing Arabs, with guns and shells supplied by America and Israel. It is Beirut."

"So we're in Lebanon."

"Syria. But not far from the border."

"All right. What I wanted to ask—why are you holding us?"

"We are preparing to bargain," said Harisah. His face had closed, now, into the look they had once seen by the light of torches. "But to deal with capitalists one needs something they want. What do we have? Nothing—all we owned was stolen. So you are what we will trade."

"Trade for what? What do you want?"

"I think you must have some idea," said Harisah. He went to the window, looked down; Susan noted the furrows at the corners of his eyes, the way he sagged his tallness into the casement, not for support, but as if for reassurance that solidity existed. He searched his pockets but came up empty. "Do any of you have cigarettes? I am out of Luckies."

"No."

"You?" he asked Cook.

"Don't do it, sorry."

"Very good Americans, health-conscious, none of you smoke." He snapped at one of the others, and took the pack the man held out. He lit one and sucked smoke in angrily, still gazing out over the little courtyard that made a space between the buildings. "Look," he said, taking the cigarette from his mouth and pointing over the square with it, toward the hill. "They don't come near the building."

"The soldiers? We saw them. Who are they?"

"Syrians."

"Your allies?"

He threw a look of contempt over his shoulder, but said only, "They are Russian dogs. No more, no less."

"You won't tell us why you're holding us?" Moira asked him.

Harisah shrugged, his back to them. The distant rumble lent weight to his next words, as if he were speaking in thunder. "Sure, I'll tell you. Why shouldn't I? It will be more helpful if you understand us, so we can work together. Perhaps I will have you to make tape recordings later on. To prove at least that you are alive, and to speak through your words to the many."

Susan caught Moira's narrowing eye. No, Ox, she thought. Just listen. If she flew off the handle now . . .

"A little background for the Americans. Background—

the right word? Good. English comes back as you speak it.

"Our party is called the Wihdah. The Unity Party. We are freedom fighters, for our own land first, but also for all the countries under Zionist-imperialist domination. Your diplomats know of us. We have made ourselves known by our steadfast battle.

"The Turks, your country's friends, have in prison several members of our party. We want their release. Beyond that, we want an end to America's arming of the Zionists. We want our country back, to build a progressive democratic state."

"Your country?"

"Yes. The country we lived in for a thousand years, and were ejected from in one. Our land sold by the landowners to the Zionist rich, the poor driven out into the desert at gunpoint to make room for the Jews. Palestine."

"You mean Israel," said Moira.

The Majd stared at her again. "You seem very interested in 'Israel,' " he said.

She shrugged. "That's what we call it in America."

"Here we call it by its true name."

Moira fell silent. The younger man came back, carrying a plastic bowl. Harisah motioned, and he set it on the bed. Nan looked toward it. Susan lifted it, took a cautious sip—it was warm but welcome, pure water—and held it to her daughter's lips.

The Majd watched her, his face still. "Anyway," he continued after a moment, turning again to the window, "I will perform my assignment. I would like to do that without hurting any of you. I don't want to do that unless I am forced. Or unless you disobey. You tell your daughter that. Maybe it will all come out all right."

"And if it doesn't?" said Cook. "If the Turks don't do what you want—"

"Oh, it's easy enough. America orders the Turks to release them. Your allies are dependent on the Americans for weapons, money, ammunition. They will do as they are told. So, our friends are released and flown here. You go back on the same plane, leave Syria, leave the Middle East for home."

"Ah," said the Ox. For a moment gunfire was the single sound in the room, that and the sound as Susan sipped water for herself. It was warm but clean and she drank the rest of the bowl without stopping for breath. Only then, too late, did she remember Moira and Cook, and felt guilty and selfish. Then she thought rebelliously, But I got it for us. For Nan and myself. Why shouldn't I drink it?

"It won't work," said Cook. "I hate to say this—Harisah?—but I don't think the U.S. has that kind of leverage over the new regime there. Especially while they're in the middle of a war."

"We will find that out."

"And if they don't? What will you do then?" said Moira.

Nan let out a sob, just one, and they all turned to look down at her. Susan got up from the bed, holding her close.

"You had to threaten to do something to us," Lieberman repeated, lowering her head. Susan recognized her stubborn look, the one she got in class when she was ready to argue. "If your demands aren't met—if the U.S. can't, or won't, make them release these people—then you'll kill us. Isn't that right? Of course it is. Why don't you go ahead and say it?"

When he shrugged Moira turned away. "Maybe you'd better get out," she said. "Israel doesn't negotiate with terrorists. I hope no one does with you."

Susan froze. No, Ox, she thought desperately. Don't taunt him. Don't humiliate him. Don't order him about in front of his men—

But to her surprise, Harisah said nothing. Only straightened from the window and held out his hand. One of the others reached his rifle from the corner for him.

He left, not looking at them again, his back straight. As soon as the corridor was empty Moira sat down heavily on the bed. "Whew," she said. "I hate heavy scenes."

"You're sure Nancy's okay?" said Cook.

Susan slumped to the bed, too. She could feel her knee-caps trembling. "Oh . . . I think so. Aren't you, Bunny? Everybody's gone, you're all right, you're here with us?"

"I guess so," said the child, but she did not smile. Something in her face was a little too still.

"Okay, folks, show's over," said Michael to the other hostages, who had come to stand outside the door as soon as the guards had left. "Betts, you want to go back to our room?"

"Yes. Let's, please."

But Moira hung back a step, touched her arm as they filed out. "Hey, kid. A word."

"What?"

She lowered her voice. "I saw him looking at you. You better watch out for that guy."

"You mean—?"

"Harisah. I don't like it. If he's willing to kill us, what's a little rape?"

"He doesn't seem like the type, Ox. He was fair about Nan—"

"Fair?" Lieberman's eyes sharpened on her. She leaned a little closer. "Hey. Are you getting ideas, too? Forget them. This isn't the place for them, Betts Chan, and he sure as hell isn't the guy."

The suddenness of the insight, the source, and even more unexpected, the partial truth of it—she had to admit that, if only for a second, her emotions had been caught off guard—made her angry. "Don't be an ass, Moira. I assure you I have no—no *ideas.*"

"See that you don't. Remember, you have her to think about."

"I know what I have to think about, damn it, Moira! Don't think for a minute I wouldn't do anything for her! And what about you? Why did you push him like that, in front of his men? Is that smart? Snaggletooth has his gun back. Don't you have any idea what he can do to us? The only one who's keeping him from shooting us all is Hari-sah."

"Okay, okay. Maybe you're right. Hush, Betts, I'm sorry."

She tried to shake off Moira's hand, but it stayed firmly on her shoulder, guiding her out the door. Susan turned, at the last minute, hoping to see him one last time; but all that remained to sight was his broad back, far down the corridor, his hand lifted in the middle of a remark to the men who dogged his steps. And then he turned the corner, and was gone.

22
U.S.S. *Guam*

THE COMMODORE SCOWLED IN THE SIL-
ver light of approaching dusk, and shifted again in the
padded chair. There was no comfort in it anymore. The
lumpy patch one of the bo's'n's mates had sewn over the
hole poked right into the small of his back.

They'd have done better than this for their precious
Fourchetti, he thought darkly.

Well, maybe it would help him stay awake. He leaned
back gingerly against leather. The patch jabbed his kidney
this time. He ignored it, forcing his mind back to a fact
it would have preferred to forget.

He had to make a command decision, and soon.

The message he held now was clear, in its way. In the
failing light that filtered through the bridge windows he
studied it again. Pink paper. Top Secret.

*Upon receipt of this communica-
tion CTF 61 will prepare for immediate execution of an amphibious raid
for the rescue of the hostages and
associated embassy personnel suspected being held vicinity Ash
Shummari, Syria.*
*Maximum effort will be made to
achieve operational and tactical*

surprise. However, U.S. forces will avoid all appearance of hostility to Syrian and other forces, should they be encountered. Friction with Soviet land or sea units must repeat must be avoided. Deadly force is authorized only against terrorists actually holding hostages. To emphasize the limited nature of the incursion, 32 MAU will disembark with hand weapons only. Units proceeding inland will not fire unless as a last resort, i.e. self-defense against armed attack. Supporting or suppressive naval guns or air support will not be used.

If challenged by hostile forces of larger than battalion size they will, unless otherwise directed by this or higher authority, terminate the mission, retire, and reembark.

The concept of operations is as follows:

The rough plan took up only three paragraphs. Stripped to its essentials, it outlined a time-urgent landing on the coast of Lebanon, just south of the Syrian border. While part of the landing force secured and held a beachhead there, a strike element of lightly armed marines would continue inland at high speed, attempting to avoid the various warring militias. Some twenty miles inland the marines would hook left and cross the border into Syria itself. Ash Shummari, the abandoned resort where the commandeered airliner had landed, would then lie only a few miles to the north.

So far, okay. He could get Lenson to reorient his operation order from Cyprus to Syria. Too bad, by the way, that apparently his dependents were among the hostages. But he's better off not knowing, the commodore thought. He'd spend all his time worrying. And I need him. No, I did the right thing there.

But his eyes narrowed, he tilted the paper to the evening light at the conclusion of the message.

In view of adverse weather and fluid political situation in the Eastern Med, circumstances may arise which prohibit carrying out of these orders, or require delay or modification. In this case CTF 61, the On-Scene Commander, is authorized to use own judgment, informing higher authority as soon as possible. In any eventuality, excess force will not be used, nor will U.S. troops be exposed to risk incommensurate with the mission.

Now, what the hell did *that* mean? It sounded like some goddamn legal beagle had written it. He shifted on the slick leather and put his feet up on the squawk box. He regarded his slippers moodily, then craned his neck around. "Dan?"

"Mr. Lenson's below," said the operations officer, coming toward him from the opposite side of the bridge. "What can I do for you, boss?"

Sundstrom glanced at him sourly. *Boss.* The fat lieutenant was unshaven, his cap shoved back on his head; his uniform shirt strained at its buttons. "Mr. Flasher . . . what's that in your mouth?"

"Gum."

"Remove it before you talk to me, Lieutenant."

"Sure, sir." He worked free a pink wad, looked at it for a moment, whistling under his breath, and then affixed it carefully to a handy speaker. Sundstrom closed his eyes. Perhaps that, he thought, is the most irritating thing of all about him. The unfailing cheer of the idiot. Of all the unprofessional . . .

"SUROBS," said Flasher, holding out a clipboard.

"What?"

"I had Radio monitor the Kleiat airfield frequency. That's only four miles from the target beach. They got a local weather report. I calculated surf height from that and the chart."

Sundstrom felt sick. Eavesdropping on commercial radio for their intelligence. He should have a proper preassault preparation: aerial reconnaissance, an underwater demolition detachment to check for beach obstacles, minesweepers. But there was no time for that. Instead Roberts expected him to steam a hundred miles and carry out a landing on a coast none of them had ever seen before, with twenty hours' warning. But one thing was sure. It was his feet they would hold to the fire if he made the wrong decision.

"Well, goddamn it, let's have it. No, I don't want to read it! Brief me!"

"The numbers work out high, Commodore. Between six and ten feet, way too rough for the smaller craft. But I still think we can get them ashore."

"Why?"

"The combination of lee and this sandbar."

"What do you estimate?" grunted Sundstrom. He hated asking this man for advice.

"No more than five feet."

"Show me the chart again."

Flasher unfolded it for him against the window. Sundstrom leaned forward, blinking to clear his eyes; they were falling shut again. "Just a moment. Call my steward up here."

"Aye, sir. Messenger—ring the commodore's pantry, please."

"Okay," said Sundstrom. "Winds are still from the east. Right?"

"Zero-nine-five last report, Commodore."

"Sea height open sea, ten to twelve feet forecast—and we saw worse than that today. So you think—" He examined the stretch of beach between Tartus and Tripoli, trying to envision what the hydrography meant to swell formation. God, he thought then, I don't have the faintest idea what I'm doing.

But sometimes you had to act as if you did. It was the only way to keep the flunkies and time-servers honest. He stabbed a finger just south of the Syria-Lebanon border, the stretch of beach the Pentagon had recommended. "What about secondary systems?"

"Don't have any information on those. Sorry."

"If there's one from the early part of the storm, it would shoal right here at El Aabde. It could be higher than six feet."

"I don't think so. It's not that gradual a gradient, according to the chart."

"You're guessing, Mr. Flasher! Aren't you?"

"Yes sir, I sure am."

"Goddammit, I can't commit a force on that kind of information! That's not the way I operate. I need to be sure!"

"Well, you asked me for an estimate, Commodore."

Sundstrom threw himself back, staring at the lieutenant. At that moment his steward, who had come up silently behind them, set a cup of coffee and a saucer on the arm of his chair. Flasher glanced at it. Sundstrom picked it up and drank a good half of it, frowning, then set it aside.

"What about a helicopter?"

"Sir?"

"Could we send a helo ashore? Get a check on the surf height that way?"

"It's too dark now. Anyway, they'd have a hard time estimating surf height from the air."

"You're too negative, Lieutenant."

"Yes sir." Flasher grinned.

Sundstrom looked at his face for a moment longer, then

waved him away. He lifted the saucer, shaking his head, and drank the rest of the coffee, staring out at the sea. *This,* he mused, is the kind of staff support I get.

Dusk. The shrouded and dying sun, out of sight astern, penetrated the clouds for a moment as if in farewell. Its dull light threw an indistinct shadow ahead of the heaving ship. Where it fell the waves turned from storm-green to black. He could see the crests moving steadily toward them, creaming white, sliding at last under the bow, the ship rising sluggishly and then dropping. The motion was not unpleasant, in as large a ship as this. There was no roll now that the seas were on their bow. Pleasant, like he imagined horseback riding to be, moving along at a steady canter.

He twisted in his chair. To port, to starboard, ahead, steadily converging now though still scattered out of sight, the ships of the MARG would be steaming each at a steady pace, each with her own rhythm of roll and pitch. Where . . . where was their escort? He had ordered *Bowen* to stay with the flagship. He craned outward to see her coming up from astern, not more than a mile away.

She went past him at flank speed, heeling a little, slicing the waves apart with her sharp bow rather than crushing them like the bulky amphibious ships. The low hull disappeared for a moment among the seas, then heaved high on a crest. A trace of light smoke blew from her stack, and he could see spray fly along her forward decks as a larger sea threw her head up. He followed her dumbly with yearning eyes. God, what he wouldn't give to be her captain. To have clear orders to follow. No politics, no equivocating.

But his life wasn't that simple. This weasel-worded piece of flypaper Roberts had sent him, now. That was what was wrong with the Navy these days. If the boys upstairs had just said, openly and honestly, "Do it," then Ike Sundstrom would march into Hell itself with a clear conscience, eyes on the ball. He was good at following orders, none better.

But all the weasel-wording . . . his head sagged back against the headrest.

When he woke the bridge was dark. Only a faint luminescence, the faintest wash of gray, lit the sky. He sat upright in sudden panic. How long had he been asleep? There were things to be done. "Mr. Flasher!" he called. "Why did you let me go to sleep? What time is it?"

"It's almost nineteen hundred, sir."

"Who is that?"

"Lieutenant-Commander Byrne, sir."

"Goddammit, Byrne—God *damn* it." He sat up, furious. He had to decide, right now.

But still he found himself gripped by the same indecision, stymied by the same lack of information and conflicting fears. That goddamn surf—if it was ten feet, like Fleet Weather predicted, he could lose a lot of people getting ashore. The surf could roll a small boat over and over along the beach. He had seen it happen to an Italian landing craft at one of the early exercises.

But this was not an exercise, to be delayed if conditions were not perfect. He had orders to get the MAU ashore if he could. Other problems occurred to him then. "Byrne."

"Sir."

"*Ault* . . . what's her status? Is that shaft fixed yet?"

"They're working on it, sir."

"What? You're guessing. You don't know. Call them up and find out."

"Sir, they reported half an hour ago. They hope to get it on line soon, but they can't be sure."

"How far back is she?"

"About fifty miles, I estimate, sir."

"That goddamned Foster. He's had it in for me since she joined; he knows I'm an old destroyerman; they can't put things over on me like they could on MacInroe. How can I land without gunfire support? And what about *Barnstable?* Is her ramp still jammed?"

This time he felt the man hesitate. "Well?"

"I'll give her a call, sir, and check on that."

"What have you been doing up here, Byrne? You should be on top of things like that. That's what you're drawing salary for."

"Yes sir."

But the answer from the landing ship was just as unsatisfactory. They felt they could get the bow doors open once, but they might not be able to get them closed. The rocket hits had destroyed the handling mechanism. Sundstrom had a vision of one of his ships foundering, trying to face a storm with her bow doors open. He put his hands over his face, rubbed hard. He felt himself sliding off to sleep once more, and ground his back into the patched chair. No. He had to stay awake, and he had to decide.

What a goddamn no-win situation Roberts had put him in. He understood suddenly what was going on. They were lining his coffin. How had it taken him this long to catch on? They'd gotten to him, the ones who wanted Ike Sundstrom to fail. Or Roberts was doing it himself, leaving himself an out in case they lost men going ashore, or the landing was a bloody disaster. That was it, he was covering his ass. With a message phrased that way, no matter what happened, Commander, Sixth Fleet was safe. If he made the wrong decision, the admiral could point to that message. "I told him to use his good judgment. Unfortunately, Commodore Sundstrom failed to take into consideration the following factors—"

Oh, that was it, all right. That was how the big boys worked. You didn't make admiral by taking chances. Not in the peacetime Navy.

He stared at the intelligence officer's back. "Commander Byrne."

The man came back unwillingly, dislike in the very set of his neck. Sundstrom was suddenly angry. "So you don't know the status of the task force. Let's see what you *do* know, if anything. What's happening in Lebanon now?"

"Ceasefire's down the drain, sir. Heavy shelling in the Beirut suburbs."

"What about the north, up near Syria? Where they recommend we go in?"

"Things seem quieter there."

"What do you think of their recommendation?"

Byrne nodded, as if to a child who had asked an intelligent question at last. It enraged Sundstrom, but he held his peace. "The El Aabde beach, then inland along the hill road; hook left across the border, hit the terrorists in the flank—it sounds reasonable."

"I expect a more thorough analysis than that from my intel staff, Mr. Byrne."

"Yes sir." The N-2 pulled a chart from his pocket and unfolded it. "I brought it up with me, in case you asked. Here's what we know about the militia formations in the area. The nearest regular forces are a regiment of Syrian armor back here, at Homs—"

He allowed Byrne to go on for some minutes, thinking darkly there was no way he could know this much on a few hours' notice. It was a put-on, like his accent. At last the intel officer wound up. "At that point, twenty miles into Lebanon, we turn north and head up the Akroum Valley. Actual penetration of Syrian territory is both sudden and minimal with that route. The strike elements of the MAU only need to go in five miles to reach the old French hotel complex where they're being held.

"All in all, sir, it's probably as good a plan as we could expect at short notice. We make the actual landing in Lebanon, instead of a frontal assault on the Syrian coast. The nice thing is that it's relatively nonprovocative. Our political people can present it as clearly aimed only at the terrorists. If we can get the marines in and out fast enough they shouldn't meet either the Syrians or the Soviets." He hesitated. "Of course, that assumes that the Syrians are not actively supporting the group in the hotel."

"I'm more concerned right now with making it ashore at all. There's a rough surf running."

"That could cause us casualties too, sir, that's quite right."

Sundstrom grunted. *That's quite right,* he mimicked in his mind. Jesus Christ! He dismissed the man and Byrne faded once more back into the now-shadowy bridge.

The commodore writhed in his chair, under cover of the dark. Distances and advance rates crawled in his head. Then he froze: A figure loomed by his side. It was the radioman. He scanned the new message, using the man's flashlight.

It was Flash priority. Commander in Chief, U.S. Naval Forces Europe, wanted a status report. Was he going in or not? Representations had to be made to allies, to certain international authorities—

Sundstrom groaned aloud.

At last he asked for Haynes. The colonel came up at once, as if he had been waiting for the summons. His white hair gleamed in the faint light from instruments, and Sundstrom caught the smell of a cigar.

"Evening, Ike."

"Hello, Steve. You seen this?" He waved the message.

"Yes. I'm an information addressee."

"What do you think? Should we go in?"

He saw the colonel's head steady, saw the faint glow of the cigar-end describe a little circle, as if his teeth had taken hold; but the marine did not answer for a few seconds. At last he said, "That's your decision, Ike, as commander of this task force. No one else can make it for you."

"I know that, Steve. I assure you, no one wearing khaki understands his responsibilities better than I do. I just wanted to scrub things down with you . . . see if there were any rough edges you could bring to my attention." He paused, waiting, but the red glow did not move. "You've been through a hell of a lot more of these landings than I have. You're a professional, Steve, you know the kind of position this message puts me in."

"The MAU is ready to go ashore."

"I know that, Steve. But this surf business worries me.

We might not be able to support you, once you get in-land."

"We can use the helos for logistical support," said the colonel's voice, in the dark. He sounded tired. "Since they've restricted us to light weapons, that will bring pounds per man per day way down. If we don't hit resist-ance—"

"But if you do! This part of the Med is crawling with Russians. This could be a trap. And if we can't support you, if the surf rises and we can't get ammo ashore—"

"Three-four MAU is ready to go if ordered," Haynes said again, an edge to his voice. "That's about all I can do for you, Ike. The decision is up to you."

Sundstrom saw suddenly what was going on. His mouth curled on itself. Haynes, too. He wasn't going to commit himself. That way, if it ended in disaster, they could all point their fingers at him.

"That's all, Colonel," he said, his voice distant. "I'll let you know when I decide."

"Yes sir."

Alone once more, he stared out at the dark sea. He had to decide, and soon. COMSIXTHFLEET, and behind him those tall men sitting grimly in the War Room, wanted to know which way he would jump. Cancel, be-cause of the weather—postpone—

Or go in, and take the heat if any one of hundreds of things went wrong.

Out of nowhere, he thought of the air attack. Of the paralyzing fear when the planes came for them. Of flame and sound. And of the corpses, drifting past the side of the ship, bobbing in the gray cold sea. Someone had made a decision for them. The wrong decision.

If those fighters had been more heavily armed, he thought suddenly, I might have been one of them.

Sitting in the dark, gripping the leather armrests, he all but whimpered aloud. This was not the way he operated. He should have staff work. He should have clear orders. But no one would commit himself. His career—twenty-three years of hard work, sacrifice, making himself useful and agreeable—they were making him bet it all on something he couldn't control, couldn't check out, on the whims of weather and an enemy he knew next to nothing about.

On the other hand, if it worked out there could be a promotion in it. More likely than not, a decoration.

It all came down to that. It was a bet.

He could say no. What if he did? What if he sent back to Roberts, it's too big a risk, the surf estimates are uncertain, I'm postponing until the weather improves? But no, goddammit—the situation ashore demanded action. With every passing hour this hostage thing would be heating up. Politically, back in Washington. And militarily, too. This terrorist gang could have reinforcements on the way. Worse, the instant they realized what was afoot the Soviets would get their whole Med fleet underway. They couldn't let the U.S. invade one of their allies without putting up a fight. He could wait a day, maybe even two, for the weather to abate, but by then he might be sending Haynes into a war.

Or, on the other hand, it might all have been planned this way. The breakdown of the ceasefire in Lebanon. The diversion of the hostages to southern Syria, so temptingly just in range of sea power. I worry too much, he thought, sweating. But just this once, the bastards really might have set us up. The big meatgrinder might already be oiled, sharpened, just waiting for the marines to wade ashore. It could be another Tarawa. Or worse.

The ship throbbed through the night, vibrating, humming with machinery and life. His ships moved around him, a powerful engine of intervention, of force, but dependent on his will. He felt himself the center of things, the pivot, the one man whose decision would set this vast mechanism and its vast consequences into motion. He felt dimly that his whole career had pointed to this moment. Pointed to it, but it had not prepared him. He had followed orders for twenty-three years. Followed the book.

The book had never disappointed him. But now it had no answers. Now, this night, he had to find the answer in himself.

This is it, he thought. Luck, chance, had put the ball in his court at last. But now they were fencing him about, hoping to trip him up, waiting for him to slip. Then the wolves would come out of the bushes. But he wasn't going to trip. Ike Sundstrom was in charge, and there would be no mistakes.

He sat motionless, staring at the sea, and the two sheets of paper trembled lightly in his hands.

And some time later, eons or minutes, someone was shaking Lenson awake in the dark. "Lieutenant. You okay? Commodore wants you."

"What now," he muttered, turning his face to the bulkhead.

"He wants you bad," said McQueen, and Lenson heard the shadow in his voice. He sat up, too quickly, and his head slammed into the overhead. Yet it did not hurt. He realized he had gone to sleep with his helmet on.

"More planes?"

"Almost wish it was," said the quartermaster. He sounded grim. "No, he wants you to bring the operation order up. He says he doesn't like it, he says it's against his better judgment, but he's got to do it. So it's on."

"It? What?" he said. Then he knew. He had known for days.

"The commodore's ordered the rendezvous," said McQueen. "For 0200. Arrival at oparea at 0400."

"The landing?"

"That's right," said the petty officer. He reached up, something clicked, and dazzling light flooded the room. "We're going in tomorrow morning, sir, at dawn. I'd say you and me, we got a little work to do."

23

U.S.S. *Spiegel Grove*

AND SIXTY MILES DISTANT OVER THE
night sea, the sea over which so many fleets and armies
had sailed to battle, the two hundred men of Bravo Company crouched and lay and sat in the hull of a rolling
ship.

They waited. The ceaseless murmur of their steel
mother surrounded them: the rush of sea as they pounded
steadily eastward, the creaking groan of the metal fabric
that alone sustained them, the hum and whisper of ventila-
tion, the distant throb of a pump, as intimate and yet
mysterious as the heart of a woman who sleeps beside you,
no matter what the vow never yours inalienably, but only
for a moment of inestimable duration.

It's so quiet, Will Givens thought, cradling his guitar.
So filled with familiar sound, and yet, somehow, so silent.

His fingers touched the strings so lightly that through
the fresh callus he could barely feel them. Still, in the odd
quietness of *Spiegel Grove*'s troop compartment that evening, he could hear the chord hum to him. As if all the
music still to come from the old guitar was waiting, ready
for him to release it, yet willing too to bide. Yielding itself
to the future and to his will.

Above him Liebo shifted his weight, and Givens looked
up at the underside of his mattress. It shifted again, creaking.

"What you doing up there, Dippy?" he asked the ticking.

"I ain't doing nothing, goddamn it. Let me alone."

"Don't get uptight about it. I just wondered."

"Well, wonder to yourself, Oreo."

His fingers tightened on the frets. He sat up on one elbow, staring up at the close cotton striping, the dingy yellow fabric of Liebo's fartsack.

"What did you call me, man?" he said to the mattress.

Silence, and then he heard: "Sorry, Will. I'm kind of on edge, I guess. I didn't mean to call you that."

He waited, considered, and then lowered himself back into the embrace of his bunk, still feeling the pulse-hammer of arousal, but relieved that he didn't have to face the private down. But there was disappointment, too. He wanted to say something angry, strike out, hurt someone. Yeah, on edge. *We're all on edge,* he thought. That was why there was no sound in the compartment except the whine of the blowers, the distant throb of engines running at full speed, the omnipresent creak as the bunk frames warped under the weight of bodies and the steady batter of the storm. No mutter and sudden laughter of bull sessions, joking, cassette players, no grab-assing, none of the continual ritual murmur of card games.

He glanced down at the table, below where he lay. The cards were out, but no one was playing. Harner was sitting with his boots planted square on the deck, head down, whittling slowly with his Ka-bar on a swab handle. Washman had his feet up on the bottom bunk, staring blankly at a full-page crotch shot in an Italian girlie magazine. He watched them for several minutes. Harner whittled on. Washman stared at the same page. Not even his eyes moved; only his thin chest, ratitic and sharp-edged beneath the thin cotton of his skivvy shirt, rose and fell, rose and fell.

He tried another chord, but it seemed too loud. Liebo shifted nervously above him. He laid the guitar aside and pulled out the book, tried to read a page. The equations made no sense. They described somewhere else, some perfect universe of concepts and logic that had never existed, and never would. He laid it aside too after a few minutes and stared at the underside of the bunk frame for a while. At last he climbed down, taking the guitar with him. Harner and Washman looked up, jerked from their reveries by the scrape of his chair.

"Good magazine?" he asked Washout.

"Uh, yeah." The private closed it, looking guilty.

"Get that in Palermo?"

"Yeah." He hesitated, then held it out. "Want to check it out?"

He didn't. He had resolved not to look at such things again. He had prayed over what he had done, prayed over it and been, he felt, forgiven. He was clean now. But the glossy flash of white thigh as the page turned, a curve of brown into pink, had made the water start in his mouth.

There is none righteous, no, not one . . .

He took it, and flipped the stained pages. It was in Italian, but the pictures were self-explanatory.

"Oreo," said a familiar voice behind him, "what are you doing with that trash?"

"Just looking at it, I—"

Cutford's arm came over his shoulder, so close he could smell him, and seized the magazine. He snatched for it, but he was too late, and the corporal too fast. Bits of paper fluttered down over his head. Washman started up, his eyes wide. "Hey! That's my magazine, asshole! What the fuck's wrong with you?"

"Why you pushing it on this brother, then? He don't want no cheap white cunt, nor no pictures of any, either." The tearing came faster, and Washman flinched back as a wad of pages flew at his face.

"Come off it, Cutford—"

"Shut up." The corporal finished his shredding and tossed the naked spine to the deck. He swung on Givens, his eyes whited. "Why you poison your mind with this toubab shit? It's a trap for the true man, nigger. Don't you know that?"

Harner, silent, scooted his chair back. He put the chewed broomhandle behind him, holding the knife in his lap.

"Goddamn it—" began Washman, getting up. His face had gone pale, the blotches standing out in red relief.

"I'll pay you for it, Washout," said Givens, standing up, too. "Never mind."

"Fuck you will," said Cutford, swaying dangerously ponderous as the ship heaved to a heavy sea. Under the thin dark fabric his chest bulged as he lifted his fists. "He give it to you. I tore it up. Anyone want to settle anything, he settle it with me."

Givens sighed. The corporal was hungry for a fight. There was no way around it. All he could do was show Washout and the others that he was on their side, not Cutford's. The anger he had lit with Liebo, and then tamped down, licked up again. Anger was sin, but there was righteous anger, too. The long-built rage of being black yet not accepted as black, the truthlessness of stereotypes and the way men of hate like Cutford forced you into them despite yourself. And suddenly he was eager for it, too. Rage sang through his veins, tightened his calves and the long muscles of his arms. The weak points: groin, eyes, throat. The voice of the instructor at boot camp. "Like they say, troopers, you can build muscle, but not over eyes or knees." But Cutford had been through boot camp, too. And a lot more. He stepped forward warily, knowing that his enemy was both bigger and more vicious. David had won in the Book, but only with the help of the Lord.

The Lord seemed far away from Troop Berthing tonight.

"You crazy—" he was beginning, when a cry from the next bay of bunks pivoted them all around. It was Hernandez, his voice high with surprise and insult.

"What you doing in my locker, jerkoff?"

"You owe me ten bucks, man. I'm takin' it out in trade."

"Like shit you are, you goddamn thief."

"Fight! Fight!"

Givens stumbled forward, catching an edge of the table. The guitar jangled a discord on the steel deck, but he didn't stop. He rounded the bunks in time to bounce a red-haired man, one of the riflemen, head-on. There were four of them, all from the same squad. Hernandez, his back to his locker, was wrestling with the biggest. There was time only to see that before the redhead stiff-armed his head against the bunk frame. A dazzling pain shot forward between his eyes. All through the compartment, men leaped down from their racks, taking sides with instantaneous readiness. Unfortunately, that meant the mortarmen were outnumbered four to one.

The white dazzle cleared, and he came away from the frame fighting mad. He grabbed the redhead in a halfnelson, tripped him down in the same motion, and made for Hernandez. Two riflemen took him halfway, hammering him to the deck with punches in the ribs and back. They rolled in a melee around the feet of the bunk frames, he punching out at whomever he could reach, as above him the original fight dissolved in a free-for-all. Hernandez stubbornly defended his locker; Harner had his long arms around a lance corporal from the second platoon; Washout screamed shrilly as a black grunt twisted his wrist behind his back. Liebo was still going round atop that first biggest rifleman.

Then he saw Cutford. The big corporal battered his way through three men in as many seconds, snarling, leaving them sitting on the deck holding bloody faces and moaning. His assault left the mortar team in possession of the narrow space for a minute or two, then the grunts got smart and scrambled across through the racks between them. Surrounded, the squad went down under a mass of shouting men. There were too many of them, and as if realizing it, the riflemen began to fight among themselves, without pretext, and the atmosphere suddenly changed with that, as if they all realized simultaneously that it was over. The skirmish eased off into slaps and pushes. Givens found himself in a corner with Hernandez. "What the fuck, hombre!" the little man said, grinning, a trickle of blood coming from his nose.

"Too many of them, man."

"Ah, they want to fight, we fight, right?"

"They think they can push mortarmen around, they going to end up with their asses in a sling," panted Liebo.

"The brass!" somebody shouted from the far end of the compartment. There was no officer, or else he wisely decided not to come in, but they broke apart. The riflemen drifted back toward their racks, leaving behind threats and lifted fingers. The mortarmen jeered after them, but not too loudly. Givens reached up to feel the back of his head. It hurt, but he didn't seem to be bleeding. Probably leave me with a lump, he thought. It hurt when he breathed, too. Some bastards always had to go for the kidneys. But still he found himself grinning, the adrenaline happiness of a fight welling up, and he bent to help Hernandez pick up the clothes the riflemen had knocked from his locker.

Back at the card table they scraped chairs together. There were not enough and Washman and Hernandez sat side by side on the lower bunk. Liebo displayed a torn shirt sleeve, Harner grinned slowly around a bruised lip, and Givens rubbed the back of his head with a shade more wince than it really called for. They panted together for a minute or two, and then Cutford rubbed abruptly at his skinned knuckles. "I'd 've liked to take out a couple more of the fuckahs," he whispered. "Young bastards. None of them old enough to show hair yet."

The others looked up, uncertain as to whom he meant. Them? There was something strange in the way the older man sat, chafing his palms as if for warmth. Givens saw that he was bleeding, the drops thick and black as road tar against his skin.

"How old are you, Cutford?" he said softly.

"Old enough I shouldn't be wastin' my time in shitpot little troop-compartment scuffles," said the corporal sharply, yet still without looking at any of them.

"Uh . . . you fought real good," said Washout.

Cutford looked at him then, close, and his broad flat nose widened. He gathered his feet beneath him as if to get up, and a jangling musical sound came from under the chair.

"My guitar," said Givens, remembering suddenly. "Gimme it."

"Get it yourself, Oreo. Crawl under there and fetch."

Oh, sweet Jesus, he thought hopelessly, groping under the table, among the butts and scrap paper. What is it with this dude? Is there no way to pacify this anger, this apartness? Looking up at Cutford's heavy legs, the tops of the athletic socks he always wore showing above the scuffed black of boots, he felt a sudden need to answer what the corporal was continually asking of him, of all of them.

Only what was the question?

When he came up with the guitar, leaning it carefully against the smudged bulkhead where the mortar tube had leaned every morning since the far beginning of the float, Cutford was talking about Vietnam. He never had before.

"Shitpot little scuffles like this . . . we done this all before, in d'Nam," he was saying, not remotely, but to Hernandez, who was nodding, eyes intent. "Scuffle around, fart around, grab-ass in the bunkers . . . it was the heat. It got to you real quick, when you come in country. Heat, man, Alabama was nothin' to it."

Givens eased himself back into Washman's bunk, away from the level of the corporal's eyes. The other men grew silent too, waiting with him for whatever Cutford had to say.

"Heat," prompted Hernandez. "Yeah, like in the Delta, hah?"

Cutford looked to him, almost gratefully. He sighed. "Yeah. Hot like that."

"Where were you?" whispered Hernandez. "In the jungle? The swamp? The mountains?"

"Shit, the bush, man, the bush. It was jungle, man. Fucken scorpions all over, find them in the Claymore pouches, you could feel them crawling on you at night, on ambush, couldn't move . . ."

They hung breathless and alone with him, hunters at a campfire, young warriors by the bard; silent in the once-again silent compartment filled with expectant men. The ship banged and creaked. Cutford rubbed his hands.

"How long was you there, man?"

"Two tours, man."

"*Two,* Cutford? How come you went around again?"

The corporal hesitated, just for a moment, looking round at them; then reached into his back pocket.

The picture was ironed from years in the wallet, an old Polaroid, the green of jungle yellow, faces yellow, sky yellow. Over his shoulder Givens' eyes found the eyes of other marines. Hand-twisted cigarettes dangled from smiling mouths. One of them was a short man, thin, something gold gleaming yellow against his dark throat. Next to him, his arm over his shoulders, stood a gangly, grinning, friendly-looking boy Will recognized with a shock as Cutford.

"They needed me," said Cutford. "Them simple bastards I was with. Off the streets of Watts and Durham and Selma. They needed my black ass. They was going down like . . . like . . . we was going down bad. It was sixty-nine, man. They was no more grunts to come. I was a rifleman then. We just went patrol; they just kept sending you patrol, you know, no slack, no break, maybe a day back at battalion if you took heavies, but then, man, right back in the bush. After Tet the Man was scared. He knew what was coming down. It was use the grunt or lose him, and they used us, man. Used us up. I tried to learn them, them simple bastards . . ."

"The squad?" said Hernandez.

"The whole fucken squad," said Cutford, leaning forward. The little golden charm, twisting on its chain, swung out from his chest and dangled gleaming in the stark fluorescence from the overhead. "The whole fucken squad one night. Overrun by a batt of en-vee regulars. Just me. They only left me.

"That's how it was, fuckheads. The Man sends you out there, the ghost officers. They fuck up, the Man don't pay. We pay, baby, you pay, dickheads like you. I stuck the rest of that tour, and they wanted me to be a warrant. I said, no, fuck you, I'm gettin' out. And I did."

"You got out?" said Liebo, gentle-like.

"Two years."

"Why'd you come back?"

Cutford looked at him long and hard, then seemed to see the rest of them. His face changed, and he shook his head angrily. He was starting to get up when the 1MC came on. The silence in the compartment went suddenly, electrically a dozen times more silent, the men looking naked-eyed up at where the gray speakers sat screwed to the bulkheads. The boatswain's pipe shrilled, cutting through the whoosh of ventilators, and someone cleared his throat.

"THIS IS THE CAPTAIN SPEAKING.

"AS YOU KNOW, WE HAVE BEEN STEAMING INDEPENDENTLY OF THE OTHER SHIPS OF THE MARG, HEADED EAST WHILE AWAITING ORDERS.

"A FEW MINUTES AGO, WE RECEIVED DIRECTION FROM CTF 61 FOR RENDEZVOUS AND RECONSTITUTION OF THE TASK FORCE. THE RENDEZVOUS POINT IS SOME FORTY MILES AHEAD OF US, NOT FAR OFF THE COAST OF LEBANON. FOR THE INFORMATION OF OUR EMBARKED MARINES, NOT FAR FROM A TOWN YOU'VE PROBABLY HEARD OF BEFORE—A PLACE CALLED TRIPOLI.

"WE HAVEN'T GOTTEN OFFICIAL WORD YET, BUT THIS WILL PROBABLY BE OUR LAST NIGHT

OF WAITING. WE'LL BE LESS THAN TWO HOURS OFF THE BEACH AT THE RENDEZVOUS POINT. ACCORDINGLY, ALL HANDS WILL TURN TO IMMEDIATELY FOR INSTANT RESPONSE IN THE MORNING.

"I WANT ALL PERSONNEL TO CHECK AND DOUBLE-CHECK YOUR GEAR. THIS GOES FOR EVERYONE, BUT ESPECIALLY FOR THE DECK DEPARTMENT AND THE MIKE-BOAT CREWS. CHECK THE ENGINES AND RADIOS, THE WINCHES, AND THE GATES. MAKE SURE FUEL TANKS ARE TOPPED OFF AND LIFEJACKETS ARE ABOARD—THE SURF AT THE BEACH IS REPORTED HIGH, AND MAY INCREASE TONIGHT IF THIS WIND PICKS UP.

"OFFICERS OF THE MARINE DETACHMENT WILL MAKE THEIR OWN PREPARATIONS FOR DEBARKATION AS EARLY AS 0400 TOMORROW. THIS INCLUDES WEAPON AND AMMO ISSUE.

"I WILL CONTINUE TO KEEP YOU INFORMED."

The loudspeakers hissed briefly, empty as the eyes of the listening men, and then went silent.

"Ohhh, shit," whispered Washman. "Is this . . . is this the way these things start?"

Cutford got up. He was still looking at the loudspeakers, and his hands hung loose and open, palms out, fingers slightly up. A drop of blood trembled for a moment, then fell to the floor. It made a dark pool on the tile.

"Yeah," he said. "Yeah, this is how they start."

"What do you want us to do?"

"Lemme see Silky about that gear issue." The corporal turned, took a step, and stumbled over the varnished hollow curve of the guitar. It fell again, chording against ship-steel. He looked down at it for a long moment, and then bent. He held it to his face, looking closely at the pearled fretboard.

"Hey, Cutford—"

But he had already gripped it by the neck, like a bat, and aimed and then swung it, fast, the air rushing through the strings and past the sound hole, singing. When it hit the stanchion it shattered suddenly in midair into separate things, uncoiling strips of wood, strings snapping back on themselves, the pearl cracking like plastic. It was as if the music crammed inside, so tightly, years and years of it still unheard, exploded the stops and nickeled keys across the compartment, snapping and ringing against the bunk frames and deck and even the plastic covers of the light fixtures. The neck was left in his hands, strings dangling, and he swung it again, and again, against the unscarring steel of the stanchion until nothing was left.

"I told you it was too fucken big to fit in here," he said. "Oreo? Din't I tell you before?"

"Yeah," said Givens. "Yeah, Cutford. You told me."

The corporal had half-turned toward the hatch, tossing away the remnant. Givens' savage right must have been unexpected. It caught him low in the gut, unready, and he buckled over for a moment and his eyes widened. Then, too fast for Givens to see or follow, he found himself lying on the deck with his windpipe being crushed by Cutford's knee. It dug deeper, and he clawed instinctively for the man's eyes. The corporal avoided his hands easily, grinning, and pinned him tighter. Givens began to see stars. "Nice try, boy," he heard the deadly hiss above him. "A lil late, a lil slow, but at least you tried. We may make a marine of you yet instead of a Jesus-dreamin' ofay-lover."

His lips moved without voice. "Fuck you, Cutford."

"Oh, man, you just said the magic word," said the corporal. He stood up, grinning, and at his sweaty throat gold swung and glittered like a searching knifepoint. "Okay, dickheads, suit up. They's sendin' us to war."

24

U.S.S. *Ault*

"BLANEY, MASON, POLOCK—STAND BY TO heave your guts out," grunted Wronowicz. "Take a breath. Ready—"

They laid hands on lines, squinting at their knuckles, waiting for his word.

"Haul!"

"Uhh!" The held-in air left each man in an explosive grunt.

Deep in the destroyer, the four engineers strained at the tackle in frozen attitudes of timeless, tremendous effort. Muscles quivering, sweat sheening their bare arms and chests, they leaned into the lifting tackle with all their strength. Yet nothing moved, and they swayed there, locked, frozen in strain like warriors in a frieze. But they were not heroes, they were just machinists and firemen, Navymen, no different from the thousands of others afloat and at desperate work on that sea that night. Each man by himself was alone, individual, locked for the duration of a life into a single consciousness. Yet now, at last, each one of them could feel for a moment part of something larger.

Wronowicz was too exhausted to muse on or even to notice what they looked like. In the eighteen hours since the breakdown he had left the engineroom once, to wolf a sandwich and pastry standing up in the chiefs' quarters.

He had heard about the air attack on the main body of the formation, somewhere ahead. But he did not think about it for more time than it took to finish his coffee. His entire being through all that night and through the day had been concentrated on one thing.

On the port reduction gear.

The first thing he'd had to do was make sure it was really a failed pinion bearing. There were a few other things that could produce that kind of vibration. Loose foundation bolts, for instance. But when he disassembled the strainers the gleam of babbitt, trapped like placer gold in the oily mesh, told him his guess was right. High temperature, vibration, and metal ground to powder in the lube oil. There was only one thing that caused that. A wiped bearing.

He had locked the shaft, and set the black gang to taking things apart.

Only the reduction gear did not come apart that easily. It wasn't supposed to be taken apart at all, not at sea. That was why it was padlocked shut, and the keys kept in the captain's safe. And that was why in the midst of his men Kelly Wronowicz strained at a lifting tackle deep in the guts of the old ship, in the swaying heat of the engineroom, walled in by metal, floored and roofed by metal. Steel grated under the braced boots of strong men, and the roar of machinery and the sea beat steadily against their ears.

"Goddamn. . ."

"Heave, dammit!"

"Yuh . . ."

"Stewie, give her a tap . . . see if she'll move yet."

The first-class gauged the distance between himself and the casing, balanced the sledge in blackened hands, and then swung, hard, putting his hips into it. The hammer glanced off, jarring their ears even over the roar. The solid steel cover casting, connected now to the overhead by taut lines of tackle, stirred upward a bit, and then jammed again.

"Again," Wronowicz grunted, and they panted, wiped

their hands on their dungarees, and set their shoulders once more.

The sledge clanged, louder, and suddenly something gave. The men lurched backward into the dead turbines. Wronowicz and Polock hauled in line rapidly, hand over hand, gauging the roll of the ship. The tackle multiplied their strength and the chainhoist rattled as the massive hump of the gear cover rose slowly toward the lifting ring clamped to the overhead.

Wronowicz wrapped his hand in the line and leaned back, looking upward, breathing in great gasps. "Get a steadying line on it. Quick, before she rolls again."

"Right, Chief." Steurnagel twisted rope into a running loop and tossed it over a projecting ringbolt, made the other end fast to a generator mounting. Just in time; the whole fabric of the ship groaned, and the dimness of the engineroom tilted, tilted. As it passed thirty degrees the men began to slide on the greasy deckplates. They cursed, reaching for handholds, and tools slid across the gratings and splashed into the bilges. The casing, two tons of metal suspended in the air, came massively taut against the single steadying rope. Wronowicz backed away, keeping tension on the lift line.

"Blaney, keep those lines taut. If that bastard gets away from us, starts swinging, we're screwed but good."

"Right, Chief."

The destroyer reached the end of her roll and hung there. The men in her guts waited, breathing hard, their eyes on the single rope, taut as metal. They waited for it to part, to release tons of steel in an unstoppable arc.

The ship groaned, deep, and then began to roll back. Wronowicz moved instantly, sending a second line over the other end of the casing before the first one slacked. Steurnagel sent a third snaking up, and like a bound beast the jacket shifted uneasily, entwined but still dangerous under its net.

"That do it, Chief?"

"Looks like it. Stand from under."

"Right."

Now that the cover was lifted, the gearing itself lay exposed to sight. Wronowicz reached for his hand-rag. Then, on his knees, conscious of the mass suspended above him, he ran his big fingers over the polished metal, poking and prying. The hundreds of intermeshing teeth gleamed under the light, oozing yellow oil like a honeycomb. Steurnagel leaned past him with a flashlight. He tapped delicately with the sledge haft where the gearshafts came through their bearings.

Solid. Solid. He came to the one he suspected and tapped it delicately.

Solid. He rocked back on his heels, staring, and the ship rolled and he grabbed for the deck, almost falling. Damn, he thought. Isn't this it? The low-speed pinion . . . no, goddammit, where was his mind? This was the high-speed. He shook his head and closed his eyes for a moment, trying to concentrate. His brain felt like junk iron. Three hours of sleep the night before, then all day down here, it was long past dark, and he was forty-two years old. . . .

"Chief, you all right?"

"Yeah. Sure." He opened his eyes and leaned forward again, ignoring the exhaustion, ignoring the uneasiness in his throat. It had to kick up a storm now, just when you needed a steady keel. They all expected miracles of him. Well, Christ, he thought, that's what Wronowicz is here for. He breathed deeply and felt a little better. He lowered the sledge again and tapped delicately, deep in the gearing.

"There. Hear it?"

"Uh . . . no."

"There?"

"It sounds a little different, I guess," said Steurnagel, looking at Wronowicz, not at the gear. "Doesn't it?"

"Sounds hollow. Like a busted baseball bat. Hear it?" He tapped again.

"Yeah! I heard it that time."

He relinquished the hammer to the petty officer and sat

back on his heels, considering. The casing stirred above his head, the roll of the ship catching some rhythm once in a while, but he was no longer conscious of it. The black gang stood behind him, leaning across the now-cold jackets of the port turbines. They were silent, intent as he was. There was no griping, no grab-assing. Whatever he asked, whatever they had to do, they would give it. They all knew what was at stake. On Friday nights ashore Polock and Steurnagel had battered and been battered by their share of "jarheads," but now they were all the same.

Or close enough, Wronowicz thought, then concentrated on the job at hand. "Get in here, you jerks," he said over his shoulder, then, to the first-class, "Stewie, what you think?"

"Think we ought to replace the bearing."

"No spares. Remember?"

"Oh, shit, yeah."

"You and the captain, just memory wizards, both of you . . . okay, there's a couple things you can do when you wipe a bearing. Things they don't teach you in 'A' school." The half-circle of grimy faces watched him, some blankly, others with intelligence, all listening. "The best thing is to replace it, sure. That way you got a inspected, new part in there. But supposin' you can't, you don't got one, then you got to finesse it a little. We'll have to pull it out to see . . . but I strongly suspect we're going to have to do some babbitt work on this one."

"Rebabbitt it, you mean, Chief?" said Polock.

"Jesus no, we can't do that at sea. You got to have a seventeen-hundred-degree furnace, dam babbitt, pipe dope, mandrel, all that shit . . . no. That's shoreside work. What we got to do is see if there's a clear area we can scrape down and reuse, then maybe shim up with that three-thousandths stock you use on foundations. But we'll get to that. What's the first thing we got to do? Anybody know?"

"Get the bearing out, Chief?" grinned Blaney.

Wronowicz stared at him for a moment, then nodded.

"Yeah. That's right. Now look." He pointed to the bottom of the bearing. "Friction bearings are just hollow rings, like a woman's—well, like a wedding ring. They're lined with soft metal, and the shaft of the gear rests on that, inside a collar. See? Now, in a gear case like this, every time you torque up you change where the shaft pushes on the collar. So first thing we did was shut down, let everything cool to get the stresses out of it, so each gearshaft rests right at the bottom of its bearing."

They nodded, solemn and intent. The ship rolled, and they all put their arms out, bracing themselves without looking away from him. He went on. "Now, these pinion bearings are split rings. You can get them out, all right, unbolt the cover and then roll 'em out from underneath, but only if there's no weight on them. So what we got to do?"

"Lift the shaft," said Steurnagel.

"Right. How?"

"Jeez." He thought about that, then looked up at the overhead. "Uh . . . another chainhoist?"

"Right track, but way too small. What's this shaft weigh?"

"A lot."

"You ought to know that," said Wronowicz. "Anybody know? Polock?"

"Not me."

"Blaney?"

"Twenty tons."

"Holy Moses," said Wronowicz. "You been studyin', for a change?"

"Some, Chief."

"About time. No, chainhoist won't take forty-two thousand pounds. So we got to do better. How? You know that, Blaney?"

"No, Chief."

"Well, I'm still a little ahead, then. Here's how: We're gonna use hydraulics."

"Chief," said one of the men behind him, and he turned,

annoyed at being interrupted, and saw Ensign Callin. He stood with his hands in his pockets, looking down at them.

"Did you want something, sir?"

"I wanted to see how much longer this is going to take, yeah. The captain's on my neck up there every fifteen minutes for progress reports."

"We're working on it, sir."

"Well, let's concentrate on getting it done, Chief, not on school call. You can train your men later, after the landing. Okay?"

Wronowicz didn't answer, just looked up at him, and after a second or so the ensign turned away for the ladder. He turned back, though, just as he reached it. "Anyway . . . how much longer?"

"I don't know, sir."

"We're going in at dawn. You know we got to have full power then."

Wronowicz nodded. The tension between the two men, chief and officer, was like a rope strained to breaking. One more word, he was thinking, and I'm going to say it. I'm going to tell this fuzz-cheeked kid just where he can stick it.

He fought it down just once more, the ten thousandth time in twenty-two years of enlisted service; but this time it was a closer call than it had ever been before. There might not be much more forbearance left in him.

"You better get back up to the bridge," he said.

Callin looked startled; the men behind the chief were silent. The ship began its tilt, the ladder slanting, making the ensign snatch for the handrail. He opened his mouth, then closed it, seeing something in the chief's averted face, and then swung himself up the ladder and disappeared.

"Chief?" said Steurnagel tentatively. "You said, hydraulics?"

"Yeah . . . hydraulics, yeah." Wronowicz took a deep breath. Forget Callin, forget the landing. Just fix the fucking shaft. "Okay, you worthless sons of sea cooks, move! Polock, I want that Hamilton ram broke out and set up over there, ready to go under the shaft. Mason, we're going to need some bridge beams, at least two inches thick, and some good thick planks from the damage control locker. Steurnagel, break out the scrapers and bluing, and clear off that bench over there. Move, assholes! Move! Move! Move!"

They scattered, and Wronowicz leaned against the turbines, studying the naked gears; and then his gaze lifted, toward the ladder. He licked his lips. Just one drink, just a single short nip. Just to cut the taste of oil. He had a sudden image of the bottle. Nestled half-full under his mattress, only two decks up, a minute away, and then back down to work again. . . .

And against that vision, another, of marines struggling in the surf, and the waiting mouths of guns . . .

He slammed the sledge viciously into the solid steel of the bearing cap.

At eleven that night he leaned back from the disassembled gear and wiped a trembling arm across his forehead. His skin was black with oil and blood thinned with sweat dripped from his knuckles. Behind him, leading aft, the gratings had been ripped up to expose the shining length of the propeller shaft. From under it protruded baulks of timber, steel beams, wedged deckplates. The men around him lifted sweat-streaked faces as he reached for a clean rag, wiped oil and shavings from a six-inch metal ring, and held it to the light.

"There," he muttered. "See it?"

Within the steel, several parallel gouges marred the perfect smoothness of silvery lining. Beside him, the first-class nodded.

"Got the scrapers sharpened?" the chief asked him.

"Put a man on it an hour ago."

"Get 'em out. We want to get this thing running by dawn, we got a lot to do. Blaney, wake up!"

The fireman started guiltily, then his smile came back

full force; but he, too, looked tired, and his "Right, Chief," was barely audible.

"If you're so wiped out, run up and get us a pot of fresh joe out of the engineering office. If there ain't any get some from chief's mess; tell the senior chief I sent you. The thicker and blacker the better."

"Right."

"And some cinnamon buns, if they got any left," Wronowicz shouted after him, then turned his attention back to the bearing. "Stewie, we're in luck. See how these gouges are deepest in this quadrant? If we can scrape them out just right, we can seat the shaft on a smooth area when it takes power. It'll shimmy some at low speeds but at flank it'll smooth out."

"Won't that give us too much play?"

"We can bump metal to take that up. I think. And jack the oil pressure as high as she'll go. It's only got to take it for a few hours. After that, nobody topside gives a shit."

The decking began to slant under his feet, and both he and Steurnagel grabbed for the bearing. The men grabbed for handholds, and above their heads, as the ship tilted farther and farther, the gray mass of casing stirred uneasily in its web, the ropes popping and creaking as they tautened.

"Goddamn filthy weather . . . got it?"

"Yeah."

"Tighten up on this vise, I'll hold it in place."

"How tight you want it?"

"Bear down, damn it. I don't want it moving around while I'm working on it. Where's Polock? I want him to start polishing that shaft while we're doing this. A fine stone and oil, some emery cloth, get all that old babbitt off—"

"Already on it, Chief," the second-class called.

"Good . . . now, where's that bluing?"

"Over here."

"Hit that light there."

As they reeled toward the workbench, grasping at pipes

and stanchions as the ship staggered again, one of the younger men turned aside and began suddenly to retch into the bilges.

"Seasick?" said Steurnagel. "Keep a close eye on what comes up."

"Yeah?" The sailor raised a white face, unsteady eyes. "Why?"

"Just watch it. You see a little puckered red thing come up, grab it. That's your asshole."

Wronowicz ignored them. He had heard that one too many times before, and just now, with the men giving them all they had for twenty hours straight, it even seemed cruel. Especially since his own stomach was threatening mutiny. It sure is rolling hard, he thought, and then dismissed it as the lamp snapped on over the workbench. He blinked in its glare, bending his dripping face close over the steel ring. The vise held it secure as he probed at the gouged metal and then dabbed bluing out of a can and brushed it over the babbitt in a thin, even layer. He gave it a minute to dry and then selected one of the scrapers, delicate rounded blades scalpel-sharpened to cut metal. He stared at the scarred surface of the bearing, working it out in his mind. Tired, Christ. This was a shoreside job, not something you did on a rolling destroyer at night. He needed an inside micrometer and feeler gauges, not his eye. But that was all he had, eye and experience, twenty-two years of it. That was all; and just for a moment, standing there ready to begin, he thought that this was it, what he had trained for all that time; and then he thought beyond Kelly Wronowicz; this was it for real for a lot of people.

It was up to him.

He bent into the flood of light. His hands had been shaking, but somehow they steadied, now that they had to be steady, and with infinite care peeled off the first thin silver spiral.

At midnight he straightened, put his hands to the small of his back, and leaned for a moment against the bulkhead.

He felt dizzy, sick with the confined motion of the ship, two days without sleep. . . . "Polock," he grunted, not opening his eyes. "He got that polishing finished?"

"Lemme check," said Steurnagel, starting up from where he had watched every move the chief had made. He was back in a minute, to find Wronowicz sitting on the deck, his head in his hands. "He says it's as smooth as he can get it . . . say, you all right?"

"Yeah. Here, gimme a hand up. Unjack that vise. Let's give it the old fit test."

The other men stirred from half-sleep as he carried the bearing aft. Holding it delicately he split the rings apart and worked the bearing on. It had to fit perfectly, perfectly, or the vibration would begin and once begun grow and grow, the spinning shaft scouring off metal like a power grinder until the bearing wiped again, overheating, and the shaft warped or the babbitt melted or the whole box came apart in whirling shards. At full speed there was too much power to give it more than a ten-thousandth of play. Too tight, though, and it wouldn't go on at all . . . he breathed out gently as the collar slipped over the end of the shaft. "Oil," he said. "Gimme a shot of it right along the shaft, where she's going to fit."

The bearing stuck, halfway down the shaft. He stared at it, whispered curses. Five more hours, four, till they went in . . . he turned savagely to Polock, behind him. "You polished this shaft, you said?"

"Yeah, chief. I used the emery, like you said, first rough, then the finest we got. Polished it down—"

"Shut up. Steurnagel, gimme that sledge."

"A *hammer*, chief?"

"Gimme it, goddammit!"

He held the tool at the outer edge of the bearing, and felt the sweat start anew from his forehead, break from the roots of his thinning hair. His beard itched. You didn't force a bearing. That was against all the manuals, all the training. It had to slide on slick as hundred-dollar head. But the time was past for the rules; there were no hours

to take it off and blue and file and fit again. It had to fit
right now, and if it didn't there was no use trying again.
He could strip the babbitt right off doing this. He could—

He quit thinking about it and gave the bearing a prelimi-
nary tap before hauling the maul back to swing; and then
dropped it clattering to the deckplates. The ring had slid
inward a full inch. He set the toe of his boot against it and
it eased smoothly inward, a thin drip of oil purling from
around the shaft, and seated in the gearframe. He and the
first-class looked at each other, then at the shaft, and then
back at each other again, and they were both smiling; not
grins, though they both realized how incredible it was that
it fit, but the tired smiles of tired men.

"Son of a bitch," said Steurnagel. "I don't believe you
got it that close by eye."

Neither did Wronowicz, but that wasn't the kind of
thing a chief admitted. "Yeah, it takes some experience,"
he said coolly. "Now, you people, let's get hot. We only
got about four hours to get this sucker back together and
ready for power."

"Less than that," said Ensign Callin from behind them.
"Is it fixed?"

Wronowicz felt the tension in himself instantly, as if he
were taking an electric charge through the shaft he still
rested his hand on. "It's fixed, yeah," he said, not turning
around. "You better go tell the captain."

"I will. But we've got to have flank speed available
earlier than H-hour, just to catch up."

The ship began her tilt, a little bit faster than usual, the
way she did before a good roll, and all three of them
recognized it and glanced around for handholds. "Less
than four hours?" repeated the chief, looking back at the
torn-up deckplates along the shaft. "No can do, no way.
These guys just did the impossible, getting the casing off
and the shaft blocked as fast as they did. And getting this
to fit"—he waved at the bearing—"was just plain cock-
eyed luck. Tell Captain Foster we're in business, but if he
gets it any earlier than four I'll eat my anchors."

"I'm not telling him that." Callin's chin set itself; he looked down at the squatting men from all the height of a single gold bar. "You know, Chief, you're way out of line talking like that. If we got it fixed, let's get it back together. Seems to me two and a half, three hours is plenty of time to get those deckplates back in place and—"

"Jesus Christ," Wronowicz muttered.

Behind him the men stilled. "Chief, take it easy," murmured Steurnagel. Wronowicz ignored him. He wasn't taking this crap from Callin anymore. They had to have it out sometime, and this was as good a time as any for a showdown. If it went in his record, too fucking bad. He stood up slowly, wiping the oil from his hands with a gesture that must have looked menacing, because Callin backed away a step.

"Ensign Callin. You have given me one ration of lip too much. Lieutenant Jay, the captain, they know they got the best chief in the fleet in their engineroom. These engines run, and when they break we fix 'em, even without a tender, without even parts. See? And they get fixed without you. I didn't see you gettin' your white gloves dirty down here."

"I had the watch," said the ensign. His face had paled slightly but he still, Wronowicz thought, looked game. He glanced at the men, at the carefully remote faces they had instantly put on when Wronowicz stood up. "And look, Chief, in front of the division isn't the place to—"

"You're criticizing me in front of them, I'm going to tell you you're wrong in front of 'em." Wronowicz paused; he wanted to choose these words carefully. Then his finger lanced out. "Now Jay and Foster trust me and I deliver. You trust me and I'll deliver for you. But if you keep up this carping bullshit"—Wronowicz paused, enjoying the dramatic effect, the gaping men—"why, I'm just liable to lose heart. And then things are liable to break down. And you're liable to have to explain to the captain why the engines ran fine till you took over. Unless you can make them run by yourself."

"Don't threaten me, Chief." Callin was angry now, he saw, no longer surprised but mad; but he didn't back off or bluster; he stood there toe to toe. Something in Wronowicz stood apart, watching them both. Yes, he might make a good officer of this one. "You made your point. I know you did a damn good job tonight, you and the men. But—hell, if you can fix it earlier, the marines would sure appreciate it."

The ship slanted farther, and then, just when it seemed to hang at the farthest edge of it, thirty-five or forty degrees of roll, the men half-hanging from bulkheads and stanchions and catwalk rails, something else hit the ship. A rogue wave, Wronowicz thought, and even as he thought it he was wrapping his legs around a stanchion. This would be a bad one.

It was. *Ault* seemed to lose her grip on the sea, like an old car hitting a curve with bald tires. Tools broke free and leapt toward the far bulkhead. Four big drums of lubricant freed themselves suddenly from the angle irons where they had been stowed since leaving the States and came rumbling across the engineroom. The ship tipped further, further, and he shot a glance at the clinometer on the bulkhead forward. Fifty degrees! His eyes met Steurnagel's. A can rolled, sure, but there was a point where a ship did not come back. You never knew just where it was, though, until that fatal instant when she kept on going over.

"Chief! Look out!"

Wronowicz snapped his head to see the gear casing lunge toward him, then quiver, brought up short. With the ship almost on her side, its weight had left the chainhoist; it was hanging now only by the steadying ropes, and as he watched, the second one parted with a bang, and the whole immense weight of it lunged again toward him. The last rope on that side tautened, just for a moment, and then it, too, snapped. The ship staggered, paused, then began its roll back to port, but he saw immediately that the one remaining line would never stop that mass of steel once it started back.

"Clear out!" he screamed at the men opposite, forgetting the argument. Callin was staring hypnotized at the gigantic pendulum. "Get away from it!"

The last line broke and the beast was free. The men scattered as it accelerated, taking energy from the roll. Piping crumpled like foil as it drove into the turbines, slowing it not at all. A cloud of vapor burst from a shattered steam line, a hot blinding cloud through which the gear cover, like a wounded elephant, reappeared as the ship rolled again, headed back for the starboard side. At them. He grabbed the ensign's shirt, tearing it as he jerked Callin backward, and they came up against a generator. Metal dug into his back as the gear went by, fanning them with the hot breath of its passage, and severed a condensate line; a geyser of boiling water showered the deckplates. It hit the port side with a clang that deafened them all, denting a gouge into the thin plating that formed the shell of the ship, then reeled back to starboard as *Ault* careened again. A man screamed and ran from its path; to his horror Wronowicz saw thin streams of seawater burst through the bright edges of the gouged hull, joining into spurting fountains. Callin huddled against him, his eyes on the juggernaut that next destroyed a hundred-and-fifty-pound auxiliary line, triggering a deafening roar of live steam into the air. Wronowicz intuited as much as heard his shout: "Chief! It's tearing the ship apart!"

"You want to try and stop it?"

"Get a line on it—the men—"

"It'll mash a man like a fly."

Another scream burst from the far side of the compartment, followed by the crash and snap of buckling metal and electrical short circuits. With the steam in the air, neither of them could see who it was.

Wronowicz looked around the compartment. He could see Mason lying face down at the forward end, Polock throwing a terrified look his way from beside him. Steam, blue smoke, and sparks blotted out the men forward. The ship rolled again, and a rumbling noise came from forward. All over the ship it must be havoc. But right here was the worst. If they didn't get this thing stopped it would batter its way right through the hull into the sea. With a flooded engine compartment there would be no reserve buoyancy—no power to keep nose to sea, no power for pumps—

He moved forward warily, in a crouch, watching the top of the pendulum, the chainhoist. It ground and rattled as the weight under it shifted direction, gathered momentum for another pass. He had to stop it, but he did not yet see how. Get a line on it? One would never stop it. They'd have to get several on at once . . . or else stop it swinging. . . .

Yeah. Stop it swinging. He saw now. It would be dangerous. But there was no other way.

The casing reappeared, rushing toward them. He crouched, then caught a movement out of the corner of his eye. Callin was moving forward, too.

"Get back, sir!"

"What are you going to do, Chief?"

"Drop it on the deck, by the compressor. Get back."

"I'll help you. I—"

Wronowicz shoved him. Callin staggered back, recovering quickly, but a second was all that Wronowicz needed. The casing reached the limit of its portward arc, hesitated, and he stepped forward and jumped.

"Chief!"

He thought for a moment that he'd missed, slid scrabbling down the side of the casing; then his hand caught in the chain. Panting, he hauled himself upward as the casing gathered momentum, carrying him with it, a man on the back of a bull. He had a confused sensation of speed, the blur of vision and nausea of a carnival ride, and he hauled himself upright onto the mass of steel. He crouched there, reaching upward, swinging dizzily faster and faster, the engineroom rotating around him. His groping hand found the trip line of the chainhoist. The engineroom swayed. His head snapped back, searching for a clear spot. Had to time the swing, drop it away from the naked gear. There—coming up—

Now—

He yanked down on the trip. The lever clacked over, the jaws of the hoist opened with a snap; and suddenly he was weightless, riding tons of metal in its short free-fall toward the tilting deck.

In that second, short as it was, he thought of his first day at sea, so long before; of the swell of breasts, the dark eyes of a woman he would never see again; and he began to think something else, something that made sense of it all, put it all together into something shining and meaningful.

It was a machine. *It was a machine.* And the point, the goal, the product of it was—

In the middle of his thoughts came a shock and the clamor of steel. And quite suddenly Chief Kelly Wronowicz found himself lying dazed on the deckplates, watching helplessly as the immense mass of metal reconsidered, decided, and began its irresistible and savage roll toward and over him.

25

U.S.S. *Guam*

THIRTY MILES AHEAD OF THE ROLLING destroyer, sixty thousand yards closer to the moving point toward which now the darkened ships arrowed inward to rendezvous, Dan Lenson lowered his head and rubbed at the knotted muscles around his eyes.

The lamp hummed above the litter of paper that covered his foldout desk. Its white monotone spilled over the tiled deck, strewn with shoes and pencils by the motion of the ship, over the khaki shirt that swayed from a hook, over his down-turned face. The man in the lower bunk, dead asleep, had turned his back to it to escape the glare. He was Lenson's roommate, one of *Guam*'s officers, catching a catnap before going on watch again.

No naps for Ike Sundstrom's staff, Lenson thought. Behind him a radioman leaned waiting against the bulkhead. He dropped his hands from his eyes, sighed, and reached for the next stack of paper. It was like an all-nighter back at the Boat School. He saw for a moment his room in Bancroft Hall, just like this at night, compact, Spartan, his old Tensor humming just like this.

Only now he was at sea, where everyone at the Academy had known he would be some day. Where they would have to measure up, not for grades, but for real. At sea, and on his way to action.

He picked up the first sheet and bit his lip, concentrating. There was no time for polishing. This would be final, this scribble in pencil.

SECRET

FM: CTF 61
TO: All Units TF 61
Info: CTF 60
  CTF 62
  COMSIXTHFLT
  CINCUSNAVEUR
  JOINT CHIEFS WASH DC

Subj: Revised Operation Plan, Operation URGENT LIGHTNING

  1. (S) *Situation. The hostages taken at the U.S. Embassy in Nicosia have been moved by their captors to Ash Shummari, Syria, approximately twenty miles inland and five miles north of the Lebanese border. Electronic intercept of Syrian traffic suggests that the terrorists, with covert support of Syrian authorities, will play out hostage drama from there. Fulfillment of their demands is being explored, but may not be possible due to loss of influence with new Turkish government.*

  2. (S) *Mission. To resolve the crisis and rescue the hostages, National Command Authority has directed Task Force 61 to carry out an amphibious raid into Lebanon and a land penetration of Syrian territory. This assault will begin on signal this morning.*

3. (S) Execution. American in-
tervention may be opposed by either
indigenous or separately landed
forces, including Soviet troops or
warships. For this reason, upon re-
ceipt of this operation order all
units will make preparations for a
fully supported, combat-prepared
landing, although armed force
will be used only in response to
attack. . . .

He read through it once more and handed it to the radio-man. The opening part of most operation orders was boil-erplate. He had lifted the tone, if not the specifics, from the dozen others he had collected during the cruise.

What followed was harder, much harder, and more complex. He had to rewrite the schedule and movement order for the opposed approach, with units spaced for mutual protection against land-based missiles or gunfire; the combat air patrol (CAP) coordination plan, for local vectoring of the fighters that *America* might or might not be there to provide, in case there was an air threat to the amphibious group; the antisubmarine patrol plan; the electronic emission plan, to foil any jamming or radar-homing missiles; and the most technically confusing, the communications plan.

And all that was before the first man put foot on the beach. When they moved from sea to land things got a lot more challenging. To do, and to plan for.

And he had to do it all. Not Red Flasher. Him. He rubbed his eyes again, reached for a cold cup of coffee, and set to work again.

After a hasty midnight consultation with Colonel Haynes' staff, he had decided that the best approach would be two-pronged: a heliborne advance party, to pre-vent surprise by hostile forces, followed by the main, sea-borne strike, carried in the amtracs and landing craft. The air-landing zone they had placed three miles inland, on a rise where the advance party could command the road leading east. They would lift off from *Guam* and *Spiegel Grove* two hours before dawn. A half-hour before first light the seaborne strike would follow. For this the amphibs would do a "turnaway," racing in to drop the assault force and then retiring out to sea. Byrne said both the Lebanese national army and the Christian militias had U.S. howitzers, and the Shi'ites—largely armed by Syria—had corresponding Soviet equipment up to and including tanks. There was no predicting the reactions or dispositions of any side, and if they expected gunfire from the beach, the thin-skinned ships would have to be in and out again in a hurry.

The LSTs, with the shallowest draft, would close at flank speed until the bottom shoaled. He pulled the chart out to confirm the depths. They'd have to slow when they got close in, or the screws would suck the sterns right into the sand. They would steer by radar bearings on a small group of islands to the south, off Tripoli, and visual bearings on the light at Kleiat. Three miles from the El Aabde beach they would turn and parallel it at a course of 020 degrees true.

At that moment, H minus thirty, six thousand yards from the edge of land, the first wave of amtracs would roll into the sea. The amphibious tanks would form up in lines on guide boats, and then, on command, head for the shore.

Meanwhile, a mile or two farther out, the larger ships would be dropping boats. Already filled with marines, the landing craft would be floated, still safe inside the hulls, as the ships ballasted down. At H minus twenty-five, as the 'tracks began their swim ashore, the "mike boats" would move out of the wells and form for the second wave.

If all went well, they would hit the beach ten minutes after the first amtracs waddled ashore.

An amphibious landing, he had been told, was the most complex thing the Navy did. He believed it. It took exquisite timing, long practice, and fanatic adherence to plan. As the first waves moved ashore, the ships would continue out to sea in a long loop, readying the reserve boats. And then they would come back. The same maneuver, again—no, better use different courses for the second run, in case shore batteries got the range. Yes. He plotted with pencil and dividers, then covered a sheet of yellow paper with coordinates and turn bearings.

The second drop would hit the water twenty minutes after the first. Another ten boats, eight more amtracs. The third and fourth waves would carry supplies, the heavier communications gear, and the rest of the raiding force.

Lenson wrote furiously, glancing from time to time at an exercise oporder, pulling out a pub for reference, punching the phone to the marines, who were working in Haynes' cabin. How many armed troops did an LCM-8 hold? How often could you shut down and bring up a radar without destroying the magnetrons? How many tons of water, fuel, food would the MAU need per day in ninety-degree heat? He knew basically what he was doing, but he would have liked Flasher and Hogan to check it when he was done, to avoid any boners. Unfortunately Sundstrom had them both on the flag bridge, standing lookout watches. So it was all up to him; they were going in this morning, plan or not, and as if to remind him of that, his door opened and the radioman stuck his head in. Dan handed him five more pages and he disappeared again.

He no longer believed, as he once had, that Sundstrom knew what he was doing. But recrimination or protest would only get in the way. Best for the job or not, he had been ordered to get the force ashore. And that he would do.

His roommate snored on, the ship creaked around him as steel bent under the impact of the sea. The lamp hummed. He worked on.

At last he finished the basic oporder. He stapled the scribbled pages and they followed the rest into the ready maw of Radio. Next: the schedule of fires. He stretched in his chair and grinned. At last, something he was supposed to be doing.

The warning order from Admiral Roberts had said, prepare for an "opposed" landing. That meant, against hostile forces, ready and waiting on the beach. If you did that right, he thought, if you really expected the landing to be resisted, Sixth Fleet should have ordered preparatory fire. Destroyers and cruisers, standing offshore, would begin pounding that unlucky section of beach two hours before the first amphib came over the horizon. Gun after gun would spout flame and smoke, sending tons of explosive in to carpet the beach, destroying emplacements and driving any defenders deep to earth. The barrage would be continuous, and carefully calculated to make it impossible for anyone to move or aim a gun for the whole time the boats and tanks churned their clumsy way in from the sea. Only when the first marine was a hundred yards from land would the curtain lift, draw back, moving ahead of the troops at a walking pace to keep a wall of fire and steel between them and the enemy.

And overhead, at intervals, aircraft would come in to strafe and bomb any pockets of resistance.

That was the way it was supposed to go. In reality, a World War Two-style landing was impossible for the Mediterranean Fleet to support anymore. The gun-heavy old destroyers and cruisers were all but gone. Their replacements were missile escorts or antisubmarine units, not gunfire-support ships. Their high superstructures were crammed with electronics and computers, not weapons. They carried one or at the most two automatic five-inch rifles, with a high rate of fire, but too complicated for the hours of continuous bombardment you needed to soften a heavily defended beach.

But in the Navy you got used to making do with what you had. He had two escorts, and if the raid got into trouble ashore, he had best be ready to use them no matter what Roberts' message said about limited force. Then he remembered: *Ault* was no longer with them. Christ, he thought, I hope she gets here in time. She's ninety percent of my fire support.

Pulling the chart toward him, he subdivided the landing areas ("green" and "gold") into sixty-four rectangles of varying depth. These would be the target areas. Checking the coordinates of each corner, he cleared off another part of the desk and transferred the numbers to a fresh sheet of paper. This would be the beach blowup, included in the oporder as direction to the destroyers' gunnery plots.

That done, he began the tedious process of calculating how many shells per square meter per minute would suffice to keep the beach neutralized. That took half an hour, even skipping the finer points, but when it was done he had five columns of figures, each subdivision broken out by number of shells, projectile type, fuze type, and providing ship.

The radioman took it out of his hands and Lenson went on. Byrne had given him the locations of known militia forces and observation posts in Northern Lebanon, areas along the road where ambush was possible, and the disposition of the Syrian Army between Homs and the coast. These he began translating into preplanned targets, assigning numbers and coordinates so that fire could be called down instantly. Dan sweated. One wrong number could mean firing on their own troops. When it was done, that, too, followed the rest into the roaring teletypewriters.

He was working on the last section, communications, when the phone buzzed. He jerked it from its rack. "Lenson here," he said rapidly, continuing to write.

"Red, on the bridge. Commodore wants to know how you're doing."

"Well, kind of hurried, but almost finished. They've been typing it up as I went so tell him he'll be able to sign it off for transmission in about ten minutes."

"Okay, will do." Flasher paused for a moment, then said, in a lower voice, "Dan, you might be interested in a flash priority we just got. Sixth Fleet and Naval Forces, Europe just went to ReadCon Orange."

He searched his dulled mind, then remembered. "Nuclear alert?"

"You got it. First time since the Six-Day War."

"Somebody's taking this seriously."

"That's a no shit, Charlie."

"Okay, got it." He hung up and thought for a moment. Then he began writing again.

The ship pitched and vibrated around him, fighting its own battle with the sea. But his mind was not with her. His mind was forty miles ahead, on the dark coast that now waited, silent under the overcast. In a few hours the southern sky would flicker with the light of gunfire, the ships, darkened, would begin their approach. He did not think of this. He did not think of hostages, of terrorists, or of hostile militia. His attention was on the numbers. They had to be done now, and they had to be done right. Only after that would there be time to wonder whether the raid would succeed.

As to what might happen if it failed, he did not dare think at all.

26

Ash Shummari, Syria

THEY WAITED THROUGH THAT EVENING
for the promised food. Susan was worried. Nan had rested
since their confrontation with the terrorists. Quietly; but
this quietude she did not like. For hours the little girl lay
motionless on her side, hugging the pillow, eyes open yet
unresponsive to the fading light from the window. She did
not speak, even when Moira told her stories and tried to
play.

The bread came finally well after nightfall. Hard, round
loaves several days old. The hostages had no idea where it
came from. They knew only that two of their guards went
from room to room, tossing them out from a blanket as one
feeds animals. They left, too, a basin of water at the end of
the corridor. Susan gnawed at a chunk and drank as much
water as she could. It had been a hot day, despite the
overcast, and the small reserve in the toilet was exhausted.

"Look, Bunny!"

Nan turned her head listlessly to see her mother, cheeks
stuffed full.

"I'm a chipmunk. Want to be a chipmunk, too?"

But she only turned her face wordlessly back to the
window. It was all Susan could do to make her eat a little
soaked bread from the center of the loaf.

She went into the bathroom, alone, when she could put
off crying no more.

After the meal they gathered near the window. Open now, it admitted a cool wind, doubly welcome after the day's heat. Silently they looked out over desert hills shrouded in night. The distant, sad rumble of artillery had come from them all afternoon, on and off, nearer and farther away. Tricks of the wind? They did not know. A campfire glowed where Cook had seen the Syrians. To the south, from time to time, they could make out flashes, like distant lightning.

"Sure sounds like a war," muttered Cook.

Susan sat with Moira on the bed. Nan lay between them, asleep at last. Susan had given her the last dose of aspirin, rinsing out the powder in the bottom, and the bottle lay empty on the floor.

"Moira . . ."

"Yeah?"

Her roommate's voice—funny, they were roommates again, half a world away from Georgetown—was soft in the darkness. Comforting. She reached out a hand to touch her shoulder. "I was wondering . . . do you think anyone will be able to get us out of here? Will they do *anything?*"

"I don't know, Betts."

"We don't have anything to go on, Susan," said Michael, staring out. "There must be something going on, but what? Is the Majd negotiating with the Syrians? Are they supporting him or surrounding him? We don't know. Are the Turks going to release the prisoners? What kind of leverage does the States have? Since that bastard busted my radio we don't know a thing."

"So, I guess we just look on the bright side," said Moira. "He's feeding us, anyway."

"Stale bread," said Susan.

"Wait a minute," said Cook then.

"What, Michael?"

"Quiet. Come here."

They got up quietly, not jostling Nan, and went to his

side. He pointed, and their eyes followed his finger downward, into blackness.

The square below had been a handful of night, cupped by the shadowy masses of the other buildings. Within it now a yellow circle bobbed, lengthening and shortening across the pavement. The lantern showed them three men. Two wore the white shirts and makeshift brassards that seemed to be Wihdah uniform. The other, held between them by pinioned arms, was bare-chested.

"What are they doing?"

"Jeez, Betts, we don't know any more than you do," said Moira. "Watch."

The wind eased itself through the opened window, stirring her hair. She leaned forward, into the jamb, to see around Cook.

The shadows halted in the middle of the square. The bobble of light halted too, then contracted as the man carrying the lantern set it down. The two in shirts paused then, conferring. The clouds flickered, and long seconds later, the sound of a heavy barrage reached them. The other one, the one with tied hands, looked around; looked back, it seemed, at the lobby entrance.

The two men stepped up to him, unslinging the rifles. The man cringed, then, and tried to run; but they caught him easily.

"Oh, God," whispered Moira.

The rifle butts swung quickly, heavily, and the half-naked man staggered. A scream came faintly up to them. At the third swing he fell, but the others did not stop or even slow. The crunch of blows came up clearly to them.

"Oh, God . . . who is it? I can't see down there—"

"It's Snaggletooth," said Cook.

"But what are they *doing?*"

"It's terrorist justice," said the archaeologist grimly. "Pretty rapid court procedure, wouldn't you say?"

Susan watched. She could not reply. She did not know what to say, or what to feel. A part of her wanted to laugh, wanted this man to suffer. He deserved it. For one moment, when she had seen him with her daughter, she had wanted him to die. She would have shot him herself if she had held the gun.

But watching it, hearing the steady thudding of metal into bone and flesh, was different.

It seemed a long time until the beating ended. The small man lay in the flickering circle, motionless save for a slow twitching of the legs. They could see dark stains spreading on his back.

The man with the lantern picked it up. They paused for a moment, looking toward the entrance; then one of them slung his rifle and grasped the prone man under the arms. His legs dragged.

The light bobbed onward, out of their sight.

Cook closed the window and drew the ragged curtain. They sat touching close in near darkness, each grateful for the warmth of the others.

"He got off easy. They should have shot him," said Moira tentatively, glancing at her.

Susan could think of nothing to say in reply. She had seen a man beaten almost to death. She wanted to vomit. But behind that, alongside it, an older and more savage persona gloated. Revenge—yes; she had wanted that, demanded it, in the heat of the moment.

This calm, unhurried punishment, that could leave a man a cripple—she could not accept that as right. She remembered the terrible fear in the short man's face. And then her mind recoiled from pity. *Not pity but hypocrisy,* it said. *You have the right to hate, even the duty;* and she saw again the way Nan had looked toward the door as she burst through it. The terror of that lone search. The minutes when she feared her daughter gone, and knew that her heart would break.

But she could not enjoy this revenge. She couldn't. And then, suddenly, she knew why.

To almost kill a man so deliberately . . . to do that, to order that . . . what kind of person would it take?

She found herself suddenly in Moira's arms. "It's okay,

okay. Betts, he had it coming." She felt a hand on her hair, stroking it as she stroked Nan's.

"Ox . . . if he can do that to his own men, *what will he do to us?*"

It was as if, she thought blindly, not until now had she realized what was going to happen to them—to all of them. What protection, what safety could there be here? They were alone with this madness, this terror. Alone.

Oh, Jesus, God . . . my father . . . Dan . . . she thought blindly, rage and fear knotting heavy beneath her breastbone. Why have you abandoned us to this?

"Okay, okay," she heard Moira whisper in the dark. And then, a caught sob of shared fear. "I don't know, Betts. I really don't."

After a moment she pulled away, and drew the arm of her T-shirt across her face. The room was quiet for a time. "I'm going to sleep," came Moira's sobered mutter, then, "Mike, you coming?"

"Yeah."

Susan sat in the dark, on the bed, for a long time, long enough that she heard the Ox begin to snore.

She was thinking.

At last she got up and pushed her feet into her sandals. She was surprised to find them still damp from the morning's rain. Nicosia, that morning, seemed weeks distant. She adjusted the strap, hesitated, and then went out.

In the hallway the air stank of burning, and fearing fire she glanced quickly around. The guard was at the far end, near the stairwell. He had a kerosene lamp beside him, the same kind the men in the square had carried. That was what smelled. The Arab watched her by its buttery light as she went to the bucket and dipped up a cupful of water. Perhaps an inch more remained. Drink as much as you can, and take some back for Nan, she thought. If they don't give us any more in the morning, she won't cry from thirst—

"*Ahlan.*"

Startled, she almost spilled the precious liquid. She

caught the cup in midair, though, and tossed back her hair, looking toward the light.

He had come up the stairwell, out of the shadows, so stealthily that there had been no sound at all. He stood now motionless beside the guard, his face in shadow above the smoky flame of the candle he shielded in his left hand.

"Hello," the Majd repeated. "Your child is better?"

"The same." She took a breath, released it, and bent to dip up another cup. Her hand made rings in the water. She took another breath. "The water and the bread helped. Thank you."

"We had to ask for the food from the Syrians. They didn't want to give it at first. Then they agreed. Anyway, we needed it, too."

So there's friction, she thought. Whose side were the Syrians on? Did they know themselves? But aloud she only said, "So it was a beneficial trade for you."

"Beneficial?"

"Good."

He laughed, seemed to find the word amusing. His face was still in shadow. "Yes. For us it was, beneficial."

They stood silent in the slow yellow glow. She finished the drink and put the cup back in the bucket. I must be careful, she thought then. It does not matter that he punished one of his own. He did not do it for us. All fear in this place comes from him. He is the evil.

"What is your name?"

"Susan. Susan Lenson."

"You are American?"

"Yes."

There was the space of perhaps five heartbeats. "I saw the punishment," she said then, into the unquiet shadows of two flames. The outlines of a man and a woman stretched far down the carpet, their heads joined in a pool of darkness.

"From your window? I thought you might."

"Did you order it?"

"Yes. He was my man, under my orders and party discipline."

She shivered. He said it so matter-of-factly. Party discipline.

He said a few words to the guard, who nodded, and then his long body detached itself from the shadows of the wall and moved toward her. He bent at the bucket, and drank as she had, sipping at the water. She watched the golden light slide over his face, focus in onyx gleams in his mustache.

"You want to talk?" he said.

"I don't know what about," she said quickly. "I don't have anything to say. Thank you, I suppose, for your . . . discipline. But that's all."

"But still—"

"But you're still holding us here," she said. "Why don't you—why don't you just let us go? At least some of us?"

He said nothing. Just looked at her, and shook his head. His face was closed again. She knew she was taking risks, but she went on. "Then we're enemies, aren't we? Moira's right, why pretend otherwise? You're using us. We don't matter at all to you as human beings."

"Ah," he said. His face changed. "If it's a political discussion that you want—"

"No, I don't—"

"Maybe it's time for one." Harisah shrugged his shoulders then, and smiled. He lifted his head too, and for that moment, for the first time since they had begun speaking, she saw his eyes. "Sit down. Or do you refuse to talk to me?"

"Well . . ."

"Here. Just here. Sit down."

It was as if there were two of her, one wanting to flee, the other, to stay. She saw herself for an unaccustomed moment as if from outside, saw herself hesitating between which "she" she was.

Don't blow it, Betts, she thought then. He wants me to

be grateful? I'm grateful. He wants to talk? I do whatever he wants. As long as he leaves us alone.

There was an underthought to that, but she did not acknowledge it even to herself.

Meanwhile, while she stood uncertain, he had set the candle into the carpet, around a corner from the guard. "Come, sit down. I won't harm you."

She hesitated still, looking at the wax dripping into the carpet. One more consideration struck her; she turned, looking back. No, Nan would be all right for a few minutes more. . . .

She sat down. The wall was hard against her back. The floor, under the carpet, was hard against her rump. She glanced across the flame. His head was bent, a strand of damp hair clinging blackly to his forehead, his profile to her. She examined the stab of nose, the heavy chin. His mustache needed trimming; it was ragged at the line of the lip, as if he had tried to cut it himself, hurriedly, and failed. Wiry black hair curled at the neck of his shirt. His arms were outstretched, curled around his knees, and the rifle lay across his arm, opposite her. In the close light she could see the grooves at the mouth of the barrel. Arabic characters had been scratched near the trigger, near where his hand rested, where his fingers stroked it unconsciously. The wooden stock was scarred with hard use. But the metal was smooth with oil, and she could see grease clinging to it, as if it had been wiped off hurriedly with a rag. The light of the candle fell yellow over his hand, throwing the tendons of his wrist into relief.

"I am sorry. I'm out of Luckies."

She looked at the pack. They weren't American, some foreign brand in a light green pack. "I don't—I quit smoking. Years ago."

"Take one. You're too nervous."

Whatever he wants.

"Well, all right. Thank you."

The nervousness eased as he held the candle for her.

The harsh cheap tobacco, after abstinence for so long, made her head swim.

The silence was becoming too long. "This gun. Is it—where did it come from, Majd?" she said.

He exhaled smoke, his eyes sliding to her and then away. "My name is Hanna, Susan. The gun? In a way it is my father's. Now it is mine."

"Was he a—a soldier?"

Under the tangled hair she saw him turn wary, a scowl drawing the dark brows together. Something there he didn't want to remember. "He was a fighter, yes," he said, emphasizing the word. "As a young man—you have heard of the revolt of 1938? Of Al-Quasim's men?"

"No."

"He fought then, and after. He hid in the mountains, as a young man. He killed many Jews and British. His rifle was British. He took it from a dead soldier. Mine—" he patted it—"it is Chinese. Why? Because they gave it to me. I would use any other, if I could get ammunition."

"That was before the war."

"Yes."

"What did he do afterward? After the fighting stopped?"

Harisah lifted his hand and made a chopping motion above the flame. Again, she noticed, he scowled at questions he did not like. At those times he looked dangerous. "Ah, you know so little. For us the fighting has never stopped. What did he do? After the British prison he could fight no longer. They broke his legs. What he did after that, that doesn't matter, that was not an important part of his life.

"He told me, my father,"—and he held the rifle up, as if to let her admire it, and perhaps that was what he meant for her to do, she thought—"where he left his, in Jaffa. He wrapped it in cloth of grease and buried it, with the bullets, under the earth, where no one could find. And sometimes they came, and they looked."

"Who?"

"Israeli police. Troops, sometimes. I saw them beat him once. He never told. Perhaps it is there still."

"I don't understand. Why would they—?"

"Because he never stopped fighting, in his way. We hid people. He made bombs for Fatah. He did not change easily, my father. He did not . . . give up, surrender, like some of the others."

"Was that in—in Palestine?"

"Yes. In Gaza. We went there when I was small, when the Zionists forced our people out of Jaffa. We scattered— they scattered us to all the world." And with a sway of his head he indicated the world outside the walls; indicated, she realized, the south, the ancient and violent lands that to her had once been only names: Lebanon; Israel; Jordan. "He had a shop there for a little while; he repaired the clocks, the watches. He was good at that; he taught me some of it. But he lost it when the Israelis came again in 1967. We had to leave, my mother and sisters, all our . . . neighbors.

"So then we went to Jordan. To Baqa'a, the refugee camps. That is where I grew up."

"He lives there now? In Jordan?"

"Who?"

"Your father."

"No, my father, he's dead. He made trouble again, and then he died."

Died how, she wanted to ask; but the grimness that had deepened the corners of his mouth as he talked put her off. It was a warning, like a sign before a precipice, and she went extra slow, as she had driving the winding roads of Cyprus with Nan asleep beside her. She studied the glowing tip of her cigarette. God, they made her dizzy after so long. "I see . . . and your mother?"

"She lives."

"You said you had sisters. How many?"

But he only shrugged, slowly, and looked at her. "That is not important."

"No, I wanted to know—"

"Do you? What do you want to know? I know what you think of me. All Palestinians are terrorists, dirty Arab killers, cowards. Is it not right? You never ask why we fight. If your land was taken and occupied, if you were driven off to live as strangers in foreign lands, would you not resist?"

Resisting, yes, I can understand that, she thought; but hostage-taking, murder, terrorism? She knew she shouldn't argue, though. Instead she said, "I don't know much about it. But what is it you want?"

"We want Palestine back."

"But the Israelis are there now. Where will they go?"

"Where they go does not concern me. They will leave or they will die."

His face was hard now and she saw his hands tighten on the rifle.

"I don't know much about it," she said again cautiously. "What I would like to know is how long we'll have to stay here."

He shrugged. "That's not up to me; that is up to others. They will be doing the negotiating with the Turks. So far they do not respond."

"I hope—"

"I know what you hope. Don't expect it. I am not going to release you. And don't expect rescue, either. The Syrians don't want to be seen helping us, too much, but they will protect us. No, you will be here for a long time, I think."

"What if they let your friends go?"

"That is unlikely. But if that happens there are other things we want, too."

"I don't understand. It sounds like you mean to hold us anyway."

"When you have a dollar, and buy what you want for less, do you throw the rest of the money away? Anyway, I tire of explaining." He shifted on the floor. "Tell me, what of yourself? Your name is Susan. The others called you that. You are with them? The ones in your room?"

"Yes. They're my friends."

"The girl. How old is she?"

"Nan is three."

"Three years old . . . your husband, the tall one, he is good to you?"

"The tall . . . oh, no." She had to laugh, there in the warm darkness. "*Michael?* No, he's not my husband. He's Moira's friend. The brunette."

"Brunette," he repeated.

"A woman with dark hair. Like yours."

"I am a brunette?"

"Well, it's generally used in English for women. But yes, you are."

"You are a brunette."

"Yes."

"But you look different from the others."

"I'm part Chinese."

"You look a little like our women, you know. But you are American."

"That's right, buster."

"Many Americans are Jews."

"Americans are everything."

"Yes," he said. "I have seen black ones, brunette ones, everything. Buster. This is strange language, too. I studied it in the camp, to prepare myself for struggle." He was gazing at the ceiling; she followed his glance, to see their shadows caught together in the golden wavering of the candle. "I did not think to be using it like this, talking to a pretty woman."

"You speak it very well."

"I have an accent."

"A bit of one. Sure. But I can understand everything you say. You don't make many mistakes."

"No, I don't make many mistakes," he repeated. His eyes came down to hers. "Your husband, then, he is not with this group. He isn't here?"

"He's not here. He's . . . he's in Italy. I was on my way to join him."

"And what does your husband do, Susan?"

"Nothing exciting, I'm afraid. Something to do with insurance."

"An executive?"

"No. Just a—just a clerk."

"You are happy with him?"

"No," she said.

And then stopped, appalled. "Wait . . . no, I didn't mean that."

"But you said it. What is wrong?"

"I don't know. I never said it before, I mean, not to anyone." She looked at him with wide eyes. "You don't —I didn't mean anything by that. You have to understand it. I love him."

"Then why were you traveling without him?"

"His company called him away. I went to visit friends in Cyprus. We were going to meet later." Her cigarette had burned down now. She looked around, then stubbed it out on the carpet.

Harisah sank into a reverie, tilting his head against the wall. She shifted her hips a little; the floor was getting hard. She should go back to Nan. She knew that. But then her eyes found the curl of hair at the V of his shirt, and followed the tanned curve of neck upward to his jaw. There was no question that he was attractive. But he was also what Moira said. He had fed them, but for his own reasons. He was the one in charge, the one to fear.

The only one who could protect.

Very slowly, she put out her hand and laid it atop his. Her fingertips traced the tautening of his muscles, the start of a pulling away; then they relaxed, and submitted to the pressure of her palm. "Do you think," she whispered, "you could let the old doctor see my child?"

"Perhaps."

"Perhaps? How can I—"

He turned his head, and the whisper stopped in her throat. Her eyes shifted upward four inches to his. They sat like that together for several seconds.

He leaned forward, slowly, and his lips touched hers. Lightly at first, and then harder. She twisted her head back, trying to move away along the floor; yet the touch of his mouth was so warm, so hard, she felt the grating bristle of beard on his jaw, and smelled the heat of his body. She was sticky too, dirty and unwashed; she thought she must smell awful.

Vicious thoughts welled up in her mind. She turned her head away, and then felt his arms slide around her. She thought it was a hug, and stiffened, but then she heard his lips tighten as he took in air. He was lifting her, one hand under her and one around her waist. Lifting her in the yellow hot light, in the shadows that flickered in the warm night. Bearing her up like a child, as no one had since she was as small as Nan, high into the air, her feet dangling, feeling the old fear of being dropped. . . .

Weakness took her legs, her arms. "What are you doing," she whispered, close to his ear. A lock of his hair brushed across her lips with a softness that thrilled and frightened her.

He did not answer. The corridor moved by, room after room. The candle diminished to a distant spark. He shouldered open one of the doors.

She gasped as he threw her onto the bed. He stood for a moment by the door, outlined in the faint light, and she thought that he was going to leave. But instead he closed it.

Scream, Betts, a part of her thought desperately. Her mind was a tornado. Scream. But who would come if she did?

More of his men.

There was one last moment of doubt, later, in the darkness. A last surge of terror. But it passed. She made it pass, she let it go, said nothing, lay quiet. She was two minds, mind and body, mind that spun confused in the dark, body that lay quivering and silent. She did not know what to do. And then, it was too late for knowledge.

It is for Nan, she thought at that last moment. For

Moira. For all of us. But she no longer was sure whether it was only her mind whispering to her, justifying her, telling her that since she only did what was right, whatever she did was right.

And after that she did not think anymore. She put up her arms, and felt the smoothness of his hair.

I hate you.

And outside, from the night, came unheard to both of them the rumble of the guns, the roar of the wind.

VI

***

THE ASSAULT

27

U.S.S. *Spiegel Grove*

THREE A.M., AFTER THE GEAR CHECK AND map familiarization that had occupied the mortar squad till 0100, was bleary as a hangover. Givens lay half-asleep, sprawled on a nest of life preservers in a small compartment just forward of the helicopter deck.

"Got all your mortar team shit?" the Top was saying to Silkworth. The two noncoms glanced over the piles of equipment, ammunition, and weapons. Will saw the special intensity as they checked out the dozing troops.

"Looks like about a helo full, don't it?" said Silkworth, grinning at the older man.

"No jokes, Silky. You got it all, or not?"

"Yeah, Mick, I got it," said the sergeant quietly. "Can I send them up to breakfast now?"

"Soon as you've made muster and checked equipment, head them up. But leave a gear watch."

"Goddamned right I will," muttered Silkworth, to nobody in particular, since the Top had left already, hustling himself along to the next station. "Liebo! Pry your eyes open. Keep an eye on all this crap, specially the forty-fives."

"Why me all the time? I just got to sleep."

Silkworth ignored him, turned to the others. "Rest of you, go on up to chow. No grab-assing or fuckin' off. Get your butts back here by zero-three-thirty or I'll kick 'em back for you."

Givens watched Cutford flash the sergeant the finger, but Silkworth's back was turned. He closed his eyes for a second. When he opened them the corporal's perpetual scowl was looming over him. His hands tightened.

"Goin' to get som'n eat?"

Givens said, "Yeah, Cutford."

"Surprisin' me, Oreo. Figured you'd be puking scared by now. You know, in a hour we be hittin' the beach."

His mouth was dry, but Cutford was wrong about his not wanting breakfast. He wanted it desperately. He turned away through the hatch, heading for the mess deck.

Spooning up fresh scrambled eggs, nearly a plateful, he blew into a coffee mug so hot it burned his fingers just holding it. The squids in the serving line acted different this morning. They ladled the food with anxious, ingratiating smiles. Nice of them to care, now that we're leaving, he thought vaguely, sipping at the cooled edge of the cup. He stared at the Formica tabletop, as if in its random maculation he could read what this day would bring. But he was not thinking about himself.

Not yet. Instead he found himself thinking about other days, other men.

About other landings. North Africa, Iwo, Normandy, Inchon. The names you learned in boot camp. The men on those gray ships, had they looked as young, eaten in the same strained quiet as the marines around him, boys of eighteen and twenty bending shaved heads low over their plates, eyes far-focused? Had they felt the same as he did now? No matter that a dozen of his mates crowded hip to hip at the same table. Each ate alone.

They were going in. And this was where the real waiting began. It was internal, a preparation of the soul. This was the point when it became not a matter of the mass, the team, even for men who worked and drilled as a team. But of the individual.

Will Givens finished his eggs and started on the hash. A squid messman, younger, skinnier, and blotchier than Washman even, rattled down a platter of buttered toast. He did not thank him. It took several seconds before he even noticed it. He finished the hash, crunched half a piece of toast in a still-dry mouth, drained his mug to the bottom, and shoved back his plate. Before he could get up, though, the sailor was there, reaching for it.

"Want more, Marine?"

"Huh?"

"Y'all had enough, buddy? Can I get you something else?"

"No. No, thanks." He stared after the messman, uncomfortable; his politeness had just the flavor of a warden serving a final meal.

"You finished, Will?" said Silkworth, breaking into his bemusement.

"Uh, yeah, Sarge. Just leaving."

"Take your time. Have another moka joe. Just got word: movement's delayed."

"Anything wrong?"

"Don't know. That's the word, that's all they tell me. Go on, have another cup."

He muttered thanks and sat down again. He did not want more coffee, but he took some anyway. Delayed . . . he was not sure whether to be glad or not. Maybe if it was delayed enough they wouldn't go in. But then if it was delayed too much, and they still went, they would be landing in broad daylight. He was afraid even to be annoyed at the extension of the wait. Afraid because at least now, right now, he was warm, he was alive, he was safe. And in a few hours, he might wish with all his might to be back aboard the old *Spiegel,* drinking hot joe.

The messman came by and filled his cup again. Just this once, he thought, sipping, why not forget it. Don't worry, don't even have an opinion. It's too far beyond you to affect, too far even for you to understand. Did anyone at all understand what was going on? Here, aboard the ships, ashore? He doubted it.

He waited.

Helmet tipped over his eyes, blanket roll and pack strapped to his back, flak jacket hunched forward on his chest, he lay later on a pile of green lifejackets and brown cases of c-rats, staring at his book. In the diagram electrons were shown charging one side of a condenser, while on the other the little crosses of positive charges piled up, row on row.

The holding station for helo embark was twenty feet long, six feet high, and no more than eight feet deep. Into this less than one thousand cubic feet had been crammed an entire planeload, thirty men and all their gear. Washman and Hernandez lay almost indecently nestled, save that they were turned away from each other, on a stack of packs, Washman with his eyes closed and Hernandez with his open, but both looking equally remote. Harner sat apart from them, chain-smoking Marlboros. Liebo's face hovered over a tattered paperback; the title was visible; it was *School Mistress.* The others in the compartment were grunts, the three rifle squads. Their landing team was forty strong, the capacity of one of the helicopters. And that one plane would hit with eighteen, twenty other choppers. They wouldn't be going in alone. That was one of the things the crowding of them all into that small compartment meant. It was reassuring, a reinforcement as well as a preparation for the even more cramped space inside the fuselage of a helo.

Cutford and Silkworth sat near the door, together yet apart, and sitting that way too, as if their noncomness set them together and the other thing set them apart, and right now both these things were working and so they did not know how to sit. From time to time the sergeant turned his wrist to bring the face of a black twenty-four-hour combat watch into view. The compartment was silent, closed off, filled with men and then sealed, like a jar.

And all they could do, inside the invisible glass that walled each one of them off from the others, was wait.

"Time you got," Givens heard Cutford grunt.

"Five ten."

"When they gonna move their fat asses? Said we was gonna move out at four."

Silkworth said something too low for the others to hear, and Cutford grunted appreciation.

He felt his stomach move uneasily and forced his attention back to the book. Maybe the jitters, like seasickness, would back off from you if you ignored it. Let's see . . . the voltage from the battery built up a kind of pressure. It squeezed the electrons into the plates kind of like air blowing up a tire. He could see that. The higher pressure pump you had, the more air you could get in the tire. Then you sealed the tire up, and then when you needed the electrons they were there to do the work for you.

He yawned hugely, unexpectedly, and lost the page. Damn, he was sleepy. He looked over at Washman, yawned again, and was considering catching a couple of Zs himself when the outer hatch banged open, bringing in a blast of night air and the roar of descending helicopters.

It was the captain, in battle dress and light pack, the anodized railroad tracks of rank black in the instantly red light of the compartment. Suddenly everyone was awake. Silkworth jumped up, looking at him expectantly. The captain's mouth opened, but the turbines were too loud. The men stared at him blankly. He glanced over his shoulder, then half-shut the hatch. "You men—get ready to go."

"Now, sir?"

But the captain was gone, the hatch clanging steel-hollow behind his back. Silkworth turned, motioning impatiently. "You heard him. Get that gear buckled up. Liebo—where the fuck's Dippy?"

"I'm back here."

"Get that helmet on, damn it. Gear check! On your feet." As they scrambled up, their legs tangling in straps and slings, he moved through them, tightening buckles, slapping their helmets for fit. He pulled a cammie stick from his pocket and smeared more of the smelly paint under Washman's staring eyes. "Washout. You feelin' okay?"

"Sure, Sarge."

"No butterflies? No whimping out?"

"No sweat, Sarge." The Washout straightened thin shoulders. "I'm, uh, up for it."

"Good." Silkworth slapped his arm and moved on. "Givens? This is it. You ready?"

Ready. Was he? This was the moment marines were supposed to live for. The moment they had screamed after at boot camp, simulated so many times on the bayonet course, the grenade range, Combat Town; the assault tactics at Geiger and LeJeune, practice landings here in the Med. This might be it for any of them. Nobody knew what waited for him ashore. His hand slid sideways to brush the reassuring steel of the mortar tube.

"Answer up, Private."

It didn't matter a bit. Ready or not, he was going. "Yes, Sergeant, I'm ready."

"Got pins?"

"What?"

"Here." Silkworth pulled small objects from an unbuttoned blouse pocket, counted three of them out into his hand, and turned his head sideways. "See these in my helmet cover? Spares for the shells. If you get antsy, drop the pin for a round, you got one handy to safe it with."

"Thanks, Silky. That's a good idea."

The men stood waiting in the compartment, swaying to the roll, glancing down to where each had organized his gear in the same way. You griped about the manual, Will thought, but when you were doing things for real, the Corps way was best. The compartment smelled of sweat and greasepaint and gun oil, and they took in the smells in short hard breaths as the minutes ebbed by, slow as time flows as you lie waiting, anticipating, when a woman has promised herself and then left to make the preparations.

"What the fuck," said Hernandez at last. "Din't he say we were going?"

"Sound like it to me," said Cutford.

"Must've been ten minutes."

"Ten minutes sure," agreed the corporal, his face like dark stone, embittered, unsurprised by anything *they* did to him.

"Stand easy," said Silkworth. He banged open the hatch, lighting the world red, and then disappeared.

"We goin'?" asked Washman.

"Shut up," said Cutford, looking toward the door.

"Jesus, Cutford—when Hernandez or Givens says somethin', you don't tell *them* to shut up."

"Shut up, goddammit, or I'll tear your fucken throat out!"

Silkworth came back. He unslung his rifle and tossed it onto the lifejackets. When he broke the straps on his pack and lowered it to the deck too, the rest of the men began to sag back into their corners, their niches, their nests, again.

"What's the scoop?" said Cutford.

"Some screw-up . . . lieutenant says stand easy on station."

"He tell you how long?"

"Lieutenants don't tell sergeants how long they gotta wait. Even if they know . . . ah, fuck it." Silkworth seemed to give way suddenly, fold inward, not from lack of strength but from disgust at having to justify what officers did to reasonable men. He stretched full length on the deck, so that no one could move between him and the hatch without stepping on him. In a moment he was snoring loudly.

"Hurry up and wait," muttered Liebo.

"Ain't we going?" said Washman again. This time no one answered him.

Half an hour later the door banged again. This time it was the Top. He stared around at the sleeping men, then bent to Silkworth and shook him. The sergeant blinked and sat up. The senior sergeant, squatting beside him, whispered rapidly for several minutes. Halfway through he was interrupted by Silkworth's cursing, but the Top cursed him right back, into silence again, till he was done. When he had finished he stood up, only five-feet-five in combat boots, but still big enough to fill the compartment by himself. "And that's your orders. Any questions? Gear man'll be around in a minute."

"It's crazy, Top. Fucken crazy. We're going to need those tubes. There's fucken Russians ashore here, man."

"We don't know what it's like ashore. They do. And those are orders, and you're a marine. So get moving." The Top looked around the compartment once more, then slammed the hatch hard as he left. The men stirred.

"On deck!" bawled Silkworth angrily. "Listen up, listen up! We got to turn our mortars in, and like right now."

"What the fuck, Silky!"

"What he mean, turn them in?"

"Shit if I do, man!"

He waited out their griping for perhaps three seconds, then bawled louder than all of them put together, "Gaw-*damn!* You people cry like fifteen monkeys fucken' a football at how much gear you got to carry, then you don't want to leave it when you're ordered to. Give me a troop of palsied old-maid librarians in front of you bastards, at least they'd do what they was told. Shit fire, if they was free blow jobs waitin' ashore, you'd whine how you had to unbutton your flies. Now break that gear out! Cutford, count it all, make sure we leave every piece of the weapons and every round 'a' mortar ammo."

"They sendin' us in without cover," said Cutford. "You know that? How we gonna—"

"We gonna do it like U.S. Marines," said Silkworth, cutting the corporal off. "It's a tricky landing; the people here can cut us to cat meat if we piss them off, and the Man says not to take in anything but rifles. I don't get it but diplomacy ain't my job. My job is to follow orders, just

like you, and if I wanted to live forever I wouldn't be
wearin' this green suit. So shut up that wicked mouth,
Cutford, and roll out those tubes."

I don't get it either, Givens was thinking, pulling the
sleeved rounds from his pack loops. We're mortarmen—
mortars, they always said, were part of company firepower. What was suddenly wrong with them? But he took
one look at Silkworth, glaring around like Jehovah with
thunderbolts in the middle of the compartment, and decided not to ask.

The inner door opened and the armorer came in, bent
like a Christmas tree under a festoon of M-16s and cartridge bags. "Gitcher rifles here," he said from beneath the
pile. "One ammo pouch each. Sign these cards here. Can't
have the piece without the signature."

"Fuck! These ain't our fucken rifles!"

"Ain't got time to check numbers. Just grab one and
sign."

"Cutford, count 'em off."

"Magazines. Can you give us extra magazines?" Cutford asked the armorer.

"They said one each, but . . . I brought extras. Just don't
flash 'em around, okay?"

The corporal passed Givens a rifle. Their hands met
on the stock; they stared into each other's eyes for a long
intent second. Then he turned back to the armorer, and
began handing out ammo to the others. Will jacked back
the bolt and locked it to the rear, checking the chamber,
and peered down the barrel. Oily. A reserve weapon. But
that would shoot out, or he could swab it himself after
they landed. He reversed it and clicked the sights on
twelve, sixteen—standard setting when you picked up a
strange piece. *But how do they expect us to shoot with
these?* he thought, glancing at Silkworth, but deciding
once more not to speak. *Over fifty yards, we won't have
any idea where we're hitting.* The infantrymen watched
them, amused.

"This all of it?" said the armorer.

"Thass right," said Cutford bitterly. "You got ever' bit of our mortar gear there."

"Gimme a man to carry it."

"But what are we gonna *do?*" Washman muttered. "We go through all that shit training on mortars—now what are we gonna be? Just *riflemen?*"

"No, you'll never be that, buddy," said one of the grunts.

In the midst of it the lights turned to red again and they swung toward the door. It was the captain again. But this time he said nothing; just looked at them for a moment, and then jerked his thumb over his shoulder.

"Helo team thirteen, up and ready!" sang Silkworth. "Let's go!"

On the move at last. Will tugged his chinstrap tight one last time and picked up the rifle. They shuffled forward in the red light, bent like old men, weapons dangling. The black mouth of the hatch was filled with night and wind and the scream of turbines, and then with leaping men. Silkworth's face, turned backward for a parting shout: "Remember, watch the blades! Rear rotor's on the left!"

Then it was his turn. He put his arm to Washman's shoulder and they went through together.

Night, sound, and rain. They staggered onto a rain-slicked flight deck, caught icy spray on their uplifted faces. Sound struck them like a left hook, the buffeting of rotor-wash like a right. Lights pulsated weirdly in the mist, making the stumbling queues of men leap to existence and then fade to black, the strobe of the rotors slicing each second into a dozen slow-motion frames. Still pictures: men leaning forward into the rain, men looking back to the safety of the ship, two marines helping a comrade up, troops running under the burden of full combat gear. The stationary ballet of the helo deck crew, wands glowing orange, speaking in slow circles to the pilots who waited invisible for their human freight to board. And above and behind the rainswept stage, decks above, the outangled windows of Pri-fly glowed jade and ruby, silhouettes of earphoned figures leaning forward in their boxes, audiences to the dance below, directors to more machines that hovered waiting, pulsating in mist-shrouded aureoles a hundred feet aft of the rolling ship . . . the helicopters looming gigantic in red-flickering darkness, their screaming presence leaning on the men who ran, it seemed to each one, endlessly across an endless deck toward them, each one blinking through the wind-driven rain toward the loom of his chopper, each man reminding himself *Fifty-threes, tailrotor's on the left.* Picking out as he lumbered forward the blunt curve of the forward section, the flickering fatal halo of the rotor, the blue steady flame of the engines as they rounded the tail, still running, packs banging on their backs, rifles at high port. The exhaust kicked up stinging droplets from the flight deck, mixed hot blast with soaking cold rain. Givens tripped on a tiedown and felt momentary panic. He recovered with one hand to the deck and ran on, blundering against Washman as the squad slowed, bunching together, then pounded up the ramp into the lightless maw of the plane. He moved left, felt the seat jam horizontal into the backs of his legs, and groped for the belt. Not till it clacked solid did he feel secure. He leaned back gasping against the bulkhead, staring still into darkness, feeling the others close around him.

The ramp came up. The engines rose to a roar. The fuselage shuddered, rotated under them, and launched them suddenly heavy into the air. Scared, exultant, he screamed wordlessly into the wall of sound, as loud as he could, the other men screaming too, none of it audible.

They were off. The deck tilted, the aircraft throbbed, its interior so bright with sound, conversation and thought alike were impossible. The engines cut through the thin aluminum like a cleaver. A dim red bulb came on in the curving overhead, and the rows of faces flicked on as if the light were behind them, behind red translucent masks, half-hidden by the helmets. The deck tilted again and slanted to the side, hard. He caught a windowed glimpse of a lit square of deck, a pulsating ruby cauldron where the next settling wave of aircraft stirred the mist into tornadoes, the rest of the ship black against black ocean.

The first gust of raw fear tightened his hands on his weapon, lifted his head, thrilled along his back with the buzz of the airframe. It blew his nostrils wide with the smells of oil and hot metal, man-sweat and rain. Staring out between illuminated faces, his gut tight against the straps as the plane shuddered around in its turn, he thought to himself suddenly: *I will never forget this.* This was no book, no song. This was real, and he knew with absolute sureness that he would remember it all, just as it was in this moment, no matter how many years would pass before he remembered nothing. Because this was life itself, this screaming moment lit in scarlet, tilting through a foreign night in this aluminum coffin toward whatever was to come.

He lifted his head to the battle; to the trumpets he saith, yea, yea. . . .

The deck steadied. The ship rolled backward from the window, replaced by darkness and then a pearl-gray glimmer of predawn as the horizon came up. The helicopter settled, as if into grooves. It ceased climbing and tilted forward. The engines dropped to a deafening drone. The light brightened, showing each of them the eyes of the others and the expressions: Silkworth competently bland; Cutford scowling, still pissed off over the mortars, eye-whites glistening against the total dark beneath his helmet; Washman scared, mouth open, eyes fixed on Givens', but unquestioning, accepting; Hernandez scared too but alert; Harner blank-faced, eyes closed, fingers laced tight over packstraps; Liebo staring out the window, remote, dreamy-eyed.

The chopper settled and tilted, vibrating, droning in repetitive patterns through the ribbed riveted metal, through the snake-writhe of wiring and hydraulic lines that the brighter red and now a fine gray wash from the windows, not yet light but just bright enough to be there, showed their inquiring eyes around the interior of the helicopter. The Stallions were big; they carried thirty-five men at a lift, but he had the same feeling of eggshell, kerosene-smelling fragility he had in every copter since his first lift at Pendleton. It was like riding in a beer can. He hated to think how little that paper thinness would slow down a bullet. This was not practice; there might be ground fire for real. Sweat broke under his helmet-liner as thought became threat. What had they done in Nam? Sat on their helmets? He looked toward Cutford, half-wanting to ask him, just to hear someone talk who had been through it, but the black corporal was folded into the fuselage with his eyes closed, still scowling.

The helicopter settled, shaking like the stern of the *Spiegel Grove* when a sea lifted the tips of her screw out of the water. The men settled too, wedging themselves into the canvas seats, and the vibration sank into them, rattling their teeth, shaking them down like bags of loose sand into something denser, heavier, than simple flesh.

His head sank, nodding to the thrum that surged through the aircraft, and slowly his mouth sagged open.

When he jerked awake again he was disoriented, unable to judge how long he had been out. A minute? An hour? The window was just as dark, the predawn glimmer gone. The green glow of his watch dial gave him only numbers. He did not know the flying time to the LZ. He sought the others with his eyes; they looked back but words were impossible, communication was impossible; they were separated and shut off by a wall of sound so loud that it made everything silent.

Gesture, then. He caught Silkworth's eye and held out his arm; tapped his watch; looked questioning. The sergeant held up six fingers. The motion went around the helicopter from man to man. Six minutes, he thought. Not long. And as if the pilot heard him the deck tilted back. The pitch of the rotors changed and the speed lodged in their bodies surged them into the straps as the aircraft slowed. With the sick feeling of descent came sudden activity. They checked their weapons, empty chambers but magazines full ready to feed. They cinched their packs, settled their helmets, the last motion hooking their left hands under the buckle of the seat belt. They glanced toward the rear of the helicopter, checking the ramp position, then glanced at each other.

The light went out. In the darkness they fell, faster now, the whish of the milling rotor coming clearly through the fuselage. He felt his throat close, his hands tighten on the straps. The engine—had it quit? It didn't seem as loud. He couldn't hear it!

He stared into the dark, mouth open, and waited for the crash.

The engine roared again, and they became heavy, heavy. The helmet bent his head. Something red shot past outside. Before he could think it through the chopper jolted sideways and then slammed down so hard it rapped his jaw on his chest. Motors whined aft and the clack of releasing buckles rippled along the line of men as they stood up.

Off the chopper. Down the ramp, through the man-filled darkness, turn soon, got to remember turn left turn LEFT. He felt without seeing the openness of the night, heard without seeing the deadly air-flutter from the tail rotor. The man behind shoved him and he turned left. He was down, and running. His boots thudded and swished through dry grass. Dust stung his face, kicked up by the blast. Through the thunder of engines he could hear the noncoms shouting. There was a bang behind him, a scream, but it only made him run faster. He panted through windy dark, caught up in the confusion of a night landing, the minutes when everyone ran in a dozen different directions and a squad leader earned his pay.

He was sprinting full out, rifle held high, looking around for the rest of the squad, when his boot hit a hole and he went down hard into the dirt, crashing down on his face. He lay there, half-out, the pack pushing him down like a man lying on top of him, and then heard it:

the climbing whine of a helicopter coming in to land. At the same moment the ground lit up, bright, distinct, each blade of grass sharp and individual as a razor-edge. He twisted his head. They were landing lights, all right. He blinked up at them for an eternally long second, watching the three blazing lamps spread as the helo drifted down, the rotorblast pressing him into the dirt, thunder building in his ears, his muscles rigid, unable to move. He was frozen like a rabbit in headlights.

The hand grabbed his pack, left it, groped, and found him; grabbed him under the armpit and lifted him bodily onto his feet and then shoved him stumbling into a run. He heard the copter thud into the dust behind him. The tip blast shoved him along behind the big shadow that still had one arm under his. The shadow turned, and Cutford grinned in the landing lights like a black jack-o'-lantern.

"Thanks," he shouted.

"You fuckhead, Oreo. Takin' a nap on a LZ not my idea of smart soldierin'."

"Ah, eat it," he shouted, finding the grin sticking to his face, too. The corporal's hand gripped his shoulder, fingers digging in, held it for a moment, and then released. "Les' get the squad formed up," Cutford shouted above the building roar of the second wave coming in behind them. "An' get that perimeter out. Dawn comin' up soon."

He blinked, pulling his mind from what had just happened, and remembered the disposition. Marine units dug in the instant you ran far enough not to get landed on. They found Hernandez and then Harner. Then they ran into the infantry squad they had boarded with, part of the helo team, and Silkworth and Washman were with them. Silky took charge at once, starting their fire positions to the north of the LZ on a small rise. They began chunking at the dirt with their entrenching tools.

"You seen Dippy, man?"

"No."

"No, man, I ain't seen him since the debark."

The light came while they dug, gray and pale and cool. Levering the spade beneath a rock, he raised his head to look around. The hills came first, black cuts in the graying sky, and then the men working beside him, and finally the hole. When he saw the tool in his hands he knew that it was dawn. The sergeants had linked the squads up left and right to form the perimeter and now as he tamped the pile flat in front of his firing position and propped his rifle on it he could look to either side and see men strung out along the rise. Behind them, the sound dulled by distance and somehow too by the coming of daylight, helos churned downward out of the sky, the patch team waving them in with the wands. Some of them carried gear, slung beneath in nets, and he could see piles of supplies beginning to build.

So this, he thought, is Lebanon. Again he had the feeling that he would never forget what he was seeing, that he would always be able to stand here again, be as he was right now, forever, just by remembering. It was that strong. He stretched, holding the tool, and breathed in the dry dusty air, the cool morning smells of soil and unknown trees, of a foreign land.

"We're in clean," said Hernandez, interrupting his thoughts. "I dint see one shot. Now why couldn't we have took the mortar?"

"I don't know."

"It's crazy bullshit, that's what it is."

"Yeah."

"Shut up and dig," said Silkworth, pausing at the top of their holes. "This is an entrenchment? You're gonna get your asses shot off. Deeper, you crud lovers, deeper. Like Lily says, I want you in all the way, you'll break your neck if you fall off once I start."

"Aye aye, Sarnt!"

"Yowzah, yowzah, Massa Silkwort'."

"Bad news, guys," said the sergeant, looking at all of them and none of them. "Dippy got hurt coming off the helo."

"Hurt," said Givens. "How bad? What do you mean, Silky?"

"That's all I heard. Sorry. Now get that spade in the dirt."

They dug and dug, clawing up the rocky soil, gritty dust and limestone, prying up grass cropped close by goats, and spread it out before them. Dug and spread. It grew rapidly brighter. The exec came by and passed a couple of words with them, told them hot coffee was coming up, flown in from the *Guam*.

"Hot coffee?" grunted Cutford. "In whose Marine Corps?"

"Just don't get used to it," said the officer.

"We be movin' on inland, Lieutenant?" Washman asked him.

"That's the word. Consolidate here and guard the road, be ready to continue east for the target area when transport comes up."

"How's the landing going at the beach?"

The officer shook his head.

"Sir—you heard anything about one of our guys, got hurt debarking? Name of Liebo?"

"He walked into a rotor. They flew him back. That's all I know," said the lieutenant, and went on.

They dug in silence for a while. "That's got to be deep enough," said the Washout at last, and squirmed down into his hole. "Can you see me from the front, Will?"

Givens obediently crossed ahead of the line, squatted down, and surveyed the position. "Nope. Not even the top of your helmet."

"Good. Get in yours, I'll check you."

When they were satisfied with the position the squad squatted gratefully on the reverse slope of the hill, watching the helos offload another unit. "New boys," said Silkworth, glancing at them sideways.

"Not like the old Corps," agreed Hernandez.

"Geez, it's getting hot already. Where'd all that rain go? It quit as soon as we got here."

"This is the Med, kid."

"Sergeant. Muster over there with the Top. Got some word to pass."

"Yes, sir."

They sat and watched Silkworth jog off toward the helos, his pack slapping his ass as he ran. "Gonna move out soon, I bet," said Washman. "Just when I got my hole dug."

"Cigarette?" said Harner.

"No, thanks, Buck. You know I don't smoke."

"No harm offerin'." Harner grinned slowly. "Wasn't for these magnum cowboy killers, couldn't hardly take the pressure 'round here."

Givens nodded. They watched the knot of noncoms and officers. The sky brightened. The sun came into view for the first time, bursting in red-white flame across the low hills directly into their eyes. The light picked out the dust in the clear air, the brown haze of exhaust above them, making them blink and raise their arms and squint at it, as if it was something new, this morning sun.

The knot broke. "Gonna go for sure," said Cutford, staring at the sergeant as he toiled up the hill, and they all rose, dusting off their utilities.

Silkworth, as he went up to them, was looking east. Following his eyes, Givens saw in the fresh daylight that the hills they had landed on were only foothills, and that beyond them mountains stood tan against the sky. Tan, and above that the white glisten of snow.

"Holy *shit*, Sergeant! We goin' over *those?*"

But all he said, looking to the sunrise, was "Stand easy. They'll let us know."

28
U.S.S. *Guam*

LENSON CAME TO SUDDENLY, HIS HEAD coming up off his stateroom desk. A litter of crumpled paper and marked-up pubs slid to the deck. His first thought was that his neck ached.

His second was that a phone was buzzing steadily. He lifted his wrist, stared at it without thought. He could not remember where he was for a moment; only that he was very tired. Then, gradually, it came back. Deployed. The commodore. The oporder. Finally he realized why he'd looked at his watch; this was D-day, and H-hour for Urgent Lightning was less than two hours away.

He jerked the phone out, cursing himself. It was the flag bridge messenger; the commodore wanted to see him. He splashed cold water on his face at the sink and ran up to the flag bridge. Sundstrom's chair was empty. He groped his way in the dark until he bumped into a body.

"Who the hell is that?"

"It's me."

"Damn it, do I have to send you down under guard? I told you to get some sleep."

"Can't talk now, Red. He called me. Where is he?"

Flasher used a few choice words. "He's in his cabin. I guess."

"So this is it, huh."

"Yeah, that's right. Tomorrow—I mean, this morning." A red flashlight winked on and then off as Flasher checked his watch. "Oh-four-twenty. We sent your oporder mod out a little after three. We're in the approach phase now. Everything's on track."

"Do you know what he wants me for?"

"Oh, yeah!" said the ops officer. "You'll love this one. He wants a report on *Ault*'s grounding."

"*What?* I thought—"

"Thinking again? I warned you about that."

"But—oh, Christ. Now? When we're sending in the lead elements of a raid?"

"COMSIXTHFLEET didn't ask for one till now."

"Oh, well, in that case."

"Have a good time," he heard Flasher mutter. But he was too angry to respond.

When he knocked and let himself into the flag cabin he found himself in darkness. He stood uncertainly for a moment, then heard something stir in the room beyond.

"Dan? That you?"

"Yes sir."

A light showed him Sundstrom sitting up in bed. "Come in, come in," he mumbled, flipping his hand at a corner of the bunk as he reached for his glasses. "Sit down here. Read this."

Dan studied the message. It was from Admiral Roberts.

CONFIDENTIAL

Fm: COMSIXTHFLT
To: CTF 61

Subj: Grounding of Unit Under Your Command

1. (C) *Communications from US authorities Naples IT indicate that USS AULT, under your operational control, was involved in grounding*

incident during recent departure
that port. Further understand from
HF conversation with you that AULT
currently lagging main body TF 61
due to propulsion casualty.

2. (C) *Forward immediate expla-*
nation of your failure to report
grounding. Forward immediate de-
tails of machinery status of AULT.

He blinked. Even for a naval message, this was blunt.
Roberts was pissed. He looked up at the commodore.

"Now look, Dan, apparently we owe Tony a report on
this grounding business. Nobody else thought about it—as
usual."

"Sir, Mr. Flasher says we got a message from the destroyer on it."

"I know that. I read my traffic, Dan! But that was just
the letter of the law. That was just a damage report. I'm
sure Tony wants more than that. This is prime court-
martial material. If we don't take the initiative, seal it off
right now, it'll snowball right through the cracks. I want
you to write up an investigation."

"An investigation?" Lenson said. He sounded stupid
even to himself.

"An investigation. A full, factual account of what happened. You'd better—have you got something to write
on?"

Mechanically, he took his notebook out and found a
pen. Sundstrom leaned back on the pillow and closed his
eyes. "Okay. Start with the situation—the task force having to get to sea at once. I ordered that, took the initiative,
and events have proved me right. Now, Captain Foster
called me back, and said he couldn't get a pilot out of
Naples. Got that so far?"

"Yes sir."

"Now, I wanted him underway, but I was afraid something like this might happen. He thinks he's a hotshot, thinks he can drive a destroyer blindfolded. I know his type from the Pacific, believe me. So I told him, it's up to you, but safety is paramount; under no circumstances are you to attempt the channel without a local pilot unless you're certain you can navigate in perfect safety. That's what I said."

"You said that in a message, Commodore? We could reference the date time group."

"No, no, this was in a radio conversation. There's no official record. But that's the gist of it."

"Sir, I didn't hear that—I mean, I wasn't on the bridge during that exchange."

"I know. There's been a lot going on lately, and you haven't had much sleep." The commodore's voice was understanding. "I know that, and I don't hold it against you. You're doing a great job; you're the only one of the staff officers I can depend on, and I promise you I won't forget it when it comes time for your fitness report. There should be decorations too in this Syrian operation, if it's handled right. Now. *Ault*'s CO was cautioned not to attempt the channel."

Lenson watched the pen tremble in his hands. It hesitated for a long moment, then, jerkily, as if without his connivance, wrote *Captain cautioned*.

"I want a message recounting that series of events for Roberts. Add that after receiving the grounding report, I radioed *Ault* and Foster told me personally that grounding damage was minimal to nonexistent; that his ship was at that time showing no effects on her propulsion or other systems; and that on that basis, I decided not to forward her report of grounding, because it would tend to damage the career of a promising and aggressive skipper who up to then had performed well. Say that the later casualty to *Ault*'s engines was a surprise to me, due to Foster's softpedaling of the amount of damage the grounding had caused, that I was unaware of it."

"Sir—"

"Don't interrupt me, Dan. You don't understand how these things are done. This is the way the big boys play the game. Now. Despite—"

"Sir, I can't write that. It isn't true."

There was no sound in the cabin for a long moment. He raised his eyes to find Sundstrom looking at him coldly.

"Write what I said, Lieutenant."

And the whole immense weight of years, years of conditioning, of indoctrination, of salutes and obedience forced his pen down to the paper once again. He struggled to lift it, to lift his eyes again as the commodore droned on. But he could not. He was so tired. Too tired, right now, to fight. And not over this. What did it matter? This was not important. Not compared to the landing. If he didn't write it someone else would. And he would be out in the cold.

But this was the last time. He could promise himself that. He would go along no more.

"Aye aye, sir," he whispered.

He went straight to SACC after sending the commodore's Report of Investigation down to Radio. He drank six cups of coffee while they waited, tuning the radios, checking target lists against the maps, establishing comms.

At 0550 the first helo lifted off with a roar that rattled through the flight deck down to them. He and the others glanced up, paused; then returned, wordless, to their preparations.

Now it was 0610, and the Navy was doing business at last. Deep in the flagship the hiss of air conditioners merged seamlessly with the crackle of far-off speech, the squeal of transmitters, the clatter of Teletypes. The room hummed with light. It gleamed from desktops and radio equipment, from stacks of forms, sharpened pencils. It glowed over the rows of intent men, over publications stamped with warnings and classifications. A new chart of Northern Lebanon and Western Syria, brilliantly illuminated, towered above the tiered desks. The atmosphere was tense as a broker's office during what could be a rally—or a disastrous plunge.

"Green Line, this is Overkill, over."

"Coordinates, Red Three Fow-er Seven Three, White Two Niner Zee-ro Eight."

"Negative, negative, flight leader. Maintain ordered altitude. I say again, do not descend below angels eight on this radial or you will infringe helo return lane."

"Understand range is fouled. Can you close the beach? Attempt a close and report sight checks."

"Roger. Shifting to secondary freq at this time. Overkill out."

In the center of the bright room, the intent men, Lenson wrote rapidly on green paper, glancing up frequently at the mass of land, silent, waiting, that dominated it. McQueen stood in front of it, grease-penciling rapidly on the road leading northeast between El Aabde and Qoubaiyat. The j.g.'s face was drawn. His eyes met the light with the glittering intensity of fatigue, over blue stains that made him look old. His hand shook as he tore off the carbon and tapped the back of the man in front of him.

Despite his appearance he felt wonderful. The hour's nap, that or the immense overdose of caffeine, had restored his flagging energy. He felt a hectic, nervous high. He wanted to laugh or sing or sprint. After so much boredom, so much Crazy Ike, he was in action at last. Grinning suddenly, he glanced around the room.

The long tables were filled with officers and phone talkers, Marine Corps and Navy. The air crackled with radios, the terse speech of men setting into motion the plans he had written only hours before, alone in his room.

At the thought he bent forward, flipping the pages of the operations order, and began to review his assets once more. If things started in earnest he would have no time to read. He would have to know what to do.

First: naval guns. Another escort had joined the reconstituted Task Force 61 as it steamed for the beach during the last hours before dawn. *Virginia,* one of *America*'s escorts. A nuclear-powered missile cruiser, it had one five-inch mount operational forward, but he was leery of putting it close to the beach. He'd assigned her a patrol area to seaward, where she could monitor the air picture and provide cover against air attack. But even with her, Dan was worried. Along with *Bowen*'s single mount, that still made only two five-inch guns.

I need *Ault,* he thought. Need those six tubes bad. The last word he'd had from her was that she was finishing repairs and would shortly attempt flank speed. If she made it that would give him a total of eight guns. With luck, he thought, I should be able to manage with that.

And finally—he glanced at another handset, ready to his left hand, callsigns penciled above it—he had aircraft. The night before, reversing his previous statements (the air attack, he reflected, might have had something to do with that), Admiral Roberts had sent *America* and the rest of TF 60 hurtling toward the Levant at over thirty knots. She stood now two hundred miles to the west, far enough to lessen the provocation, but bringing her fighters within range. Roberts had promised two attack jets on station throughout the morning. Jack Byrne, seated just below Dan, was on the line to them now, controlling and vectoring them at Lenson's direction. His use of them was limited, Dan knew, both by range and by what bombing a Soviet treaty partner would mean; but they were there.

I'm ready, he thought. The Navy's ready. Now it's up to the Corps.

"Well, we're on our way," he said to Flasher, who sat down at that moment in the chair to his right.

"Aye."

"Think we'll have to use any of this stuff? Do any shooting?"

"Jesus, I hope not," said Flasher. "Whoever we hit, there'll be a hell of a stink. Syrians, Russians, the Girl Scouts, you name it. I just hope they back us up back in Washington."

When the first wave hit, seven minutes after scheduled

H, a muttered cheer rose around him. The first troops took the dune line and dug in quickly, ready to repel attack, but none came. The beach seemed empty. Dan stayed alert; it could have been cleared for artillery fire. The second wave beached, disgorging men who ran full-tilt for cover. The amtracs moved inland, broadening the toehold, alert for opposition or mines.

The marines were ashore. He sent McQueen up to plot the forward edge of the battle area. A few minutes later the first reports came in from the helo landing zone on Hill 1214, three miles inland. The advance party was in, dug in, and the road was clear as far as they could observe.

"Fuel state twenty," said Byrne, interrupting his thoughts.

He glanced at one of the three clocks on the bulkhead, above the map. "The jets? They're that low already?"

"These birds can't stay around long."

"No, they sure can't. We'll break them off soon, send them home. Should be two more on their way. Tell 'em to stay away from the beach—we can't let 'em even over land unless Sundstrom sends them in."

"Understood. How's the rest of it going?"

"Good progress, Jack."

"They moving inland now?"

"Let me check. Mac—get me first-wave leader."

"Click to seven, Lieutenant."

"Right. Green Bench, this is Overkill. Interrogative situation."

The confident words came back instantly, close and loud through the invisible link of radio. From that voice alone Lenson could see instantly and completely the beach; amtracs growling up the dunes toward the inland road, the radioman riding atop them, or perhaps huddled in a hole in the sand, cautious about exposing himself despite his confident, too-loud tone. *"Overkill, Green Bench here. First wave beached on time, without casualties. Forward Edge Battle Area now inland twelve hundred meters. Point units forming up on beach road, coordinates zero-four-one-eight, six-seven-two-zero, preparing to head east. Over."*

"Green Bench, Overkill: What's your estimate of surf height?"

"Green Bench; five to six feet. Rough, but manageable. Over."

"Overkill: That's great. We were worried about that. Do you see any need for preparatory or harassment fire at this time? Over."

"Green Bench; no opposing forces noted. Natives seem to have cleared out. But sure would like to have it available. If we need it we'll need it fast. Over."

"Roger. Understand," said Lenson, wishing again he had *Ault* standing by. "Please report at ten-minute intervals as per oporder to ensure comms stay up. Overkill out."

"Roger your last. Green Bench out."

So they were ashore, the assault waves, at least. Not a shot at them during the beach approach, the most vulnerable time for a landing. And Flasher, bless him, had been right about the surf. Dan leaned back for a moment, looking at the chart, the phone warm in his hand. So far things looked good. His job now was to monitor the raid's progress, and be ready for the unforeseen.

At least, he thought with bitter gratitude, *he* never comes down to SACC.

Just now, he ought to be checking his support units. He snapped the switch, snapping his mind back into place and function again in the same motion, and leaned forward again. "Thoroughbred, this is Overkill. Over," he said crisply into the transmit light.

No response. He stared at the map.

"Thoroughbred, Overkill . . . Thoroughbred, Thoroughbred, over." Where the hell was *Bowen?*

The frigate came up at last. *"Thoroughbred. Over."*

"Request your position. Over."

"Uh, this is Thoroughbred . . . stand by . . . position, two thousand yards west of Point X-ray, ready for call for fire."

"Two thousand! Interrogative failure to maintain assigned position."

"Uh . . . captain wanted to move closer inshore."

"Negative! Return to assigned position." Lenson considered, then added the justification. "There's no resistance on the beach itself. Any calls for fire will come from further inland. We need you backed off to be able to shoot over these hills, damn it!"

"Thoroughbred, roger. Will pass that word."

"Report when back on station. Overkill out."

He tried calling *Ault,* on the off chance, but there was no response; she was still out of range. He shook his head.

Well, air support next. Two Intruders, with four thousand pounds of rockets and bombs each, had been describing wide circles over the sea west of the task force since five-thirty. As Byrne had warned him, they'd be running low on fuel soon despite external tanks. He clicked the dial to the Tactical Air net. "Hot Dog, this is Overkill."

"Hot Dog," said the bored voice of the A-6 pilot. *"Go ahead."*

"Understand your fuel state is low. Confirm? Over."

"Another fifteen minutes. Then we got to beat it for the barn."

"Relief enroute?"

"Say again your last?"

"Are other aircraft on their way?"

"That's affirm, affirm. Two more enroute. Callsign is Blazing Saddles."

"Copy callsign. We have no requirement for your services at present. Might as well head back."

"We'll hang on for a few more minutes," came the pilot's voice; Lenson could hear the whine of jet engines in the background. *"Just in case. Haven't you got any place we can deliver these groceries?"*

"Negat, flight leader, negat! We have firm word no combat aircraft over land without clearance from Sixth-fleet. Take it back and save it, it costs money. Overkill, out."

"Hot Dog, out."

No commodore, no supervision, no drill . . . just the real thing, at last, what he had trained for so long. Through the whole deployment SACC had been a place where the staff went during GQ to nap and go through meaningless exercises, reading to each other from slips of paper. Now it was different. Here in this bright room he controlled all that the Fleet had to give the Corps; here the dusty, already tired men ashore could find support against the heavier weapons an entrenched enemy could muster. Naval guns, aircraft, and later this morning batteries of Marine Corps artillery; these were the power backing the thin shells of the amtracs and assault helos, the unprotected, step-by-step progress of the infantry, the grunts. An amphibious operation, a thrust ashore from the sea, was an unnatural thing for a modern army. It stripped it of its most potent weapons. And so the ships had to protect them, guide them, and supply them, until they could build up enough power ashore, man by man and weapon by weapon, to meet an enemy on something like equal terms.

And given even approximately equal terms, Lenson thought, I'll bet on the Marine Corps every time.

He leaned back and stretched, conscious of a sure, steady pulse of power and excitement. He had trained for this moment since the day he entered the Academy. The falsity and strain, the endless worrying over appearances, had dropped away. This was what was important, and this, by God, he would do right. If only he felt more alert. Only a little more sleep . . .

So far, though, it had been easy. Almost, except for the knowledge that it was real, like practice landings at Fort Lauderdale or Gythion or Sardinia. No one had yet fired on the men who rolled or waded so vulnerably ashore; who ran from the squatting hulls of helicopters; who were forming themselves now, at 0623, to thrust inland toward the hills of Syria.

He hoped fervently that it would stay that way. He had

guns and aircraft, but too few to hold a determined enemy. If the marines ran up against the Syrian Army, trained, careless of losses, and backed by Soviet power, there would be a lot of casualties.

And those two thousand men were all there were. It was all riding on one column, one lightning thrust inland with the whole force. Haynes had not left a single trooper aboard the ships that waited now, empty and anxious, off the low beach, flat and blazing in the morning sun.

No, goddammit, he thought fiercely. This has to work.

"Coffee, Lieutenant?"

"I guess another half a cup." He stared at the mug as the petty officer tilted steaming fluid over the dregs of the last six. He knew now, forever, he hated the taste of the stuff. "Thanks, Mac."

"You look like shit, sir."

"Thanks for the beauty tip, too." The staff quartermaster, he saw, did not look much better. The hours of close navigation during the beach approach had taken their toll on him.

The intercom blared suddenly at his elbow; he winced and turned it down. "Mr. Lenson? Commander Hogan here. The commodore wants to know if you can come up to the bridge."

"We're pretty busy here, sir."

"I think you better come up, Dan."

Oh, Christ, he thought, what now? He hit the key savagely, petulantly, wanting to punch something. "Yes sir, I'll be right up."

The flag bridge was filled with light. He had thought SACC was bright, but he blinked back tears and shielded his face with his hand as he mounted the last few steps of the outside ladder. The overcast that had shielded their movement was gone at last. The morning sun, two hands above the land, was burning straight through the windows, turning the closed bridge into an oven. The watch team was in full battle dress, helmets and life preservers, buttoned up tight. He felt sweat break on his forehead as he came up to the commodore's chair from behind. Sundstrom was relaxing, his feet up on the intercom. His helmet and life vest lay on the deck by the chair. A covered tray with the remains of breakfast sat on the chart table near him, and a half-full cup of coffee was balanced precariously on his knee. He stood there for a moment, studying the familiar folds in the back of the task force commander's neck. He had to breathe deeply several times, tamping down rage, before he could speak.

"Sir, you wanted to see me?"

"Dan. Yes." Displeasure crossed Sundstrom's face as he leaned back. "Why aren't you in battle dress? We're at general quarters. We could come under missile or air attack at any time—"

"I was in SACC, sir."

"What is that supposed to mean? You mean *nobody* down there is in battle dress?"

"No sir," Lenson said, and heard the strain and viciousness in his own voice. "We can do our job better there without it."

The commodore noticed it, too; the look of displeasure deepened, but strangely his voice went softer. "Well— when you go back down, pass the word. All hands, and that means your people, too. Let's look like professionals, Dan."

"Aye, aye, sir."

"Now. What's going on? I'm not getting the information I should be getting. I want reports up here! That's the only way I can exercise positive control!"

"Yes sir," said Lenson, his face wooden. "Leading elements of the first wave are moving up the road inland. They should reach the advance party at the LZ shortly. Neither report contact nor resistance so far. It looks like we've achieved surprise."

"Good, good. Do you think they'll hit trouble?"

"I don't know too much about the political situation

here, sir. Maybe Commander Byrne could answer that for you."

"I doubt it. Anyway," said Sundstrom, raising his binoculars, "I want to make sure you know not to fire any weapon without permission. Tony was most definite on that point."

"Yes sir. You told me that at midnight."

"I remember what I say, goddamn it! I'm reemphasizing it!"

"Aye aye, sir."

"This whole raid is juggling nitroglycerine," Sundstrom said slowly. When he lowered the glasses Dan saw worry in his eyes. "Tony liked my scatter-and-rejoin idea. He said that was the key to getting the raid approved. But now they know we're here. You can bet your boots every Russki sub and destroyer in the Med is making knots for us right now. And there's a lot of Syrians starting up their tanks. You know—"

"Sir?"

Sundstrom hammered the binoculars softly against his knee. "I still think this could be a trap. But if it is they've tied my hands, Dan. We're under direct control from the War Room now. I can't do a thing to help those boys ashore without an explicit blessing from Washington."

"What about the increased ReadCon, sir? Doesn't that mean they'll back us?"

"What—the nuclear alert? Maybe. But it would be just like them to back down on me. Lead me and Haynes down the garden path, then saw it off on us—"

Sundstrom worried it like a toothless dog with a bone for several more minutes, then said suddenly, angrily, "Okay, that's all. You'd better get back on the job." Lenson turned away instantly at the dismissal. His eyes crossed Hogan's as he went for the ladder. Lenson nodded to him—he had no easy job, up here all alone with the commodore—and undogged the hatch.

He paused for a moment on the ladder, seventy feet above the blue, blue sea, and looked out toward the land.

Lebanon. It was the first time he had seen it. At ten miles' distance it was bright and beckoning, untouched by strife or war. To the south rose the white buildings, a few hotels taller than the rest, of Tripoli. According to the Port Directory it had once been a lovely place . . . directly to port and twenty thousand yards distant from the slowly moving ship was the beach, a strip of sand backed by dunes and, far beyond, the distant blue of hills rising to the mountains of the Liban. Save for plumes of smoke and dust there was no evidence of the men ashore. Asia had swallowed them, leaving as trace only the wheel of a helicopter across the sky, turtle-slow, coming back empty from a supply drop.

Clinging to the rail, staring toward the land, he thought of the marines. Aboard ship they and the Navy lived apart; segregated, almost; and he thought how strange it was that they had inhabited the same steel world for months on end, and still he could not say that he really knew a single one of the men who were now rolling toward those distant blue hills. What would they find there? He did not know. There might be battle, there might be death.

Just as none of them knew, just as no man knew . . .

Why am I standing here? he thought then. Why am I thinking about them? I have my orders. Make the men put their helmets on.

He was turning away from the brightness when a flash from seaward caught him. Something to the south, not one of their own. He shaded his eyes.

The trawler rolled even in the lee of the land, and he saw the familiar rust streaks. The flash came again, sunlight reflected from the bridge windscreen. It was bow on, headed back to rejoin them, like a dog that has tracked its master for miles and now pretends for a moment, as it approaches his leg, that it is shy.

He thought for a moment of reporting it. Then he thought: I'm not a lookout. To hell with it.

He turned from the brightness, and went below.

29
Ash Shummari, Syria

SHE WOKE EARLY THAT LAST DAY; WOKE
to an immense silence, an immense heat. She could see by
the utter blue beyond the window that the days of cloud
were past. The wind had stopped and the sun was thrusting itself into the closed room like a magician's sheaf of
swords. The mattress was damp against her back and as
she swung her legs to the floor; sweat trickled down them.
There was another wetness, too, and she went into the
bathroom, away from Nan and Moira and Michael,
snatching up her purse as she went.

Thank God for mascara and eyeliner . . . and most of
all for cold cream. She repaired the wreck in the mirror
as well as she could, then brushed her dirty hair till it took
on a dull sheen.

When she came back, wishing that the gathering mess
from four people could be flushed away, the others were
awake. Michael stood by the window, stretching. She
could hear his joints crack. Moira sat on the bed looking
haggard, not even glancing up as Susan said "Good morning."

Nan lay motionless, her face flushed. Susan knelt beside
her, feeling a rush of guilt and apprehension so intense it
made her knees weak. Her child was sick, and she was
worrying about her appearance.

Oh God, *God,* when would this be over. . . .

"Baby. How are you doing this morning?"

She moved only a little under Susan's hand, without opening her eyes. "Oh hot again. Mommy, I want water. I itch."

"I'll get you water. Where do you itch?"

"Down in my throat, like."

"Oh. Guess you can't scratch too good there, can you?"

"I guess not." She smiled a little. "Mommy . . . I had a dream. About Daddy. When is he coming to get us?"

"You're so good, you're such a good girl. I don't know—but I hope soon." She got up quickly, tears making the image of her child waver. She blinked them away, angry at herself. Nan's condition had no connection with what she had done. She loved her, she would do anything for her, but guilt was not an appropriate response. Not to this.

But someone within her was not convinced. It was all too ready to blame her for her daughter's suffering. Illogical . . . but depressing. She pressed her hand to her own forehead, unconsciously mimicking her gesture to her daughter, and went out into the hallway.

The corridor was full of sunlight and bedraggled people. She took her place in line in front of the bucket and fell with relief into what passed for conversation.

"Did you have a good night?"

"More water, excellent. I came out here around midnight, and it was all gone."

"Someone's thinking about us," suggested a woman, her voice desperately hopeful. "Aren't they? They aren't like you were saying, so ruthless, are they?"

"Has anyone seen breakfast?"

Susan joined the rueful laughter at that remark. Breakfast . . . her stomach began to growl just at the word, as if it needed a sign to become hungry. We're reverting, she thought. Water and food, avoiding danger, that's all that concerns us now. She looked at her fellow hostages. They were apathetic, listless, their faces limp and pale. They reminded her uncomfortably of a PBS special she had once seen, on public mental hospitals. She dipped two glasses of water, sloshed a sip around in her mouth. The rest would be for Nan.

She was in the bathroom again with her hair, fighting out tangles and cursing at the flies—they were persistent and thus ultimately successful like all lower forms of life—when Moira came in and closed the door. Susan did not look away from the mirror. The broken veins under her nostrils looked so ugly. Her nose was oily, her lashes stuck together, dirt showed at the collar of the T-shirt she had worn now for three days.

"I'm a mess," she said aloud, her back to Moira. She heard the hollow clank of the toilet seat and then the rattle of the Ox pissing.

"God, it stinks in here."

"Moira . . . are you all right? You don't sound well."

"I'm all right." Lieberman, still slumped on the seat, ripped off a stingy piece of *American Archaeology* from her purse and rubbed her face with it. "It's so goddamn hot . . . no, I think it's the diet that's getting to me. I wanted to lose ten pounds, but this is doing it the hard way."

"We'll get more food soon. Hanna—"

Her heart jumped. She knew it was too late then, but stopped anyway as she realized what she'd said. Moira reached back automatically to flush, but the handle only rattled loosely. "God damn it," she said.

Susan thought: She didn't notice. Her heart began again. "Yes, it's a mess . . . good thing you brought paper, though—"

"Betts."

Uh-oh, she thought. "What?"

"This Majd character."

"What about him?"

"I woke up last night; you weren't in your bed. I don't want to pry, but I saw how he was looking at you yesterday. Did anything happen last night I ought to know about?"

"Nothing happened last night." She heard the defensiveness in her tone, and saw that Moira heard it, too. "I just talked to him for a while."

"Talked to *him?*" Lieberman stood up, looking alarmed.

"Don't get excited. There's no harm in—"

"Susan. You're not a kid, don't act like one." Moira moved up beside her, looking over her shoulder into her face, into the mirror. She saw that she was not the only one who looked tired. Her roommate's hair was scraggly, there were dark heeltaps under her eyes, her cheeks sagged. She looked like a three-week drunk. "This isn't the place to play around, Betts! This bastard is out to kill. He's said that, hell, they've done it in front of us. *What happened last night?*"

"It's none of your business," said Susan.

They looked at each other in the mirror. "Betts," Moira said at last, low, "what is happening to us?"

"I don't know what you mean," she said again. They looked at each other, and knew they knew, and there was nothing more either of them could say.

There was so little to do, she thought later. Except wait, and sweat, and try not to think.

Getting up so early made it bad. The weather made it worse. Susan could hardly credit how storm, rain, and cool had become airless and choking heat practically overnight.

She lay on the hot mattress, feeling sweat crawl like ants over her ribs, and thought.

"When is Daddy coming to get us?" Nan had said.

When is Daddy coming . . . that was the child speaking. When will someone rescue us from this; when will someone deliver us from uncertainty, fear?

He won't, babe, she thought, lying in the fly-buzzing heat, feeling the thud of her heart and the occasional fruitless slap of her hand as her only distinction from a corpse. She felt angry and so sad she wanted to cry. No one will come. We're here, and we're helpless.

She rolled her head to her child. Nan lay as if thrown on the bed, facing away from her, giving only the curve of her cheek and the line of her closed eyelids. Susan studied a bead of sweat on her forehead. She mused on the unfinished, pert curve of her nose, half-Asian, half-European, the inward dip between the eyes she had often congratulated herself on as more practical than the vision-obscuring Caucasian ridge. Yes, she did look like Dan . . . and like her . . . and altogether like herself, not a mixture but something different and new and precious. She contemplated with wonder the fact that something once part of herself had become separate and distinct and new, dependent now but not forever. In a way it made her feel that the child was not her own, but belonged to someone else, someone she could not know.

She mused on that for a time, drifted into a doze, and woke again seconds or minutes or even an hour later. But nothing had changed. The room was close and hot and flies rose from the corners of her eyes as she opened them. Conversation murmured from the corridor. Arabic, but too faint for her even to separate its fluid rapidity into words.

Unbidden, brought perhaps by the voices, she found herself thinking about him.

About the Majd.

She lay motionless for a long time, her only motion to blink when the insects returned. She was trying to understand how she felt, and to justify what had happened the night before, in the dark, in an empty room.

She did not lack excuses, rationalizations, and coldly, in turn, she evaluated each. Weren't hostages often attracted to their captors? Stockholm. Patty Hearst. But this was not an emotional response. She had submitted deliberately, to gain his protection. For insurance. That was what she had told herself the night before. But her mind was less certain in the daylight. Danger made you want sex . . .

didn't it? She lay and her hand moved gradually downward. No, the others were awake, sitting up . . . her hand came to rest on her midriff. She scratched at a pool of sweat in her navel, and half-turned again, switching her hips down into the hot ticking.

She had been faithful since she was married. It wasn't the end of the world, even if—and she knew that this was one thing it was not—it had been a random fling, a sideshow enjoyment. It was how you felt about a person that mattered, and not whom you slept with, once in a while. Dan, conservative as he was, would be horrified at that attitude. She knew he felt more strongly about fidelity than she did. But she had accepted that, accepted that it was important to him, just as she had stopped smoking because he disliked it.

But now that was over. Not the way she had sometimes fantasized it: a chance meeting at a bar; the daydreams she had dozing at the beach about the blond-stomached, long-limbed Frisbee players. But in a way not so different. Because she hadn't planned it, hadn't really thought about it, before it happened. What was that phrase of Erica Jong's . . . it had been his idea. She had not given herself. She had been taken.

No, that was not true, either. She rolled to lie on her side, hearing a trapped buzz beneath her that quickly died. She had talked with him, sat with him. Then she had made that remark about her and Dan. With his Arab ideas about women he would take that as a blatant come-on. She should have known that. And there at the end, when he lifted her, a part of her had wanted him. It had not been rape or anything like it.

Stay with the truth, Betts, she told herself sternly. It's going to be hard enough getting through this without lying to yourself about it.

"Mommy—"

She groaned and got up for water. Coming back she thought, Why try to sleep anymore? She sat on the bed and dispiritedly watched the sun-faded tatter of curtain stir to a breath of air so faint she could not even feel it.

"This is crazy," she said.

"That's the way the weather is around here," said Cook. Like a caged animal, she thought, he paced and stared out, stared out and paced, switching an invisible tail. It made her nervous. Now he was leaning his forehead against the glass, rocking on his heels, his face drawn into a frown. "This strip of coast is too narrow to generate its own weather. It just takes whatever comes off the sea."

"What are you looking at out there?"

"I'm not sure . . . I can see one of those jeeps once in a while, over between those buildings. They're moving around, but I don't know what's going on."

Nan said, "Will they shoot us?"

They stared at her. "Of course not," said Moira brightly, going over to the bed. "Aunt Moira can promise that. Nobody would hurt a little girl as pretty as you."

"Ox, please. I don't want her to get that kind of image of herself."

"Sorry, Betts . . . Yes? What do you want?" she said, her voice suddenly rising, hardening.

Susan turned. Harisah was standing in their doorway, alone.

"I've brought you some bread," he said, holding out the loaf to Michael. It was the same rough meal as the day before. "Can you use it? There is fresh water in the hall-way."

"Thanks," said Cook, his voice guarded. As Harisah turned away his glance swept the room and found hers. She felt herself stiffen, felt her back actually flatten against the wall against which she leaned, like a cat hiding from thunder. She held his dark eyes only for a second, but in that time she felt a sense of danger and tragedy so imma-nent and personal it was as if the veils of culture and inculcated prejudice that separated their two worlds had disintegrated like nightweb on a branch tossed into flame. She knew for a moment that yes, it had happened to them, what must happen between men and women. And at the same time—at the same time—she hated him, his single-mindedness and cruelty, and was afraid.

It was unlike anything she had felt before, and it, or the heat, made her dizzy for a moment.

The Majd said, turning his eyes away from her to Cook, "There may be some changes today."

"What do you mean?"

"The Turks are considering our offer. The Syrians tell us that. So, there is some hope they will answer our demands, if they are convinced we'll do what we say."

"Meaning, we'd be released?"

"It's possible."

"Why don't you do it now?"

"I can't do that," Harisah said. His eyes took on the hardness. "I won't do that. I am waiting for a messenger from the committee. One is to come today, this morning, soon. He will give me instructions on how to proceed."

"Committee? I thought you were the leader," said Susan. Moira glanced at her.

"I am *za'im* of these men. That is, a leader in battle. But there are others. Some of us fight; others are better to do the negotiating."

Harisah went to the window, lowering his rifle as he passed Cook, and peered down. It was the same position of body, the same attitude, that the American had taken, but Susan saw how much more fluently the Palestinian leaned, how his shoulders drooped naturally and without tension. How his muscles bunched under the damp cotton as he lifted his arm to lean against the pane. How the edges of his eyes crinkled as he peered upward into the sunlight, then downward to the square.

"There's a jeep coming," said Michael helpfully.

"I see it." The terrorist peered down at it for a moment longer, and then turned suddenly. His shoes rattled briefly on the stairs. Then the hot silence returned, marred only by the slow patrolling of flies and then the nasal beep of an automobile horn.

Susan elbowed Michael, and felt Moira join them at the

window. Side by side they looked down at the wide sweep of square. Empty asphalt, cracked, and beyond that, small between them and the hills, the glitter of sun off the immobile aluminum of the abandoned plane. The only movement was the eddying of air as heat shimmered up, the only sound the mutter of the jeep's engine.

It waited in the center of the open space, an open boxy vehicle. The red-white-black Syrian flag drooped from the aerial and another—Palestinian?—from the left bumper. The two men in it, foreshortened by height, wore short-sleeved suntans and officers' caps. As far as Susan could see they were unarmed.

"What are they doing?"

"Waiting for our fearless leader," said Cook. He pointed. "And there he is."

Harisah stepped into the street, into their sight. He was not alone; two of his men tagged a step behind, to left and right.

Susan saw that he was still carrying the rifle.

And suddenly she knew what was familiar. It was straight out of a John Wayne. The windless heat, the tense, loose way the men sauntered toward the jeep, the motionless intensity with which the officers watched them approach.

"It's some kind of confrontation," said Cook.

"You felt it too—"

"Shut up and watch," said Moira.

The talk seemed to take forever. After the first few minutes it became animated. The distant figures waved their arms, pointed back to the hotel, and the shouting came faintly up to the watchers.

"I don't get it," said Moira.

"It's the messenger he was talking about," said Cook. "Can't you see that truck? Back beyond the hill?"

"No. You know I can't see that far away."

"Well, I guess there's some trouble. The Majd is—"

"Wait," said Susan.

Harisah had turned away, shrugging his shoulders in

exaggerated disgust. If this weren't the Mediterranean, she thought, we couldn't tell what was going on nearly as well; the pantomime was transparent, even from this far away.

What was not clear was the appearance of two more guards, and in front of them, edging forward apprehensively across the blazing, silent square, two old people.

"The Stanweises!"

"That's them, all right."

"Where has he been keeping them? They weren't on this floor."

"Look—she's still got her dog."

Susan turned to make sure that Nan was not watching. No, she was still in bed, her face turned to the wall. She watched for a moment more, just to catch the rise and fall of her chest, then turned her attention back to the light-filled square.

The two Americans were being prodded forward. One of the young men behind them carried a rifle, the other a grenade. They stayed closed up, as if the old people might try to run. But neither of them can, she thought.

The horror of it was gradually overtaking the three spectators. They were quiet now. "What is he trying to do?" Moira muttered. "God—I wish I could see better. What does he look like? Is he smiling?"

"No," said Cook. "He's frowning."

Susan leaned against the casement, staring out.

Turning, far below, the tall figure pointed back at the couple, then confronted the uniformed men once more. There was renewed talk, then more shouting.

"They won't let it through."

"What?"

"The truck. The cordon has it. Harisah wants it."

"Or?" said Moira.

"I think that's what we're about to find out," said Michael, and raised his hand to shade his eyes from the sun.

The old couple, prodded forward, came to a halt a few feet away from the jeep. There was more talk, a lot of it.

Then, suddenly, Harisah stepped back. He made a sweeping gesture with his free arm.

The guard with the rifle raised it to Mr. Stanweis' silver hair.

"No, you bastard," Susan heard Cook whisper, beside her. Moira was muttering something under her breath, something long. And she herself stood frozen, horror under her heart like an iceberg that once congealed there would never melt. There in the heat, sweat running into her eyes, she felt the touch of death as surely as the old doctor, who stood stiffly, back bent but still dignified, the muzzle just behind his ear.

The tableau was still for a minute. And then, slowly, one of the officers in the jeep nodded.

Harisah nodded too, and the Palestinian behind the old man lowered his gun. Stanweis raised a shaking hand to his face. Susan thought then: He knew. Had known and had said nothing, done nothing. Just waited, for life to continue or end, there on the hot loneliness of asphalt, in a strange land, with his wife and dog.

"Thank God," she muttered.

"He'd have done it," said Cook, his voice tight. "He was ready. He was going to do it."

"I'm not sure," said Susan. "Maybe he just—"

"I think you're right, Mike," said Moira. "Jesus . . . let's close the fucking window. I can't watch any more of this."

"Wait. Here he comes."

A second jeep barreled across the square at top speed, canvas top fluttering, a battered blue panel truck not ten yards behind it. Both vehicles squealed to a stop beside the first. From the interior of the truck two men unwound themselves, hopped stiffly down to the pavement, and walked toward Harisah. When they met they hesitated for a moment and then shook hands, oddly formal.

Harisah turned then, motioning to his own men. "Junior," as they had taken to calling the boy terrorist, waved the truck by. It headed out toward the plane, raising a dun cloud as it bounced and wavered into the desert mirage. Behind it the party began to walk back to the hotel.

Halfway back they stopped. They stood in a close circle, for just a moment.

A white-haired figure broke away, into a shambling run, back in the direction of the jeeps.

"What the hell—" breathed Moira.

The shot cracked in the stillness like a breaking rope. Stanweis did not take the next step; instead he jerked forward. He moved twice on the hot pavement as a man eases himself in bed, small from their height, insignificant. The dog began to bark then, high and spoiled-sounding. It leapt from the woman's arms and ran across the empty square. Too stricken to speak, their eyes followed the moving animal, its little legs working too comically rapid for its speed, until it came to a bewildered stop above the old man's body.

"Ninety-three of us now," Mike Cook whispered, squatting beside them on the worn carpet of the corridor.

Susan patted Nan's hair, again and again, and said nothing. She was afraid. Even though she could see that her nervousness, the fear around them in the mass of refugees crowded under the eyes of their possessors, turned itself in the little girl's mind into terror, she couldn't argue or numb herself away from it any longer.

At least Nan had not seen it. Susan was glad of that. But though she'd been asleep something of it had communicated itself to her. Some change in the way people talked, or did not talk; some new vibration in the air too high for older eardrums. Susan remembered, a little, what it was like at her age. You were an antenna, but you did not understand what you received. You knew emotionally, perhaps as an animal knows, but you didn't know what it meant.

And knowing only that you were threatened, and were helpless, dependent, you were afraid. And so Nan huddled herself close against Susan, just as she had when she was tiny, and looked out at the people around her silently, with large frightened eyes.

"That's all? I thought there were more," Moira whispered.

"Counted them twice."

One of the guards detached himself from the wall and went over. "Quiet," he said to Michael, gripping him by the shoulder.

Cook shook off the hand. He said something just loud enough to hear.

"*Skhot'!*"

"Michael, for God's sake—"

Cook nodded and fell silent, looking at the carpet. The guard hesitated for a moment, watching them through hostile eyes, and then went back to the wall and leaned against it.

The captives were massed together, seated, in the second-floor corridor. Pushed and shouted out of their rooms, they had been forced close together, crammed thigh to thigh, for more than an hour. Now the heat, the closeness and smell, were becoming unbearable. Susan felt sweat drip from her chin, and wiped it from Nancy's cheek. Nan didn't move. Her mother's hand came away dirty. We're all filthy, Susan thought. Her skin itched.

Nan stirred uneasily. "Mommy—"

"Wait, baby. Be quiet." The guard was looking their way again. She hoped he did not understand Cook's muttered curse.

"Got to *go*. Go to the *bathroom.*"

"Wait, baby. You have to hold it this time."

"Go bad," the child whispered again, but obediently did not say anything more. She looked in a frightened way toward the guard who had shouted at Cook.

A few minutes later the waiting was ended by the ring of boots on concrete, the jingle of metal, and the chatter of voluble men. The stairwell door slammed open and several of the terrorists came out. All were armed. One of them was the Majd. Beside him, looking angry, were the men who had come that morning.

They talked among themselves for a few minutes. Then, with an abrupt, impatient gesture, Harisah stepped out, almost within the front row of sitting hostages.

"You Americans, you British," he said loudly, "you are being prisoner here. And now, because of the stupidity and arrogance of your governments you are in great danger. It's time for me to tell you why.

"These fighters, these men,"—he swept his arms around at the guards, who straightened—"are *mujahiddin,* fighters for the freedom of Palestine and the unity of all Arabs. They aren't paid; they fight of their free wanting because they have nothing left but guns. They fight against injustice of the invader. The Jews have taken our country and oppress our brothers. And America arms them against all of Islam.

"They are here to fight this, to regain freedom for our comrades and justice for the Palestinian people. They will do it here more surely than in the front lines.

"We fight also, shoulder to shoulder with the others who battle for freedom, against those whose puppets the Turks are; against American injustice and imperialism."

He paused, putting his hands behind him, a little grandiloquently, Susan thought. He strolled to the window and looked out. Every eye followed him. He's had training in speaking, somewhere, she thought.

She noticed then, half-amused and half-horrified, that for a moment she had felt proud of him.

He turned, and his face had become dark. "Believe me, I do not like to shed blood. If your government had been reasonable you would all be safe. But now our friends tell us the imperialists have tricked us. They talked; and talked; and now the American marines are landing in Lebanon."

He paused, waiting perhaps for a response from them; but none of the crouched hostages moved.

"They will not reach here, whatever they intend. We

will use you to stop them, to drive them out. How? The same way we wanted to use you to release the freedom fighters they hold prisoner. It will work; we have proved this already. The Turks did not wish to talk. Now, under American pressure, they are meeting with our leadership in Yemen.

"When that is done, we go on to remove all the Jews from Palestine, the same way."

"*All* the Israelis?" she heard Cook whisper. "That's not even PLO doctrine. These guys are some radical fucking splinter—"

"Goddammit, Mike, not now," hissed Moira.

Harisah paced back and forth. "You may say, how will we do this? We started by taking the embassy. But now that the Americans are taking foolish risks we must go further. How? By harsh measures."

He paused again, but no one said anything, no one gasped, no one moved. The flies buzzed sleepily above his captive audience.

"I have carried out the first execution. The Syrians have been told that there will be another at nightfall. This is for transmission to your people. Another at dawn. Another at noon tomorrow. This will continue until our demands are met. When the Americans withdraw and our men are released, executions cease. When our comrades arrive here with us, or at one of our camps, we disappear one night, and you all go free.

"Executions will be carried out in the square, in view of witnesses, among whom will be the American and Turkish ambassadors to Syria and any news persons who may wish to come."

"This is crazy," Cook whispered tensely. "He can't mean this. The Turks are busy in Cyprus, and a new regime isn't going to start out by knuckling under to foreign terrorists. They've got enough of their own. No way."

"Goddammit, Cook, *shut up.*"

"To help this plan work faster," Harisah went on, raising his eyes to them, "you are going to help me. You can save people of your group, perhaps yourself, by letting the British and Americans know that we mean what we are telling them. We have a recorder here. You will make tapes, speak to your families if you wish, or to the American authorities. We will deliver your messages at nightfall, before the second demonstration.

"And for that demonstration, I think"—he raised his arm high, pointing—"that tall young man in back, who talks while I am talking—"

"Michael! No!"

Moira punched wildly at the first guard to reach them, but the man simply pushed her over; off-balance, she fell into the other hostages. There was a tangle of arms and legs, shouting and crying. Cook did not struggle; he stood up, face paling, but not fighting the men who beat him out from the crowd with their rifle butts. The others shrank back as his guards pushed him forward. Harisah waited, looking grim, and then turned his head to speak briefly to the two men.

Susan sat rigid, unable to believe what was happening. She could not move, could not speak. She held Nan tight, and wondered that she did not whimper. She felt like whimpering herself.

"Goddammit—let me up. Mike! Mike!"

And then Moira was on her feet, running through the still-cleared path behind the guards. Cook turned at her shout. He started to wave her back, and then his arms were twisted behind him and he was pushed toward the stairwell.

Harisah nodded, and two men stepped in behind Moira. And at that Susan was up too, holding Nan tight and screaming: "Majd! Hanna! Not her, too!"

Harisah looked in her direction. As they caught hers his eyes became opaque, the gaze of a stranger.

"Of course," he said, "the Jewish woman may also die if she wishes."

And Susan sat, slowly, unable to think or speak. She lowered her eyes. Fear and guilt rose in her throat. She had thought, somehow, that her sacrifice would protect them. But it had not been a bargain. What had Moira said—you can't bargain with a terrorist—

She did not want to look at him again, ever.

Harisah looked around, at all of them. "There; you see I mean this business. Now you can go back to your rooms. Do not open the windows. Do not leave rooms. The guards will bring the recorder to you there."

He paused, looking toward the stairwell. From the open door a shout floated up, but so faint that she could not tell whether it was Michael or Moira, or even a man or a woman. The Majd's scowl deepened. He turned from the stairwell to them.

"You should know me well enough by now to know that the Majd does not lie, he does not bluff. Make your messages convincing. It is the only way any of you will escape death."

30
Northern Lebanon

THE WAY TO ASH SHUMMARI WAS A
storm of noise, sunlight, heat, and dust.

From the high safety of outcroppings of white limestone
an occasional lone figure—a shepherd, perhaps—could be
seen looking down on the narrow, winding road, clinging
to the hills like a snake to its prey, that had made its way
from village to village across this ancient land since Hel-
lenic times, since Cretan times, since before there was a
Bible.

The marines in the van of the raid saw Lebanon that
morning in an hours-long, jolting blur of speed and heat.
They saw it with the clarity of fear at twenty-five miles an
hour, more on the downhills; saw it with the hollowness
in the belly that comes expecting attack at any moment.
They did not talk. They did not watch the road. They
watched the hills that marched with their progress,
watched ceaselessly the white-shuttered windows of the
villages they sped through in a clatter of treads, a howl of
engines.

Will Givens saw it holding desperately tight to the
welded manholds on top of an amtrac, so sun-hot he could
barely close one hand on them. In the other he gripped his
M-16, empty, but with a magazine ready in the unbuttoned pocket of his blouse. His boots dangled over the
edge of the rolling tank, over the terrifying squeal of bo-

gies. Beneath him, beneath the other riflemen (for that was all he and the rest of the mortar squad were now, riflemen) who clung to the top of the amphibious tank, the engine roared as if designed to deafen them, and steel treads clawed sparks from the stone. Behind them came a jeep, then another amtrac, and then a long string of them.

Three-two MAU was on its way to battle.

The squad had waited out dawn dug in at the LZ. Some time after sunrise the rumble of artillery to the south brought a renewed tension to their breakfast of cold rations. As they waited, since no one had any clear idea of what was happening, they began to invent scuttlebutt. The Syrians were good soldiers; no, they were bums; the Israelis had chewed them up a dozen times. The Russians would be waiting for them across the border; no, they would pull out and leave the terrorists to face the music; no, the Soviet Navy would sink the amphibs behind them and cut them off here in a blazing Chosin. At first they passed the rumors as a joke, but some gained the sound of truth. Will had listened to them with a hollow feeling, gripping his rifle and wishing again he had been able to zero it.

At 0730 the lead amtracs had rumbled up from seaward and the squad had clambered aboard with the rest, leaving their dug-in positions with a feeling already of regret.

Will clamped the rifle, still unaccustomed to it, in the crook of his arm. His hand came away from his face gray-white with caked dust and sweat. He could not believe how much dust there was. It came up like smoke from the 'tracks in front of the column, mixed with diesel fumes in an oily stink that overlay the warm smell of the land. He grabbed hastily at the weapon as it started to slide; they were jolting over a particularly atrocious section of road, nearing a town. People . . . there must have been thousands of them along here, he thought, not long before. But now the invading marines looked fleetingly down alleys where golden heaps of oranges lay in rotting piles, where laundry flapped sun-dried but forgotten.

Stores gaped blank-fronted, their windows empty, those that had not been shuttered or barred. There were no cars, there were no people, there weren't even any dogs. As he blinked past Cutford's shadowed bulk he saw that the buildings they were passing now—taller, the city center—were hulks, shattered by shellfire. . . .

He stared around from the 'track, forgetting fear, seeing what war had done to Lebanon.

It might have been any of the resort towns along the coasts of the blue Mediterranean. Towns the ships had sailed by, or dropped anchor at briefly, not permitting the men ashore. It might have been downtown Palermo, the better section. It looked most like Greece, though.

Or must have once. The buildings had been new, in light colors. But now the modern fronts stared empty and the terraces were filled with smashed brick and glittering shards from the empty windows. The black stains of fires stood above them like eyebrows. The streets had been wide here, lined at ground level with shops and offices. Now piles of shattered masonry leaned outward, closing half the road, and the windows were blank and the shops were empty and the cars, those that were left, lay like the husks of long-dead insects: burnt, overturned, flattened by fallen walls. The very air was disquieting, heavy with smoke and the cave-smell of shattered plaster and the chemical stink of recent explosive.

It was the smell of ambush. He shivered and craned round, maintaining his deathgrip on the hot metal, to look for the others. Hernandez; Harner, looking sleepy, stretched out against the gunner's cupola on the opposite side of the vehicle; Silky, seated facing aft, his helmet pulled low to screen his eyes from the sun; Cutford, sleeves rolled over heavy muscle, his face lifted toward the upper windows of a four-story apartment block as they rolled by. Washman wasn't aboard, but Will could make out his pale face, open mouth, through the dust, on the next 'track back.

And Dippy Liebo. Where was he?

He decided not to think about that right now. It was too freaking hot; he felt sick from the motion and the jolting, and he had to stay alert. With that thought he realized suddenly what Cutford was looking for, and the knowledge, coupled with the slow thunder early that morning, made him sit up straighter and try to blink the dust and sun from his eyes. Maybe you'll see some action today, Will, he thought. Somehow the prospect was less appealing than it had seemed in boot camp. Or even that morning, on the ship.

Have I any pleasure at all that the wicked should die? saith the Lord God; and not that he should return from his ways, and live?

Above them, between the building-fronts that walled off the road, a plume of smoke blinked from the hillside. He tightened his grip on the rifle, staring upward; it was dust, not smoke, streaming behind a single vehicle that paralleled their progress along the lower road. A flank guard, most likely. He craned left to look past Cutford's shoulder down into the valley and saw, yes, a left flank of two jeeps and a 'track below on the dry bed of a river. They stopped as he watched, and men leaped out to clear something from the path; then they rolled on again, the 'track taking the lead, tiny as a green bug from his height.

The lights on the tank ahead glowed red as it slowed for a curve so sharp the vehicle ahead of it had disappeared. He opened his mouth, but the pause of thought made speech too late, even if the driver could have heard him. He got his legs up just in time. Inertia jerked him forward, almost tearing his arm off, and the hull of the 'track bonged as its snout collided with the rear of the one in front. Glass shattered above the diesels, and when they moved again he saw that their headlights had been crushed flat. Too much noise for communication, even in a shout, but when he glanced back his eyes met Hernandez'; that was enough, to share it with someone else.

He faced forward again and stared up at the corner building as they edged around it, backing and filling to get past. He inspected each window, watching for movement, for shadows; and beside him the corporal did the same. Though no one stirred behind the dust-filled glass he still felt the coldness.

But if ye will not obey the voice of the Lord, but rebel against the commandment of the Lord, then shall the hand of the Lord be against you.

By noon they were deep into the hills, and still had seen nothing and no one. The only sign of human life had been a crack-windowed Mercedes full of local militia, who hastily pulled onto the berm when the lead amtrac came barreling down the middle of the road toward them. The terrain became steeper after that. The ancient folding of the land grew more violent, less welcoming, if any of it was welcoming, until the left flank dropped back out of sight. The villages they clattered through became smaller, the buildings older, and then they were in the mountains and there were no more villages at all.

The road stayed good, though. It was a new-looking two-laner, and they could see at curves where the rock had been blasted away in white gouges and left to fall toward the river. From atop the 'track the view was dizzying. The elevation was no greater than he was used to back in Western Carolina, but here the hills were unrounded, unclothed with green; they fell precipitously, eroded faces of bare white rock, gullies with thin brown grass over what soil had not been leached away. To him it looked ancient, blasted, barren. The open sky blazed blue light down over them, shimmering the asphalt with heat, the breeze of their motion offering no coolness but only drying their eyes and parching their open mouths. The roar of their engines echoed back from the faces of the hills until it seemed that an army, not half a battalion, was winding its way upward into the highest passes of Lebanon.

It was a little after midday, and the feeling of danger, of threat, had worn thin. They were toiling in column up a long grade, the overheating engines whining. He was clutching his M-16 between his legs and sipping at his canteen between jolts, letting it swing with his arm so that not a drop of the hot fluid would be lost, when the first detonation sounded far off and faint beyond the top of the hill.

The mortarmen knew it instantly. Silkworth twisted round in the frozen instantaneity of surprise. Givens dropped his canteen, the water slopping warm over his thighs and crotch, leaving a dark streak down the dusty green hull of the track. It bounced once heavy off the roadway and then splintered, crushed, flattened by the rolling steel of the treads. Cutford slammed his riflebutt on the hull, swinging himself down to the roadway as the 'track began to slow.

"Incoming!"

The first round exploded below them, down along the drop of the ravine, blasting rock and dust outward through the clear air. The column slowed, 'tracks slewing sideways trying to stop in time, slamming into one another, crushing in the fenders of jeeps as officers scrambled out. Horns beeped and echoed from the hill. The distant thunking of several more rounds on their way precipitated a general dismount and a scramble for a shallow ditch against the upward slope.

"Mortars," he said stupidly to Hernandez, whom he found beside him, leaning against the bare hot stone. "They sound just like our eighty-ones."

"Man, we shoot back?"

"Can't see anybody to shoot at."

"Well, let's get some fire out, man. Get their heads down maybe."

He watched Hernandez pull a loaded magazine from his trou, and it was suddenly the obvious thing to do. They were shooting at you; you fired back. The click of the thirty-round magazine engaging, the slam of the bolt feeding the first cartridge sent stiffness into his spine. With a loaded weapon in his hand he felt like a marine and not like what he had been all that morning—half-tourist, half-target. Behind him one of the 'tracks loosed a burst from its turret machine gun. Craning his head back, he could see it tear puffs of stone from the upper curve of the hillside.

"They're on the far side."

"Yeah. They got us in defilade. Nice setup."

"For them."

"That's what I meant. Wish we had the tube here."

"Yeah, toss a few back . . ."

"But we don't," shouted Silkworth, just behind them, startling them so that Will almost dropped his rifle. "You two fuckups leave your brains on the ship? Spread out under fire! Christ! Hernandez, clamp that chinstrap, you're losing your helmet. Givens—"

He ducked suddenly, the two privates half a second behind him to the ground, and the whoosh came down on them and exploded ahead of the lead 'track. Rocks rattled off the hull and skittered along the asphalt toward the stalled column. The shock patted his face and he raised his hand to it, coming a little out of the numbness and unreality that had begun the moment that first faint chug had come from the other side of the mountain.

"Eighty-one all right," said Silkworth loudly into the aftersilence, pulling himself to his feet.

"Sarge—is it Syrians, or Lebanese?"

Silkworth stared at him as if he were crazy. "I don't know, and I don't give a shit. Do you?"

He had to admit it, the sergeant had a point. He pulled back his head and looked up toward the crest. Nothing showed on the ridgeline. He looked back along the road. Two of the 'tracks had maneuvered almost to the cliff-edge, cupola MGs at maximum elevation, and were firing tentative bursts into the blue. The foot marines, all disembarked except the men actually inside the 'tracks, leaned in the ditch next to the hill-slope, looking upward.

Another shell exploded into dusty life, still below them, but closer than any before it. Fragments whicked past. "Jesus Christ," said Silkworth angrily, looking back along the column. "They're bracketing us. We just going to sit here? Sooner or later one of them motherfuckers is going to hurt somebody."

A jeep edged around the firing amtracs, between them and the hillside. A man in back pointed a flexible 7.62 upward, his eyes white in a dust-smudged face. As it neared them, Will recognized the man beside the driver: the Colonel. He had seen him only a couple of times, but he had a face you didn't forget. At this moment he looked interested, but not excited. The jeep squeezed past their 'track, scraping metal to metal, and went fifty yards farther up the road; then stopped. Haynes stood up in the front seat, looking down into the ravine, and one of the officers ran up from the ditch, not saluting, and began pointing out where each shell had fallen.

The colonel pointed too, back up the hill, and then a flurry of faint thuds floated down to them and with no lag at all, as if the noses of the shells had distanced the sound of their firing; two flame-hearted tulips of smoke and dust leapt simultaneously out of the hillside fifty feet above their heads. The blue light of sky turned brown, dark, and dirt came down and rocks, flying free down among the crouching men, banging off the hulls of the tanks, which fired now steadily up into the dust. Will found himself firing too, blindly, and along the hill the other men lifted their weapons uncertainly.

"Knock it off," shouted Silkworth. "Save ammo, fuckheads. You can't see a thing. Hernandez! Put your safety back on."

"What's wrong with shooting back, Sergeant?"

"I didn't say to, that's what." Silkworth glanced toward the colonel, saw that he was still standing, still looking up at where the dust was settling toward the column. Anxiety came suddenly into the corners of his eyes. "Helos . . . he ought to call for gunships. Where are they? I haven't seen one all day. Air support . . ."

"Unless he know something you don't," said Cutford,

who had crawled up behind them while Silkworth was talking.

"What's that mean, Cutford?"

"I mean, they ain't gonna be no helos. No support. Why else they took away the mortars? No, man—this another of those fucked-up political actions. We just here to die, man, just here to die."

"Shut up," said Silkworth. "Just shut that up now, Corporal." He looked away.

The colonel sat down; the jeep's engine revved; the lieutenant ran back toward the lead 'track, his holster slapping, helmet bobbing. The mortarmen watched him run past them, watched as the colonel reached back to take a microphone that the gunner handed him.

"Into the 'tracks," the junior officer shouted to Silkworth, not stopping. "Get 'em in."

"We movin' on, Lieutenant?"

But he was gone, past, shouting and waving at the next knot of men huddled into the hillside. Silkworth looked back toward Haynes, then upward, squinting into the eye-clenching brilliance of the Mediterranean noon; hesitating, reaching out to hold Givens and Hernandez back as they started to stand up, so that they froze too, looking upward.

Thud. Thud. Thud. Thud.

"Jesus," breathed Will Givens, deep in his chest. He recognized the sound, not of one mortar, but of a battery of them.

Far above them, high up in the brilliance, tiny blacknesses, like steel tears wept by the sky hung turning, deciding; and then winked out.

"Disappear," shouted Silkworth, and Will hit the ground at his feet, scrabbling down into the deepest part of the ditch. More bodies slammed in on top of him. There was time only to hope desperately that the rest of the column had someone like Silkworth to warn them, and then the rounds went off, the sound not outside but within his head, like a train passing a foot away. The ground jolted and concussion cuffed at his chest. Things pattered and pinged above him, and in the middle of four explosions so close they were one explosion, someone began to scream. "Barrage," someone yelled above him, and he thought *Barrages yes they're firing in salvos now, not like we do but then this way you get to spot your fire as a group, you don't get confused between tubes the way we would;* and he knew, too, they must have someone spotting for them, someone on the far side of the road, on some bare crest, with binoculars and a radio—the radio probably just like theirs.

Shit, he thought. Shit. Shit. Jesus!

It all took about half a second, two seconds at the most, and then the roaring stopped and he was up and running for the 'tracks, stumbling over a fresh hole in the roadway, the stink of explosive cutting his lungs like one of Harner's Marlboros. The other men were running too, the ramps of the 'tracks were coming down. Two marines carried another between them, his feet dragging uselessly. He looked awake but dazed, and his boots left blood on the asphalt. At the head of the column, through the dust and smoke, he saw the colonel staring still upward, holding the handset absently away from him.

Will Givens hesitated on the ramp, looking back. He was looking at his first field of battle. He looked closely, seeing it all whole and clear; the men, the helpless vehicles, unable to turn on the narrow road, the striating clouds of blue smoke and white dust that tamped down the hot heavy air above the roadway.

The colonel stiffened and swung the handset toward his mouth, looking upward. Givens saw now, looking down at him from the ramp, that he held a map in the other hand. He leaned back, peering through the smoke. The amtracs had stopped firing. Whoever had been screaming stopped. In the sudden silence along the road all they could hear was the faint serial concussions of another volley beyond the hilltop, and a tinny voice quacking from the radio in the jeep.

"No, I can't spot," the colonel was shouting back. "Area fire. Area. It's rock up there, so HE's just as good as VT. As long as it goes in right now."

The tinny voice crackled back, and the marines waited, looking first at the man in the jeep, at his erect back, turned to the hillside, and then upward at the sky. Then the explosions came again, louder this time, and the ground shook and pieces of rock came loose from the cliff above them and slid downward.

"Get the *fuck* in here, Oreo, you idiot," said Cutford, appearing beside him.

"Let go of me."

"You want to catch a frag? Get your ass in here."

"What's happening, Cutford? Does he want artillery?"

"You listen with those ears, numbnuts? We got no arty ashore."

He understood then, and a shiver took him. He raised his eyes to the smoke that blew off the other side of the hill, from the hidden mouths of mortars, and felt suddenly how immense it all was, how vast was the machine that had put him here, deep in a ravine in Asia. Vast and unpredictable, vast and unknowable. Some distant decision-maker had placed a black private first-class here, like a checker nudged forward by an old man in the pine-smelling dimness of a lumberyard. But that anonymous counter was Will Givens, sometime guitar player, some-day engineer. The machine used him. Would it stand behind him? Or did it even know, recognize, that the man inside this uniform felt and knew just like the ones who sent him, suffered fear and yearning and desire?

The last men came running from the ditch, bent low, aiming themselves for the amtracs. Will recognized Washman's tubby figure, his lowered head. He was heading for the next 'track back. He craned out. "Washout!" he yelled.

The private looked up, pimply face dirt-smudged, and saw him and changed his direction.

Will was craning around the hatch of the 'track, watching him, when the volley hit the column. Five, six shells, dead on in range and spaced along the road. The hull of the LVT behind them vanished and in disbelief he saw bodies in the air, smoke, flame; it must have been a dead hit. Another went off at the same instant directly in front of him. The shock was so close and hard he was unable to move, only watch, frozen, as twenty feet away Washman straightened, arched forward, like a clumsy diver from the side of a pool, and then rolled to a bloody stop on the roadway. One side of his head had been blown free, left behind on the asphalt like a discarded rag.

"Washout!" he screamed, starting forward.

"Get in here, shithead!" Cutford shouted in his ear, jerking him back. He stared, unable to look away, as the ramp ground upward, cutting off the light. Something shoved him, something he dimly recognized as a heavy hand, and he stumbled back into the shelter of the amtrac.

The eyes of the others met his in the dimness, and huddling together they waited for the shells to fall.

31
U.S.S. *Guam*

LENSON STRETCHED IN HIS SEAT, LOOK-
ing across the crowded, bright compartment with a premonition of triumph. A fierce grin crimped the fatigue
lines tight around his eyes. He had forgotten his days
without sleep, forgotten the months at sea, forgotten Isaac
I. Sundstrom.

Urgent Lightning was rolling like a well-oiled machine.

The marines were solidly ashore, and moving rapidly
inland. Not a shot had been fired, and they had taken only
one casualty, a man who ran into a rotor during the helo
insertion. Lenson could hardly believe, even now, that
sitting deep in the steel vitals of the flagship he held a
handset that linked him with live men, real ships. He was
remembering all the times he, and the others with him,
had practiced this. The schools, the months of drills,
study, exercises.

Now it was for real—and it was working.

For the first hour after the leading elements crossed
their lines of departure, he had kept the whole team on the
edges of their chairs. The first wave to hit the beach had
rolled out of the amtracs and dug in instantly at the first
dune line, covering the troops in boats behind them. But
the beach was deserted. He had followed the cautious
probes inland, putting the wave commander's frequency
on a loudspeaker so that everyone in the compartment

could hear. But there was no resistance. No troops or even civilians were reported on the beach.

The second and third waves hit and moved quickly up to the front line, consolidating the initial toehold and then leapfrogging forward onto the beach road.

At 0700, when the mobile column, sorted out and remounted, launched itself inland toward Qoubaiyat, the atmosphere in SACC relaxed. Men slouched back in their seats. They stayed alert, but the excitement waned. Lenson laid down his phones and stretched, glancing at the map. They were by no means home, though the landing itself, the most vulnerable moment in an amphibious raid, had gone off well. But perhaps this would go more easily than they'd feared.

He rubbed his eyes and focused them on the chart, opening the operation order to check reported positions with those he had assigned for the postassault phase.

Ships first. The amphibs, empty now, were steaming slowly in separate boxes of sea ten miles out. To seaward of them *Virginia* patrolled; she was now at the northern edge of her area. Good; any Syrian air strike would come from that direction.

Farther inshore, the two escorts were lying to only a few thousand yards off the beach. *Ault* had reported in at 0700. He had swiftly established comms and briefed her gunnery team by radio. He felt far more confident now: Her arrival had quadrupled his seaborne firepower.

He blinked, and shifted his attention landward. The militias and regular army units that Byrne had sketched in from Sixth Fleet intelligence reports worried him. Several of them lay between the MAU and its goal. He knew that some of the positions and strengths reported were guesswork. And no one could predict their responses when faced by an unexpected body of fast-moving U.S. troops. Some of the Lebanese, the Maronite militias, should be friendly, or at least neutral. Even the Syrian-backed Shi'ites might not interfere—if the diplomats had done their job.

I'll worry about that when it happens, he thought. We've got our plates full here. He stretched again, feeling good, and thought for the first time that day about food.

At 0730 the column of amtracs from the beach reached the ALZ, and the two forces joined. Lenson relaxed a bit more. The heliborne troops probably hadn't realized it, but out on their own above the road, unable to move except on foot, they'd been prime targets.

Byrne, beside him, was staring into a pub and looking worried. Dan turned down the speakers and punched him lightly. "Jack, what's wrong? Somebody split an infinitive?"

"Real droll."

"What's that you're reading?"

"Intel summary on Syria."

"You're worried about them?"

"Aren't you?"

"They pay guys back in Washington to do that, I thought."

"I hope they do," said Byrne. "The action back at State must be fierce. Think about it. The obvious course would be to get word to Damascus that we'll be coming ashore this morning, that our target is the terrorists and only them, and that opposition will bring retaliation in overwhelming force. But they had to time it: allow them enough hours to warn their troops and client militias, but not tip our hand so far in advance that a leak would lose us the element of surprise when we hit the camp in the final assault."

"That's obvious?"

"Of course. But then, if you warn the Syrians, they might just as well decide to defend their border. In the last analysis, it might depend on which way the USSR, their protector, advisor, and overall Big Brother, tells them to jump. So if some junior Middle East expert makes the wrong decision—or makes the right one and the President overrules him, if *anybody* screws up, *anywhere* along the line . . ." He let his voice trail off.

"I get it now," said Dan grimly. "Instant powdered MAU."

"Or worse," said the intel officer. "If the Soviets back them up and we don't, or can't, back down. Why do you think we went to nuclear alert? I guarantee you, every missile boat we have at sea is checking its firing data right now."

Both of them looking worried now, they looked back at the map. And above it, the clock whirred on.

He was gnawing at a leg of cold chicken a few hours later, part of a box lunch sent up from the mess decks, when things began to go sour. He had his first intimation of trouble when Flasher stiffened and sat up, phone pressed to his ear. He was on the circuit to Haynes, near the head of the column.

Dan stiffened too, and laid the drumstick down. "Red— what is it? Damn it, pipe down, you guys."

Flasher waved his hand; wait. The buzz of conversation stopped, and men turned their heads to listen.

"Put circuit eight on the horn," Lenson said to McQueen.

When the speaker cut in, the tension in SACC snapped instantly back to high pitch. Every man in the room could hear the landing-force commander's deliberate voice firsthand. No. More than that. Lenson swept the table in front of him clear, pulled a fire form to him. They could hear the rattle of small-arms fire and the crunch of mortars, terrifyingly close. Every man in the room had reached for his handset then, by reflex, and so had Lenson; but at the last instant he snapped his selector switch to a dead portion of the spectrum.

"Goddammit," he shouted. "Everybody back to your own net. I'll handle this. Regular procedures!"

"Dan, I got two Intruders orbiting—"

"What's their fuel state?"

"Ten minutes."

"Christ. Mac! Where's Haynes' grid position? Leading

element?" At the map, the petty officer reached far into the hills, laid his hand on a curved segment of road. Lenson half-rose, squinting to make it out. "Forget it, Jack. It's too far inland now for them. We've got to use the guns."

"Use them, then."

"No," said Lenson again, still holding the switch closed. "Not yet. He hasn't requested it."

"He will," said Flasher.

Haynes did, then. Lenson screwed the handset into his ear; the circuit had gone faint for a moment. But the next words came through clearly.

"Overkill, this is Green Bench Leader. Call for fire. Indirect. Grid location, North, four three seven seven. East. Niner four zero zero. Fragmentation, variable time. Will control. Over."

"Green Bench, this is Overkill. Roger your call for fire." He scribbled. The pencil snapped and he dropped it and grabbed the next. "Indirect. Grid North, four three seven seven, East, niner four zero zero. Fragmentation, variable time, will control, over."

"Green Bench, roger, out."

"Mac! Check those coordinates!"

"Nothing on the map, Lieutenant."

"Double-check. No houses? No roads?"

"Bare ground, sir. Nothing but the other side of the hill."

"This has to be a test, Dan," said the intel officer urgently. "To see if we'll support them with force. Hold this for me," he snapped to one of the other men, handing off his handset. "Be right back." He shoved his way past chairs and ran out of the room.

"Let's get it on the air," said Flasher. He reached for the form.

"Hold it, goddammit, Red. We got to get Sundstrom's permission."

"Screw that, Dan! Those guys need cover!"

"I know. And they'll get it just as soon as I have the

commodore's chop on it." He bit at his lip and flipped the intercom on. "Flag bridge, SACC. Commodore, please, emergency."

A moment's pause, seeming like minutes, though it could not have been over four seconds; then Glazer's voice. "He's listening, sir. Go ahead."

"Commodore. Lenson here. We have a call for fire from Colonel Haynes. He's under attack."

Silence. Then, "Mr. Lenson, Commodore wants to know what kind of attack."

"Hostile fire, sir! We need clearance to use *Ault*'s guns."

Another pause, then, finally, Sundstrom's voice. Nice of him to push his own talk button, Lenson thought. "Dan. Let's all keep a cool head, now. That's what it's all about. Is this a serious situation? I'm not going to release heavy weapons just for snipers."

"It's not snipers, sir. Sounds like mortar fire."

"*Sounds* like? Better find out, Dan. A mistake here could get us in real hot water. I can't give permission to fire without knowing all the facts. I'm not going to fly off the deep end like that."

"God damn him," muttered somebody in the silent room. They were all quiet, listening to the dialogue over the intercom.

"Lieutenant," said McQueen, "Colonel Haynes wants an acknowledgment."

"Acknowledge. Tell him we're getting it cleared," Lenson said, very fast. To the intercom he said, "Sir, Commander Byrne—I mean, I believe they're testing us. If we don't respond, they've enough forces in the area to destroy the MAU. It's urgent that we support the troops ashore."

There was a moment's hesitation. Then, "I agree, Dan, to the utmost. You're preaching to the choir when you tell me that. But we have other requirements laid on us, too. This is a touchy situation, diplomatically. I have to bear that in mind. Call him back—call the colonel—and ask him for an estimate of the numbers and armament of the force he's encountered."

"Do it," snapped Lenson to McQueen; then, letting up on the "press to talk" lever, so that his voice would not reach the bridge: "Red, get on the net to *Ault*. Their callsign is 'Gunslinger.' Give them the target coordinates. Double-check those numbers and make them read them back! Have them load with VT, fuzed for air burst, but make sure they understand not to fire till they get a 'batteries released' from us."

"Roger," said the N-3.

Byrne came back, panting, and slid into his chair. He thudded a weighted briefcase on the table and began hauling out folders. "Jack," said Lenson, "double-check defilade fire for five-inch thirty-eight. Make sure trajectory for full-charge load will clear seventeen-hundred-meter hills at a range of twenty-nine thousand yards."

"Right. Dan—"

"Sir," McQueen interrupted, "Colonel Haynes says he can't see them. He doesn't know who they are. But they have at least four heavy mortars, and they've got the column pinned down. He can't advance till the road ahead is checked for mines. They're getting plastered there; he's got casualties. He wants fire now."

He could hear the mortars, booming out of the still-open circuit to the interior. He could hear the growl of amtrac engines, the rattle of rifles, sporadic, as if the marines were firing at random. Faintly, a thin tremolo over the bass of battle, a scream laced the still air of the room.

"Trajectory checks out okay," said Byrne.

"Right."

"Dan," said Flasher, very softly, and Lenson turned his head. Their eyes met across the room. "*Ault* reports ready. We ought to fire."

"No, Red," said Lenson, just as quietly. "You heard him. This is the commodore's decision, and he has to make it."

"Lieutenant Lenson?" said the intercom.

"Here, sir. Haynes estimates four mortars, sir, and that

means at least twelve men. Probably more to carry ammo."

"Can he see them?"

"No sir, he says he can't see them. They're over the top of a hill from him."

"What's on the other side of that hill, Dan? Has anybody bothered to think about that?"

Lenson bit back anger, focused dutifully on the chart, checking once more. "Nothing, sir. We double-checked the map. No houses or anything shown."

"But they could be there. A map doesn't show everything. I could be authorizing fire into a village. That's a favorite terrorist tactic, decoying our fire onto the population."

Lenson couldn't believe his ears. He recognized the familiar whine. Sundstrom was digging in. Next would come the bluster. He would deny everything, distrust everything they told him. He glanced at the men who watched him, and said weakly, "Sir, this is a new map. They don't build villages that fast in the hills of Lebanon."

Byrne was digging furiously in the briefcase.

"Let's send the air in for a look. Don't we have recon helos standing by? I can authorize that. Let's use those, Dan. Use your head."

"Sir, we don't have time. It would take fifteen or twenty minutes for them to get to—"

Byrne emitted a cry of triumph and shoved a photograph in front of him. He had circled an area in the upper right-hand corner. Peering close, Dan could make out a winding road, a cliff, a hilltop. The hillside beyond was bare, littered with rocks. A reconnaissance photo, taken from high altitude. The coordinates, neatly typed on the edge below the Top Secret marking, matched the map.

"Sir, wait a minute. Mr. Byrne just showed me a satellite photo. It's the hillside. There's nothing there."

There was a hiss from the intercom. He visualized Sundstrom's face, close over it, holding down the button. Surely that was enough. Surely—

"No," said the commodore. The suspicion was open in his voice now. "Byrne? He's not on my side, Dan. He's pulled the wrong picture. I'll guarantee that. No way I'll authorize fire on *his* say-so."

But Dan had stopped listening to him. He was listening to the speaker from shore. It was Haynes, sounding, for the first time, frightened.

"Commodore Sundstrom. Are you there, Ike? We need fire now. For God's sake, we need support. We need gunfire or air. These 'tracks don't have overhead armor and I don't have room to turn around. Ike, can you hear me?"

"Sir," he said into the intercom, "Colonel Haynes is asking you personally to fire."

There was no answer. The intercom clicked once, twice, and then came on again.

"Tell him I'm on the line to Admiral Roberts."

"Christ!" said Byrne. His face had gone white. "That's the mission. He's giving them up."

Flasher sat with the phone in his hand, staring at Lenson. McQueen stared. Everyone in SACC was looking at him. Slowly, he released the switch.

What should he do?

All his life he had tried to do what was right. What was right now?

"Flag bridge, SACC. Commodore, we need you down here, right now."

"He's on the radio, Dan. He says to wait." Stan Glazer's tight voice came back.

Lenson hesitated for another long moment, looking back at the eyes; and then he reached out.

He turned down the speaker. The sound of gunfire, detonations, faded into the still air, faded into the metal of the bulkheads. And one by one, he watched each pair of eyes go distant, go far away, and then drop or turn aside as each officer and enlisted man in turn shifted in his chair, looking away, looking down.

They were sitting like that, quiet, all of them staring up at the point on the map where a red arrow marked the last position of the MAU, when the hatch ground open. Lenson turned.

It was the commodore. He was in fresh khakis, open at the neck, his eagles gleaming silver. He paused in the hatchway for a moment, then came two steps into SACC, looking up at the map.

"Sir?" said Lenson.

"He can't authorize fire without clearance from above," said Sundstrom. He stared at the map as if drugged. And no one else said anything.

"*Sixth Fleet* can't, sir?"

"He has his orders," said Sundstrom. His voice sounded dead. "Just like I do. Just like we all do, Dan."

"Sir, we can't wait for them to kick it all the way up to the White House and back. Let's put a few rounds in, at least. Whoever's firing might pack up if they think we're spotting, going to pour it on in a minute."

"I can't give permission for that."

"Sir, you're responsible for this landing—"

"Goddammit," shouted Sundstrom suddenly, lowering his head from the map. "I said no! I have direct orders, no heavy fire, no tactical air on the beach!"

"Sir," said McQueen softly, "The colonel says the mortars have the range."

Flasher stood up then, shoving back his chair. He swung himself over the desk, heavily, landing next to Lenson. He held out his hand. "Give me the handset."

"No, Red."

"Mr. Flasher! Get back to your post."

"Commodore, I'm giving that order, if you won't." Flasher's voice was quiet, no trace of anger, no trace even of strain. Lenson felt admiration and terror. He looked up at the two men, face-to-face, the lieutenant and the commodore; one heavy, sloppy, his uniform pulled out at the shirttails; the other crisp and neat, tailored, self-controlled only with great effort; looked up at them both. . . .

"Sit down, Mr. Flasher," said the commodore again.

"Lieutenant Lenson—the colonel is asking for you on the line," said McQueen.

Lenson picked up the handset. He turned the selector dial, clicking it from net to net. He stopped at one, began to depress the talk button, and then let it up. He looked at Sundstrom's face, at the sweat that had suddenly sheened his forehead.

He turned the selector one more notch.

"This is Overkill," he said. "Batteries released."

Flasher started. Both he and the commodore looked down together, toward him. He depressed the button again, watching the transmit light wink on, forcing himself this time to speak slowly and distinctly. "Gunslinger, this is Overkill: I authenticate, juliet romeo. I say again, batteries released. Out."

"Dan," said the commodore.

"It's done, sir," he said, and as if to underline his words a tremor came through the steel of the ship, carried through the sea and through the metal hull up to vibrate faintly under their feet.

"I told you not to fire," said Sundstrom. 'Goddammit, I told you not to fire!"

"We had to, sir."

"I gave him the order, sir. I'll take the responsibility," said Flasher.

"That's immaterial. Order them to cease fire. Right now! Do you hear me?"

"Yes sir," said Lenson automatically, but though his fingers jerked he did not lift the handset. The guns slackened for a moment—that would be the first salvo gone—and then picked up again in a continuous fusillade, like the drumming of rain on a metal roof.

The shells were going out . . . he visualized their flight, fifty pounds each of steel and trinitrotoluene hammering out of the stubby barrels of the old destroyer in great pyrocellulose flashes of light and dirty smoke, traveling upward and inland at two thousand feet per second. Crossing the beach still headed up, spinning, as the next salvo came up from the magazines and slammed into the smoking breeches. Spinning, spinning . . . the glass-cased batteries smashed into life by acceleration, the complex and sensitive fuzes waking into their brief span of consciousness, suddenly deadly. Then the peak, high over Lebanon; the bitter brown of dry land whirling by beneath them; and then the descent. Range, twenty-nine thousand yards; time of flight, forty-three seconds. And then the fuzes, plunging downward, would sense solidity, earth. Calculating instantly the time of their remaining life, they would send a tiny current back through their metal bodies. . . .

A rumble came through the speakers, and he reached out to turn it up. The commodore, who had gone quiet, lifted his head to listen.

"They sound close," said Flasher.

Sundstrom said, "You're firing right over their heads. If *Ault* has a short round—"

"I told them to shoot long and walk them up, on his direction."

It was as if Haynes could hear them; the colonel came on the circuit then, his voice exultant. *"Overkill, Green Bench Leader; that sounded close! Drop two hundred, go to rapid continuous fire. I can't spot exactly from here, but keep them coming."*

"Give him a roger, Jack," said Lenson. He did not look up at the silent commodore, but he could feel his eyes.

"Lieutenant, we have two more aircraft reporting in on my net. Full tanks, full racks of ordnance. Should they orbit?"

"No. Send them in. Dogleg to the east, tell them we have naval gunfire going in, max ordinate five thousand feet."

"Aye."

"Report to Haynes for direct support, Tacair Net, when they're in range."

"Aye, sir."

It was done and irrevocable. He looked up then, words struggling against each other for his lips; then, together, they died away, leaving him voiceless. He could not justify what he had done. Successful or not, that did not matter. Whether it was right or not did not matter. He had defied a senior officer. He and Sundstrom looked at each other for a long, silent moment. Neither spoke. His hand began to shake, and he set the handset down, feeling it rattle on the desk before he let it go. Haynes' jubilant voice talked on over the net, but he did not hear it. From somewhere a fragment came into his mind; something he had memorized, long before, at the Academy.

Every law is as naught beside this one:
Thou shalt not criticize, but Obey. . . .

He saw the commodore's hand on the desk before him. It, too, was trembling. Before he could speak Sundstrom said in a low voice, "I hope you don't regret this, Mr. Lenson. All of your life."

"I don't think—"

"You will."

Byrne stood up then. "Tell him, goddamn it! I'm not keeping quiet any longer."

He stared at them. From the way they looked—

Byrne leaned forward. He spoke quickly, his eyes riveted to Lenson's. "Dan, your wife and kid are in Ash Shummari. They were taken hostage in Cyprus with the others. *He* ordered us not to tell you. He thought it would affect your performance."

For a moment he almost laughed, staring at them. Then he saw from Sundstrom's averted eyes that it was true. The disbelief, then the numbness, lasted only a moment.

He felt himself begin to shake. He had been ready to apologize, explain; but now it dissolved in anger white-hot and uncontrollable. He stood suddenly, and the commodore started back. Speech ran now through his mind, angry, lashing words. He wanted to say you bastard, you liar, coward, liar; but the strange control and separation that had always affected him in anger, sliding down smooth and deadening as a fire-curtain, separated him then from the rage, left him cold and observing.

Aloud he only said, in a voice that sounded to the men around them toneless and inhumanly controlled, "Sir, you do not deserve your rank."

A moment later that control broke; but by then he was at the hatchway. It slammed open against the stops. Then it was empty, the door swinging slowly back to latch with the slow roll of the hove-to ship. The men in SACC did not look at Sundstrom, who sat motionless by the desk, one hand still raised and forgotten before him.

After a soundless moment Flasher picked up the handset. "Green Bench Leader, this is Overkill," he said slowly, staring right at Sundstrom. "Over."

"Green Bench, over."

"Has hostile fire ceased? Over."

"Green Bench. That's affirmative. Over."

He clicked the dial. "Gunslinger, this is Overkill," he said steadily into the bright and silent room. "Cease fire. I say again, cease fire. Your mission is complete."

32
Ash Shummari, Syria

THE SQUARE WAS FILLED WITH LIGHT like a mountain pool with water. And as the pool in its depths turns the clear stream by mysterious alchemy to blue, so the afternoon sunlight, trapped between the silent buildings under a cloudless sky, turned to heat. The pavement shimmered, seemed on the point of melting. The boiling light of buildings, desert, the distant mountains eddied upward into her brain.

Susan leaned out over the balcony, feeling the love of the immense earth begin the acceleration of her body. Leaning forward, only a pressure of her hands holding her back, she stared down to where the old doctor's body lay crumpled and irrelevant as a discarded tissue.

But she was not seeing it. She was remembering another hot day, years before.

It had been a year after Nan was born. Dan's ship was back from deployment, and her parents were glad to sit Nan while they drove to Atlantic City for the time together that she always wanted, but that the Navy never seemed to want them to have.

But that weekend, as if by magic, they were alone. They found a motel south of the resort strip and walked to the beach in the same dizzying heat, the same silence. The sky had opened overhead in the same way, and there had been the same sense of expectancy, of waiting.

They had walked alone for an hour. The flat brightness of the Atlantic glittered beyond the dunes, edged with a litter of wrack and driftwood. Behind them, inland, stretched a neglected tangle of scrub pine, thorns, and wild grapevine.

She had not really been surprised when he had led her downward, neither of them interrupting the heavy stillness, their feet sliding in hot sand. There were shadowed caverns under the vines. Hot, sand-floored grottoes where pale sand crabs scuttled back, claws raised like kung-fu masters. She had not wanted to lie down. She was afraid of ticks. But at last she had, and then, a little later, given him what he wanted: a wordless token of her loss of self; and then he had lost himself too, shouting hoarsely above her into the bright empty sky.

And the brightness remained with her a long time, seared into her eyes as she lay staring upward, into the all-seeing sun.

A faint grumble came from the distance, from somewhere beyond the hills. She shaded her eyes and looked, but there was nothing to see. Nothing moved below her. The watching jeep, she realized, was gone. The distant bass muttered on for some minutes, individual detonations at first, then running together into the continuous rumble of an alpine avalanche.

Again, again, again, she thought angrily and wearily. When would men finish their madness? When would this end—and how?

Behind her, a child began to cry.

When she closed the window Nan was sitting up, watching her. Her eyes were preternaturally dark, the pupils widened till the irises all but vanished. The bare mattress creaked as Susan sat beside her. The guilt and the terror she felt as she smoothed her daughter's hair made her feel faint. Her child was ill and helpless. Totally dependent on her. And that, at last, was what decided her.

"Bunny, Mom's got to go downstairs for a few minutes." Her voice sounded faint in the thin hot air. "You won't mind staying here alone for a little while, will you? You won't cry? You won't go out?"

Nan's eyes did not alter. For a moment Susan wondered what this was doing to her; what nightmares, what vein of dark terror was being laid down that she would carry all her life. Then she thought, It's not my fault. I've done all I can to protect her. More, I know now, than I should have. I will have to depend on her for the rest.

"Nan? Did you hear me? I—"

"I heard you, Mommy. I be quiet. You come back, won't you?"

"That's right, Bunny. I promise." She crossed her heart solemnly and pushed her hair back. "Want anything before I go?"

"No."

"I've got someone I have to talk to. Maybe he can help us."

"Daddy?" she suggested, without hope.

"No."

The child said nothing more then. After a moment Susan bent and kissed her, tasting the sweet salt, and went out of the room. Halfway to the stairwell she remembered that she was filthy, unkempt, her T-shirt soaked through with sweat; but she threw her hair back again and went on anyway. There was nothing to be done about it. There was one guard in the stairwell, lighting a cigarette. He looked startled to see her, and grabbed for his rifle, coughing the cigarette out of his mouth.

"I want to see Harisah," she said, spacing the words so that he might understand.

"Harisah? El-Majd?"

"Yes."

He did not say anything more, simply looked at her stupidly, so she shoved by him and went down. Her thongs flapped on the stairs. The stairwell stank of urine. They've been doing it right here, she thought. Disgust and fear slowed her for a moment at the foot of the stairs, but then she took a breath, lifted her head, and went out into the lobby.

Crowded through it the morning before, she had seen it only briefly; had gained a confused impression of luxury long abandoned. But now she could see that the lobby, the carpet, was littered with trash. Crumpled plastic and bits of metal and empty glasses lay around a Russian-style water machine. Its coin mechanism gaped open, unlocked with a bullet. Razored fragments of mirror snapped beneath her feet. Crumpled cigarette packs, heels of bread and empty juice bottles lay about the lobby.

Across it, by the propped-open entranceway, she saw the men. They were standing under the portico. Their backs were to her; they were watching the airstrip and the desert beyond. They all held guns. As she stood there, waiting, another rumble came in faintly from the mountains. For a moment she fancied it seemed closer than before.

She moved forward, glass cracking underfoot. And then she stopped again.

He stood at the center of a group of his men, hidden from her before by a corner of the building. He was talking to the others. He gestured; none of them moved. He shouted, made violent blows of his fist in the air. She wished she could understand the Arabic. His listeners shuffled their feet on the dirty marble of the steps. They glanced toward the mountains, at each other, and then, as if drawn, back toward the leader, as if they could not take their eyes from him or their attention from his impassioned speech.

Susan waited alone, in the middle of the empty lobby. She felt tired, but unafraid.

At last the group broke up. He was second through the door. His head lifted and a wary look took his face as he saw her.

"Go upstairs."

"I came down to talk to you."

"I can't help you."

"I want you to talk to me."

"We have nothing to say."

"Oh, yes we do." She took a breath. How to make him listen? She remembered something Dan had told her. His "command voice," the tone he used aboard ship when he gave orders. Another of the inanities they taught him at Annapolis, she had supposed.

"Look, you bastard. You're going to talk to me, and now. First, I want to know why you took my friends."

"Oh," he said. His expression changed. He glanced backward, then nodded unwillingly. "In there."

My God, she thought, *it works.*

The bare walls of the stairwell echoed, and she lowered her voice, remembering the guard above. The *za'im* leaned against the wall, his eyes on his feet. He looked hostile, like a man cornered by a debtor who asks for more.

"Hanna—this is not right, what you're doing."

"I think you do not understand what is going on here. I am a fighter. This is a war for our country."

"I don't care what it is. This isn't the way to fight." She took a breath; no anger, no emotion now; she had to be calm, she had to reason with him. "Yesterday you shot, your men shot, a doctor, a harmless old man. Today you're going to shoot two archaeologists, one of them a woman. This is a war? Wars are fought between armed men. You think that's going to make the Turks release your men? That's going to make the Jews leave Israel? Not a chance. This isn't even terrorism, Hanna, because it hasn't any chance of working. It's just murder."

He kept looking at his shoes. He scowled.

"Hanna—"

"Ma kint lazim hinte'i."

"What the hell does that mean?"

"I should not have made love to you."

"What?"

"It was not a right thing to do."

She saw suddenly, and cursed herself for not seeing it before: what his reluctance and averted face meant. He was an Arab. To him, now, she was just a whore, a soiled piece of female flesh. A sudden need to laugh hysterically came over her. She glanced up the stairwell, its dimming upward flights, and had a sudden feeling that this was, had to be, unreal; arguing with this stranger, this terrorist, the same way she did with her husband; having him turn guilty and perverse on her, the way Nan did sometimes. . . . "Look," she said, forcing her feelings inside somewhere. She put her hand on his arm, feeling at the same moment his heat and the trickle of sweat along her own ribs. "Leave that aside, what happened last night. Just listen.

"I don't know what these other men, this committee, are telling you to do. But these are *your* men. Not theirs. You can refuse to go on with this. They tell you to do it now, but when—when peace comes, you'll be a criminal."

"It is my duty," he said, turning his eyes upward, away from hers.

"Duty doesn't mean murder! Someday you'll make a mistake, and they'll catch you and hang you. Terrorists don't live long, whoever wins. And I don't—I don't want you to die."

She could not say herself, now, how much of what she was saying was true. And it didn't matter. She would say anything, do anything, if it worked.

"I don't care about my life. If the party says that what we do will win us back Palestine, that it will bring the Revolution one day closer, then it is my duty to do it."

Duty. The word rang heavy in the stairwell. Where had she heard it before? "But this is crazy," she said again, then stopped. She was failing. It was true, what Moira said; they were too imbued with hate to see reason. Or what an American saw as reason, anyway, she reminded herself.

There remained only one way, and it was easy; so easy that she felt ashamed, both for her and for him. She reached up slowly to brush his dark hair back. He stirred at her touch, but still looked down, away, not at her.

She drew his lips downward to hers, and felt him resist. Resist; and then yield.

They stood together in the heat and stench of the stairwell for a long time.

"You'll let me talk to my friends, at least, won't you?" she asked him at last.

He took his hands away from her, nodding, looking relieved. She followed his broad back, wanting to touch the patch of sweat between his shoulder blades, out into the lobby. They went past the desk and down a short hall to a door marked *établissement* in faded lettering. A guard, the youngest one, stood up from a squat as the Majd came up, grinning and giving him a half-salute. Although he carried a rifle it still shocked her a little to see one so young with a cigarette in his mouth.

"He's in here," said Harisah. "They both are. Now I have to go. Things may be happening soon. Go back to your room when you're done with your friends. Go back to your little girl. Susan—"

"What?"

"I may not see you again."

"What do you mean?" She glanced at Junior; he was still grinning, glancing from her to his leader, but it was evident from his expression that he did not understand their words.

"The Syrians have left. I think that means we may be attacked soon."

"Attacked—" she stopped.

"If we are," he said somberly, "I will fight till I and all my men are dead. That is *sharaf*—honor. I became a soldier, a fighter, to fight this battle. There are others in our party than those here. You see? If we fight here, even if we lose, we strengthen them for next time. And we may win. I can die for that. I have to; I have promised."

So neat, so wrapped up, she thought. There's no way he can lose, even if he dies. And abruptly she felt angry. It was so fucking masculine. Soldier or terrorist, it was all the same. "Duty" and "glory" and "victory," and meanwhile people dying, with families, with dreams of their own. Or just people . . . like old Stanweis. And Moira. And Cook.

And he was so eager, not just to take the lives of others, but to give his own. That was the tragedy.

"Yes, I see," she said, forcing a smile. "But if you think we'll be attacked—what happens to us? Can't you let us go? Won't you? For me?"

He hesitated for a long time. Then he said, "I wish . . . I wish now I had done that. But I was angry. I can't now. Not in front of my men."

"Won't you at least think about it? If we're attacked?"

"I will think about it."

"Thank you," she said. "Thank you. Thank you."

"But one more thing," he said.

She waited, in the close air of the corridor, smelling him and herself.

"If fighting starts here, stay in your room. Understand? There are men like Ihab"—he jerked his head back toward the boy—"and the man I punished, who have been told that you are our enemies; and I cannot be everywhere. *Don't* come down to help your friends. Don't come down to the lobby. Wait till it is over, until it stops. If we win, I will come and find you. If we lose, don't go back to the plane."

"The *plane?*"

"Even after the fighting is over." He leaned closer over her, lowering his voice, although the guard still looked on blankly. "Do you understand?"

"No, I don't. Why not? If anything happens, why shouldn't we try to get out?"

"Listen to me, stupid woman! I am trying to help you. Don't go out of your room. Don't go back to the airplane."

"I'll go wherever we'll be safe," Susan said. She straightened her back, and a little of her courage came back from wherever it had gone when she saw old Stanweis die. "I'm responsible for my daughter. I'm not promising anything where she's concerned."

"All right, all right." He waved one hand in an irritated gesture. "Are all American women as stubborn as you? Look. I will make you a deal. All right? If you stay here, in the hotel, I will try to protect you. You and the child. You see? If you stay in the room with her I will make sure no one hurts you. Is good enough? Will you be happy then?"

"You'll protect us yourself?"

"That's what I say. Yes."

And it was strange. It was what she had wanted, yet not dared to hope for. It was more than he had any reason to promise. Yet now as she looked up at his face in silence, in the cavelike dimness of the corridor, despite what he was, she did not doubt him at all. He would stay with them and protect them. It seemed natural. It was the way it should be. And she knew that despite his unwillingness to acknowledge it, it had not been only hers, that feeling of last night, that sense that there was something unspoken and complex between them. He felt it too, and he would stay. The knowledge flooded her, made her light, free, until beside her the guard sniffled and she remembered Moira.

But you could push a man, this man, only so far. "Thank you," she said again. "I knew you . . . cared for me."

"I care only for my people," he said stiffly, but she knew that he was not really speaking to her now; it was for the guard, or more truly for some yet-unyielding part of himself. The way he stood, his hands gripping and releasing the stock of the rifle, told her that.

"Can I see them now?" she asked him.

"Yes. Go in. I will tell the guard to let you come out."

Lieberman and Cook were sitting behind an incongruous oak desk, the manager's, apparently, looking out a barred window into the square. The guard followed her in. They both moved silently. As she came up to the desk, feeling the hot, still air cut at her face, neither of them heard. They were not speaking, not moving, just sitting together in green leather chairs. She saw just before she reached them that their hands were locked.

From outside, through the bars, a stutter of distant shots filtered into the room.

"Ox?"

They both turned, but their hands stayed together. Moira's face was streaked with tears, glistening trails through the dirt, and her eyes were wide and wet.

Susan went to her and hugged her, and then, almost as an afterthought, kissed Michael. She paused then, uncertain what to do. She wanted to tell Moira about Harisah's promise, but that seemed cruel. Instead she perched herself on a corner of the desk and said, too brightly, "Well, it's not so bad down here, is it? There don't seem to be as many flies."

"No." Moira didn't smile.

"What's happening?" said Cook. He looked excited, his cheeks flamed with color; she had never seen him so keyed up. "Can you see anything? Who's doing all the firing?"

"We can't see anything. It's coming from out in the mountains. Harisah says there might be an attack."

Their eyes sought hers for a moment; then the falsity of hope, the futility of it, struck them all at the same moment. There was a small space for silence. Susan looked down at the desktop; Moira looked away; Cook played with the dial of a rusty safe, left and right, left and right.

"How's Nancy?" muttered Lieberman.

"All right . . . she's all right."

"She's the one you have to watch out for," said the Ox. "This can really scar her, Betts. Forever. Trauma—"

"Right now, I'm going to worry about keeping her from physical danger, Moira. That's enough for me, right now. And there isn't anything I wouldn't do for that."

Her friend lifted her head, and for a long moment they looked at each other across the desk. Susan knew what she was thinking, knew what Moira thought she meant. Well, that isn't the way it is, she thought. But it's a simple way to explain. And one not even the Ox can fault. Let it stand.

"Betts. I want you to be real careful with him."

"I will be."

"He's a murderer. He—"

"You've said all that before, Moira. And I'm not disagreeing. I know you're right, now. I don't think he's all bad. But what's good in him is enlisted in the service of evil—like all the Germans who fought for Hitler."

"All right. I won't argue about that. But there's one more thing. What are you going to do about Dan?"

"Dan?"

"Remember him? What are you going to do when this is over?"

"I guess . . . I guess, Moira, maybe that's over, too."

It was the first time she had said it, even to herself.

The Ox narrowed her eyes at her. "If that's your decision. But I want you to do something for me, if we make it through this. Because I care about you. And that's this: Think about it again, later, when this is over. Just be sure. To find someone you can love through . . . good and bad, well, that's not so easy anymore."

She and Cook turned back to each other, and Susan stood for a moment in the hot silence, feeling suddenly excluded, left out. She watched their hands creep together across the desktop, creep and meet and intertwine again, tight, tight.

They were still together, waiting, when the sound crept into the room. At first it was a humming, a far drone, just below the threshold of hearing. But it grew. Cook noticed it first, as if his senses were more finely drawn than theirs; he lifted his head, turned toward the window.

"What is it?"

"I don't know. There's something out past the airstrip. Raising dust. A car, maybe—"

It grew swiftly, climbing the scale as it neared. Grew, and then was lost in a popping vibration that made them all look at one another, suddenly, and then jump forward to the sill.

Out of the southern sky a moving thing buzzed forward,

drawn as if along a wire from the open desert valley toward the hotel. It grew swiftly, and then, suddenly, resolved itself into a small helicopter. It dipped, and as their eyes followed it, a gout of smoke blew free from its engine and unrolled toward them. But then their eyes dropped from it to something beyond, moving across the desert beyond the airstrip.

"It's a goddamn tank or something," said Cook.

"Where?"

"Beyond the plane. We couldn't see it coming because it was behind it. Wait. There's a whole fucking line of them! Jesus! Do you think they're ours? Do we have green things with pointed noses?"

At that moment the clatter of the aircraft turned to a roar as it passed over the square, and the world outside disappeared in a whirling storm of dust and black smoke.

"Susan!" Moira turned to her, her face white. "Get upstairs. Get with Nan! Now!"

And with the sound of beating wings in her ears, terror in her heart, she fled through the empty corridors of the hotel, tears streaming down her face.

33

Ash Shummari, Syria

THE STRIKE ELEMENT ENTERED SYRIA
that afternoon without knowing it. Baked within steel
boxes, jolted half-unconscious over mountain roads, there
was no way they could have known.

Will Givens couldn't tell. In fact he was asleep. Fatigue,
heat, and the reaction to his first hostile fire made a powerful soporific. He snored through the last miles, slumped
against another trooper on the hard bench inside the
'track. At times he would open his eyes, on the worst
stretches of downhill road, but he never came fully awake.
Only halfway, to a fevered place of dreaming, where
he would linger and then slide back again into the hot
maw of darkness, seeing again and again a bloody scrap
of flesh. . . .

He did not see the border station, its white-and-green-
striped crossing-guard down, but its windows empty,
abandoned; did not see the lead amtrac take it at full
speed, smashing the poured-concrete guard post, tearing
through wood and glass and barbed wire.

At some indeterminate time Cutford jerked him awake
in the roaring din of the 'track's interior. No. Not roaring.
The engine was at a high idle, and they were squatting
stationary on level ground. As Will realized this the ramp
banged down aft. He ducked his head to look out, catching
a breath of hot fresh air, and said "Where are we, man?"

"I think it's the place we're going to," said Hernandez seriously to the whole interior of the 'track.

"Better stay inside," the A-driver called back, as Cutford made a move for the hatch. "They're talkin' on the radio. They ain't sure this is the right coordinates."

"Fucken officers. They sure it's the right country?"

The driver straightened back into the turret, his back stiff. Cutford turned round once more, like a dog about to lie down, and lowered himself unwillingly back onto the seat, glaring out the open rear of the 'track.

Givens watched him briefly, nodding, and then curled back into sleep. Or tried to. But the change of air had brought him back to wakefulness. As he peered past Cutford's shadowed bulk he saw mountains in the distance, the range they had crossed.

"Noncoms dismount," someone shouted outside. "Muster for precombat brief."

"They love to jerk their jaws, don't they," muttered Silkworth. Will looked back at him. The Silk grinned for just a moment, just as he had in a cathouse in Sicily; and then he swung on the rest of the men and was a sergeant again. "Come on, Cutford. Rest of you boys, hang tight."

Will saw the corporal pause for a moment at the hatch, as if unwilling to leave the shelter of metal walls, and then move into a lope, lifting his M-16 to high port. Through the open rear hatch, as if in a frame, he could see the noncoms from the other 'tracks arrive two by two and form a rough circle around the command jeep. Silkworth and Cutford joined them as the colonel, with two other officers beside him, spread a map out before them on the hood of the vehicle.

Will looked at the sky. It was still blue, still clear except for smoke a few hills over. He relaxed for a moment, glancing at Harner, who had lit a cigarette and was sucking smoke into his nostrils, and then looked out again at the sky. On the ship it had meant freedom, the only thing in his life that was the same as home. Now he found himself remembering how the projectiles had appeared against it, nothing more than specks, like the negatives of stars, but aimed at him.

As if to reinforce his unease the popcorn rattle of automatic weapons sounded some distance off. The marines, packed close, yet drew slightly closer. Givens began to feel a primitive need. He was debating jumping out of the vehicle, just for a moment, when the sergeant reappeared in the open rampway. One of the colonel's staff officers, a major, had come back from the jeep with him, and now stood behind him.

"Listen up!" Silkworth shouted, staring in at them. "We're two miles past the border, and three miles from the objective. This is all the briefing you're going to have preattack. So listen good.

"We're in Syria now. The Syrians have backed off to let us in. We don't know for how long. Looks like we'll be alone with the terrorists, for a little while at least. But everything has got to go fast, and I mean fast.

"Assault will go as follows: Over the crest of this last hill is a two-mile-wide valley plain. Airfield on the far side. Plane on the field, probably deserted, but one rifle squad from 'track seven will take it in combat order. On the far side of the airstrip is an old resort compound. The hotel itself is the tallest building. That's probably where the hostages are.

"We'll stay in the 'tracks the whole way to the buildings. Dismount there in cover. Most of the force will provide a base of fire from the front. That's the holding element. The maneuver element—that's us, this 'track and two others, with Major Wasserman here in charge—will flank left in open order and carry out an assault through and into the objective proper, which is the hotel. We don't know the layout, so keep your eye on me and the major. We'll move fast and hope we don't hit anything we can't handle. Any questions?"

"What about when we get in the hotel?" asked Cutford. The men looked at him. He had reversed his rifle so that it hung upside down by the sling, and Will remembered the way the men in Nam used to hold them on TV. In Nam, when he had been a child . . .

"Major?" said Silkworth.

The officer moved forward, a radioman moving with him, as if they were attached. "There's been no time to plan that," he said, folding a map and stuffing it into his blouse. His eyes were slits in the sunlight. "Squad leaders will have to act on their own initiative. Coordinate your men with those of the other units. Normal urban-combat procedures."

"Okay." said Silkworth, taking their attention, their obedience, back with the single word. "Weapons loaded, safeties on. Out fast and take cover instantly when the ramp comes down. Driver! Close this fucking barn door and put her in gear!"

At that moment, sweeping in great circles a mile behind and three hundred feet above Givens' 'track, Dan's back suddenly prickled.

He leaned forward, his forehead touching the windscreen, and swept with his eyes the entire column. The vehicles, strung out along what had become no more than a dirt track. The knot of men around the jeep, breaking and scattering as their briefing concluded. The dry hills, the mountains behind, ahead the last rise before Ash Shummari. And all around them, above them, open and empty sky.

He had not stopped to think after he left Sundstrom and SACC. Instead he had gone straight to the *Guam*'s helo deck. He knew the air plan. He'd written it. His orders had been no armed aircraft over the beach; but Haynes had asked for two of the unarmed observation choppers, fitted with smoke generators, to be over the hotel when the column hit. He had gotten to the flight deck to find only one warming up. The other had a casualty to the transmission. Dan had sprinted across the deck, yanked the hatch open even as the crewmen turned, surprise on their faces, and thrust himself behind their seat. One of them pushed aside his throat mike.

"What's going on? Who are you?"

"I'm on the squadron staff, and my wife is in there."

"I don't have any—"

"Get going, damn it! Look at your operation order!"

That stopped them; he knew damn well none of the pilots read anything but their own flight schedules. The man turned his head front and began flicking switches.

Then, quite suddenly, they were in the air.

The chopper passed low over the inshore ships, barely higher than *Ault*'s mast. Low, gray, grim-looking, the old destroyer rode seemingly close enough to touch the land; from the helo he could see sand ridges fingering out toward her under the glittering surface. Then she flashed past, and he was over the beach. He looked down on the rear guard, digging in among the dunes a mile inland. Machine-guns and antitank missile launchers, here and there a tank crouched in cover, ready to hold a beachhead through which a retreating force could withdraw.

Beyond that Lebanon seemed empty of life. But through the whole flight inland the pilot and copilot swiveled their heads, searching that blue sky. After a while, his back itching at the thought of a Syrian fighter, or an antiaircraft missile, he started doing it, too. They kept low, flashing so close over hill and valley that sheep scattered beneath them on the crests. Sometimes he had to look up to see them. Despite that there was no guarantee they would not be fired on, and he knew that now, as they hovered almost exactly over the border, they were in as much or more danger as any of the men in amtracs below them.

His back prickled again. He leaned forward and reached up to slap the copilot on the shoulder. The man turned.

"Are we going in?" he shouted.

"Any minute, soon as we get the—"

"Smoke!" the pilot shouted at that moment. The copilot

started and reached up to thumb a switch. The helo tilted forward.

They leapt over the last crest no more than fifty feet up, and at two hundred miles an hour Ash Shummari burst into sight.

The 'track's engine roared and its treads dug into the sand. Will's rifle was jerked from his hand and clattered on the deck. He snatched it up, feeling sick, and checked it. It looked okay. He loaded, as Cutford had ordered, pointing it at the overhead as he put the safety on.

The nose rose, and then dipped. The engine roared, cut as the driver shifted, and then howled again at maximum rpm. The men inside couldn't see a thing. Givens tried desperately to visualize what Silkworth had said. An airstrip—a compound—a hotel—

At every moment, as they swayed and roared across suddenly flat land, he expected the jolt of an antitank rocket. How well armed were these terrorists? He had no idea what a terrorist looked like. Did they wear uniforms? Beards?

Were they black or white?

Harisah was standing in the lobby, talking to the men from the committee, when the shout came from outside. He heard at the same instant the whock of helicopter blades, the growing whine of turbines. He knew instantly what it was, but restrained his first impulse to run for the door. That would be natural; they might have expected that, and targeted it. Instead he lowered his head slightly, and said, "They are here. Your advice?"

"The battle, strictly speaking, is not our responsibility, Majd," one of them said. "What are your intentions? Where do you want us?"

"I will hold them off if they are few, or attack stupidly; and move to the upper floors if they penetrate. We will use the hostages as shields. If I judge the fight is lost, we will kill them all. The pickets and barricades should hold them long enough for me to make the decision. You will draw arms and fight with the rest."

"We understand. Go with God."

"Insh'Allah."

He turned from them, dismissing that now from his mind. Now was the time for battle. He thought for just a moment of the American woman. In a way she was right. This was honorable war, to fight those with arms in their hands. He hoped for victory, that he might not have to kill so many of the innocent.

But victory or defeat, life or death, for him and for them, was not in the hands of the Majd now. For all would be, could only be, as it was willed.

Without thought, emptying his consciousness the way he had once crawling beneath the wire into Israel, he slid back the bolt to feed a fresh round. From outside came the sound of his men firing, shouting: "God is great!" He paused at a window, looking out. Then crouched, smashing out the glass, and picked out his first target.

Two floors above, Susan stood half-hidden at the window, looking breathlessly out and down. From this height she could see far out across the desert. She turned, again, to look back into the room. Nan still slept. She turned back to the window.

There was no doubt in her mind now. She was watching an attack on the compound. The helicopter had disappeared, passed out of her sight, but the smoke it had laid blew along the desert floor, eddying dark around the jetliner, then hiding it. The pulsating drone of many engines grew behind its curtain.

Then, all at once, six, twelve of the green vehicles burst out of the murk. Bigger than she had thought, they swayed roaring across the level sand, throwing up wakes of dust. At the same moment, below her, she saw men race back toward the hotel, saw them stop, turn, and throw up their weapons to aim.

The first cracks of rifle fire split the hot air. She paused a moment longer, watching, then ducked below the windowline and crossed to the bed.

"Get up," she whispered. Then, above the rising clamor outside, said louder: "Get up, Bunny. Mommy needs you with her now."

Bullets clattered suddenly on the hull. The men in the amtrac stiffened. One half-rose, reaching for a firing port. Cutford slapped him back into his seat without a word.

A few seconds later the engine faltered. It cut out, and the 'track glided for a moment almost soundless; then came the snarl of the starter. The engine caught, roared; they began to reaccelerate; and then something ground viciously beneath their feet, like an animal clawing at the floor. Without thought Givens lifted his boots to avoid it. An instant later the 'track slammed upward, scraping and screaming across something hard, and came to rest tilted up and canted to the left.

"Drop the ramp!" he heard Silkworth shout, dragging on the A-driver's leg. The wall fell away and light hit the interior of the tank. All the men leapt for it.

Will pounded down the ramp, rounded the flank of the LVT, and dropped with the rest. Hugging the bare ground, pumping its hot dry chalky smell rapidly through his lungs, he squinted quickly around in the sudden brilliance of day.

Their 'track had run up over a low retaining wall of cut stone. It loomed above them to their right with its snout cocked in the air. Bullets hummed overhead; it was drawing fire. One whacked into it as he watched, blasting off a neat oval of green paint. The men were crouched partly behind its immobile mass, and partially in cover of the wall.

Givens half-rose for a second to look over it, then ducked back down. Through the smoke he had made out an open space, a paved plaza. In the center of it was a ruined fountain. Around it was grouped three main buildings and behind them several smaller, lower service buildings. In that second-long exposure he had seen the flashes of small arms in the windows of the central building, the tallest, directly across the square. He hoped they didn't decide on a frontal assault.

No, flank left, Silkworth had said . . . a space behind the building, perhaps an alley or service road, opened in that direction; he saw the sergeant, ahead of him, pop up his head to examine it.

'Tracks were still arriving to their right, men dismounting. The din of engines and fifty-calibers was deafening. Givens realized the plan was already going wrong. The LVTs couldn't get to the hotel itself; the retaining wall was too high for them to climb. Instead they were dropping their troops behind it, then pulling back a hundred yards or so to provide suppressing fire with bursts from their cupola MGs.

He felt his need again then, and this time it was undeniable. Guiltily he pulled down his trousers and crouched for a moment in the cover of the wall. The relief was immense.

"Advance!" Silkworth's voice penetrated the ringing in his ears from the collision. Harner threw a just-lit butt away with a disgusted motion and swung himself easily over the wall. The others followed, rushing one or two at a time. Will got his pants up, clambered over the wall with two other men, and sprinted full out for the first building. Flashes from the far side of the square . . . rounds sang overhead, ripped trenches in the asphalt at his feet, and then he was behind it and in cover.

Ahead, standing erect at the mouth of the alley, the sergeant slapped his hands over his head and spread them; open up. "Mortar squad, follow me! Givens,"—he started, still trying to get his belt buckled—"you take point to the left, Harner right. Hernandez, you're tail-end Charlie. Staggered column, five meters apart. Use doorways, trash bins, whatever cover you can find. Keep your weapons pointed outboard."

Will was moving to obey him when he felt his arm

gripped. It was Cutford. "I'll take point," the corporal muttered.

"Silkworth said—"

"Hey, *fuck* Silkworth. You think he cares for a brother like I do? Shit he does. Follow me."

And there was nothing to do but fall back, watching the broad neck darken as Cutford lifted his rifle and slid toward the first doorway in a narrow lane. He acquiesced in it, but he didn't like it. *That Cutford,* he thought again, as he had so many times since the float began. *Why doesn't he leave me alone? Why is he always on me, giving me a hard time? This 'brother' baloney . . .*

"Come on, buddy, move," whispered the guy behind him, some rifleman he didn't know, and he flinched and started forward. Ahead of him, already into the alley, Cutford moved from door to door in sporadic rushes, eyes on the windows of the larger building to their right. Givens tried clumsily to imitate him, trying to recall the drowsy lessons in the troop spaces on street fighting.

"Spread out, fuckheads!" Silkworth called behind them, and he froze for a few seconds, letting space seep between him and the point. Cutford was twenty yards ahead now, ducking into what must once have been a loading dock.

They moved like that, leapfrogging warily along the alleyway, for two or three minutes. Once one of the guys let off a burst at a window, and got his head chewed by Silkworth. They weren't supposed to initiate fire, not till they reached position. Givens took advantage of the halt to tip back his helmet and wipe his forehead, scratch his sweat-soaked hair. It left his brow feeling naked and he tipped it back down quickly. He realized then that the mortarmen hadn't been issued grenades. Silkworth got them moving again and he concentrated on the next doorway, on the windows above the fire team. Was that someone moving? . . . no, only a curtain, flapping in the wind through a shattered window.

Cutford . . . Hernandez . . . himself . . . Silkworth . . . Harner. Had Liebo made it? Walking into a blade sounded pretty fatal, but with a quick lift back to the ships they said you had a good chance of surviving anything but a head shot. From here, too? Where would they put a helo down here? Well, probably on the airstrip, if one of them took a sniper round. But they wouldn't. Then he remembered Washout, and the other men, those who had screamed back on the road, under the mortars. Where were they? He'd seen no medevac for them. It had happened to his friend—it could happen to *him*—

Pay attention, Will, he told himself. Sweat dripped from his nose. *Jesus, your head is all over today, isn't it.*

No. I shouldn't say His name like that. I'm sorry.

The alley ahead turned, angling off to the right, and as they crept closer he saw it.

Barricade. A mass of debris, mattresses and boxes and bricks piled from wall to wall across the narrow way ahead. He lingered, checking it out, but it was Cutford, still twenty yards up, who saw danger first. He pumped his rifle twice above his head as he dropped and rolled.

"Covah! Hostiles!"

From above them, from the second floor of one of the buildings, came a sudden blast of sound. The pavement where the corporal had been flashed sparks and gray dust. Givens lunged for a doorway, fear squeezing his chest like a tightening rope. M-16s barked high-pitched around him, five, six weapons at once. He found himself firing too, the rifle kicking, tracking up the building. Blue smoke formed a cloud. He saw his bullets join the others as the window and the frame around it burst into fragments and dust. A weapon flashed from the barricade then and he jerked his sights down, still firing, and aimed into it. Something whacked into the concrete above his head and he ducked. He triggered the weapon again, stood momentarily surprised as nothing happened, then released the magazine. It thudded empty off his boot and he slapped in a full one. Thirty rounds don't last long, he thought. I better start conserving ammo.

"Cover fire! Covering!" someone was yelling, and he

aimed at the barrier again, then saw something move to the side. He swung, then jerked the rifle up just in time to miss Cutford. The corporal, on his belly, was tight against the leftmost wall, just where it curved. He was feeling at his chest. Givens ducked out, fired a burst at the barricade, ducked back, checked the window. Nothing moved.

Cutford rolled back a foot or two, raised himself on an elbow, and tossed a grenade overhand. It went up and over the barrier. The explosion boomed away, echoed, and in the sudden silence that followed they heard a man cry out.

"Move up, pal," said the rifleman, rolling into his niche. "Quick, quick. I'll cover you."

Me? he thought for just a moment, and then he was running, bent low, hearing the ripping fire behind him. Another rifleman was moving up on the opposite side of the alley, head lifted, eyes wary. Givens ran, his boots jarring on the pavement, tripping on loose bricks. As he reached the barricade, Cutford got up and sprayed a burst over it, moving his rifle in a figure-eight pattern, and they went over it together.

Three men were running down the lane beyond. Two were ahead of the last, who was moving crabwise, bent to one side. Cutford paused and raised his weapon. His rifle barked once, then the bolt locked open. But the limping man was lagging even further, dragging himself along. The others looked back, but when Will fired too, they ducked away and disappeared.

The lone man jerked to a halt, whirled round, and fell to the pavement, dropping something. Will spun, only then remembering their rear, but there was no one else behind the breastwork.

Hernandez edged through it, hunched like a scared turtle under his too-large helmet. Silkworth appeared behind him, then two of the riflemen and then the major, Wasserman, holding his pistol with the slide back. His face was set and pale. Silkworth looked pissed. "Cover, you turds!" he bawled. "You don't double-time in like that! Jesus Christ! Fire and cover!"

"Sergeant's right," said Cutford. He lowered his rifle, looked up at the blank faces of the buildings, and started back to the left. He ran gracefully for a big man, holding his weapon like a toy. Will followed him, stumbling a little because his legs were suddenly weak.

"Where'd you get the grenade?"

"Say what, Oreo?"

"The grenade, Cutford. Where'd you get it?"

"Bummed a couple off the riflemen. You better get some, too."

"Right," said Will.

"When you can."

"Right."

They came up on the man they had shot. He was face down, moving his arms as if trying to crawl. His left side had been shredded. Casualty drill, Givens thought from somewhere frozen in his mind. Silkworth kicked his weapon away. It was a Soviet-style carbine. Will booted him over, not too gently, then stepped back, drawing in his breath.

This was their enemy. No more than fourteen, not even a smear of mustache, dark eyes blown wide with shock and fear. Silkworth had aimed his rifle at the prisoner's head. Now he lifted it. One of the M-16 rounds—Cutford's, or Will's?—had hit the boy low in the back. The exit hole was the size of a catcher's mitt. Will swallowed, unable to look at it, unable to take his eyes away. He smelled blood and shit and powder smoke.

The major came up with the radioman lagging a few steps behind. "He alive?" he said.

"Not for long," said Silkworth. "Look, sir, he's nothin' but a kid."

"Old enough to carry a SKS. Check him for documents."

"What, sir?"

"Documents, Sergeant!"

"Aw, Christ, sir, he ain't going to be carrying any documents."

"Don't tell me that till after you check his pockets," said the major. "And disable that weapon. The rest of you, keep moving."

"Yes sir. Goddammit, you mungbrains, *spread out!*"

The sound of renewed firing came from ahead. Oily smoke from somewhere billowed dark and nearly motionless between them and the sky. As they moved forward, faster now, the air quivered from an explosion. Givens ran his tongue around the inside of his mouth. It scoured his teeth like steel wool. He was glad to leave the dying boy. He thought of asking the man behind him for a swig from his canteen but was afraid to take a hand off his rifle. A small helicopter roared by low overhead, filling their narrow slit of space with the beat of its blades. The smoke was coming from it. It disappeared on the far side of the complex, dropping slowly toward the ground.

"Hold up here," said the major to Silkworth.

The sergeant signaled and Will crouched. Wasserman huddled with the radioman in a doorway. The men waited, looking up at a building they could see now above them to the right. It was five or six stories, a good deal higher than the others. That, Will thought, must be the hotel. He hoped they would not have to fight all the way to the top. The bamn-bamn-bamn of a heavy machine gun came from the far side, from the smoke. After a few minutes Will turned his head and made a gesture to the rifleman. He got the cap off after a couple of tries, and allowed himself two swallows of water; and then a third.

The huddle broke; the firing on the far side swelled in volume, became a roar. He could distinguish, now, a rifle-sound different from their own. "Listen up!" shouted Major Wasserman. The men, strung along both sides of the way, turned their heads to show they were listening.

"Here's the situation. The main part of the force is at the front of the plaza, where we dismounted. They'll constitute the base of fire, keeping the hostiles occupied. We're somewhere around the back of the hotel now. We'll go in slow till we see where the firing's coming from, or see some means of entrance; then lead with grenades and go in fast. Assault upward from the first floor. Everybody'll be in civvies, remember. Don't wait till it's too late, but don't shoot Americans by mistake."

"Oh, shit," muttered Cutford.

"Don't use grenades to clear a room unless you're sure there's no hostages in it. Estimate is thirty to forty enemy. We're in a good position to take them. Any questions?" He looked at their faces, then nodded once. "Sergeant."

"Let's go," said Silkworth. He still looks pissed, Will thought. Maybe he always does in combat. He wondered how he looked himself.

They moved forward. Givens felt urgency now. The sound of firing grew louder to their right. The men ran, bent low, trying to keep cover from overhead.

They passed a side entry to the plaza, and for just a moment he saw the hotel plain, framed by the arched doorway like a postcard picture. It looked like one in any town, the upper stories the same gray concrete and glass as any other building of the mid-twentieth century, the lower part of it faced with gray stone. Smoke was streaming out of two of the lower windows.

He ran on, and lost sight of it; but he could still make out the upper stories, through the smoke, above the building that still masked them to their right. The helicopter reappeared suddenly from behind it and flew in a long tilting curve out toward them, the throbbing drone of its engine blotting out the crackle of small arms.

A stream of tracers leapt upward from one of the windows. Before the aircraft could alter course the fiery lines met the fuselage, disappeared into it. And suddenly the blurred disc of its blades, the green body, flashed into an orange bloom of flame. The men stopped involuntarily, looking up at it; it was overhead.

The thunderclap reached them then, ringing out across the desert, and the flame became a ball of black smoke and the helo fell out of it toward them, shedding parts, the smoke whirling downward with it in spirals. The fuselage fell free the last hundred feet and crashed into the alleyway, behind the barricade, where the squad had been no more than two minutes before.

Will found his legs again and ran after the others. The chopper was fire now, a glowing shell being digested hungrily by flame. Choking smoke swept toward them. They ran within it, trying to hold their breaths, but needing it too much from the running, and at last it rose and they emerged into clear air. He saw Silkworth ahead, coughing, pointing up to where the tracers had come from. The rattle of gunfire was steady now and he could distinguish several calibers.

The alley ended at a service entrance, the door half-open. It seemed to be part of a lower wing of the main building. Harner and Cutford flattened themselves on either side. The corporal tossed in a grenade. Fire flashed and they hurled themselves inside. Givens ran after them.

In the interior, glass crunched under their boots. They slowed at a corner, Will and the riflemen, Silkworth, Cutford, then looked round it down a carpeted empty corridor toward what must be the lobby. It was straight and they could see through it to the far side. Several marines lay beyond it in the plaza, behind and beside the fountain. Pinned down, or dead—they couldn't tell. They had only a second to look. Then the major was among them, shoving and cursing pretty well for an officer, Will thought. "Take it!" he shouted.

The fire team leaped forward. A face showed itself briefly at the door to an office; someone fired, missed; he bolted across the corridor and disappeared from sight. When they reached the lobby it was empty. Wasserman showed himself briefly at the entrance. Two or three shots from outside starred the remaining glass, then the firing slackened. He reappeared, waving, and some of the men by the fountain leapt up and ran toward him.

There were at least twenty marines inside the hotel now, with rifles and light antitank rockets, all panting and blowing so hard from the sprint and the heat and their loads, there was no breath for talk. Givens, looking out toward the plaza, noticed two stone lions flanking the entrance. Their heads were pocked and scarred by bullets.

"That's it," said the major. A wet patch showed dark between his shoulders. "Blow all that fatigue out. Gonna go on in a minute."

"Let's go now," said Silkworth, straightening, his face taking on that pissed-off look again, and Will thought: *Is it really the combat he hates? Or is it the officer telling him what to do?* He sucked air and looked around.

The lobby was a shambles. Shattered glass, layers of it, lay on torn-up blue carpet, and spent cartridges gleamed amid the sparkling shards. One side of the lobby's marble wall—it must have been elegant once—showed where flame had licked it. Paper, trash, empty bottles lay inside the door, right where, Will figured, a guard must have stood up till the assault began.

He was standing there, gazing around a little stupidly, when the thud of gunfire came faintly from above.

On the floor above, standing with his remaining men, Harisah edged his head round a casement to look down at the square. He could make them out: a hundred of them, perhaps more, firing steadily from cover of the tanks. As he watched, a squad of ten or eleven broke cover and dashed forward. He edged the assault rifle around the corner of the window and triggered a burst downward as they passed the fountain. At the same time he heard his men firing from other windows, on this floor and above. Three of the runners fell. The rest disappeared beneath the entrance overhang.

He caught the movement just in time, the elevation of a turret on one of the green vehicles, and hurled himself to the floor as the windowframe and the wall opposite shattered under a hammering blizzard of heavy machine-gun slugs. Plaster-dust filled the air and flying glass sliced at his back. With the others he scrambled on his belly back into the corridor.

The Majd considered there for a moment, lying prone, feeling their eyes on him. The barricades had not held. The lobby was open, and perhaps the rear of the building as well. He had left guards at the stairwells, but that was only a holding action.

It is not my fault, nor that of my men, the Majd thought passionlessly. Someone above me misestimated the situation, or those we thought our friends have turned traitor, as to Ali so many years ago. The enemy came too fast and in overwhelming numbers. Whatever the cause, the result is this: We have lost.

He glanced up. Intent, sweaty faces stared back; some frightened, some resolute; but all of them alike ready. He smiled. They were good men. Was there a vale of pleasure waiting beyond a warrior's death, as the *mullahs* said? He doubted it himself. It was a salutary fiction, no more. But he did not care. This moment was enough. He smiled at them, his comrades, and they smiled back.

The Majd said, "It is time. Kill them all."

The men picked themselves up, still crouching, and began running down the corridor. Doors slammed open. Then the shooting began.

Harisah got up, his legs disgusting him with their sudden weakness, and walked rapidly in the opposite direction. He no longer understood why he'd given his word to the woman. He wished now that he hadn't. It was sentimentality, foolishness—and for someone unworthy of it. But as soon as she was safe he would resume the fight. Perhaps he could escape. Most likely he would die. But he could not be taken. No, he must not permit himself to be taken. His cause could use martyrs, but not prisoners.

A woman ran from a side door, then froze, turned toward him, her hands thrust out imploringly. Harisah recognized her. The American official, Freed. She was in his way. He shot her down and began to run.

"Stairway," said Silkworth instantly. He looked around the lobby. The men stared at him, then understood, and scattered to search. Harner found it around a corner, past the open but motionless doors of the elevators. Silkworth put his hand on his shoulder as he started through. "Not you, Buck. I want riflemen in the lead. Two little fast guys, with plenty of frags. Volunteers?"

Two of the riflemen exchanged glances and lifted their hands slowly. "Yeah—you two."

"Listen," said the major, cocking his ear upward. They lifted their heads. The firing above had stopped. Then, as they listened, it burst out again more rapid and sustained than before. Faintly beyond it they could make out shouting and screams.

"Let's go," said Silkworth to them all, jerking open the door.

Givens started for it behind the sergeant. At the jamb he was pulled back. He jerked around. "What the hell—"

The lightless face was bent close to his. The corporal held a small green sphere close to his chest. It was a fragmentation grenade, pin out. Givens' eyes shifted to it. "Cutford—"

"Hang back," said the corporal.

"What?"

"I'm goin' first, Oreo. You're new at this. Listen up or lose teeth."

The stairway. The first thing that struck him about it was the smell: It stank like a country privy. Behind the sergeant, behind Cutford and the riflemen, he took the risers two at a time. His heart hammered, dragging leaden legs upward. The air burned in his throat. First flight. Second. The concrete well, unpainted and bare of the carpet and glitter of the lobby, echoed the scuff of boots and the harsh panting of climbing men. A hollow clatter came down to them, and Silkworth and Cutford slowed, holding the rest up. They looked at each other. "What was that?" Silkworth whispered.

"I dunno, man."

"Gimme your frag."

"It's live, careful."

"I know that, dickhead."

"Christ, hold the fucken spoon, then!"

Men shouted above and simultaneously with it a burst of fire deafened the marines in the closed stairwell. The bullets blew craters out of the concrete walls, whanged and spun in the narrow well. Givens flinched as one flicked at his trouser leg.

"This one for the Corps," said Silkworth. "Ready?"

"On your ass, Silky." Cutford turned his head. Givens saw familiar white-rimmed eyes, yellow teeth grinning. "Rest of you fuckheads, we catch one, just keep on going over us. Don't even think 'bout stoppin'."

Silkworth swung his arm back and popped the grenade. It hung hissing and smoking in front of Givens' eyes for as long, it seemed, as all of boot camp had lasted, and then the sergeant threw it, snapping it hard upward so that it hit the wall and bounced around the corner. An instant later the flat crack hit their ears and fragments slapped the wall.

"Go! Go! Go!"

The two riflemen screamed together and rounded the landing, clattering upward side by side, both firing from the hip. Givens, his heart bursting from the climb and battle, ran upward after them. An ugly little man lay screaming at the landing doors, a civilian—no, a pistol lay near him on the floor. He had been wounded before the grenade-burst; bandages were wound around his back. Silkworth kicked the weapon down the stairs, shot him, and ran on into a corridor.

They tripped on bodies. There were three of them. A woman, two men. One of the men was still conscious. Cutford glanced down the corridor, where it took a right angle.

"Soldier—"

"What, man," he said rapidly, bending a little, but keeping his eyes and the rifle barrel pointed toward the angle.

"Keep going," the man muttered. "They shot us. They're going to shoot everybody. I heard them say so."

"Let's move! Down the hallway!" Silkworth shouted. The point team moved forward again, pounding down the carpeted passage, and turned the corner. There were two more bodies, still writhing, and blue smoke in the air. A stout unshaven man looked up from them, startled, and began to raise his arms. Hernandez swept him with a burst; the impact of the 5.56s knocked him down and sent a pistol flying. Another door opened and Givens raised his M-16, ready to kill, and then ran on as a blond woman looked out at them, eyes wide in a chalky face.

The firing was suddenly close, right down the hall. He saw the two riflemen ahead, and beyond them caught a glimpse of white shirts, green armbands. Flash of gunfire. The marine ahead of him shouted hoarsely and fell to the floor. Will ran past him. There was more firing; people appeared at the doors behind them, and some of the marines stopped, checking out the rooms.

But Silkworth kept the mortar squad and the two riflemen going, running ahead of their disturbance down the long hall, empty as early morning, toward where the gunfire came loudest. Cutford disappeared around the end of the corridor just as Will passed the last door on the left. As he ran by it, boots thudding into the carpeted concrete, it swung slowly open, and he saw its interior from the corner of his eye: registered it instantly and completely in that fraction of a second. A man. A woman.

Saw it, and understood. The man had a weapon. He glanced ahead. The others were far down the corridor now, or lying where they had fallen. There was no one else near.

He turned in mid-stride, glanced off the wall, staggered a step, and ran back for the open door, checking that the safety was off his M-16. The door started to close and he hit it running, kicking it in and going down rolling in the same motion, the way they showed you in combat town. He came up weapon ready, facing the woman. Asian! He almost fired but instead froze. No, she was dressed American, one of the hostages. But where was the man? He swung the barrel to check the room. Gone.

"Where is he?"

"Who?" she whispered.

"The guy, the *guy.*" He gestured impatiently with the rifle. She wasn't bad-looking. Dark eyes, heart-shaped face, makeup smeared. She was hugging a child, he saw suddenly, a small girl with startlingly wide eyes; she was staring at him, Givens, in terror. His mind jerked back. "Come on. These people is shootin' hostages. They was a man in here. He one of the Arabs? Where'd he go?"

She hesitated, said nothing; but her eyes slid, inadvertently or not he could not tell, to the open window. Following the look, he took two steps and shoved the curtain aside with the flash hider of his rifle.

A story below, a man looked back up at him from the roof of an attached building. He had, Givens saw, an assault rifle of some type in his right hand. He was swarthy, dark-haired, tall. An open, dirty white shirt. Will felt his breath stop as the man's eyes steadied on his, and he saw the fear and challenge in them.

This was the enemy he had traveled so far, waited so long, to meet in the hot deadly silence of a strange land.

He was stepping out onto the balcony when the woman, behind him, said, "Wait. Please."

"Ma'am?"

"Wait—don't go out there. He just wants to get away. You—"

But he had stopped listening, was already outside, with one leg over the railing. He saw how the other had gotten down. An air-conditioning duct led down to the roof, a steep incline, but better than a drop. He swung his other leg over, holding his rifle with one hand, the other gripping the balcony.

"Don't," he heard the woman say again, behind him.

"Stay in the room," he shouted.

"No!" It was a scream, full-throated, pure terror; and

thinking it was a warning, he looked up from the duct, his eyes blasted open with sudden fear.

The bullet came soundless. No muzzle flash, no bang; he heard nothing; felt only the incredible force of the blow. He heard his rifle hit the roof-gravel below. He looked down at it, tiny and far. A lost weapon. A marine could not lose his rifle. . . .

Then he was falling, the surprise still too great for him to do anything but watch. He hit the roof with a scream still in his ears, his own or the woman's, prolonged, endless, he couldn't tell. Hit hard, knocking the breath out of him, almost knocking him out

But he didn't go. He blinked to clear his head, staring at the black gravel of the rooftop. It was sun-hot against his cheek and he could smell it: like the hot tarpaper of a roof. Then he tasted salt. He licked his lips for a moment, wondering, and then shoved himself up with his arms. Something moved in his chest, something heavy, but it did not hurt. He rolled over, groping with blind urgency for his rifle.

The woman was shouting something; it was in English, but he couldn't make it out. And the man, he saw him, he was still looking at him. He was raising his weapon again. He was smiling. Then he lifted his eyes. His expression changed.

"Givens!"

A deep voice, a roar of rage and pain.

"Oreo—goddamn it—where the fuck—"

Cutford's sweating face came over the edge of the terrace and looked down at him. It became suddenly still; then foreshortened to Givens' darkening sight as it looked up, to a young man in a loose shirt running across the rooftop, headed for the next building. His shoes kicked up spurts of black grit that rattled as they fell.

Cutford's face disappeared, swung back. The slender barrel, the cylindrical flash-suppressor of the corporal's M-16 steadied itself on the bar of the balcony. Steadied, paused, and then jerked twice, three times.

The running man threw his arms up, his legs straightening suddenly from the run, as if he was leaping. Givens saw his face, angry, despairing, triumphant, for only a moment before he disappeared over the edge of the roof.

Not a hundred feet away, but below them, Lenson crouched against an outside wall, unable to move.

The helicopter's pilot had put him down in a ravine about a quarter-mile from the compound. He had ended up, after a fear-filled sprint off the desert, in an alley on the eastern, blind side of the complex. At its end there was only one small door, and when he tried it, it had been locked.

Now he was terrified. Pure unreasoning anger had driven him inland, away from Sundstrom. But the noise and smoke and screams had leached that pure emotion away, leaving him with a shocked, incredulous awareness of where he was. At any moment a rifleman could lean from the balconies above and destroy him as casually as a man sweeps away a spider. Susan or not, Nan or not, if they were really here, he had made the wrong decision in coming. The marines were armed and trained for this. While he was a naval officer, untrained in land combat, still in his shipboard khakis and without even a helmet. I should have stayed aboard *Guam,* he thought. Done what I knew how to do.

He stared at his hand. The yard-long chunk of reinforcing iron he'd picked up in the alley seemed ridiculously inadequate in the storm of automatic-weapons fire that roared from the far side of the hotel.

In that moment Lenson thought despairingly that he had made all the wrong decisions. He was not a military man. He felt none of the lust of battle he had read about.

He huddled trembling against the hot concrete as close as he had held anyone. But it was not fear that held him there. It was the scream he had just heard. A woman's scream, terrifyingly familiar, from above him. He stared upward helplessly. There was a fire ladder there. A metal lattice, but with the familiar counterbalanced last stage, so that he couldn't reach it from ground level.

At that moment there came to him the stink of burning fuel. And at that nightmare-familiar smell, something in his mind began to bend.

He stared at the empty end of the alleyway. A form was emerging, slowly, from the swirling smoke. He lifted the steel bar in reflex, like a man armed in a dream, even as he realized it was a figment, a hallucination, the creation of a mind five days without sleep. He fought to disbelieve. But above him the crackle of firing built to the roar of a monstrous pyre. Behind it he heard now faint but clear the shriek of tearing steel, agonizing as your own body being torn apart; the screams of abandoned, drowning, burning men.

"Oh, God, no," he said aloud.

From the whirling smoke the bow of a carrier took shape. Huge, gray, head-on. And from the advancing bow, remorseless, inexorable, rolled out once more a solid, advancing sheet of living flame, rolling *toward him*—

He was flattened there, staring at the curling smoke, when a rattle came from above him. He started, tore his eyes away, and looked up again.

Someone was descending the fire ladder, coming down it from the roof.

Lenson moved quickly, sliding sideways along concrete till he was directly beneath the platform. A moment later the rattle paused, and a face appeared, looking down. It looked out to right and left, but missed him; Lenson was too close to the wall. Dan waited, resting his face against the wall and breathing deeply, staring at the concrete. After a moment he felt something warm on his shoulder. He turned his head slowly. As he did another patch of it appeared with a little plop. It was falling from above him. It was blood.

Harisah paused, crouching, and looked again upward. He was pleased that there was so little pain yet. Only a crushing numbness where the black marine's bullet had hit. A nice shot, that, when he'd been running . . . it could as easily have found his heart. He thought coldly that he would lose the arm. But that did not concern him now.

Listening to the firing from the floor above him, the cries and screams, he judged that his men were taking the worst of it. He'd planned to stay a few minutes with the woman, then lock her door and supervise them in dealing with the remaining hostages. But the marines had come through the corridors too fast; he'd had to leave. Fortunately he had done a thorough reconnoiter when they moved into the hotel. He'd known the fire escape was here, though it couldn't be seen from above. He'd taken a round enroute, but, he thought, thanks be to God! The Majd is still alive.

Now, out here, he had two choices. He could descend to the alley below, turn left, and thread his way out toward the desert. The smoke would aid him now. If he made it to the broken system of ravines to the east, he'd have a good chance of reaching the Syrian lines. They were not friends, not after this betrayal; letting the Americans cross their borders unopposed; but not quite enemies either, for they were, after all, Arabs. From them he could expect repatriation, return to his people to the south. He might even fight again, if the UN-funded doctors were skillful.

Or he could turn the other way. Right, and emerge at the front of the hotel, taking the marines in the plaza on the flank. They'd be exposed to his fire for several seconds, till they reoriented to the new threat. He squatted motionless, weighing how many he could kill. It might be a fair trade for the life of the Majd; a fair ending to his long struggle against Zionism, oppression, and imperialism.

His mouth twisted. He glanced upward once more, toward the slackening sound of gunfire. It was almost over. Then downward, toward the alleyway. Still empty. Still the choice to make: escape, or attack.

Well, either way he would need every drop of blood. The pain had begun too, creeping at last through shattered nerves into his brain. But he could ignore that for a few minutes more. Crouching there, he tore off the green armband. He rolled it into a rat's-tail and knotted it tightly round his ruined arm.

Harisah checked his weapon then. Awkwardly, one-handed, he pulled the clip free to check and was immediately glad; it held only one cartridge. He tossed it over the edge of the platform and thrust in his last full magazine.

Ready for his final battle, the Majd straightened from his crouch and moved downward on the steel stair.

Something clattered on the pavement. Glancing at it, Lenson saw that it was the magazine to a weapon. He took a long slow breath and raised the bar, steadying it with both hands.

The counterweight lofted slowly and the ladder came down. Steel kissed asphalt with the toll of a gently struck bell. Dan watched numbly from beneath it as the man descended. His back was to him, but the butt of a rifle was easy to make out. He held it awkwardly, pointing down; Dan saw fresh blood on his arm. When he stepped off the last tread he paused again, his back still to Dan. He half-turned left. Then he paused. At last, as if he had decided something, he pivoted suddenly full toward the front of the building. It was then he caught sight of Lenson.

They faced each other, frozen for a moment. They were no more than six feet apart. Facing him Dan saw a man as tall as he, young, dark-faced, with blood soaking the sleeve of his shirt. Though his mouth looked slack, dazed, his eyes were sharp. They grew wide as they took in Lenson, then narrowed in sudden calculation.

"American!" he said. "You're my hostage. Move to the—"

"Bullshit. You're mine," said Lenson, and brought the bar around into him with all his strength and will.

The rifle went off at the same time, aimed low, but coming up. The bullets blew concrete dust from the wall behind him, stinging his neck. Then steel met steel with a shock that numbed Lenson's hands. Something snapped, and metal clattered at their feet. Another round, wild, hit the wall, then the rifle clicked. Dan cocked the bar again; the man looked down, his expression surprised. There was no magazine to his weapon.

"Drop it," said Lenson, holding the bar like a baseball bat. "Drop it!"

The man nodded. Just for a moment, he looked tired. He held the rifle out, muzzle down. Dan reached out.

The next moment it came flying at his face. His arm came up instinctively to guard. Before he could bring it down again to swing, the other man had slammed forward into him. He heard the iron clang on the pavement. But there was no time to look down. He blocked the groin-kick with his leg, but missed the chop to his throat. Lightning flashed in his head. He struck upward with his elbow, catching what felt like a jaw, and then punched out into the body. He battered his way into him, again and again, till the weakness was too much. At the last blow the man folded and, holding a bloody hand to his arm, sagged slowly and with a look of disbelief to the pavement of the alley.

Lenson reeled back, then fell to his knees, grabbing at his own throat like a madman. Above his head the storm of gunfire abated, trailing off into scattered shots and then a sudden silence. But he was not listening. The world had gone a bloody dark, and his heart had paused terrifyingly in his chest. He was struggling to draw air through a crushed windpipe. At last he got a breath. Then another. When he was able to see, he crawled toward the fallen man.

He was bent over him, slamming the rifle butt into his face again and again, when the marines came round the corner of the building.

Will Givens came back.

He thought, surprised, that the action must be over. He could hear no more firing. No more shouting, the deep short brutal "Oo-rah" of marines in assault. No more screams. Only the low sobbing of a woman, and hoarse breathing from above as Cutford found the duct. Combat boots scraped hollow metal, and then the familiar, hated face was close above.

"Oreo. How is it, blood? You fall?"

"No. Hit."

"Hit bad? Feel numb, like?"

"Yeah . . ." The sky beyond Cutford reddened to scarlet and a wave of dizziness supplanted the emptiness in his chest. He wanted to cough but was afraid to. It might jar loose the heavy, numb thing on his breast.

"We'll get you medevacked," the voice came faintly through the dark. Behind it, now, he could feel the thing, hear it. Thud. Thud. Maybe it was his heart, but it felt different. Slow. Thick. The thing in his chest was heavy on it, drifting over it like fog over the deep valleys of the Smokies in the cool nights of October.

"Hear, man? You got to hold. Hold that old fuckah Death back. Don't give in, Oreo. Can you hear me, brother?"

He could hear, but he did not respond. It was Cutford. He hated him. Cutford had broken his guitar.

And he was thinking. About a lot of things. About the woman. She had tried to stop him, tried to save his life. Or . . . had she screamed for him, or for the other? Her eyes . . . so dark, so full of secrets.

Eyes; the eyes of the child, the woman, the eyes of the terrorist, of the corporal. Secrets, all of them, deep as the sea as you hung over the rail of a ship, staring into depths you would never know, that no one knew.

His book said it all turned out to be math. Equations. The world was all in books, and all you had to do was learn it. And if you studied, learned hard enough, you would not be a nigger. You would not be a small-town laborer in North Carolina. You would be a college man, and never be poor again.

He was remembering the feel of a guitar, the smoothness of the wood and bite of strings, the way that first chord sobbed out in "Amazing Grace."

And then, as if a curtain had been ripped apart, he knew what he was meant for.

He was not an engineer. There were enough engineers. He was not a guitar player. He had not been meant for that.

He had the Call.

"Oreo. You got to hold on, man. We gettin' a corpsman. Open your eyes. That's a fucken order!"

That Cutford. He had to grin, at least inside. Won't he never let up on me?

No. He wouldn't. He was like Someone Else. He called and called, patiently, never taking no. And when you were ready, you had to understand.

Finally, finally, Will Givens understood why he had been set apart. Made different from the rest.

For thus saith the high and lofty One that inhabiteth Eternity, whose name is Holy; I dwell in the high and holy place. . . .

"Givens! You son of a bitch, answer me!"

Cutford. Another of the lost, those whose lives were endless, goalless, whom he had been sent to help. Had he helped them? Had he brought them to certainty? He had not. He had not even tried. And now his journey was at an end.

Follow peace with all men, and holiness, without which no man shall see the Lord . . . and be not conformed to this world; but be ye transformed by the renewing of your mind. For the Lord seeth not as man seeth; for man looketh on the outward appearance, but the Lord looketh on the heart.

"Will!"

I guess I better answer him. He sound like he almost care.

"Okay, brother," he whispered.

Or only thought he did. For within him, somewhere, the dark hand of Jesus had already joined his. Despite himself, despite his failure and sin, he was loved and accepted and taken. And with joy in it, joy and surcease from pain and fear, he yielded to a delight that passed anything, anything, he had ever known.

VII

THE AFTERIMAGE

34
U.S.S. *Ault*

SO THE OLD POLISH-IRISH LUCK STILL held, Wronowicz thought, relaxing back into the bunk after the doctor left.

Still held—kind of. He knew he was in bad shape. His head swam with the dry-mouthed euphoria of morphine and he could think only in snatches. His legs were heavy as ballast pigs and there was no way to move them. He was busted up bad. But alive, that was the kicker! And that was goddamned lucky when a two-ton gear casing had ironed you out twice before the black gang got it wedged down with shoring and lines.

Kelly Wronowicz looked up at the distant blue overhead of after officers country, and wondered where he would be now if he had died. Or if you died would you ever know it, would the only way you knew it be that you didn't?

With the thin silver song of the drug in his ears even that did not seem too awful.

When he woke again the song had gone away and he came up hurting. He stood it for a while, then whistled. A minute later the long, professionally blank face of the *Ault*'s corpsman, a first-class whose name he ought to but could not recall, leaned in. He watched Wronowicz for a minute or two, then his glance went to the dripping bottle that tilted with the gentle sway of the ship. Gentle? Storm must have eased off, Wronowicz thought. Or else I been tits down longer than I thought.

"How you feeling, Chief?" said the medic at last, edging the rest of his body into the room.

"Not too good." He tried to push himself up and caught his breath. "Whoo . . . that smarts."

"Lay down, damn it. You remember what the doc said?"

"Doc? I remember somebody . . . don't remember what he said. Wait a minute. We don't have a doc aboard."

"Shock, probably." The corpsman sat on the bunk and reached for a pulse. "He came over in a gig from the *Guam.* You got three broken ribs, hip, leg in two places. Internal bruising, some hemorrhage. You got blood in your urine, too."

"I guess that's why I feel so rotten," Wronowicz whispered. It was getting worse; he blinked sweat out of his eyes. He tried to concentrate. Broken ribs. Hip. Leg . . .

"Yeah," said the corpsman, wiping down his forehead, "time to put the quietus on that old pain again."

"A shot?" said Wronowicz. "Forget it. I can take this."

"You sure?"

"Yeah. I don't want no more of that dope."

"Well, how about some aspirin, then? At least?"

"That would be okay."

When he had them on his tongue he could taste that they weren't aspirin. He'd been tricked. But he swallowed them anyway. He twitched his fingers and then dug them into the sheet. "Hey. How long I been here?"

"It's 1700. Five in the evening."

"Oh. Landing . . . ?"

"It went all right. We even got to fire the guns. If you're wondering why you haven't been medevacked, Foster was on the horn as soon as we pulled that thing off you, but they were warming up to launch the air assault and there just weren't any to spare. He was cursing a blue streak but the commodore wouldn't give him one, said to stabilize you and he'd divert one when things calmed down."

"So when's that?"

"When's what?"

"When am I going?" Wronowicz muttered. It was getting bad, worse than he thought it could be. Whatever the white pills were they weren't working. "This goddamn tub . . . hurts every time we roll."

"Should be pretty soon. Kind of sorry you woke up, though, 'cause getting you up those ladders and through the hatchways is going to hurt like hell."

Wronowicz closed his eyes.

"Tell you what. I'll give you a reduced dose. How's that? You'll still be awake, but it won't be as bad."

"Oh . . . all right," said Wronowicz, reluctantly and gratefully.

Strapped like a mummy into a Stokes stretcher, he sweated his way up the ladders, fearing with every jolt that they would drop him. But they didn't, and once they hit the 01 level, four men could carry him horizontal and that was better. On the *Ault*'s little helo deck Polock and Steurnagel and Blaney stood around him, watching the dusking sky. It was warm and windy, the flags on the signal bridge snapping above them, the turbulence aft of the funnels snatching down stray streamers of stack gas. The throb and hum of the blowers was music. He moved his fingers and the first-class bent down.

"Stewie. How's the engines doing?"

"Passable, Chief. We was busy as a dog with two dicks for a while, but we dropped the cover back on, bypassed the aux steam line, soft-patched the condensate line and a couple of others, and welded up the bulkhead. She's running, for a while, anyway."

"Did Foster get his thirty knots when he wanted them?"

"I had them flat out flank for three hours," said the first-class. "I didn't hear him complain."

"You done good, Stewie."

"*You* done good, Chief. That fuckin' casing would have wiped out the whole engineroom."

They looked at each other in the warm wind, and the gas from the stacks made Wronowicz's eyes tear.

"Bird's incoming," said Lieutenant Jay, coming up to the stretcher and rubbing his hands. "You'll be on your way in five minutes, Chief, a nice clean hospital and sweet little nurses. By the way, before you shove off—skipper can't leave the bridge, but he said to tell you the yeoman's looking up the requirements for a Navy Cross."

"Thanks," muttered Wronowicz. He was feeling drowsy. That tricky bastard had fooled him again, given him a full shot. . . . "Sir?"

"Yeah." Jay bent to hear him over the roar of the approaching chopper.

"Steurnagel . . . he done a damn nice job of work getting that plant back together."

"I hear you," said the lieutenant.

"ON THE DASH DECK. EVERYONE BACK OF THE LINE EXCEPT FOR PATIENT AND CORPS-MAN."

The amplified voice was familiar. He rolled his head to see Ensign Callin's hand lift inside the control booth. Strange. He hadn't known Callin was helo-deck qualified.

"Well, so long, Chief."

"We'll see you back aboard in a couple of weeks."

"Yeah. Yeah, g'bye."

They retreated, waving. The swollen hugeness of the chopper settled warily toward the stern of the destroyer. It hovered over the after gun mount, gauging the motion of the ship, and then lowered the last few feet. It touched, bounced, and then was down, leaving not an inch of room to spare. The engines drummed at his ears. He was lifted and slid in with a click. A crewman leaned over to strap him in, and then he was heavy with the upward rush of the floor.

* * *

"Want to see out?"

He could barely understand the gargoyle in helmet and throat mike; there was no hope of his shouting back loud enough to be heard. So he only nodded. The crewman loosened a strap and edged him over to the window, and he looked down from three thousand feet on the entire operation.

Land, and the sea. The beach was gold, fringed with white lace of surf, an arch of gold from horizon to horizon. Far to their left were a few fishing smacks, the same ones you saw all over the Med, and the haze of a small city. Below, though, it was almost vacant; just gold, and that fine, fine lace.

Then he saw the boats.

Or amtracs, either one. He looked for but couldn't see the ships of the task force; they were on the seaward side of the chopper. All he could see were the boats, coming out. Fine lines of white, the wakes, each one arrow-tipped by dark gray or green. They crept with painful slowness over the intense purple of the sea, leaving behind the golden arc of land. They were no longer in formation; they were just sea-trucks now. The backload must be starting.

Jarheads down there. As the helo crossed the surf line he could look down on them, the spiderweb crisscross of wheeltracks on the sand, moving jeeps and a bulldozer with its blade lifted, the tiny dots of men. Another dozer was working at the dunes, scraping out a ramp. Beyond that amtracs were coming down the road from the hills, their treads throwing a plume of dust that the wind spread silently (from this height) along the beach.

The helo banked, for some reason; Wronowicz heard the sound of rotors change; the drug told him not to worry.

He looked out, blinking as the sun wheeled through his line of vision, and then saw the ships.

They lay dark against the blue sea, gray against blue. He had never seen anything so beautiful. Nearest him the foam-waked silhouette of a frigate rolled, her missile launcher pointed inland; beyond her was the tubby hull of an attack transport, hove to or at anchor; he couldn't see a wake. Beyond her were more amphibs, all hove to or moving slowly. His eye picked out an LST; was that *Newport,* or *Barnstable County?* Boats clustered around her stern.

Then he saw her: low, fine-hulled, gray, riding close in, her six guns pointed shoreward. The sea glittered around her, the declining sun showering her with powdered gold. It's her, the goddamn *Ault,* he thought. So suddenly was he parted from her. He knew her better than any other thing on earth, more intimately than his own body. She was his home. He wondered if he would ever be back. Stove up as he was, it would be months before he could climb a ladder, scramble into the bilges, take a strain on a line. Maybe longer. At his age . . .

He pushed the thought away, but it came back. Maybe they won't find me fit for sea, he thought. This time fear cut through morphine. Maybe they won't give me another ship at all. Shoreside duty . . .

He could not imagine it. The idea of Kelly Wronowicz beached in West Ocean View was so incredible that he was able to stop thinking about it. His eyes moved on to a grander silhouette, high and square, the gnat-flickering of helicopters between it and the beach, and recognized *Guam.* And beyond her, tiny against the flaming western horizon . . . a cruiser, one of the nukes. That meant there was a carrier out there somewhere, far out to sea from the toehold, but ready with all her power to strike wherever it was needed.

The world wheeled. More of the land came into view, dry-looking mountains rising miles inland, the white buildings closer now. His mind, dimming, tried to creep away from him. He called it back, reluctantly, with questions.

Where are we going?

The hospital, they said.

Hospital? Where?

Does it matter?

Will they fix me up all right?

They'll weld you up, he reassured himself. It'll hurt, but you can take that.

Will they send me back to sea?

He lay there for a little space with his eyes closed, and mused. I'm forty-two, he thought over the roar of the engine, the silver piping in his brain. I'm divorced. My son is a queer. I met a woman I could have loved, but I left her. There's nothing else but my ship. And now I've lost her, too.

The crewman was bending over him. "How you doin', pal?" he shouted.

He moved his lips, not bothering with voice. "Beautiful."

"Anything I can do?"

"No . . . don't think so. Where we headed?"

"*America,*" the crewman shouted. "All the casualties bein' flown out to her. But they won't keep you long. Navy hospital for you, prob'ly Naples."

He opened his eyes. "Where?"

"Naples. Italy. Ever been there?"

"Yeah."

"Figured you had. But you looked kind of surprised." The crewman grinned, popping gum. "Whassamatter? Don't you want to go to Napoli?"

"Yeah," said Wronowicz again, drowsily. He thought for a moment of a brass bed, heavy, gleaming, solid as time and love, lashed securely where no harm would come to it. His eyes closed again. "Yeah. I want to go. In fact . . . got somebody there I mean to look up."

And bit by bit, trustingly, forgetting the ship, forgetting past and future both, Kelly Wronowicz let himself slip at last into the black oil pool of sleep.

ASH SHUMMARI, SYRIA

This land, the commodore mused, was neither as bleak nor as unlovely as he had expected.

In fact it was beautiful. The road, five hundred feet below the hurtling helicopter, was a speeding ribbon, winding along picturesque hills, passing through quaint villages.

Ike Sundstrom cracked a vent, letting wind cram itself into the cockpit. It was cool at this height, cool and clean. He leaned back and took his helmet off, cradling it in his lap. Annoyance crossed his face as he saw the seat belt wrinkling his freshly starched fatigues. He flipped the collar points up, glad that he had thought, back in the States, to buy the anodized eagles that went with battle dress. Silver insignia would have been an instant giveaway to snipers that he was an important target.

I don't have to do this, he thought then. My assigned station is back aboard. But no—his place, really, was with the fighting men under his command.

Besides, his presence on-scene, in Syria itself, would reflect well in any subsequent citation.

He settled deeper into the seat, watching the ground rise into mountains. The pilot, beside him, tilted back the control and the helo began to climb.

Really, he thought, it wasn't as bad as it could have been.

A quick raid, limited to ground forces and unarmed recon helos. Less than an hour of fighting and the hotel and airstrip had been secured. According to Haynes' last report, just before Sundstrom lifted from *Guam*'s deck, hostage evacuation was underway. As soon as the last civilian was gone the withdrawal of troops would begin.

And after that, he thought savagely, let them settle their own goddamn squabbles. Palestinians, Maronites, Cypriotes, Syrians. Let the UN do it. We'll be well out of it and that's where we should stay.

The pilot was shouting something. He lifted the headphones and leaned toward the man. "Yeah?" he shouted.

"Sir, coming up on the border now."

He raised his head. The sun was still up, but the sky was reddening. Dusk before long. He thought this swiftly, and then he saw the smoke. It rose above the still-hidden camp, fanning upward to a capped cloud of brown, thinning where the wind was moving it outward, toward the sea.

They came over the last hills and saw the airstrip and then the hotel complex. He saw that it was still burning, scattered fires, each sending its own pillar of smoke upward toward the approaching helicopter. The pilot pointed. Yes, Sundstrom thought, that's it. The tallest building. The thickest smoke was coming from there.

When they reached it he patted the pilot, made a circling motion. The man looked over at him.

"Let's take a look around."

"We'd do better to minimize time over the LZ, sir. This is where we lost the other helo."

"Okay, use your judgment. Let's go right in."

As they settled he saw a square, the glitter of smashed glass. The open space was filled with vehicles. He could make out amtracs, jeeps. As they came in, the buildings swooping dizzily up toward them as the helo rocked on updrafts, he saw men between the vehicles. Green rectangles—he recognized them then. Litters.

"Are you flying out casualties?"

"Yes sir. Two planes inbound behind us."

"No, I mean, what are your plans for this bird?"

"We're at your disposal, Commodore, far as my orders go. Do you want us to pick some of them up, get them back to the ship?"

"Not right away," said Sundstrom. "I want them to get the best of care, of course, but I may need a chopper at any moment. Just put me down and stand by. Oh, and better have your copilot accompany me, too."

"Aye, sir."

They set down, the rotorwash blowing smoke away

from the open space where skids met asphalt. He put his helmet on, tried to get out, then remembered the belt. He released it and jumped to the ground, bowing his head under the roaring rotors.

"Hello, Commodore. Welcome to Syria."

Sundstrom returned a major's salute, glancing around. Haynes wasn't in sight. "Good afternoon. Where's the colonel?"

"He's in the hotel, sir. They're checking all the rooms one last time before we pull out. He should be out any minute."

"What's the situation? Give me a report."

"Well, the objective is secured, sir. We seem to have gotten here in time to save most of the hostages."

"What about my men?"

"Your men, sir?"

"That's what I said, Major. What kind of casualties did my marines take?"

"Lost eight ground troops in the assault. Two officers in the recon copter. About a dozen wounded."

"And hostages?"

"Eight dead so far. Still counting, but somewhere between eighty-five and ninety souls rescued alive, sir."

"Not too bad."

"No, they could have killed a lot more than that," the major agreed.

The commodore looked toward the buildings. "That the hotel? That one on fire?"

"Yeah, that's it, sir."

"What's the hostile body count?"

"I don't know, sir. Maybe the colonel does. Frankly, we're badly exposed here. I think we'd better just get the hell out and leave the toe-counting to the Syrians."

"I hope we got all the bastards."

"We're pretty sure none of them escaped. By the way— you sent one of your staff out, Lenson? His family was here?"

"I didn't send him anywhere. He deserted his post

aboard ship, in direct contravention of my orders. Where is he?"

"With his wife and daughter. He was pretty disturbed when we found him. He got one of them, though, killed him with a piece of pipe. Turned out when we searched the body he was the leader. Intel's getting pictures before we pull out."

"His family make it?"

"Yeah."

There was, for the moment, nothing more to say. The officer had things to do and the commodore let him go, asking him to send Haynes by if he saw him. He stood off by himself, watching the troops move in and out of the building. The hostages were coming out now, men and women, a few children. The marines were helping, but most of them were walking without assistance. They didn't seem to have much baggage.

"Come on over here," he said to the copilot, who was still standing behind him. "Here. You mind—it's set, just push this button."

"Yes sir," said the officer, taking the camera.

Two of the civilians were clinging together, a blond young man with dried blood on his face and a heavyset brunette. Sundstrom put his hand on her shoulder. "Hello. I'm Isaac Sundstrom, in command here. Are you two all right?"

"Moira Lieberman. Yes, thanks, we're okay."

"You're in charge of these soldiers?" said the man. "We're glad as hell to see you. They were going to shoot both of us at sunset. When the firing started we hid inside an old safe. Snaggletooth—one of them—came in after us, started looking around, but by then your guys were coming in the back. So he ran. I understand they got him, upstairs."

The beat of another incoming chopper swelled over the plaza. Sundstrom stood a little straighter, patted the holstered .45, and settled the helmet tighter on his head. He thought of fastening the chinstraps, but decided not to.

Still holding the woman's shoulder, he turned to face the copilot for a moment. The shutter clicked. He patted her and let go. "You go on ahead. Those helicopters putting down over there are for you. You'll be safe aboard a Navy ship soon."

They thanked him again. As they rejoined the line an old woman left it, moving out from the group of civilians; she was carrying a dog in her arms. He watched her as she came toward him, came up to him.

"Ma'am?"

"God bless you," she said.

He nodded, surprised, and she turned without another word and went past him, toward the helicopter. He looked after her thoughtfully.

Four men trotted by with a litter. He saw the face: a young marine, dead, one dangling arm bouncing with the bearers' pace. There were two corpsmen on the poles in front and two marines on the back. One of them was short, swarthy, the other a tall gaunt boy with a cigarette dangling from his lip. Sundstrom gestured to a trooper who seemed to be with them. The man scowled, but left the group and came slowly over to him. He was black. He had an air of command, but the commodore saw that he was only a corporal. The others set down the body to wait for him.

"Sir."

"Are we boarding KIAs already? Are all the wounded taken care of?"

The man's look was flint-hard, opaque and hostile. Sundstrom dropped his eyes. "All our wounded are off-loaded. Sir. That man on the litter was the last casualty, from up on the roof. One of my men. One of the best."

"I'm sorry."

"That all you wanted?"

"Yes. Thank you, Corporal."

The man walked away. As he rejoined the others, Sundstrom heard a mutter, then a bark of sardonic laughter.

He ignored it, staring up at the hotel. Smoke was still

streaming out of the second-story windows. He looked around him. Helos came in, squatted briefly, then lifted in a racket of sound and exhaust. Men crouched or leaned against the hulls of the 'tracks, grasping weapons with an exhausted but still-wary air.

Standing there, watching, he reviewed the day. It had gone well. Goddamn well, better than he had dared to hope. Haynes had probably called a frontal assault—he was not a man for finesse—but in spite of that there were not too many losses. Ten marines dead for ninety-some hostages rescued would read well in the *Post* and *Times.*

Not a debacle, as he'd feared, after all! The worst part had been that morning, the naval gunfire snafu. Lenson and Flasher, his own officers. It made his face tighten just to remember it. It had been rank, blatant disobedience in action.

But goddammit, that, too, had turned out all right. Now, considering it with a cool head, he did not think explaining it would be insurmountable. The clearance to use supporting fire had come in half an hour after the 'tracks got moving again, all the way from Washington via CINCUSNAVEUR and then Roberts. Half an hour late.

A passing thought made him smile tightly. Bureaucracies. That very slowness of decision was probably the reason he'd succeeded. They had moved faster than Damascus and Moscow could make the decision to stop them. Yes, he'd definitely surprised them. Obviously no one had anticipated that the U.S. might resort to force.

But as yet—his mind returned to his central concern—no one up the line knew that *Ault* had fired before the authorization arrived. He had not reported his use of gunfire and air strikes until after the leading elements of the MAU were actually at the objective.

I'm sticking my neck out, he thought. But then, he would be writing the after-action report. The times could be adjusted, or better yet, just left off. Yes, and the same could be said of *Ault*'s grounding. Success had many fathers, and if Urgent Lightning was a success, no one up the line was going to be too interested in finding fault with it.

No, he decided, there was no use in dragging it all out into the open. There were people who would use it to make him look bad, look like he had not exercised leadership. The men concerned were, after all, his officers. He could deal with them quite adequately in his own way.

He felt abruptly weary, then, sick of the whole business. The dodging and second-guessing and ass-covering. It was not what he had thought the Navy would be like when he was Lenson's age, or before that even, in Officer Training, so long ago. No, he thought, I lost that goddamn innocence, that naivete, a long time ago. The Navy was politics like everything else, and although he knew he was good at it he still hated it. It was not the way it should be anymore. Maybe it never had been. No, none of us in the Navy are supermen, he thought. We're just people.

But we get the job done, he thought.

He looked around. The hotel—the plaza—he decided to check the airliner and started walking toward it. Marines stood outside, smoking, their weapons draped over their arms. Behind them, by the cargo door, he made out the bumper of a parked pickup.

He was still a hundred yards away when the group scattered. Three men came tumbling out of the doors.

"Bomb squad!"

That single hoarse shout, and then the jet erupted behind them in a crash of light and smoke that, in the instant it took for the sound to reach him, darkened the strip and mowed down the men in front of it. He hit the ground by instinct and the shock wave banged his helmet into it. Face twisted to the side, he saw the air filled with debris, heard metal hit and clang around him. He pressed himself into the ground.

Goddamn it, he thought.

When the ground stopped quivering he got up quickly and ran back toward the hotel. What remained of its glass had been wiped away by the blast, but the low wall in front still stood. Marines, shielded by it, were staggering up. The air was heavy with smoke and dust. The last man got up and brushed himself off. He reached them. "Anybody hurt?" he shouted, and was surprised to find that he could not hear himself speak.

"All right."

"No—think I'm okay."

"Say." One of the men came up to him, bent to look under his helmet. Sundstrom strained to hear, caught a few of the words. "Think you caught something there, pal."

He felt the trickle then and wiped his forehead. His hand came away bloody. He took off the helmet.

"Scalp," said the man, and turned away.

Haynes came out of the lobby, running. He caught sight of Sundstrom and stopped. In what the commodore thought was an unwontedly cold tone he said, "Ike. Are you okay? How did that happen?"

"I don't know."

"We checked the plane in the initial attack. There was no one in it. It must have been a timed demolition."

The colonel paused, looked around; the others had drawn away; there was no one else in earshot. When he turned back to Sundstrom the anger in his voice was unmistakable. "What the hell are you doing here?"

"What am I—?" Sundstrom frowned. "I happen to be the commander of this Amphibious Task Force, Steve. And I don't appreciate your taking that tone with me."

"We're ashore now. I'm in charge here. But that's crap, that's games. Let's get something out in the open right now, Sundstrom. I consider your conduct of this operation unsatisfactory. Your delay in providing gunfire support cost me seven men. Almost as many as I lost in the final assault. I intend to include that fact in my after-action report, and I will recommend a court of inquiry be convened to investigate it."

Sundstrom felt cold. He put a hand to his scalp. "Colonel—Steve—now just hold on a minute. You don't have the full story. My hands were tied."

"Don't make excuses to me," said Haynes.

"Better not go off half-cocked on this, Steve. There's a promotion in this, decorations. You'll need my recommendation for that—"

"Go to hell," said Haynes. "You're responsible for my cover and logistics right now, and instead I find you here sightseeing. I'll mention that too, believe me. See that chopper coming in? I want you on it. Or I'm telling my men to throw you aboard."

"All right, all right. Wait a minute. Do you have a corpsman?" said Sundstrom. He wiped his face again. "I need a bandage or something, keep the blood out of my eyes."

Haynes turned away, his back rigid. "Corpsman! Over here."

Ike Sundstrom tilted his head back, letting the blood drip. He tried to concentrate but could not. He felt sad and empty.

So Haynes, too, is against me now, he thought.

The explosion, he saw, had cleared the square even more. The men were loading into the amtracs now, engines were starting up. As if on cue, thunder reverberated to the south. It was a moment before he recognized artillery.

The corpsman came over and began working on him, not saying a word. Sundstrom tilted his head back obediently and the man sponged away blood. The sky was fading red and brightness beyond the smoke.

"Pulling out?" Sundstrom asked him.

"Yes, sir. Colonel just passed the word to mount up. He wants us across the border in an hour and backloaded out of Lebanon before dawn."

"Okay," said Sundstrom. He settled the helmet over the dressing gingerly. He turned and found the copilot still behind him. He was still holding the camera. "Let's get one more, here, with the medic," he said. "Then we'll get the hell out of here."

"Aye aye, sir," said the pilot expressionlessly, and in his hands the raised lens glittered in the setting sun.

U.S.S. *GUAM*

Rolling easily, the escorts traced their curving white wakes on blue, like skaters on deep ice. Their bow waves widened, shallowing as they ran outward, till they lapped at last on the deep gray hulls that lay hove to, waiting, several miles off the shore.

Dan leaned against a lifeline near the *Guam*'s bomb elevator, looking downward at the sea. Under his empty eyes the last red-gold rays of a westering sun penetrated it deeply and effortlessly. The ship seemed to float less on a fluid than on light that sank inward, downward, fading as it fell to chrysoprase, then sapphire. The silent radiance was broken only by the fluttering fins of the fish that clustered around the overboard discharge.

He was remembering the meeting in the plaza.

One of the marines, a sergeant, had led him with surprising gentleness away from the body. Lenson had raised his head when he reached the plaza, to see them, coming hesitantly out of the hotel between two shattered statues of lions. He had called; had seen her lift her eyes, then break into a run, coming straight to him. He opened his arms and she slammed into him, and he was holding her, Susan—she was thin and filthy and hot, sweating and crying into his smoke-smelling khakis, holding him with strength he never knew she had. And Nan was holding him by the legs, crying and crying as she had not cried since he could remember. And he held her tight and stared blankly over her shaking shoulders. At last her sobbing slowed, and he'd lifted her face, looking down into it, almost afraid to believe that she was here, that they were both alive.

"Susan . . ."

"Dan—it's been terrible, it's been—"

"It's all right, babe. It's all right, now. Nan, baby. How are you? Are you all right?" He bent to his daughter. But she had not responded. Only clung to him, silent, her eyes squeezed closed. . . .

From landward came the pop and clatter of helicopter blades. He stared downward still, without sight or hearing, until it grew close, harsh, chopping the ephemeral peace to bits.

The last CH-46 of hostages came in low over the water, its graceless sausage of fuselage heavily loaded. Faces crowded the ports. Dan lifted his hand, waving them a welcome, then leaned forward again, resuming his silent study of the sea.

He had left *Guam*'s sick bay after talking briefly with a doctor. Susan and Nan were still down there, getting a thorough checkup. He had stopped in SACC, but Flasher and Byrne were firmly in charge. Red had told him that with each passing hour the situation for a smooth extraction looked better. The Syrian Army had finally moved toward Ash Shummari, firing a few indifferently aimed shells after the marines as they withdrew. Doubtless tonight they would be claiming credit for repelling an American invasion. As for the terrorists, the results of the hotel action seemed to have shocked their organization into silence. According to Byrne there were no reports of activity, nor had their leadership as yet even issued a statement.

They would regroup, Lenson thought. And the subterranean war would resume. Terrorism was not defeated in one battle. It would be a long war, the worst kind for Americans; they bored easily; they did not care for sacrifice. But we are growing up, he thought. Perhaps this time we will find the will and courage to win. For now at least, we haven't done so badly.

And now they were withdrawing. The wounded were back; he had seen them below in the medical spaces; and the dead. The last hostages were aboard. By dawn, they were rolling seaward as fast as they could, the entire MAU would be back aboard.

And then the ships would sail; offload the men and women they had rescued at some friendly port; and then, resume patrol. Resume the endless drill and preparation. For the deployment was still only half-over. The days would settle back into the dreaming, hard-working grooves of sea time. And it would be as if Cyprus and Lebanon and Syria and the waiting and terror had never been. . . .

So many goddamn contradictions, he thought, scowling at the sea.

Flasher said Sundstrom had been quiet since his return aboard. No one had any idea what he planned to do, and he had given no hints. Instead he stayed on the bridge, twisting restlessly in his patched chair, snapping orders at Hogan when he had to, but otherwise just frowning toward the darkening mountains, his eyes narrow under the gold crusting of his cap.

Maybe, Dan thought suddenly, he'll let the incident in SACC go by. Especially since it had worked. The outcome of the raid must have Sundstrom boxed in. He couldn't both accuse his staff of disobedience and take credit himself for their success. That would be setting himself up as a fool, and he'd spent enough time around the commodore to know he didn't relish that role.

But that did not mean he would forget. He knew Isaac Sundstrom would never forget a slight, a defiance, whether it was real or the product of his own paranoia.

He put that worry aside, and tried again, as he had all that evening, to formulate the other thing that was worrying him.

He had killed a man. True, a man who'd tried to kill him; the most dangerous and experienced leader of a terrorist organization with a history of outrages from England to Israel—true. But he hadn't done it rationally, or even, strictly speaking, in self-defense. He had just . . . lost control. So that, too, was morally equivocal. Perhaps the dark man deserved death. But he did not feel like congratulating himself. Should he feel guilt? Or conclude that, somehow, he had done his duty?

No, he could not trace his previous concepts of right and wrong through this maze. His solutions were inadequate. And so the question reformulated itself to him now as: Was there any right? And was there any wrong?

It was a frightening question. But at my age, he thought, it's time I faced it.

He had always believed that there were two paths in a life. He had resolved early to take the one that led upward. It was clear, it was well-defined, and although he saw it as the harder, he felt deep inside that it was the only way for a man to live. His decision for the Academy, unexpected as it was for the son of a beat cop, fitted. It promised a rigorous but an honorable life; of self-abnegation, of subordination leading eventually to command.

Above all else, the Navy had offered a career of clearcut choices that might not be easy but were at least plain. There seemed no room for waffling, for duplicity, or for the greedy scrambling after dollars that made the American military secretly yet deeply contemptuous of the civilians they defended.

And he was good at it; he fitted it. The watches of the night, the responsibility for sleeping lives, millions of dollars in ships, was the most exciting thing he had ever imagined. He knew he was a good conning officer.

And then—the collision.

And now this.

There's so much I don't understand, he thought, watching the graceful maneuvering of the fish for offal. He could not understand faithlessness, either studied or casual. He could not understand prejudice, lies, laziness. And so when he counseled men who drank, who fought, who borrowed more than they could repay, he was gentle in approach but ultimately inflexible because he had never understood how they could do such things. It seemed so clear that they led where no one who respected himself would want to go.

Now it seemed different, murky. A shading, a tone of gray had crept in.

He wrestled with it for a few minutes more, then put it away, feeling angry and depressed. He stretched, rubbed at his face—the weariness seemed to have infected his bones—and wondered what to do now. They didn't need him in SACC, and he didn't think it would be wise to rejoin the commodore on the bridge just yet. He decided to go below, back to his wife and daughter.

He was standing there, staring blankly across the deck, when he saw her walking toward him across the hot steel, through the dying sunlight. His heart lifted. Men stood above them, watching from the carrier's island. He didn't care. They had survived a terrible thing. He opened his arms as she reached him, and put out a hand to lift her lips to his.

She turned her head away at the last moment.

"Where's Nan?"

"With the doctor."

"How is she?"

"They're giving her an antibiotic. Physically she'll be okay. Emotionally—she'll need a lot of love, Dan. I shouldn't leave her now, even for a minute. But we have to talk."

"Now?"

"Yes."

He looked around. After a moment he stepped to the edge of the flight deck, and jumped down, into the catwalk. When he put up his arms she hesitated, just for a moment, and then let him catch her.

They sat side by side on a pyrotechnic locker and looked out over the sea. Toward Lebanon, now only a dark strip against the evening sky.

"How's your throat? You sound hoarse."

"The doc gave me a relaxant for the spasms. It's all right," he said. Then waited.

"Thank you for coming after us," she said at last. "I know you weren't supposed to."

He lowered his head. "I had to, Susan. Once I knew. Was that what you wanted to say?"

"No. Dan—this is going to be hard. For both of us. That man you killed—"

"How did you know about that?"

"The people in sick bay were talking about it."

"The Majd."

"Yes. Him. Dan, I slept with him."

He stared at the sea. Uncomprehendingly. "You what?" he said at last.

She said, "I made love to him."

"You mean he—"

"No. At least, not entirely. I've tried to figure this out. I even wondered if I should tell you at all. This is the best I can do: Part of it was fear. To keep us safe. But only part of it. The other part is, for a while, for a little, I wanted him."

He sat silent, a black silhouette against the first stars of night. Staring up at him, she wanted to take his hand. Reach out to him. But she was afraid to.

"You don't—" he began, and then seemed to choke.

"I do love you, Dan. That's the truth. And I'm glad he's dead. But the other is true, too."

"I don't understand."

"Neither do I. Look—is there anything you want to say? Anything you want to call me? I deserve it."

"Damn you! What do you want me to say?"

She closed her eyes, shivering at the pain in his voice. "Whatever you want. But let's talk it out, Dan. We've got to do this now. For us. But most of all, for her. Do you still love me, in spite of that? That's what you've got to decide."

He didn't move. But after a long time their hands crept across the gray steel. And then they were crying, head to head. She felt his body heave. A moment later he broke free and went to the deckedge.

She leaned back while he finished being sick. She felt empty, as distant and emotionless as the tiny lights in the sky.

When he came back he slumped there for a long time. Beside her; but he did not move to touch her again. At last he said angrily, "Are you sorry?"

"For hurting you. That's all."

"I see."

"What are you going to do, Dan—about the Navy?"

He passed a hand over his eyes. "Oh yeah."

"You were going to decide, Dan. Whether you were staying in or not. That matters as to—as to whether or not we're staying together."

"Yeah," he said again. Then, after a long time, "Yeah. I thought about it. Let's see. It's like this.

"The Navy has its faults. What can I do? I can leave, or I can stay in. But even if I leave, it's still going to be important to me.

"See, Sundstrom's always talking about 'professionalism.' I think what he means by it is careerism—what gets you promoted. But I think it's something else. A military man is responsible for the lives of others. That's why he takes an oath, like a doctor. And that's why it's important for him to know his job, and insist that the right things are done and the wrong things uncovered and stopped, not hushed up.

"Sundstrom, and the guys like him, don't see it that way. They're in business for themselves. But if we leave the Service to them, we can't bitch about its failure or waste or unreadiness. And then when we need it, it'll fail, and we'll lose everything we have.

"I don't care anymore about my career, Susan. I know I won't make it very far now. But I'm going to stay as long as I can."

"What about us?"

"You're important to me," said Lenson. "But I think this is more important. And that's what you're going to have to decide—whether you love me enough to stay with me, on those terms."

And after a pause she said, too, "I see."

"So that's it, Susan."

"I guess so."

"What do we do now?"

Susan thought about it. She felt empty and sad. "Take care of Nan, I guess. She's going to need both of us. For what comes after, between us—we just go through it, Dan. Just go through it. And see what's on the other side."

"Okay," he said.

"Shake?"

"Shake."

They shook hands, awkwardly. She got up. "We'll talk more later. I'm going back to Nan now."

"I'll be down in a minute."

She left him standing alone.

Whatever happens, he was thinking, it will be all right. If they made it or not. It would be hard either way. But there were some things that could not change, could not become murky or gray. And one of these was the fact that he loved them both, so much.

He followed her into the ship. And behind them, out of the sudden darkness of the Mediterranean evening, the helicopters settled, dark petals slowly falling from a windy sky.

D. C. POYER

AUTHOR OF *THE GULF* AND *THE MED*

"There can be no better writer of modern sea adventure around today."
—Clive Cussler

The tight-lipped residents of Hatteras Island aren't talking about the bodies of the three U-boat crewmen that have mysteriously surfaced after more than forty years. But their reappearance has unleashed a tide of powerful forces—Nazis with a ruthless plan to corner the South American drug market, and a shadowy figure with his own dangerous agenda.

Whatever's out there, someone besides salvage diver Tiller Galloway is interested. Someone prepared to bomb his boat and kill any witnesses. And when Tiller finally meets face-to-face with his pursuers, it's in a violent, gut-wrenching firefight that climaxes hundreds of feet below the surface.

"I couldn't turn the pages fast enough!"
—Greg Dinallo, author of *Purpose of Evasion*

HATTERAS BLUE

HATTERAS BLUE
D. C. Poyer
_____ 92749-5 $4.99 U.S./$5.99 Can.